It is 1914. As war engulfs the British Empire, Royal Navy gunner, George Royal awaits his next ship in his home port where his best friend falls in love with beautiful Carrie, a woman with secrets. When she is attracted to George, she brings the two men into conflict.

Unprepared for war, Britain's leadership is severely tested. Even during Cabinet meetings, at which his bickering warlords make fate-changing decisions, the Prime Minister is preoccupied with his love for a young woman.

George Royal epitomises the young men who collectively brought Great Britain safely through the conflict and never questioned or knew of the circumstances of the warlords who worked in white stone buildings in London and placed them in danger every day throughout the war.

Through the personal lives of Britain's leaders and George's coming-of-age, love triangles at home and ferocious battles at sea, the story reveals how the machinations of leaders influenced the course of the Great War and the fate of those fighting it.

For Chris Evans
With best wishes

William Daysh

Nov. 2013

Front Cover Artwork © Mike Peers 2011
Cover Design © U P Publications Ltd

The right of William Daysh to be identified as the Author of this Work has been asserted by him in accordance with the Copyright, Designs and Patents Act 1998
First published by Libros International ISBN: 1-905988-40-0 978-1-905988-40-2

Author's Note: Although many of the characters in 'Over By Christmas' are fictional, some really did exist and are central to the events described in the book. On my website, www.williamdaysh.com the Image Gallery 'link' leads to photo galleries of the historical characters, events, and ships relevant to the story, as well as an audio recording of Lady Margot Asquith. However, whilst built around real historical events and documented correspondence this is an entirely fictional interpretation of events and characters.

Excerpts (1038 words) from "Asquith's Letters to Venetia Stanley" edited by Brock, M & E (©1985) By permission of Oxford University Press 2011 http://www.oup.com

This edition published by U P Publications Ltd
25 Bedford Street, Peterborough, UK. PE1 4DN

A CIP Catalogue record of this book is available from the British Library

ISBN 978-1-908135-03-2

Printed in England by Lightning Source UK Ltd Milton Keynes UK

SECOND EDITION

www.uppublications.ltd.uk

www.williamdaysh.com

Over by Christmas

William Daysh M.B.E.

U P Publications
2011

In memory of all those who died in the Great War,
regardless of nationality,
and dedicated to my late father,
Lt. Charles George Daysh, RN
whose long naval service inspired me to write about the Royal Navy of WW1.

Chapter One

GOSPORT, HAMPSHIRE
Saturday, March 21, 1914

Close to the Horse Sands Napoleonic Sea Fort in the Solent a grey destroyer of the Royal Navy heading east for the English Channel encountered the Imperial German Navy's substantial dreadnought *Nassau* heading west for Portsmouth harbour. This was not a conflict. The *Nassau* was on a public relations visit and as the ships passed at speed they observed traditional courtesies and trained their guns away from one another.

The big dreadnought had a noticeable bow wave at her nose but, as she neared the harbour mouth, she slackened her speed and turned to starboard. Hissing serenely through the short and narrow stretch of water between Gosport and the naval city of Portsmouth, she entered the harbour. From stem to stern, the guardrails of her upper deck were lined with smartly dressed sailors standing with their feet uniformly apart, facing outward and motionless. Although broad in the beam, and chubby, the 19,000-ton ship sat low in the water, lending her hull a slim, graceful profile. Her impressive armoury comprised at least twelve heavy guns in six turrets. Painted a darker shade of grey than the Royal Navy's ships, *Nassau's* fresh new paintwork, tinted by the low sunlight, looked spotlessly immaculate and the sailors standing on her deck shoulder to shoulder, with unsmiling faces, looked like a continuous chain, unblemished by irregularities in their height or the daylight between them.

Nassau left a distinct image of professionalism and efficiency in her wake as she was led by fussing tugs to her allotted position among the other warships resting peacefully in the naval dockyard. Some of these were belching the dense coal smoke that was filtering hazily through the latticework of masts and cranes outlined against the early evening sky.

On the Gosport side of the Portsmouth harbour mouth a young sailor, George Royal, leaned on the quayside guardrail and watched *Nassau's* arrival intently before setting off for his home in St Mark's Road, Gosport for a special occasion. According to his mother, it was a very special occasion. Lieutenant Jack Royal, George's father, a gunnery officer in the Royal Navy, had returned home after a long tour of duty at sea, and his wife, Emily, wanted to celebrate the fact that, for the first time since their son George had also joined the Royal Navy, they were all in the same place at the same time. The old cruiser, *HMS Good Hope* (Jack's ship) had just returned to Portsmouth Dockyard, where George was stationed.

For a time, at least, Emily felt secure. She had the comfort of knowing that by strolling to the jetty at Gosport and gazing over a short stretch of water, the very reasons for her existence were within her sight among the dockside cranes of the busy port. She'd been dying to lay on this special dinner. It was the roast beef and Yorkshire pudding, roast potatoes and thick brown gravy that the men in her life dreamed of during their long months at sea. This was traditionally a Sunday lunch but, as Emily knew from having two naval men in her life, she always had to seize special opportunities when they presented themselves. Another day in these uncertain times and who could know what might happen.

As there was just enough room for four at her table, she'd invited George's closest friend, Bill Guy, to join them. Living by himself in the centre of the small naval town of Gosport, Bill Guy never refused an invitation to one of Emily's meals. The Royals were the only family he had.

In their now rarely used dining room of lovingly polished wood and a faint hint of mothballs in the air, the men sat in formal silence staring at the crisp, white tablecloth and Emily's Sunday-best cutlery and crockery. They tried to ignore the delicious aroma that reached out from the kitchen and clawed at their stomachs, and smiled stiffly. Inhabiting very different worlds and meeting only rarely these days, they had to search harder now for things they had in common. Jack and George were in the Royal Navy; Bill was a civilian. George was a gunnery rating; Jack was a Gunnery Lieutenant, and although George was with his own father, in his own home, he was strangely and newly conscious of Jack's rank. It was a nonsensical unease he was feeling – a bizarre effect of the indoctrination of naval discipline.

Jack swigged his beer and finally broke the silence. 'I see we've got a German battleship in the dockyard?'

'*Nassau,* you mean?'

'Yes. The Kaiser's pride and joy!'

'Yes, I looked her over as she came in,' said George, pleased that the inertia of conversation had been overcome. 'Blimey, she's big. She's got six turrets and twelve big guns. I reckon she'd give us a good pasting if we came up against her!'

A fatherly smile creased Jack's weatherworn face. 'The *Nassau* is nothing to worry about, son. Even though your last ship, *Dartmouth*, was a light cruiser, she could show that one a clean pair of heels, believe me. Anyway, *Nassau* is not all that she's cracked up to be. Did you notice that short freeboard of hers – how low she is in the water? The two turrets either side, amidships, they're far too close to the water. First sign of rough weather and those muzzles will be right in it. Useless, they'd be. And did you see how she's only got her fore and aft guns on the centre-line? That means they're the only ones she's got that can fire both sides. Her four midship turrets can only fire two to port and two to starboard – so it's impossible to fire a broadside with all of her guns. Big design flaw, that. Anyway, for some reason or other, they've gone for eleven inches when most of our guns are twelve and a half now – going up to thirteen – even fifteen inches in *Queen Elizabeth*.'

George raised an eyebrow at his father's knowledge as Jack went on. 'But I'll tell you one thing – never underestimate the German gunners. Bloody red-hot, they are. That's what you'd have to worry about, if ever you came up against them – accuracy. You can smell the efficiency in that ship from the dockside: always shipshape and Bristol fashion, the Germans. Can't imagine being at war with them. They're pretty good blokes really, just the same as us. We've had some good parties in each other's wardrooms.'

'What do you think is going to happen, Mister Royal?' asked Bill, feeling left out of the conversation. 'About war, I mean. D'you really think it'll happen?'

'I wish I knew, son. We're still friendly with the Germans at the moment. That's all I know. They've certainly been building up their navy over the past few years, but as far as I know they haven't done much with it yet. But "Their Lordships" up there at the Admiralty aren't taking any chances. That's why we're here right now. It's not just for the Spithead Review in July. That's just a convenient excuse to keep the Grand Fleet in home waters until the trouble blows over. I hope it doesn't come to anything, I really do. But you never know.'

Jack's ready smile faded momentarily. He glanced at George and lowered his voice. 'If it does, you'll have to get along at home without me, son. After a bit of a refit, we're off to the Falkland Islands, I'm told, to join the South Atlantic Squadron: another Christmas away.' He looked down at the table. 'Your mother's a bit touchy about it but you'll be here to look after her, won't you? Unless you get a new ship, of course.'

'I really hope I do. Being shore-based drives me nuts.'

'Look, son. It's all right to talk between us about this kind of thing, but not in front of your mum. She's worried about war and all that. So let's all put a sock in it when she comes in – OK, lads?' Jack took a deep breath and embraced the smell coming from the kitchen. He closed his eyes and smiled. 'You know, that's what I miss when I'm abroad. There's nothing in the world like your mum's roast.'

He turned to Bill. 'Haven't you found yourself a nice girl yet, young man? How old are you now?'

'Twenty-four, Mister Royal. No, not yet, I'm too busy running the shop. Living by myself, I never have the time to go looking. Anyway, there's hardly any single girls left in Gosport. They all go for sailors in uniform, like George here.'

'Well, you keep your eyes open. Something – someone – will turn up one day, when you least expect it. Life's a bit of a jigsaw puzzle I always think. It's Fate's jigsaw puzzle. You never quite know when she's going to pick up the pieces that have your name on them, but when she does snick one of your pieces into her puzzle, things start to happen for you. It'll happen to you one day, believe me. Anyway, a man needs a good woman.'

Right on cue, Emily bustled in with the roast beef and proudly set it down before the master of the house. As Jack began carving the golden, sizzling beef, she ferried in the rest of the meal then stood back before sitting down to join them. Unseen by the men, she quickly dabbed a tear from the corner of her eye. Jack never knew how strongly his voice carried into the kitchen.

Apart from murmurs of appreciation, there was little conversation until the main course was well and truly downed, but then Jack had something on his mind. 'Anyway, I've been wondering why you don't try to get yourself promoted, George.' There was no response from George. He swigged his beer instead. 'You must be twenty-three now, so when are you going to try for a commission? I know it's good to have experience on the lower deck, but it's far better at the other end of the hawse-pipe, believe me.'

Jack was not to know that one particular wardroom expression "coming through the hawse-pipe" virtually summed up everything that was holding George back from trying to become an officer. It was a reference used by the snottier direct-entry officers to describe other officers who had been promoted from the lower deck, i.e. from the ranks. In harbour in the old days, rats could board a ship by climbing its mooring hawser and then scampering through its hawse-pipes – the tubes through which mooring ropes passed through a ship's side. George could picture some acidic aristocratic son, with easy access to rank, inventing this hurtful distinction for officers like Jack who came to the wardroom the hard way, up through the ranks.

Even while his father was talking, George was thinking about it and his ire rose. *Christ, if ever I made it to the wardroom and some upper-class sod implied that I had sneaked in like a rat up a mooring rope, I'd floor the bastard before I could stop myself.* He had thought about wardroom snobbery often and, like a ball and chain, it was still weighing down his motivation for potential promotion but, for his father's sake, he had to keep it to himself. 'Oh, I don't know, Dad. There's plenty of time for that later.'

'Maybe, but take my advice, son – have a go as soon as you can. As you know, I came up from the lower deck and when I think of the years I wasted...' Jack shook his head. 'If only I'd had the sense to push myself sooner!'

'It's all the studying that puts me off.'

Jack looked into his son's eyes, to make his point. 'Look, George, life is what you make it. If you stretch a bit you can often reach things that you perhaps thought were too high for you. Your mother and I wanted you to have a better education than we ever had. Do yourself a favour, son – listen to your old man and start applying …and keep on applying until you get there.' He looked sternly at the young man he could hardly believe was his own son. He seemed to have grown into a man while his back was turned. 'Please,' he said, sincerely, 'for us.'

George looked at his father. He could feel his conscience pricking him. 'OK, Dad. You're right. I'll go and see someone about it.'

'Great! There's a new officer cadet scheme coming out for bright young lads like you. Having an officer for a father won't get you through the exams, but it will help you on your way. Alright?' George nodded and Jack began to smile again.

'So, what's really going to happen?' George asked the unanswerable question again. He seemed concerned but excited about the prospect of a war. It was a subject that pierced Emily's heart like a sharp sword.

THE SAVOY HOTEL, LONDON
Saturday Evening, March 21, 1914

At this point in time, H H Asquith, the 59-year-old Prime Minister of Great Britain and her extensive empire, happened to be the world's most powerful statesman. However, in spite of this and being a father of five, he also had a weakness for intelligent young women — and he was in love. Although the Prime Minister appeared to be enjoying himself, he was uneasy. The young woman with whom he was in love was somewhere in the crowded room... and so was his wife. The irony of a certain dinner toast ran through his mind – *"To wives and sweethearts; may they never meet".*

The object of his desire was 24-year-old Venetia Stanley – the unmarried daughter of Sir Lyulph Stanley, 4th Baron of Alderly and 4th Baron of Sheffield – who was also a close friend of his own eldest daughter Violet, His obsession with Venetia Stanley had begun in a single instant on a crisp Sunday morning in February 1912, in a house on the edge of the New Forest in Hampshire

Relaxing in the dining room after breakfast, chatting with Venetia while his wife Margot and his children were out walking, he looked at his guest and experienced a moment of revelation that changed his life. He later wrote of it:

"...We were talking and laughing just on our old accustomed terms. Suddenly, in a single instant, without premonition on my part or any challenge on hers, the scales dropped from my eyes; the familiar features and smile and gestures and words assumed an absolutely new perspective; what had been completely hidden from me was in a flash half-revealed, and I dimly felt, hardly knowing, not at all understanding it, that I had come to a turning point in my life."
©

Out of this single moment grew a strange affair that was destined to leave him emotionally drained and distracted at a critical time later in his life. However, for now, it kept him happy and affected his leadership only positively, he claimed. In any event, it was a non-sexual relationship, as he was keen to point out to anyone who broached the subject. It was a claim that was left unchallenged. He also claimed that it did him no end of good by moderating his drinking habits and focusing his mind more clearly on matters of national interest. It was, therefore, kept out of the public eye.

Initially, Venetia was flattered by his attention and drawn to him by his power and position. What attracted him to her – apart from the fact that she was young and female – were her great intelligence and her interest in his work. He responded by providing her with frequent insights into the workings of the Cabinet and the foibles of its members. By this means, she was drawn further into the relationship. By frequenting the public gallery of the House to see him in action, she soon had enough knowledge of his world to offer opinions of her own about his political problems, which he eagerly accepted. Gradually, he came to depend upon her for comfort and counsel, while she became privy to the business and secrets of Government.

In isolation, the relationship was not a threat to the nation. However, with seismic changes afoot, Britain was desperately in need of strong and decisive leadership, and Asquith was certain to be tested as never before. But instead of working cohesively, his senior warlords were already bickering among themselves at the very time that his relationship with Venetia Stanley had become truly obsessive. In the event of a crisis with Germany it seemed that the direction of Britain's war effort could be left in the hands of decision makers wracked by divisive argument and led by a lovelorn Prime Minister who himself could be distracted by personal emotions. These very politicians, advised and counselled by military leaders, were at the core of the decision-making process, and whatever they decided would dramatically affect the lives of thousands of ordinary people who were most likely to be at the forefront of a war, should it happen.

Ultimately, it was the aristocrats who manipulated the levers of power in Britain and ordinary people such as Jack and George Royal would, as always, implement their decisions. Historically, momentous decisions of this nature are rarely based solely on cold facts and the well-reasoned logic of seasoned commanders. Frequently, other factors are at work in the form of the human frailties and personal weaknesses of some leaders. Therefore, in March 1914, much now depended upon how cohesive Britain's decision-makers would be in the face of the looming major crisis.

On this particular evening, the Savoy ballroom was buzzing like an enormous beehive, filled as it was with the conversations of countless lords and ladies, diplomats and politicians. Their preoccupation with Germany's warmongering and the embarrassing prospect of coming face to face with one particular guest, the German ambassador, had been put aside for this glittering event being held in the name of charity.

The abundance of Prime Minister H H Asquith's silver hair looked incongruous among the clipped hairstyles and neat military moustaches of other male guests, but it added a touch of character to his otherwise stately demeanour and served the purpose of making him instantly recognisable.

Winston Churchill, the youthful, 40-year-old First Lord of the Admiralty standing beside him, was delivering a peroration on Germany's new and controversial method of warfare. Completely wrapped up in matters closest to his heart – the defence of Britain and the Royal Navy – his pale blue eyes were sparkling with boyish enthusiasm. In spite of his defective, short-tongued pronunciation of the letter 's', he managed to 'shhss' through sibilant sentences without embarrassment or concern. It was a minor affliction, considered by most to be an attractive part of his colourful personality.

'As you know, Prime Minister,' he went on, 'the Huns have a large fleet of submarines, but the general view is that Germany is a civilised Power, and is not a vile enough nation to adopt systematically such methods of sinking unarmed commercial vessels. Indeed, Lord Sydenham mentioned recently that even in the most barbarous of times, unarmed ships were not summarily dispatched to the bottom.'

As Churchill's preoccupation with German submarines rumbled on, Asquith's attention began to wane. 'Mmm. Splendid,' he murmured, his attention drifting elsewhere. A white-coated waiter, misinterpreting the Prime Minister's anxious glances, burrowed deferentially through the tightly packed guests bearing a tray of tinkling champagne glasses.

Across the room, Margot Asquith, the wife of the Prime Minister – a small, intense woman with an air of brooding melancholy and sharp, nervous features – seemed to have become stranded some distance from her husband, in a conversation with two gentlemen. Their expressionless faces suggested that they were by her side out of social duty. Margot seemed to be only half listening to the one speaking, Edwin Montagu, Financial Secretary to the Treasury. He was droning on about national budgets, and she was hiding her wandering attention behind a bland smile. But her eyes betrayed her. They were flicking anxiously between Asquith and Violet, her young stepdaughter, who was laughing and talking with her friends in the centre of the ballroom. Among the offspring of nobility gathered around Violet Asquith was Rupert Brooke – the impossibly handsome and fashionable young poet – and a young lady by the name of Venetia Stanley.

That Violet Asquith was infatuated, if not in love, with Rupert Brooke was obvious to all around her. She was gazing up at his face with large, adoring eyes, and clung to his every word as if it were a precious gift to be treasured for all time.

Margot Asquith's disapproving stare could have been mistaken as having been directed at her daughter's adulation of the poet. But this was not the case. Her attention was focused firmly on Venetia Stanley. Dressed in a fashionable full-length white silk gown with a low neckline, Venetia looked striking, if not actually beautiful. Her elegant pearl-drop earrings accentuated the fine line of her pale neck, while a slim gold band around her forehead and black hair added a touch of fashion to her elegance and made blatant statements about her youth and aristocratic background.

Margot seethed quietly when her husband craned his neck to peer at this lady in the obvious pretence of smiling at his daughter. When Venetia's dark eyes coyly and self-consciously made contact with Asquith's, Margot noticed a certain longing in Asquith's gaze. She was fully but quietly aware of his peculiar affair with Venetia Stanley.

Just then, Lord Rosebery, the distinguished, silver-haired former Prime Minister standing next to Margot suddenly winced and pressed a hand to his stomach, breaking her concentration on distant events. A torrent of dark irritation flashed across her eyes and her features immediately stiffened into a matronly expression. 'Lord Rosebery,' she snapped, 'if you have a problem with your stomach, for God's sake, man, why do you not take pure liquid paraffin every day?'

In more relaxed circumstances, Margot's comment would have been delivered with wit. But in these circumstances it came with a barbed tone and her unsolicited advice left Rosebery speechless. He made his excuses and hastened away, leaving Edwin Montagu at the mercy of her sharp tongue. Not in the best of dental health, the unfortunate Montagu was an easy target for her anger, and he was obliged to suffer silently as she chastised him for not paying attention to his teeth. He shifted nervously and stroked his thick black moustache, as if patting it down might hide his dental shortcomings.

On the other side of the room Venetia leaned forward to speak confidentially into Violet's ear. 'Your stepmother is glaring at me again. Did you see dear old Rosebery scooting off, looking very grumpy?'

'Oh, she's been up to her usual tricks, I expect – annoying everybody as usual. It's quite normal. I don't know how Daddy puts up with it. Poor Daddy!' She sighed, looking around and catching his attention. He smiled and gave her a little wave from across the room. Venetia's eyes coyly searched for space between the heads to make contact with his. He gave her a look that said '*I love you*'. She smiled self-consciously and turned her attention back to her friends.

Still standing beside Asquith, glass in hand, was Winston Churchill with a frown now fixed to his rosy, soft, schoolboy features. He was enjoying the opportunity of having the Prime Minister to himself. His solemn expression contrasted sharply with Asquith's airy demeanour, and he seemed intent on continuing to discuss serious matters while the Prime Minister was naturally more concerned with enjoying the evening and performing his duties as host. With a smile fixed to his lips, Asquith continued to concentrate on putting names to faces as they came by, giving each their due share of his attention.

'Old Jacky seems to have gone to ground again,' Churchill rumbled on. 'I find it extremely frustrating trying to bring him back to the table.' The 'Old Jacky' he referred to was the notoriously irascible old former First Sea Lord, Admiral Lord John Arbuthnot Fisher G.B, First Baron Fisher, of Kilverstone. But Churchill's heartfelt concerns over matters of national importance were wasted on Asquith. His attention was elsewhere, keeping a longing eye on Venetia and a watchful one on his wife. Just then, a loud aristocratic laugh and guffaws like naval gunfire drew Asquith to the more jovial group in which his daughter, Violet, was among close friends. Unable to resist any longer, clutching a fresh glass of champagne, he smiled polite apologies and wandered towards it.

When Margot finished berating Montagu about the state of his teeth, she glared at him quite distastefully. He was not an attractive man. His complexion was pallid and his large, drooping moustache clung to his upper lip rather like a drowned rodent, she thought. She had long since drawn her own conclusions as to why Venetia Stanley had turned down his proposals of marriage, but it came as a blow to Margot when Venetia did that because, had she accepted, it would surely have ended her husband's obsessive affair. However, it was not to be, and all who knew her understood Margot's obvious frustration. With Montagu out of the running and no other suitors in sight for Venetia, peace of mind for Margot was a long way off, even though Montagu still harboured smouldering hopes for a second chance with Venetia.

The fact that Margot Asquith was aware of the former but

ignorant of the latter gave rise to the state of her mind on this occasion. 'See how those girls conspire,' she hissed to Montagu. 'If Venetia had an ounce of truth and candour… I should smile; but she is even teaching Henry to avoid telling me things. I'm far too fond of him to show him how ill and miserable it makes me. Good God, to think you proposed to her! A woman without refinement or any imagination whatever. Oh, if only Venetia would marry. How I loathe girls who can't love but claim and collect like a cuckoo for their own vanity. Venetia's head is completely turned.' Montagu coughed nervously and stared into his glass.

Asquith, meanwhile, had taken a circuitous route through groups of nodding and smiling guests to be by Venetia's side. Margot immediately abandoned the clearly wounded and diminished Montagu as she swept across the room like a destroyer at full speed and rammed the group of young people. Smiling stiffly she wedged herself between Venetia and Asquith. 'Well, children, I think it is high time that you got on with your social duties,' Margot said to the astonished group. 'You must circulate. It's so rude to remain in a clique, I always think.'

Her matronly manner was not to their liking, and furtive glances of frustration flickered between the young people. After polite words with the deflated Prime Minister, they dispersed among the guests like grouse put to flight. Alone with her husband, Margot smiled with contentment having regained control of the situation. 'Henry, my dear – I trust that you are not overdoing the champagne,' she said. 'There are many guests deserving of your attention. Look over there. I think David Lloyd George needs to be rescued from that dreadful dancer friend of his. That awful woman should never have been allowed in.'

Clucking nervously, she tugged Asquith's sleeve and bore down upon the Chancellor of the Exchequer, but the wily little Welshman had spotted her coming and ducked away with his sensuous companion. They disappeared into the crowd before Margot could reach them. 'That, I am afraid, is typical of your colleagues,' she confided in Asquith. 'Always looking out for themselves.'

By then, however, he had already slipped from her grasp again.

DORCHESTER RAILWAY STATION
March 29, 1914

Just a week after his lunch with the Royals, Bill Guy began to believe that Fate was indeed toying with his piece of the jigsaw puzzle, just as Jack Royal had assured him she would. It happened while he was at Dorchester station on a train standing at a platform. As he took his seat and gazed idly out of the window, the sight of a young woman on the platform took his breath away. He could tell that the pungent coal smoke and the clamour of steam engines were jarring her senses and he imagined that the atmosphere of the station contrasted sharply with the clean fresh air and tranquillity of whatever she was more used to. She was bewildered and desperately alone in an unfamiliar world, with her heart in the pit of her stomach, he imagined. She was checking with porter after porter that she had the right train, and looked apprehensive of wherever it was about to take her.

He felt an instant urge to help her; to protect her from this cruel world. As he watched her, he willed her into his compartment. When she struggled in with her suitcase, he could not believe his luck. He leapt to his feet and took it from her. 'Here, Miss, let me help you with that.' Heaving it onto the luggage rack, he smiled warmly and sat down again.

'Thank you,' she said, offering a thin smile.

The fresh, youthful beauty of her face entranced him. He saw in her hair the colour of autumn sunlight and, in her eyes, the pale green hue of tender young grass. He was smitten instantly and, for the first time in his life, began to think romantic thoughts. She unbuttoned her coat and pulled her arms back to remove it. His eyebrows rose subconsciously as her breasts thrust forward, and his furtive glance flicked over her shapely body as she put her carefully folded coat on the seat and sat down beside it.

The shrill shriek of the guard's whistle startled her and a look of panic momentarily passed across her face as the train moved and slowly pulled away from the station on its eastward journey, but soon she became engrossed in the sight of the town and then the Dorset countryside flashing past the windows. Although still preoccupied, she gradually relaxed and her gaze drifted back to what was inside the carriage, namely Bill Guy. They glanced at one another, casually, coyly, sizing each other up.

'Off for a holiday?' he asked with a smile, suddenly catching her off guard. His accent was far removed from Italy or some other exotic country in which she had already placed him according to the shiny black hair brushed straight back from his forehead and his deep-set brown eyes.

'Yes ... visiting an aunt in Gosport. Do you know it?' To Bill, her voice sounded like a Dorset cornfield sighing softly in a summer breeze. The thought of a common destination tugged the corners of his mouth into a smile.

'I live there. I have a business there,' he added, rather proudly. His gaze shifted to her clasped hands, searching for rings. He extended his hand. 'My name is Guy, by the way ... Bill Guy.' He was relieved to see no rings.

'Caroline Palmer.' She spoke quietly, as if she wished to keep it a secret. 'Friends call me Carrie.'

'Staying long in Gosport?' The hope in his voice left the end of his question dangling embarrassingly in mid-air. She suddenly seemed nervous about answering questions, and he imagined that some disaster had recently befallen her. Perhaps life was suddenly moving too quickly for her. He had to remind himself that they were complete strangers.

'I don't know really. I'll have to see,' she said, demurely. It told him nothing.

'You don't have to work, then?' He knew immediately that he had overstepped the mark; the message flashing in her eyes was clear – it was a question too many, too personal. 'I'm sorry,' he said, hurriedly, 'that's none of my business.' There was an awkward silence. She was obviously not going to tell him her life story, but she seemed reluctant to put him off altogether.

'That's all right.' She gave a theatrical shrug that had an air of forced sophistication. Raising her chin, she closed her eyelids slowly and softly, like a giraffe. 'I don't really have to work... and I haven't made up my mind quite what I'll be doing. I just need to rest for a while,' she added, rather grandly.

Confused but relieved, Bill turned the conversation. 'Do you know Portsmouth?'

'I've never been there.'

He smiled. At last he had a topic he could run with, and he did. By the time he finished his colourful description, Carrie was convinced that the drab naval city that was Portsmouth was the most exciting place in England. Their conversation eventually drifted onto his personal circumstances. He was twenty-four, he told her, and he had a successful greengrocer's shop in the main street of Gosport, left to him when his father died three years ago. He also spoke of his mother living in Dorchester with her sister, and explained that his shop was not far from the Portsmouth ferry terminal in Gosport. He made it very clear that he lived by himself in his own apartment above the shop. She listened intently.

As the conversation progressed, Bill came to the realisation that she was perhaps too innocent and inexperienced to be on her own. Wherever she had come from, whatever her past, it had given her no experience of life at all. This puzzled him, but he was pleased to see the nervous apprehension that had earlier dogged her eyes was fading fast. They shone brightly now. But what was she afraid of? What was she running from? It was a puzzle that occupied his mind until the train pulled into Portsmouth Harbour Station.

He could hardly believe they were there. The two-hour journey had seemed like two minutes in her company. He felt relaxed and comfortable with her, and was prepared to spend his whole life on the train, if he could just be with her. As they stepped onto the platform, his mind raced to think of ways of not saying goodbye. 'Let me take this for you,' he said, reaching for her case. 'We can cross on the ferry together then I'll show you where to get a taxicab. We've got to get over there first.' He nodded at Gosport, across the short stretch of water that was the mouth of the harbour.

It was obvious that she had never experienced a bustling dockyard before, or a boat. This was normal routine for him, but for her it was new and thrilling. She chattered like an excited child during the crossing. At the Gosport side, he carried her case up the ramp to the taxicab rank in the cobbled square, and explained what she should do. Pointing to the street where his shop was, he invited her to drop in to see him sometime. Standing at the taxicab rank, clutching a note of her aunt's address, Carrie began to look forlorn again and Bill had a sudden urge to put his arms around her, but the taxicab was there before he knew it, and he was holding out his hand for the address.

It happened too quickly. There was no time for him to collect his thoughts. He was suddenly telling the driver where to go and standing by the window saying goodbye to her. 'I've really enjoyed meeting you, Carrie.' She stared blankly, stuck for words. 'Perhaps we could meet again?'

She gave a wide grin as the taxicab pulled away. 'I'd like that,' she called, 'in about a week's time. Keep the address!'

He intended to, anyway. There was a broad smile on his lips and a spring in his step when he walked home but there were questions rattling around in his head. This wonderful, mysterious girl who had dropped so unexpectedly into his life disturbed him – in the nicest way possible. She had indicated that she was financially independent yet she didn't have the upper class airs and graces to go with it. She was too warm and friendly to be aristocratic. He shook his head as Jack Royal's words of wisdom about Fate popped into his mind once more.

At Ethel's house, the taxicab driver put Carrie's case down on the pavement and stood with his hands on his hips while she rooted through her handbag. Knowing nothing about tipping, she handed him the exact fare. He stared at the collection of coins and grunted then carefully fished out a ha'penny and handed it to her. ''Ere Miss, I reckon you need this more than me,' but his sarcasm was wasted on her. She stood in the quiet suburban seaside road and inhaled the air as she stared at the neat terraced house with its small rose garden at the front. Its crisply clean lace curtains hung motionless at the windows, and there was no sign of life.

She walked up the path and rang the doorbell several times, then knocked loudly. There was no response. With a sigh, she sank forlornly onto her case and stared vacantly at the garden, wondering what to do next.

'Yoo-hoo... Hello!' A middle-aged neighbour with a kindly face, was peering over the hedge. 'If you're looking for Mrs Carson, I'm afraid she's away, my dear.' The woman watched Carrie's face fall even further. 'She's on holiday for a week. Did she know you were coming? Ethel is getting a bit forgetful these days.'

'No,' said Carrie, barely hiding her desperation. 'It was going to be a surprise. I'm her niece, you see.'

'Oh my goodness,' exclaimed the neighbour, noticing the size of Carrie's suitcase. 'Have you come far?'

'Well, yes. From Puddletown, in Dorset.'

'Oh dear. Whatever will you do? She won't be back until next Monday. Have you got anywhere to stay?'

Bill Guy immediately sprang to mind. Dare she ask him for help? Could she be that brazen? Before she knew it, her mind was made up. She would go to him – she had no choice. 'Yes, I have,' she said. She was startled by her own recklessness. 'But I need a taxicab.'

The woman pointed down the road. 'If you walk to the end of the road, there is a grocer's shop. He's got one of those new telephones and he will call a taxi for you. Leave your case here, my dear, I'll look after it until you get back.'

Thirty minutes later, Carrie's taxicab was pulling up outside Bill's shop. She was wondering if she was doing the right thing, and very concerned about what he would say. But he was already a friend, of sorts: the only one she had in the world. At least he would know what to do. She felt low again, and fought back the tears that seemed determined to come. Bracing herself, she picked up her case and marched into the shop where there were wooden boxes everywhere and a heavy scent of oranges and cabbages, apples and parsley in the air.

A boy aged about fifteen, wearing a striped apron, looked and smiled at her. 'Yes, Miss?'

'Mister Guy. Is he here?' She could not mask the anxiety in her voice, but she hoped he would not notice. 'Could I speak to him, please?'

'Yes, Miss. He's upstairs. I'll get him for you.'

He disappeared through a door at the back and Carrie waited with her heart pounding, suppressing urges to run away. Bill suddenly appeared. Without his collar, tie and jacket, he seemed more rugged and handsome than she remembered. His face lit up immediately. 'Carrie! I didn't think I would see you again so soon.' He hastened to button his waistcoat and shirt then noticed her strained look and the case by her side. 'What's the matter? Please come through.' He picked up the case and led her up a linoleum covered wooden staircase to his small but functional apartment. He came over to her and looked quizzically into her eyes. 'Come on, tell me what's gone wrong.'

She opened her mouth to speak, but dissolved into tears instead. Without hesitating he put his arms around her and held her tight. The picture of serenity she had left him with crumbled like a flimsy façade under a torrent of tears, but he was not to know that they were not new tears; they were old ones that had been forming for years. He waited patiently while she sobbed and when there was nothing left but the wet patch on his shirt, they sat down and she told him why she was there. It solved some of the mysteries flitting through his mind, but not quite all of them.

'I'm not really on holiday. I've left my job and I was hoping my aunt would put me up, but she's on holiday – she didn't even know I was coming. I've got nowhere else to go.'

'Why leave where you were, then?' Bill looked puzzled.

'Well, it's a long story.' She looked nervous about telling him the truth, but he waited for her to go on. 'When I was very young, about thirteen I think I was, my mother got me a position in service with a squire – Squire Farleigh of Puddletown, where we lived. My mother had been in service at Farleigh Manor too, ever since she was young. It was a good job, in those days.'

She dried her eyes and began to look more composed as she unburdened herself. 'Anyway, when both my mum and dad died of typhoid, I had nowhere else to live, and I've been there ever since. It wasn't a bad job, really.' She sniffed. 'The squire's housekeeper, Mrs Trimble…'

'Trimble?' He smiled as if it were a made-up name.

'Yes, Trimble,' she said, not smiling. 'Well, she thinks that being a housekeeper is like being God or something, and she really had it in for me. She must have been with the Squire for more than forty years and she was always saying that I was too ambitious for my own good and calling me a rebel because I always believed that there's more to life than being a servant. She made my life hell …especially because I was friendly with the squire's son, Master Edward. You see he isn't much older than me and we sort of grew up together. We had fun together sometimes. It was probably the only real fun he ever got. Then, when his mum died, old Mrs T took charge of everything. Like a bloomin' mother hen she was then, and she was always putting me in my place and going on about servants not mixing with their masters.'

'What did the Squire have to say about it?'

'Oh Squire Thomas was all right. He just left everything to Mrs T – that was the problem. He never really got over the Mistress's death though. Fell off her horse on the estate, she did.'

'But surely, that was no reason to leave, was it?' Bill asked pensively. Carrie fell silent and hesitated. 'There's something else, isn't there?'

She sighed. 'Yes, there is. I can't lie to you.' She summoned enough courage to look him in the eye. 'D'you know what goes on in big houses like Farleigh Manor?'

'Haven't a clue. You tell me.'

'Well, sometimes girls in service, like me, are expected to…'

'What?'

'They're expected to…you know…'

Bill was getting frustrated. 'Go on, Carrie, go on. What are they expected to do?'

'Surrender to important guests, that's what!' she exclaimed.

A quizzical frown tugged his eyebrows together. What was passing through his mind was unthinkable. 'You mean… go to bed with them?' She nodded. 'Good God!' He was genuinely shocked.

'And I had to do it with a guest. Someone so important that I can never say his name.' Bill stood up and went to the window where he stared out in silence. Anger like a gathering storm clouded his features. 'The trouble is, I got pregnant,' she said in a small voice. 'I'm going to have a baby. The Squire was so angry that he threw me out. It was Mrs Trimble's fault. She's the one who put him up to it.'

'I can't believe this.' Bill's face looked grim.

'It's true, Bill, I'm not lying.' She was certain that Bill was going to throw her out too when he spun around and quickly came to her, but he moved with compassion and his anger was not directed at her.

'No, not you, Carrie. It's not your fault. I just can't believe that toffs do that sort of thing. It's disgusting. It's immoral. It's just…bloody awful.'

'The Squire said he was very sorry, but said I had to go. He's made an allowance for me, to bring up the baby. Forty shillings a week he's going to pay. That's more than artisans get. But I must never tell the child or anyone else in the world the name of its father, or it'll be stopped.' As her head dropped forlornly, Bill's heart pounded with sympathy and anger.

He sat beside her and put his arm around her shoulders. 'Carrie, you can stay here as long as you want. You can have my bed. I'll sleep on the couch. You'll get no improper advances from me, I assure you.' It was not exactly what he had in mind when he first saw her, but he meant what he said. Far from being unsettled by her sudden reappearance in his life, he was overjoyed, in spite of the circumstances. She was special, and he had no intention of abusing her trust. Feeling protectively manly, he embraced Carrie's misfortune and made it his new mission in life. He knew not where it would lead, but he dared to hope for a happy ending.

'Thank you, Bill,' she murmured softly against his chest. 'I didn't know what to do.'

'It's all right, Carrie, you've done the right thing. I'm glad I found you. There's room enough here, and you'll be safe with me.'

His soft generosity brought more tears, but of a different kind. 'It's only till Aunt Ethel gets back, Bill, I promise.'

'I know, I know,' he said, comfortingly.

Chapter Two

10 DOWNING STREET, LONDON
Monday, March 30, 1914

Asquith came back to London from a dismally wet weekend at his private residence, the Wharf at Sutton Courtney, to throw a bombshell into the arena of the House. He proposed himself as the new Secretary of State for War, with the intention of combining this office with his position as Prime Minister. He knew little of war, but felt that he could acquaint himself with it by reading whatever material he could find concerning the War Office and the Army. Having taken up the office, he was obliged to vacate his seat and seek re-election as MP for East Fife, which he expected to achieve unopposed. To many colleagues and opponents, there seemed very little point to Asquith's appointment as Secretary of State for War – except that it gave him access to War Office notepaper, as well as that of Downing Street, for his love letters to Venetia Stanley.

His move, however, failed to obfuscate his political difficulties over the complex and unresolved Irish Question and the continuing, ever more desperate agitation of the suffragist movement, the aims of which he opposed. The parliamentary Ulster Volunteer Force swelled its ranks to 100,000 men, and a civil war in Ireland was now a real possibility. Whatever course of action he decided upon for handling this situation, he had to keep in mind the fact that he depended greatly on the support of the Ulster Unionists for his parliamentary power. As a result of the problems with Ireland, his premiership had reached an all-time low, and was heading into crisis.

With the pressures piling up on him, he needed the calming influence of Venetia more than ever. Referring to the previous Friday afternoon's customary drive along the Embankment holding hands with her, he wrote to her with his latest news:

"Dearly beloved,
Your letter, which I found here this morning, was the greatest solace
& joy, as the thought of you & our delicious drive has been all thro'
the wet dreary Sunday at the Wharf. I drove away from you in
solitude & missing you so much, but the memory of things you had
said "flashed upon the inward eye".

I started the idea of the two offices at once, & I need not tell you
that Winston's eyes blazed, and his polysyllables rolled, and his
gestures were those of a man possessed..."©

THE ADMIRALTY, LONDON
Tuesday, April 28, 1914

Finally, after months of pleading and cajoling by Winston Churchill,
Admiral Fisher[1] finally agreed to meet him to discuss submarines and
other naval matters. Churchill's recent "black dog" – one of the bouts
of depression to which he was prone – immediately lifted. At last, he
was back in contact with the man to whom he had recently written:
"Contact with you is like breathing ozone to me".

It was because Fisher had once enjoyed the admiration and
friendship of monarchs and statesmen that he had become resentful in
the autumn of his years, particularly of those who stood in the way of
progress. For this reason he had a smouldering respect for Churchill's
youth and progressive ways, and had come back to give him some
advice.

Churchill sat at his desk, beaming a smile at the admiral and

---

[1] **Admiral Lord John Arbuthnot Fisher G.B, First Baron Fisher, Of Kilverstone.**
During his earlier term as First Sea Lord, between 1904 and 1910, Admiral Fisher became
the Navy's own "Industrial Revolution" by applying his dogged determination and immense
talent for improving things to virtually every part of it. Nothing escaped his attention; from
new guns that brought more firepower to bear on targets to new levels of training for naval
officers and ratings. But his most significant achievement was the introduction of a
revolutionary class of armoured cruiser, Dreadnought, *which set new standards for all future*
warships and gave the Royal Navy a lead that all navies had to follow. Fisher – known
variously behind his back as "Jacky", "Old Jacky", "the Old Boy", and "the Old Malay" on
account of the strange yellow tint of his skin – had a talent for improving things that knew no
barriers, and Churchill respected him for that.

searching the yellow face for any indication that he was past it all, but the old boy had lost none of his sparkle and his slightly bulging blue eyes, redolent of frogs, were still twinkling brightly. The pugnacious droop of his mouth suggested that he was ready for anything. Churchill cleared his throat, wondering where to begin with the delicate matter at hand. 'John, there are a few points from your excellent paper on which I am not entirely convinced.'

'Oh? What are those, precisely?' Fisher thrust his chin into a more challenging position.

'Well, like you, I am disquieted about our submarine development and agree that we must make a greatly increased effort to counter the enormous building programmes in which Germany has been indulging for the last six years.' Fisher maintained his bulldog look, waiting for the main point.

Churchill was at pains to tread carefully through this conversation. 'The greatest uncertainty I have is the question of the use of submarines to sink merchant vessels. I do not believe that this will ever be done by a civilised Power such as Germany. If there were a nation vile enough to do such a thing then it would be justifiable, and indeed necessary, to employ the extreme resources of science against them, but at present I see no evidence of such a nation. Therefore, there is nothing to support the prominence assigned to submarines in your...aah...most excellent paper.'

The old boy shifted in his seat, ready for battle. 'I have said all this till I'm sick, Winston! There are idiots who lecture at the Naval War College that Tirpitz won't use his submarines to sink merchant ships! They say that the civilised world would execrate him if he did...*ABSOLUTE NONSENSE!* Did not Skobeleff exterminate the Turcomans – man, woman and child? Was he recalled? The Mexican generals...they murder ad lib! What has the civilised world done about that?' Churchill went to speak, but was shouted down.

'For God's sake! The essence of war is violence – moderation in war is *IMBECILITY! La raison du plus fort est toujours la meilleure.*' Jacky sat back, huffily, resting his case.

'But, John, you must appreciate that increasing the budget to pay for more submarines is extremely difficult when the matter has little appeal for the Prime Minister. Remember, also, that it was at your own insistence that all available resources have been applied to building up the surface fleet.'

'He has already invited me to dine with him,' said the admiral, dropping his gaze in a gesture that indicated Asquith was of little consequence to him. 'But I've declined. I already know his views, and I am well aware that our highly civilised bridge-and-booze Prime Minister finds the whole subject of submarine warfare unpalatable, but the threat of submarines sinking our unarmed merchant vessels will not lessen, just because it happens to offend his delicate sense of nicety! Take my advice... if necessary, drop a Dreadnought from the programme and use the money to build more submarines...or you will live to regret it!'

He prodded the desk to emphasis a point that seemed to linger in the air long after he had gone.

GOSPORT, HAMPSHIRE

For Carrie the week with Bill seemed like an idyllic fantasy holiday. Just being with him and free from Mrs Trimble's oppressive attention and the situation at Farleigh Manor was like being released from prison. Never in all her life, had so much personal attention been paid to Carrie, and every day was filled with something new and exciting. With a fresh happiness that seemed as if it would never end, she looked with new optimism at the changes forced upon her. Fate, it seemed, had brought her to this place to meet Bill.

Bill left the week's business to his young assistant and revelled in Carrie's company. He could hardly believe that she had only seen the sea twice before, on rare family Bank Holiday visits to Weymouth beach, and revelled in her compulsion to see it every day, now that she was surrounded by it. She loved the smell of it, and the hissing noise of its waves retreating from the pebble shore. On the beach one day, she noticed the ferryboats bustling across the Solent. The next day, as a surprise, he took her to the Isle of Wight on one of them and they spent the day drifting through the shops of Ryde then stopped at a harbour-side teashop before returning to Gosport. It was as close as Carrie had ever been to having a holiday abroad.

Returning on the ferry in the fading sunlight, they stood together in pensive silence at the guardrail, both reflecting on the enjoyable day that was coming to an end. Bill gazed at her with a look of wonderment in his eyes and a soft smile on his lips. With big sparkling eyes, she was watching the bustle of boats and ships mingling in the Solent. Low rays of sunlight shimmering off the sea turned her hair gold and brought translucency to her eyes. They were shining as if they had a soft green light behind them. Being with her was stirring feelings he had never had before.

'You're staring, young man. What's the matter?'

He pursed his lips. 'Nothing. I was just thinking. It's one of those days I don't want to end.'

Her warm hand slipped into his, and gave it a squeeze. I know, me too, but there will be another tomorrow.'

He could not remember a time when he had felt happier.

On their last day, they went up Portsdown Hill in Bill's buggy. It was a clear, bright day following two days of bad weather and the view from the top of the hill took Carrie's breath away – a bird's eye view of fifty miles of Hampshire and Sussex coastline. At her feet, Portsmouth and the Solent, Chichester, Southampton and the Isle of Wight, looked like a patchwork quilt nestling in the silvery sea, on which some child had left his toy docks, cranes and warships.

Bill explained that the ships she could see crawling imperceptibly along the Solent waters might be bound for anywhere in the world – across the Atlantic to America, to India or China, or to Africa – and some would be bringing home the fruit he had to buy for his shop. With her face beaming exhilaration, and her golden hair flowing in the breeze, she stretched out her arms and breathed deeply, inhaling the scene. 'One day,' she said, 'I'm going to live right here…on top of this hill. Anyone living here could never be unhappy.'

He laughed and pulled her arm gently. 'Come on, dreamer, it's time to go. You'd have to have a fortune to live up here.'

'I know…I know. But why shouldn't I have a fortune one day?'

'Because life isn't like that.'

She gave him a pretend frown and a playful dig in the ribs. 'Life, young man, is exactly what you make it. If you can't imagine what it's like to have a fortune… if you can't picture it, smell it, taste it, you'll never have one. I can...and I will, one day. You'll see.'

A frown flickered across his brow. For a fleeting moment, there was a glint of conviction and avarice in her eyes that he had not seen before – then she laughed – and it was suddenly gone. She pretended to gather up the scene at her feet, to take away with her, and playfully pushed him down into the wet grass. Like all the other days they had spent together, this one swept away her troubles and ended with kisses and laughter. In his bed that night, she showed him just how happy and grateful she was, and asked him not to sleep alone anymore.

It changed everything for Bill. His heart soared away like an eagle wheeling in the uplift caused by her presence in his life. Then, with a suddenness that came as a shock, their time together came to an abrupt end and Aunt Ethel was back. The more Carrie thought about having to explain why she was there, and asking Ethel for help, the more she dreaded it. The cold reality of her situation – banished for a whole week – had returned to spoil everything.

That evening, subdued and thoughtful, she was quietly packing her things when Bill came into the bedroom and stood behind her. He put his arms around her waist, without speaking. They stood there in silence for a few moments, looking at the half-filled case on the bed. 'It's been terrific, having you here this week,' he said, nuzzling into her hair.

'Mmm...hasn't it?' There was reluctance and resignation in her sigh. 'It was wonderful, Bill. I'll never forget it.' There was a reflective pause as they thought about the week. 'But I have to go,' she said, abruptly. Her words fell to the floor like pellets of cold lead, where they examined them in silence. 'But we will see each other, won't we?' she said, turning quickly and catching his solemn expression.

'That's what I wanted to talk to you about, Carrie.'

Her smile faded quickly.

'I've been thinking. You and your situation... me and mine.' She was anxious about what was coming next. 'The trouble is...' he mumbled awkwardly, looking everywhere but into her eyes. 'I know it wasn't how these things are supposed to happen...' He looked directly into her eyes. 'Carrie, I don't want you to go,' he said, suddenly. 'I want you to stay here, with me.' She turned away, close to tears. 'Carrie, what's the matter?'

'Nothing,' she said, softly. 'I can't tell you how much this week has meant to me. I'll never be able to thank you enough.'

He frowned. 'So what's wrong, then? I don't understand.'

'It... it was a holiday…just a holiday. I don't want it to end. But it has to.' He was crushed. She could see it on his face.

'Why?' He quickly put his arms around her. 'It doesn't have to, Carrie.'

She pulled away. 'It has to, Bill. I can't stay here forever.'

'Why not? If I *want* you to.'

'You haven't thought about it properly. I'm pregnant...with another man's child. You're a really smashing bloke, Bill, but you can't take me on – I won't let you…not like this. It wouldn't be right. In a while I'll be all fat and horrible, like a beached whale. You won't want me then. And then there will be a screaming baby to take care of in the middle of the night – someone else's – and nappies on the line. What would your mother say – and your friends?'

He looked into her eyes. One short week ago he was simply getting on with his life, but now he was in love – and nothing else mattered. 'Carrie, I don't care what people say. I only care about you. I want you to stay with me... I'll take care of you, and the baby. It's part of you – and that's what matters. I really like kids.'

She smiled. 'You're terrific, Bill Guy. You make me really happy. Come here and give me a big hug.' She wrapped her arms around him. 'I want to stay...and I'll stay, if you want me to.'

'I do, I do.' With a silly grin creasing his face, he gave her a hug that almost squeezed the breath out of her. Over his shoulder, Carrie could see the whole of Bill's apartment at once: the bedroom and, through its doorway, the living room and kitchen. The only thing she could not see was the lavatory in the back yard. It was not exactly Farleigh Manor, but it felt homely and solid, like Bill. In the warmth and safety of his arms, she felt secure and contented with the turn her life had just taken. She had someone to love her and watch over her, and she was not alone anymore. However incredible the events of the past nine days, this was no dream. It was real. There was a man in her life now. Hers and hers alone, and without a trace of guilt or danger she could reach out and touch him whenever she felt the need. She could feel him now, holding her in his strong arms. It brought a soft smile to her lips and swelled her heart with contentment.

As the weeks went by, Carrie's pregnancy began to show, and Bill proved to be as good as his word. He was tender and caring, and he did everything possible to make her feel happy and secure. His friends accepted their circumstances without hesitation and treated Carrie as if she were his new wife.

It was Aunt Ethel who found the situation impossible to deal with. Finding out that the daughter of her dear departed sister was "living in sin" was bad enough, but for her to be having a baby by an entirely different man at the same time was downright shameful, she said. She agonised, long and hard, torn between her sense of responsibility for Carrie and her disgust with such an unsavoury situation – but then, knowing Bill to be an otherwise decent and respectable local man, she finally softened and extended the hand of friendship.

In the light of Carrie's new life, Farleigh Manor had already faded into past memory, and she opened up like a flower. Unshackled from the constraints of domestic service and watchful housekeepers, Carrie's real personality came shining through. Bill's friends became her friends, and they came visiting to be with Carrie as much as they came to see him. Her first meeting with George Royal, Bill's best friend, seemed to come with an unspoken requirement to get along with him. In his new domestic bliss, Bill was keen to repay the past kindness of George's family. They socialised together a number of times and George became a regular visitor to the apartment when he was on leave or stationed in Portsmouth Barracks.

With her allowance from Thomas Farleigh duly being paid into her Post Office account and living rent-free with Bill, she had money to spare for new clothes for the first time in her life. It was then that her desire to become the woman Edward had promised that she would become began to burn. With unerring intuition, Marjorie Thompson, a good friend of Bill, sensed the deepest of Carrie's needs the moment she met her.

Marje was herself a stylish, magnetic, vivacious woman who had a genuine affection and admiration for Carrie and her fresh, natural beauty. Marje was two years older than Carrie, but seemed at least ten years more mature, and she had an upper-class attitude to life that Carrie adored. She was natural, but pleasant and attractive in her own way. What Marje lacked in beauty she made up for with her stylish worldliness. Nothing about men or the world seemed to faze her, and she could be relied upon to sail through everyday matters with clever, sardonic comments and effortless decisions. However, the main attraction for Carrie was that Marje had a flair for fashion that left Carrie in awe of her.

The women were drawn to each other like magnets the first time they met. It was clear from that moment on that Marje was going to be her best friend and confidante, and mentor to the metamorphic changes that Carrie was determined to make to herself. As weeks went by, with Marje's help and encouragement, Carrie developed an eye for fashion of her own. In spite of her expanding waistline, she was soon dressing more stylishly, taking more interest in her appearance, and conducting herself with studied elegance.

Suddenly, there was new purpose to Carrie's life. She felt comfortable with her new situation and she was happy with Bill. He was not as handsome as the man of her dreams, nor was he as polished. But he was rugged and dependable. More importantly, he provided the warm glow of security that she had always longed for. She helped in his shop, keeping it clean and tidy, serving customers and arranging the produce more presentably. The partnership was good for business and Carrie fitted perfectly into Bill's life. Their lives seemed idyllic, with nothing to cloud their contentment.

Bill had jokingly warned Carrie about George Royal's reputation with women before he came to supper that first time. When he arrived in his uniform, she could see why. He seemed too good-looking for his own good, with clean, angular features, fair hair, bright blue eyes and a golden tan. He had more than his fair share of attractions, and looked athletic and self-assured beyond his twenty-three years as well. Any man like that, she decided instantly, is going to be self-absorbed and vain; and she seemed determined to show that he was, but when she spoke to him, her pupils were fully dilated all the same.

With Carrie in his life now, Bill was not as keen to go drinking as he once was. Instead, he gave George an open invitation to visit them whenever he could, to enjoy Carrie's excellent cooking. George took up the offer and came round frequently, bringing a different girl more often than not. It seemed to Carrie that there was one serious flaw in George's character. It was his preoccupation with his naval career and himself. He was full of himself and naval stories and, having been in the Royal Navy since he was fifteen, was unable to talk about anything else. His stories about his experiences and travels fascinated her, however, as did he, and envy gleamed in her eyes whenever he spoke of exotic places about which she could only dream.

'I would give anything to see it,' she purred one day, absorbed by his colourful description of Malta. 'And those huge guns you operate. How glamorous!' "How glamorous" was one of those useful expressions she had picked up from Marje, with others like "marvellous!" and "darling". It was an innocent enough remark, but it fluttered down upon George's self-absorbed exposition like a piece of frilly nonsense, and attracted a dismissive glance from him that was not the appreciative response she was hoping for.

'Glamorous? A ship's turret! You call something that wreaks death and destruction *glamorous*? You really have no idea. *Bloody murderous* is more like it. You can't begin to imagine what it's like.'

George's response seemed unnecessarily harsh, clumsy and inconsiderate to Carrie, and there was an embarrassed silence as she gathered her thoughts. A deep blush crept up from her neck and reached her cheeks. 'Well excuse me, Admiral,' she spat, venomously, 'for not appreciating the tremendous power you have under your command! How stupid of me. I thought this conversation was between a few silly civilians…not your hairy naval messmates!' She rushed from the room, offended and hurt.

It occurred to George that she was right, straight away. He had forgotten himself for a moment. In the mess, the cut and thrust of conversation could be quite vicious without causing offence, but here, it was out of order. Bill shrugged to his friends. Marje shot a reproachful glance at George and hurried after Carrie. George looked sheepishly apologetic and sighed. It was all very embarrassing. As George never did look far beyond the physical attributes of his women, the well-hidden message in Carrie's innocent comments was wasted on him. Her naïve attempt to tell him that it was *him* she found glamorous, not his job, went over his head – but Marje understood.

It was an awkward, stupid incident that set Carrie against him. Of all Bill's friends, it had to be with George that she felt prickly. She suddenly resented his intrusion, invited or not, in the life she had created with Bill and she became jealous of the bond between the men. Apart from having to cook for his numerous girlfriends, the arrogance she saw in him set her hackles on end the most. It made her angry, for no reason that she could explain to herself.

As time went by, she found herself spitting cutting remarks about his looks and vanity. It irritated her madly that he was so obviously used to adoring admiration from his women, and very clearly not short of it. Part of the problem was that she had never met a man quite like him. Neither had she had a proper relationship with a man of her own before. Now that she did, it was being marred by an expectation that she should automatically like Bill's closest friend, even though he had a remoteness that seemed cold and impenetrable. Until Marje mentioned it one day, it never occurred to Carrie that perhaps he, too, might be finding the situation difficult. But whatever the problem, it caused tension between them that dogged Carrie's every effort to get to know him better. She began to wonder if they were ever going to be friends. There was, however, something going on inside Carrie that even she could not understand. She wanted George to want her, and he did not. As ridiculous as it seemed, even to her, she craved his attention. In spite of her pregnancy and her contentment with Bill, she needed to know that George desired her.

It was fortunate for all three of them that George was completely unaware of this. According to Marje's understanding of him and his reputation, he was likely to have taken advantage of her confusion, whether she was pregnant or not. Then something else happened to make the situation worse. He and Bill were having a deep discussion one day, about Germany's military intentions, and in the middle of this, Bill suddenly announced that he believed that war was inevitable and that he would definitely volunteer for it, if it came. Everywhere in Britain, he said, men were getting excited about the chance to take part in a short war, and he was no exception. For Carrie, the fact that he wanted to be part of it would have been bad enough. But when George egged him on with all the crassness of a single, unattached man, her patience reached breaking point and snapped explosively.

'You selfish pigs!' she shouted.

They were both startled by her outburst. No one had seen her as angry as she was with George. 'So you, you selfish bastard, with no family of your own to worry about...you think it's all right for him to go off and see the world, do you? What about me and my baby? We can be left, can we? And the business? Who's going to look after that? What if he was killed or maimed? I don't suppose you thought of that, did you? God, I could knock your stupid heads together.' She spun on her heel and stormed out of the room.

The men shifted uneasily in their chairs, stunned by the outburst that fizzled out as quickly as it began. She regretted it, instantly, because her angry outburst had laid bare the secret fears and concerns that she had been trying to keep to herself. More significantly, it revealed to the men the extent to which she believed Bill was committed to her. Until then, he really did not think that he was. But George was fuming about being treated like a child.

Any regret he may have had about unwittingly causing trouble between them was swamped by his anger. Suddenly feeling unwelcome, he mumbled an unrepentant, tight-lipped farewell, stood up, and left hurriedly, looking unlikely to ever return.

Carrie's anger quickly dissolved into remorse, but the damage was already done. It took several days and as many apologies to persuade George to visit them again. When he did, he was unable to relax around Carrie. Their friendship gradually repaired itself, but it was never quite the same again. He seemed subdued, and his attitude towards her changed. But for her, that was not all bad. He became more attentive, and began to notice her glances and the sensuous way she moved when Bill's attention was elsewhere. She never let her pregnancy get in the way, and she began a flirtation with George, passing messages with her eyes and turning her head whenever he gave her a parting peck on the cheek, to bring his lips closer to hers.

He was confused and uneasy about the strange messages written in her behaviour, which were tiny, but quite obvious to him and him alone. A sparkle of satisfaction shone in her eyes when she realised that, at last, she was disturbing him.

LONDON
14 June, 1914

After the worst thunderstorms in living memory, in which four inches of rain fell on London in a mere three hours, the city felt refreshed and reinvigorated, if somewhat flooded and puddle-strewn. The Thames was in full flood. From the Embankment, the turbulent brown floodwater rushing by seemed to emulate the Bismarkism of the German Government – raw, pent-up power, relentlessly pursuing new territory in which to expand.

June and July slipped by with no indication that Germany was prepared to step back from her threatening position. For those monitoring the situation closely, the real prospect of war began to loom larger. Disappointed with the lack of information emanating from leading ministers, the *Daily Chronicle* began to probe Whitehall at all levels but it was with great fortune that its Editor chanced one day upon the Secretary of State for Foreign Affairs, Sir Edward Grey, at Grillons. Stopping by Sir Edward's table, he succeeded in obtaining permission to send a correspondent to see him for a short interview.

Sir Edward had previously shunned members of the press and was known to be the most insular of statesmen. It was said that he hated foreign travel and knew less about foreigners than any other Minister in the Government. These seemed to the press rather odd little idiosyncrasies for a Foreign Secretary.

It filled many with apprehension that the man whose responsibility it was to prevent Britain from slithering over the brink into unwanted war should also dislike meeting foreigners, foreign travel and negotiations.

The correspondent dispatched to find out from Sir Edward if all that could be done to avert a war with Germany had been done was greeted with icy resentment. However, he gained an initial impression that Sir Edward could perhaps be the "strong silent man" of the Government. Characterised by a mouth like a ruled pencil line, steady eyes and chiselled features, his face gave the impression of a steel mask. Combining this with his uncanny reticence of speech and even tone, he quickly gave the impression that he would be a good man to have in an emergency. The correspondent began by asking if he believed that Britain's stance on the German threat was likely to result in war.

Sir Edward steepled his fingers beneath his nose in the manner of a schoolmaster and sat silent and unblinking – seemingly taking care to phrase his reply. 'No,' he said, abruptly, after some time. There was a long patient wait for the rest of his words of wisdom, but none came. The next question was pressed more firmly:

'It is the opinion of Mr Lloyd George that the Kaiser wishes to avoid war with us and that given a clear indication of the precise point at which we would take up arms against him, the Kaiser would not go beyond it. Has this been made clear to the German Government?'

Sir Edward clearly resented the question but his face remained expressionless. 'Defining Britain's position in the manner you suggest would be unseemly and lacking in diplomacy,' he said, dispassionately. 'I will not do such a thing. It is not my place to issue threats of war on behalf of His Majesty's Government.'

'But surely, Sir Edward, if such action could avoid war...' The correspondent was cut off, mid-sentence. Grey continued in his toneless way.

'We have nothing to fear. It is calm on the diplomatic front. The Kaiser is reported to be on a sailing holiday in the Norwegian fjords; the Head of the German Foreign Office is enjoying his honeymoon; the Head of the German Army, von Moltke, is currently visiting a foreign spa. This should be assurance enough that nothing untoward is about to happen. Now, if you will excuse me, I have pressing matters to attend to.' With that, he terminated the interview.

The correspondent left the Foreign Office with a feeling of dread, remembering Lloyd George's comment that Grey preferred holidays in his fishing lodge in Hampshire to negotiating with "ignorant foreigners". He returned to the *Daily Chronicle's* Editor with the personal opinion that Sir Edward was better suited to the administration of an office than averting war – an aristocrat who had simply stepped into his position without the usual rough and tumble of politics – and was lacking imagination.

The article never appeared in print.

THE SAVOY HOTEL, LONDON
Late June, 1914

In London, the concierge of the Savoy Hotel was ready when the black motorcar swept up the driveway and stopped at the main doors. The chauffeur opened the door and handed out his passenger. The concierge stepped forward and politely welcomed the tall, gracious lady of mature years.

'Lady Sheffield. We are honoured. Allow me.' He bowed slightly and swept his arm towards the doors. They opened as if by magic. He led her through the foyer and into the restaurant. Waiting impatiently at a corner table was Margot Asquith, who greeted Lady Sheffield with an unusual degree of warmth. Then, with a waft of her hand, she dismissed the fussing waiters settling Lady Sheffield into her seat at the table. The two women looked and smiled at one another, as if wondering how their lives had come to this, and where to begin. A waiter stepped forward to pour water.

Margot dismissed him with a glare and poured it herself. 'Thank you for coming, Lady Sheffield,' she said. 'We find ourselves in a strange situation.'

'Indeed. I wish it were not so. When I received your impassioned letter, I felt compelled to come – in spite of not knowing what I can do.'

'Lady Sheffield, there must be something you can do to bring to an end this ridiculous romance between my husband and your daughter Venetia. I find myself awake at night, worrying about the situation – sick with anxiety and at a loss to know which way to turn.' Lady Sheffield looked intently at the dark rings beneath Margot's dark, deep-set eyes, and gave a gracious smile.

'You have my sympathy, Mrs Asquith. I do not envy you, but I cannot see that there is much I can do to relieve your suffering. My daughter is extremely headstrong. I've had strong words with her, of course, but the relationship will not be finished until she finds a way of ending it herself.'

Whatever hope Margot had had, slipped away instantly. She straightened the cutlery and moved her rolled napkin to one side then leaned forward. 'I had hoped that by making Venetia aware of the heartache she is causing, you might be able to stop this nonsense before it ruins Henry. The poor, silly man is completely besotted with her. My God, if some vindictive newspaper editor chooses to print the story, Henry's career would be finished. Both our families would be shamed. Surely, you could make her understand the seriousness of this situation?'

'Mrs Asquith. Margot – may I call you that? – My husband and I are very well aware of such a possibility, and we both feel as you do, but Venetia is twenty-seven years old, and very independent. I can only suggest that it is your own daughter, Violet, who is best placed to make Venetia see sense. After all, they are very close, are they not?'

Margot sighed. 'Violet is my stepdaughter. She will always be her father's child. Since she lost her mother to typhoid years ago, she has grown so close to Henry that she applauds everything he does. Try as I do to create a family around her, I remain the "wicked" stepmother – an outsider – to Violet. Although Henry is tender and loving towards me, it is Violet whom he loves most dearly, and she idolises him. I can do nothing to alter that – not that I would, if I could. So you see, hidden behind the public face of the country's first family there are divisions.'

'How ghastly!'

'So I beg you – implore you – to steer Venetia in another direction. Are there no suitors?'

Lady Sheffield shook her head wearily. 'Neither is Venetia concerned. Few men have caught her eye, and of those who have, none seem interested. She is such a comradely girl, more than she is feminine: almost masculine in her behaviour. A veritable tomboy: and eligible men tend to take fright and see her just as a friend, rather than as a lady wife. There was of course Edwin Montagu…'

'Yes indeed,' said Margot, with renewed interest. 'A most suitable candidate.'

Lady Sheffield's expression said that he wasn't. 'For years, Edwin has desperately sought her hand but he is, as I am sure you are aware… unattractive.'

'I admit that I have seen better looking men.'

'No, I don't mean unattractive…I mean "*unattractive*". You

know, "of another faith".'

Margot suddenly remembered that Montagu was a Jew. 'Oh that. But surely …he is from a well-founded, wealthy family. Is religion an insurmountable problem?'

Distaste stiffened Lady Sheffield's expression. 'In order for Venetia and him to marry, one of them would be forced to go through religious conversion! Clearly, that would not be Edwin, although the dear man offered to do this himself, in exchange for Venetia's hand – but that would not do. If Edwin were to give up his faith, his family would automatically disinherit him and he would be penniless. It would therefore fall to Venetia to renounce her Christian faith and become a Jew.'

'How ghastly!' said Margot, with a touch of well-concealed mirthful sarcasm. 'So marriage is out of the question then?'

'Precisely.'

'Pity.' As the ladies nibbled their light lunch, Margot continued to press for action. Lady Sheffield promised to do whatever she could…but held out little hope of success.

Chapter Three

GOSPORT
June 29, 1914

It was on Monday June 29 that an anxious customer came into the shop with news of "The Crime of Sarejevo". Headlines glared from every newspaper billboard that the Habsburg heir, Archduke Franz Ferdinand of Austria-Hungary had been assassinated the day before, deepening concerns about the mood in Europe. Bill sent his shop boy out for a paper and he and Carrie read the account of the killing with mixed emotions.

It said that while the Archduke and his wife were on an official journey through Sarajevo in an open motorcar, a 19-year-old Serb student, Gavrilo Princip, had stepped from the crowd and shot them with two point-blank shots from a Browning automatic pistol. There were reports of frantic activity in diplomatic circles as the consequences were evaluated, and of the shock reverberating throughout Europe. It all seemed so unreal. After such a long period of peace in Europe, to most people the news sounded more like a *moment critique* from a new novel about "Jack the Ripper".

From July 18th to the 20th, the Royal Navy assembled for the King's inspection of the fleet. It was the Spithead Review and over thirty miles of warships, including fifty-eight battleships and battlecruisers, filled the Solent, but this display of naval might did nothing to weaken Germany's commitment to war. After the review, all leave was cancelled on orders from the Admiralty and the Navy mobilised itself immediately. As a precautionary measure, the Grand Fleet took to its base at Scapa Flow and prepared for the worst.

After weeks of diplomatic negotiation, the full significance of the Sarajevo assassination became known, but ordinary people in Britain carried on as normal, aware that there was trouble in Europe, but still not bothering to take it seriously. It all seemed so far away.

On the other side of the world, a small but significant occurrence caught the attention of the Admiralty at Whitehall. Two German warships, *Scharnhorst,* the flagship of German Admiral Maximillian von Spee, and *Gneisenau* departed the waters of the Far East on August 3 and headed into the South Pacific Ocean, not to return. To the Commander-in-Chief of the Royal Navy's China Station these movements were ominous, and he reported his concern that something was afoot.

In Europe the crisis deepened. In spite of Britain's efforts to mediate and negotiate between the posturing nations, Germany invaded the neutral countries of Belgium and Luxemburg, without warning. Britain immediately aligned herself with France and Russia to condemn Germany's aggression, protesting and negotiating all the while but it was to no avail. On August 4, 1914, as people came back to work from the August Bank Holiday, they learned that Britain was on the brink of a war with Germany.[2]

LONDON
The Evening Of August 4, 1914

Thousands of cheering Britons gathered outside Buckingham Palace, as if intent on making its stately presence the focal point of their patriotic fervour, while millions of others lined the streets of London. Approaching midnight, a taut silence settled on the people waiting in their thousands outside Buckingham Palace. Clutching their notebooks, reporters moved slowly along the fringe of the crowd, observing the body language and expressions of the people, witnessing history in the making. The tension made the nape of many a neck bristle as people stood amongst the faint smell of coal gas

---

[2] *THE INEVITABLE CONFLICT*

The First World War – the "Great War" – began between Germany and Britain but many nations were sucked into it. The causes of the war were complex and had been brewing for many years.

At this time, Kaiser Wilhelm II ruled Germany and his ambition was nothing less than the ultimate conquest of the globe. The Kaiser was bent on war. The British Government tried to negotiate but finally sent a note to Germany that if the Kaiser did not withdraw from the brink by midnight on August 4, 1914, a state of war would exist between the two countries.

drifting down from a faulty streetlight and the homely aroma of horse manure under foot. The crowd held its breath. Apart from the occasional consumptive cough, there was no other sound, but the anticipated last-minute response from the German Government never came.

At midnight, the sonorous tones of Big Ben reverberated over the rooftops of London, echoing with the sound of doom. As the bell rang out the hour with sombre, dramatic clangs, Europe seemed to be slipping over the edge into the black abyss of war. The twelfth strike of the great bell resonated through St James's Park and died away. A roar immediately erupted and ran along the Mall then up Constitution Hill. The uncertainty was over. The worst was known. Euphoric, bright-eyed young men cheered and threw their hats into the air. It was now August 5, 1914: the first day of war in Europe, and they were keen to get on with it. When they'd exhausted their patriotism, they headed for the West End to celebrate. Other people filed away quietly.

In an hour, the Mall was empty. Brimming with patriotism and far from sleep, some wandered aimlessly, gravitating towards the West End. For many, the tiresome monotony of everyday life was about to make way for something altogether more exciting. Others drifted off with the dark shadow of impending doom embedded in their glassy stares, deep in private thought.

There was a fever of confused activity as people dashed this way and that. They seemed to be unable to cope with their dramatically altered conditions. Suddenly, the security and stability of years of peace was snatched away and life, as it had been, ended.

At least for Britain's Prime Minister, the war was a blessing in disguise, in purely political terms. The two major problems that had been dogging his premiership, the Irish Question and the Women's Suffrage Movement, evaporated overnight. All sides in Ireland agreed to put their differences and grievances aside for the duration of the war, and made a commitment to the defence of the Empire.

In a similar display of patriotism, the Suffragette family of Emmeline Pankhurst immediately offered the services of its supporters to more constructive endeavours. Having been conducting a ten-year urban guerrilla war against the Government in pursuit of a woman's right to vote, the Suffragettes agreed to defer their campaign of bombing and hunger strikes in favour of peaceful demonstrations.

That day, August 5, 1914, Asquith invited Lord Horatio Herbert Kitchener to become the Secretary of State for War. Earl Kitchener of Khartoum was then aged 64, He accepted the position readily and took over the War Office immediately. In the light of Kitchener's reputation as a cold, if not callous military leader with notable mistakes as well as successes to his credit, the appointment was viewed as a daring experiment but, as far as British soldiers were concerned, if one man could bring Britain successfully through a war it was their God-like leader, Kitchener.

Others were left wondering.

The war had begun.[3]

In spite of everything else that was going on around him at the time, the intensity of the Prime Minister's preoccupation with Venetia Stanley shone through his frequent letters to her. Writing every day, sometimes as often as three times in one day, Asquith kept her abreast of developments, particularly in respect of his feelings for her. On August 8, he wrote:

"My darling it was the greatest of joys to be with you again & see you & hear you talk & feel that you were near & the same. Only it was all too short. I wish you hadn't torn up your letter. I wonder if you were as glad to see me again? Please write to me tomorrow & tell me exactly where you will be. I like to know every hour...
...I love & prize you with all my heart."©

As the realisation of war tightened its grip on the collective British consciousness, the atmosphere in London became unnaturally taut. On behalf of the people, journalists looked to the country's leaders in search of inspiration and hope. But they searched in vain, seeing instead a Government reeling beneath the weight of its new responsibilities and the pace of developments. One inadequacy after another came to light, and the confidence of journalists flagged under

---

[3] *The Navy's plunge into war was both rapid and dramatic. The German Navy commenced hostilities as soon as formalities were over. The official time for the commencement of the war was midnight on August 4. At 6.30 am on August 6 in the southern half of the North Sea, the British cruiser AMPHION struck a German mine which broke her back and cost the lives of some 147 British sailors and 24 German prisoners*

the difficulty of gleaning information from Ministers stretched to their limits.

Firstly, there seemed to be a problem with guns. Stocks of ammunition were woefully inadequate and not enough had been ordered, or made, for a full-blooded war. Secondly, there was a shortage of manpower. The British Army was neither large enough nor adequately equipped to match the massively manned and fully equipped German Army. In feverish haste, a programme of recruitment was undertaken. Within a matter of weeks, almost half a million volunteers increased the Army's strength and the British Expeditionary Force landed in France.

Ordinary people whose lives, until then, had been sheltered, simple and parochial suddenly found themselves fighting for King and country in places they had never heard of before. One journalist, wishing one newly recruited soldier good luck as he departed for France only to discover that he had never before ventured out of Staffordshire, was dismayed by the soldier's response. *"Don't you worry, sir,"* he said, in the best of spirits. *"We'll give them Belgiums what for!"* The journalist's heart sank and he could only hope that someone enlightened the poor chap about who he was up against, before the first bullet left his rifle.

In Europe, battles and troop movements occurred at such a pace that it was difficult to keep up with them; such was the tardiness of news reports. At the Admiralty, Their Lordships remained wedded to the view that submarine warfare was an "extremely ungentlemanly way to fight", but their Lordships were soon obliged to think again. Britain's coastal waters became saturated with German submarines and mines, and the Navy was ill-equipped to detect them. As a consequence, captains and admirals of the Grand Fleet turned their attention to the unseen enemy beneath the waves and away from what was on the surface.

News of the number of British ships being sunk by torpedoes or mines came flooding in, with very few reports of German ships lost in return. Frustratingly, reports of losses were bowdlerised by the Government for reasons of propaganda, and the papers were unable to inform the public of them. For the first time in their lives some British correspondents felt the cold breath of defeat fanning their necks.

In Gosport, Emily Royal was sick with anxiety for the two men in her life. In the peacetime past, she had always missed them and wished she could be with them, but she had wearily accepted their long absences. Now, with war's constant dangers, she had no idea how she could survive the agony of waiting for news, never knowing where they were or what would be happening to them. She dreaded the time when they would leave for the war.

On August 6, 1914, Jack Royal's ship, *Good Hope,* was ordered to raise steam for her deployment to the naval base in the Falkland Islands. George, meanwhile, was recalled to Portsmouth Naval Barracks to stand by for his next ship. There were tearful farewells when Emily went to stand on the jetty beside the Renown pub with the other wives and mothers dressed in their best Sunday dresses and hats. Watching *Good Hope* leave Portsmouth Harbour for the long, 10,000-mile journey to the South Atlantic Ocean, with tears in her eyes and a tightly knotted wet handkerchief clutched against her cheek, she prayed quietly to herself that Jack would come home safe and sound. She went home with an all-too-familiar feeling of emptiness.

Bill, meanwhile, in a rush of adrenalin, wanted to head straight for the Army recruiting office to enlist with the rest of his friends. Carrie was distraught, and pleaded with him not to leave her alone. His emotions were in turmoil. He was torn between his concern for Carrie and the feeling that it was his duty to go. All he could think of was how he could possibly look friends in the eye as they went to enlist, if he did not go himself. He sat in the pub and listened to people talking about the war. Most of them were young bachelors with nothing to hold them back. He was no longer in the same position. He had new responsibilities, he reminded himself, as he enviously watched every fit person he knew setting off for the Army's recruiting centre.

After anguishing for some time, he finally made up his mind. What swayed him towards enlisting was the cheerfully optimistic view prevailing in the Government and in the street that this was going to be a short war. *"It'll all be over by Christmas,"* everyone said, and it convinced him that leaving Carrie at home for such a short time, safe and secure, would be easier to live with than the stigma that would inevitably come from not volunteering. When it was all over, he told everyone who would listen, and he was back with Carrie and the baby, all her anger would be forgotten.

Early in the morning on Friday, August 7, tight-lipped and determined, he went to enlist with an excited gleam in his eyes. He did not tell Carrie that he had decided to go, but she sensed it. Disillusioned and feeling let down, she kept herself busy and said nothing more about it. Four hours later he was back again, with disappointment written all over his face and his eyes dulled by dejection. The Army had declined him. A heart-murmur, which he never knew he had, rendered him unfit for any service, and neither the Army nor the Navy would take him.

He was in despair at first, and muttered that he felt like a second-rate man: a failure. Carrie, whose own relief gave her strength to spare, consoled him and told him that at least he would be able to look his friends in the eye with a clear conscience.

'Rotten luck, Bill!' they all said.

'Thank God!' Carrie breathed with relief. Realising how badly he felt already, she forgave him his selfishness and they got on with their lives.

Over the next few weeks, with friends gradually leaving for training camps, the people left at home felt the wind of change blowing through their lives. It felt cold, stark and lonely. Gosport, where Carrie and Bill were trying to adjust to a new way of living, became a centre of increased military activity. Across the water in Portsmouth, the dockyard bustled, as warships put to sea and soldiers and sailors streamed through the dockyard gates to embark in them. The Army set up mobile guns and occupied the old forts along the coast. Defence of the beaches and harbours had to be taken seriously.

Everywhere, faces looked set and people moved about with an air of chirpy determination. "*If we get on with it, it will be over that much sooner,*" was the general attitude. However, their Lordships still had no idea how to deal with submarine attacks and the infestation of mines in Britain's coastal waters.

The awesome potential of the submarine was demonstrated very clearly a few weeks after the loss of *Amphion.* In the North Sea on Tuesday, September 22, three British armoured cruisers, *Hogue,*

Aboukir and *Cressy,* steaming slowly at ten knots off the Hook of Holland without escort, were spotted by the German submarine *U-9.* The *U-9*'s first torpedo hit *Aboukir's* magazine and she exploded, going to the bottom in two pieces. *Hogue,* turning to assist her sister-ship, was hit by the second torpedo and sank within twenty minutes. Zigzagging away to safety, *Cressy* was struck by two more of *U-9's* torpedoes, and went straight to the bottom. Within one hour, a single German submarine dispatched three British cruisers to the bottom, with almost 1500 British officers and men.

Thankfully, no submarine had yet strayed beyond home waters. Distant sea battles were still going to be waged between surface vessels, where the outcome would depend upon the number, the relative speed, and firepower of the ships involved. The Admiralty persisted with a belief that a decisive, Armageddon-like, naval battle between the two mighty fleets would occur in the North Sea, and kept the Navy's best ships in home waters, in preparation for this but their Lordships were in a dilemma. It was in these very waters that British ships would also be most exposed to the peril of the German submarine.

THE FALKLAND ISLANDS
October 8, 1914

For Jack Royal, now 10,000 miles away at the Navy's southernmost coaling station in the Falkland Islands, there was no submarine threat, but the war was about to catch up with him all the same. Fate was already fiddling with Life's Great Puzzle and toying with the piece that had his name on it.

The protagonist of the piece was Admiral von Spee of the Imperial German Navy. It was von Spee who left the China Station on the very eve of war, and he was now loose in South American waters. With no permanent base of his own, he was roaming unpredictably in the Pacific Ocean, attacking allied shipping lines and bases at will. His squadron was small but effective, and his orders allowed him to rove the seas like a buccaneer.

Never knowing where he was or where he would appear next, the

Royal Navy could not get to grips with him. The only certain way to find him in such a wide area was to sweep it with a large number of ships, at the expense of weakening the defence of Britain's shores. The greatest fear now, however, was that sooner or later he would be obliged to force his way into the Atlantic to make his way home to Germany, and that he would destroy the Falklands base in the process.

Foreshadowing the developing drama, telegraphed signals that took several days to arrive began to chatter between the Admiralty and the two British admirals in the Atlantic Ocean. The senior of them was Rear Admiral Sir Christopher Cradock, flying his flag in the cruiser *Good Hope* – Jack Royal's ship – in the Falkland Islands. The other admiral, Rear Admiral Stoddart, was stationed at Abrolhos Rocks off the East Coast of South America, several thousand miles north of the Falklands. Stoddart had two cruisers: his flagship, the armoured cruiser *Defence,* and *Carnarvon,* and he was at Abrolhos Rocks primarily to protect allied shipping, but he was also looking for von Spee, and expected to run into him eventually.

On October 8, 1914, Admiral Cradock's 4th Cruiser Squadron was lying at anchor in Port Stanley of the Falkland Islands. *Good Hope* was being re-coaled. *Monmouth,* another cruiser of the squadron, was also there beside the armed merchant vessel *Otranto*. The other two of Cradock's ships, the light cruiser *Glasgow* and the old battleship *Canopus,* were somewhere out in the Atlantic protecting British shipping. A signal for Cradock arrived from the Admiralty, dated October 5, with a report of intelligence gathered in London. It informed him that von Spee was working his way across the Pacific Ocean towards South America, with his two cruisers *Gneisenau* and *Scharnhorst.* Their Lordships at the Admiralty then ordered Cradock to gather his small fleet together and go out and find the German ships. Cradock was worried.

His own intelligence told him that there were now five ships in von Spee's squadron: not just the three the Admiralty knew about. It was obvious to him that engaging them with his inadequate fleet of older, inferior ships would be pure suicide. He needed more ships, better ships. Responding immediately, he reported his concerns to the Admiralty, and asked that the most modern and powerful British ship within reach of him, Stoddart's flagship *Defence* at Abrolhos Rocks, should be transferred to him in the Falkland Islands.

His signal reached the Admiralty on October 11. In it, he informed Their Lordships of the latest intelligence reports he had received, confirming that three other German battlecruisers had now joined von Spee: *Nürnberg, Dresden* and *Leipzig*. He also voiced his fears that if von Spee should evade him, the Germans could go on to destroy the Falkland, English Bank and Abrolhos Rocks coaling stations in turn, and possibly reach the West Indies. Without this part of the network of British coaling stations around the world, the Royal Navy would become powerless in these waters. His signal ended with: DOES *DEFENCE* JOIN MY COMMAND?

The Admiralty was slow to respond. Unbeknown to Cradock, something was going on in Whitehall that was destined to cause indecision and delay there. The First Lord of the Admiralty, Winston Churchill, was in the process of sacking the incumbent First Sea Lord, Prince Louis of Battenberg, a nephew by marriage of Edward VII. Churchill found it necessary to do this because Prince Louis' handling of the Royal Navy, it was said, had been impaired by cruel criticism of his German ancestry in London that had made him ill with depression. It was to be effective from October 28.

This could mean "divine intervention" for Cradock, because the very man Churchill had it in mind to replace the prince with was none other than the infamous and decisive former First Sea Lord, Jacky Fisher. Churchill had been actively cajoling the mighty Fisher to return to the Admiralty as First Sea Lord, and had at last succeeded. Not that it took much to persuade the old boy.

There was also confusion at the Admiralty concerning Germany's naval tactics. Now would be the time to dispatch several British dreadnoughts to the South Atlantic Ocean, to support Cradock. But most dreadnoughts were being held in home waters in anticipation of an expected invasion of Britain, or a cataclysmic North Sea clash, neither of which had materialised. So far, the German fleet had seemed reluctant to come out and fight, and confined itself to shelling Britain's eastern coastal towns and cities under cover of darkness.

Chapter Four

GOSPORT
October 13, 1914

Considering there was a war on, life at home had been bumbling along normally enough. Letters from ships based in the Falkland Islands took several weeks to reach home, and deliveries had been sporadic. Emily had received just two letters from Jack since he left, and the last one mentioned only his boredom and great concern for George's safety. There had been no hint in his letters that any dangers were brewing in Jack's part of the world.

Carrie Palmer had worked on until she felt that her baby's arrival was imminent. Then on Tuesday, October 13, just as she was clearing supper away from the table, she had her first contractions and Bill rushed for the midwife. At 01:03 am precisely, Carrie's screams ended abruptly and her new baby girl struggled into the world. When Bill was finally permitted into the bedroom, he had no idea what to do, or how to show what he felt. He looked pale and worn out, as he gathered Carrie and the baby in his arms and held them. Beaming with pride and relief, Carrie kept staring at her baby, unable to believe that she was real. She was exhausted, but to Bill, they both looked wonderful. He wanted to feel part of the experience, but she knew that he would never be able to share what she herself felt as she held the tiny creature in her arms.

'What are you going to call her ... do you know?'

'Yes I do know,' she said, smiling tenderly at the baby. 'I've been thinking about that. Isn't she beautiful? I'm going to call her Catherine. Catherine May Palmer. That's a nice name don't you think? Kate, for short. *Kiss-me-Kate*!' They laughed together, and Kate screwed up her tiny face and tested her new lungs.

The following Saturday, October 17, George and his mother went to see the new baby. Emily was thrilled to hold Kate, and went into a self-indulgent reminiscence about George's infancy, to his acute embarrassment. Although she had come to offer congratulations, she seemed preoccupied with the war, and was clearly worried that her husband and son were now both going to be involved in it.

George kissed the corner of Carrie's mouth as he left, and put a tiny silver bracelet in Kate's wandering hand: a birth present from him and his mother. He was joining his new ship the following Monday, he said, to go back to sea again: this time, to war. It seemed ironic that George, who had been the only one of the group of friends actually serving when war broke out, should be the last of them to go to war. But that was simply because he had been under training in Portsmouth, for his promotion to Leading Gunnery Rating. Carrie felt the tears coming when he kissed her goodbye.

She knew she would miss him and worry about him, but his departure felt more poignant than that. It signalled the beginning of an altered way of life at home. The idyll she had been enjoying since she came to Gosport seemed to be crumbling away. With friends away and preparations for war being made at home, the warm bright days of summer were over and winter was closing in. A cold, grey emptiness gathered around those left at home, as they sensed an era coming to an end.

For the entire night of October 19 at 32 St Mark's Road, Gosport, George had hardly slept at all. Excitement had been to blame. That day he was to join his new ship, *HMS Inflexible*, in Plymouth Dockyard, and he had been thrilled to bits. At last, he was off to war in one of the Navy's newest and best battlecruisers. It was just what he had been hoping for. Like his friends, he would be doing his bit for King and Country. Fumbling in the darkness, he had found matches on his bedside table and struck one. He could just make out the face of the mahogany "grandmother" clock across the room. It was 5:00 am.

He had felt ragged, but eager. At home, he always had trouble sleeping at night. It was different to sleeping in a ship: quite the opposite, in fact. In a ship there were always soporific noises in the background: hissing ventilation systems and humming machinery to lull him to sleep, cocooned in his hammock. The silence of home felt uncanny, as if something was wrong, and it jarred his senses. The penetrating tick of that wretched clock had kept him awake for most of the night, as its pendulum slowly swung the hours away.

Finally, as if to end his tormented night, the smell of fried eggs and bacon seeped through the bedroom door and stirred his stomach. He heard his mother downstairs in the kitchen. His room in the tiny terraced house felt chilly. He got up, put on the light, and peered out between the curtains. It was dark, but he could just make out the outline of the heavy clouds rushing across the daybreak sky. He was inclined to jump straight into his uniform, which had his new Leading Rating's badge on its arm, but first, he needed hot water for washing and shaving. He threw his uniform greatcoat around his shoulders and went down to the tiny kitchen.

Emily was cooking breakfast on her shiny, black, coal-fired stove. She had a vacant look in her eyes. Her slate-grey hair was drawn into a neat "bun" at the back of her head, and it accentuated the paleness of her kindly face. She looked worried and tired, as if she might have been awake all night, too. She handed him a kettle of hot water from the top of the stove. 'Mornin', son.' Her voice cracked as she forced out her first words of the day. 'Your breakfast will be ready in a mo'.'

George noticed how intently she was concentrating on the frying pan. He gently put the kettle back on the stove and stood behind her for a moment, with his hands on her shoulders. He sat down at the small pine kitchen table, now white from years of scrubbing. 'Look, Mum, it's going to be all right,' he reassured her. 'I know what you're thinking, but my new ship is fine... she'll outrun anything.' He tilted his head to see if she was convinced. 'She's as safe as houses... I promise. Loads of heavy armour, new navigational equipment, bigger guns than anyone else's, torpedo tubes, and the latest steam turbine engines... she's got everything. Anyway, it's not as if we're going straight into battle. We're only sailing around in home waters. Just up there in the North Sea... you know, Scotland, Mum. Not much is going to happen in Scotland, is it?'

Emily's stony expression showed that nothing would convince her. She concentrated on her cooking and George noticed her wiping a tear from her cheek. He stood up to put an arm round her shoulders. She looked up and gave him one of her weary half-smiles. 'I know,

George. I know you've got to go', she said, quietly. 'But that doesn't stop me worrying about you, you know... or your dad.' She scooped a fried egg out of the pan and placed it carefully with the bacon and fried bread on his plate. 'Having both of you at sea is just twice the worry. That's all. There you go, son,' she said, trying to brighten up, 'be sure to get that down you before you set off. I'll make you a nice cup of tea, when you've finished with the kettle.' She wiped her hands on the apron she was wearing over her ankle-length grey skirt, and left the kitchen.

George's gaze wandered around the kitchen as he ate his breakfast. He knew he would not be seeing his home again for some time, and he wanted to take as much of it with him as possible. He finished eating and pushed the plate aside. For a moment, he sat back with his hands clasped behind his head, soaking up the neatness of the homely room and the spicy smell of the cakes Emily was always baking. This was home. He had grown up here, but it was a place he had not seen much of, since going to sea. It seemed impossible that it could be seven years since he first set foot inside the training establishment *HMS Ganges* – but it was.

On the black-painted, cast iron mantelpiece, high above the stove was a small, framed photo of his father, Jack, proudly resplendent in his Royal Naval Lieutenant's uniform. It had pride of place among the pieces of souvenir china lined up on the crisp white lace runner. Tidily arranged around Jack were several mementoes of Queen Victoria's Diamond Jubilee.

Hanging on the wall beside the pine dresser was Jack's pride and joy, a magnificent painting of the 1897 Royal Spithead review, with the old British Fleet at anchor in the narrow waters between Portsmouth and the Isle of Wight: Warship after warship, 165 in all, decked out with flags and looking like an endless queue of majestic liners, dominated by the mighty flagship, *Renown*. Each ship was painted uniformly – black hull, orange band at the waterline, white superstructure, and beige funnels and masts. George always enjoyed the painting and found something new each time he studied it.

This neat, clean and tidy kitchen was what George remembered most when he was away from home. It was the sweet smell of his mother's cooking that stuck in his mind, and the surfaces covered in crisp, white doilies, pictures, and mementoes of the Royal Navy. Like the rest of the house, it was "shipshape and Bristol fashion", as his father would endlessly say. George never did know where the expression came from, but he knew what it meant. This simple scene would sustain him and his father through whatever their time at sea might bring. If ever he imagined home and his mother, when he was away, he saw her here. He sighed deeply and wondered fleetingly if he really would ever see it again.

He shrugged and took the kettle up to his room, to get ready for his departure. When he was finally at the front door, smartly dressed in his uniform and ready for anything, Emily was there. She looked up at her son with sad eyes, committing his face to memory. He bore an uncanny resemblance to his father and had the same full mouth, well-defined cheekbones, pale blue eyes, fair hair, and a strong jaw line. When he was growing up she had noticed, as only a mother does, how much of Jack was there, inside him. The way he held a cigarette, the way he crossed his legs, and the look he had when he was puzzled.

It affected Emily more than she cared to admit. Watching George could make her spine tingle, as crystal-clear images of Jack would come flooding into her mind – even when he was thousands of miles away. A face to break a woman's heart, she thought, and sparkling eyes that no red-blooded woman could resist. In his uniform, he looked even more special, and she was so proud of him. In an unusual display of emotion, she wrapped her arms around him and kissed him. 'Take care of yourself, son,' she said, the words catching at the back of her throat. 'Come back safe and sound.'

With his parting words, he picked up his service seabag, and was gone. Emily closed the door behind him. For her it would be another day of reflection and tears. She locked the door and busied herself with being alone again. For George it was different. Although he hated seeing his mother upset, for him, it was exciting going off to the war. Right now, it was all he could think about.

He made his way through the town to the ferry terminal. The streets were dry but a blustery, gusting wind made it feel chilly. The last of the autumn leaves were airborne in a tumbling dance, flurrying horizontally across the cobbled street to find a place to gather in the corners of walls and buildings. The roads were already busy. Horses pulling drays clopped along the main streets in convoy with the lorries and buses chugging to and fro. Ladies, struggling to keep their long coats and dresses down, and hats on, made their way through the town.

When he reached the ferry, he joined the queue of sailors, soldiers and civilians waiting to board the next boat for the Portsmouth side. Once on board, he lit up a cigarette and stood at the guardrail, watching the world pass by. The ferry clanked slowly across the mouth of the harbour, passing close to the stern of a grey destroyer heading purposefully into the Solent. As daylight began to lighten the sky, the dockyard's skyline bristled with spiky masts and the angular superstructures of many ships tied up there. Clanking and chuffing, slowly moving dockside cranes were hoisting bundles of arms, stores and provisions high into the air and down into the ships. Tucked inside the main harbour were several submarines, their sleek black hulls casting sinister, shadowy shapes against the docks. Deeper inside the harbour, two cruisers were at anchor, and ships' steam pinnaces left murky white wakes in the choppy grey sea as they ferried men to their ships. The whole dockyard area was alive with bustling activity. As the ferry reached the jetty, George slung his seabag over his shoulder and walked up the wooden ramp onto the platform of Portsmouth Harbour railway station. A hundred or so sailors were already waiting for the special train to Devonport Dockyard, his Plymouth destination. Finding himself a place to stand, he gazed out over the harbour area and drifted into thought. He was excited to be part of all this.

Like Devonport Dockyard – the place farther west along the South Coast that he was heading for – Portsmouth Dockyard was heaving with activity. Its seemingly endless walls dominated the city: stout high structures of red brick and pale grey granite with huge, ornate arched gateways set into them at intervals. Some rail lines carried trains straight into the dockyard, through their own gateways, where they pulled up beside ships and unloaded tons of equipment, shells and provisions into the holds and hulls of waiting freighters and warships.

The thousands of workers who built, repaired, and serviced ships in the dockyards, lived in and around the city, coming and going at all times of the day and night. Uniformed soldiers of all ranks and regiments moved about in buses, on foot, on trains or on lorries, embarking warships bound for the battlefields of Europe and beyond.

Portsmouth Harbour station was mounted on a stout wooden structure with massive piles driven deep into the mud of the harbour bottom. From the platform, George watched a group of small children, stripped to the waist in spite of the chilly morning air, begging bored passengers to throw coins into the slimy mud shallows. Known affectionately as "mudlarks", they were there every time he came to the station. The children, local beggars, never seemed to lose the coins they were thrown, even though they had to trawl the shallow water and thick jellied mud to find them. Someone on the platform threw some coins in a long arc over the fence. The boys leapt down from the wooden mooring posts they were sitting on, into the muddy water, like penguins diving for fish. They surfaced seconds later, with white eyes and teeth gleaming from faces blackened with mud "like tanners in a sweep's ear", as Jack once described them, triumphantly holding up the coins to the cheers of onlookers.

Watching the activity in the harbour, George pondered over his fascination with ports and the sea. He looked at the pungent, jellylike, clay sediment of the harbour bottom, redolent of all periods of history. In there, he imagined, lurked traces of Roman times, the rubbish discarded by Henry VIII's men, and memories of Admiral Lord Nelson. Smells of tar and rope, burnt coal and fresh paint, fuel oil and steam engines all fused together with wood, smoke and seaweed. It was part of the port's character, its aromatic backdrop, pervading and unmistakable: offensive to the uninitiated, and homely to the sailor. It was as much a part of Portsmouth as its bustling atmosphere, and to pass through it was to remember it for life. George saw several grey warships entering and leaving the harbour. One had ugly scars from a brush with the enemy; another limped in, seriously damaged. A far cry, he thought, from six months ago, when every ship of the Royal Navy looked pristine.

For the locals and the servicemen in transit, this was a time of transience. Relationships were fleeting. A friendship struck one day could end abruptly the next, as comrades and friends went to war to die unexpectedly. It was the dawning of the age of "living for the moment". The train arrived, jolting George out of his daydream. There was a clatter of carriage doors being flung open, and crowds of chattering servicemen, with kitbags, seabags and backpacks, tumbled out. They stamped their studded boots on the platform, shaking out the creases of a long journey, straightened their uniforms, and then headed for the nearby dockyard gates.

George and the other waiting servicemen clambered into the train and settled down among cases and kitbags, and the carriages quickly filled with the smoke of freshly lit cigarettes and pipes. A good-natured cheer went up when the guard finally waved his flag and blew his whistle. Belching acrid smoke into the roof of the station, and hissing steam at the track, the train slowly moved off, taking George to a place of new adventure and unknown consequences. He gazed wistfully across the water to Gosport, and wondered what his mother would be doing.

The train lurched slowly through old Portsmouth and snaked past the city centre, its wheels clanking and screeching on the rails. The city looked shabby and grey, but alive and busy. George sat back and thought of his childhood as familiar sights passed slowly by the windows. Things were changing. The omnipresent Naval and military buildings in the city seemed more prominent now. Bustling with activity, it was as if these inanimate structures had suddenly come to life, anxious to play a part in the war. Uniformed policemen and sailors and soldiers wearing black hobnailed boots and white belts and gaiters were guarding every wrought-iron gateway, with .303 army issue rifles slung over their shoulders.

Men and women in the uniforms of all services were on the move everywhere, and khaki-coloured machines and equipment mingled with the omnibuses, trams and horses in clouds of dust and fumes. It seemed that every serviceman and woman in Britain was destined to pass through Portsmouth, at some time or another.

As the train moved through the suburbs, it pulled slowly past a row of shops on a road beside the track. There was a muddle of commotion at one of the shops. Two policemen were trying to control a crowd of twenty or more anti-war demonstrators hurling bricks and stones at a shuttered shop front belonging to some German settlers.

Sailors in the next carriage flung open a window and hurled abuse, urging the crowd on. Leaving the outskirts of the city, the train headed west through Fareham and rural Hampshire, where the countryside looked strangely peaceful and untouched by war. Although most of the farmhands had already gone to the war, the owners were working the fields themselves. Feeding the war machine was now as important as fighting on the front.

'Want a fag, mate? Got a light?' The voice broke George's thoughts. It was the friendly-looking sailor sitting opposite. George pulled out a box of matches and accepted a cigarette. A quick glance at George's cap tally told the sailor that George had just left barracks and had not yet joined a new ship. 'What's your ship, then?' He had a genuine "cockney sparrer" accent, thick enough to be cut with a knife, and the manner of a cheeky sparrow.

'*Inflexible*,' George replied, 'and yours?'

'*Invincible*, mate. Best in the fleet. You're a shell 'ed, ain't yer?'

'Yep,' said George, smiling at the reference to his gunnery specialisation. 'Where are you from?'

'Can't you tell? Lunnon, of course... Big Smoke... Old Kent Road. An' you?'

'Back there ...Gosport.' George jerked his thumb over his shoulder.

'Blimey, bit posh down there, innit? I could tell you was a bit posh. I've bin there myself... 'aslar 'ospital. What's your moniker then?' George was not sure which question to answer first.

'Royal, George Royal – Haslar Hospital, that's not far from my home.'

'Royal? Funny name, that. We 'ad a Royal in me last ship... *Good 'Ope*. A lieutenant 'e was.'

'What was his first name, d'you know?'

'Nah... never 'ad much to do wiv 'im. He was a gunner, though.'

George smiled. 'That was my father in *Good Hope*.' "Sparrer" was incredulous.

'Getoff... you're jokin', ain't ya? Your ole man! Well, there's a turn-up. I'll tell you what, mate, don't tell yer mum I said so, but he'll be 'avin a bloody good old time now, out in Sarf America... lucky dog. I was right pissed off when I was drafted off 'er. Had to go into bloody 'aslar 'ospital... sorry, *H*aslar *H*ospital, just before *Good 'Ope* sailed. 'Ad to go and fall through an 'atch, didnt' I? 'Urt me back and busted me shoulder. Cor, what a carryon. Missed the best trip ever, if you ask me. All that Sarf American crumpet. I was dyin' to get me hands on summa that. Now look what I got. Bloody *Invincible*... bloody Rosyff. Not exactly yer Buenos Aries, that lot, is it?'

George laughed. The cockney lad was loud and difficult to understand, but there was something dependable and solid about him that he liked. 'Well, you've got a pretty good ship now. You never know your luck. With the Navy going everywhere now, you could still get in a trip like that.'

'I should cocoa,' snorted Sparrer. 'Not much chance o' that. It's bloody dangerous where we're goin', mate, let me tell yer. The geezer in the next bed to me in *H*aslar 'ad just bin pulled out the drink cos 'is ship went down in the North Sea. Hit a mine, they did. There's bloody mines everywhere. Then, if it ain't mines, it's bloody 'un subs sneakin' about down there where yer can't see 'em. Anyway, this geezer reckoned we got a free-to-one chance of coppin' it, up there. And the Scotch gals ain't exactly givin' it away, neever. Seems all they want is to get married an' all that stuff. Roll on Christmas!'

'May be all over by Christmas,' said George, hoping to change the subject. 'Have you been in for long?'

'Yeah, bin in the navy for five years now. Before *Good 'Ope*, I was aht in India for a coupla years. Good there, it was. Loadsa sun. Good run ashore. But could it bloody rain! Bloody war ...got us called back 'ere. 'Ere, George ...dunno 'ow we're gonna cope with this lot, d'you?' He leaned forward and nodded towards a group of very young sailors at the other side of the compartment. It was obvious from their brand new uniforms that they were new recruits, "straight out of the box".

'I feel a bit sorry for them myself,' said George, looking at their fresh faces. 'They won't know what's hit them when they get to sea. Still, we all had to go through that, didn't we?'

'Yeah, you're right there, mate. But if the bloody ship's gonna sink, they're just summink else to think about. I wonder 'ow many of 'em will come 'ome to see this again.' Sparrer looked out at the countryside rolling by and his mind drifted off.

The conversation petered out and George was pleased it had, because he felt his bad night getting the better of him, and the warmth and rocking of the train made his eyelids as heavy as lead. In spite of the noisy clattering of the train and the chatter in the compartment, he sank into a deep sleep.

A sharp, accidental jab in the ribs woke him up. It was a stray elbow of the sailor sitting next to him, who was fishing a packet of cigarettes from his pocket. Mumbled apologies were accepted and George re-surfaced to find that he had slept through the whole four-hour journey. Having been specially commissioned by the War Department, the train had not stopped on the way, but was now screeching and clanking straight into Devonport Dockyard. 'Well, 'ere we are, mate.' Sparrer, bright-eyed and chirpy, was looking at the line of warships and freighters tied up at the docks. 'Take yer pick!' George wiped condensation from the window, looking for *Inflexible* among the confusion of grey funnels and superstructures.

From the smells and the activity at the docks, it could have been Portsmouth again. But the sun was shining now and everything looked brighter and more colourful. Lines of troops with enormous packs on their backs were snaking up the gangways of one large ship. A hospital ship was disembarking wounded servicemen. Some were walking carefully; some were carried on stretchers into the buses and ambulances waiting on the dockside.

There was a constant clanging and hammering of metal on metal coming from where dockyard workers were busy with several warships, and the blue and white light of acetylene welding torches. In one dry dock, a very large new ship's keel had been laid down, and building was underway. Several loutish soldiers in the carriage scrambled for the windows, to ogle the nurses tending the wounded. The train finally came to rest at a makeshift wooden platform and the clatter of carriage doors being flung open ran down the length of it.

George tumbled onto the platform with Sparrer and the rest of the men, slung his seabag over his shoulder, and tried to find his bearings. Spotting a crudely written sign nailed to a post, he found *Inflexible* and *Invincible* on the list, with an arrow pointing to one of the docks. They trudged along the cobbled quay with a number of other sailors, Petty Officers and Chief Petty Officers, to where both ships were tied up astern of each other. They looked magnificent, and George's heart skipped a beat. He could see from the thick grey smoke rising lazily from their funnels that they had steam up and were ready to leave.

'Cor, wot a sight,' said Sparrer, echoing George's thoughts.

Only eight years old, the sister ships were new, for warships. Both were "post-dreadnoughts" and products of Jacky Fisher's earlier efforts to modernise the Navy. Together with the other ship of the same class, *Indomitable,* all three had just completed a refit to raise their fore funnels and cure an earlier smoke haze problem.

With a displacement of 17,500 tons, *Inflexible* was much bigger than his father's ship, the old cruiser *Good Hope.* Her hull, nearly 190 yards long, looked sleek, modern, and majestically businesslike. George's new work place, her four 10-inch thick armour-plated steel turrets, dominated her decks. He had to pause and admire the huge guns. She had eight of them, and each one could hurl shells with the girth of a large dinner-plate more than twenty miles.

As he looked, the idea of firing guns at a target beyond the horizon seemed inconceivable.

'Big buggers, ain't they?' was Sparrer's only observation. 'See yer, mate. Good luck. See yer in Scotland.' He waved and walked on towards *Invincible's* gangway.

George waved back, wondering if they would ever meet again. 'Same to you, mate. Good luck.'

As he went up *Inflexible's* gangway, he noticed there was not a trace of rust in her fresh new coat of light grey paint. At the top, he stepped onto the armoured steel plates of the upper deck and turned towards the quarterdeck. In the manner required by tradition, he saluted the White Ensign flying at the stern of the ship. A smart Royal Marine NCO with immaculate uniform and glistening toecaps demanded his name and papers in the staccato tone of military authority. Peering down the impossibly vertical peak of his cap, he found George's name on his clipboard, and ticked it off.

George stepped into the ship through a doorway and made his way down to the mess deck he had been directed to, two decks below. He found an empty locker for his kit, reserved some hammock hooks, and then gazed around his new home. It was spacious, compared with his previous ship and everything looked clean, neat and tidy.

"Shipshape and Bristol fashion", he could hear Jack say. The smells in the air made him feel at home: fresh paint and rope, laced with hammock canvas and teak oil. He dumped his seabag in the locker and went off to find the Master at Arms' office, where he reported himself aboard and handed in his draft papers.

That was it: he was back at sea, serving in one of the best battlecruisers afloat! Pride and a sense of excitement ran through him as he looked around on his way back to the mess. It was a feeling he would not have swapped for anything. Later that day he met his new Chief, Gunnery Chief Petty Officer John Huggett, who came across as a competent, levelheaded man of considerable experience, and the other three leading gunnery ratings.

When the rest of the gun crews congregated in the mess for a talk by the Chief, George and another leading gunner were given joint responsibility for the mess. George looked at the list of turret crews on the mess notice board and took a note of who would be with him in the forward turret.

With no leave granted that night, the men were soon rigging their hammocks, to sleep. "Slinging their hooks" sailors called it. George and "Chalky" White, the other leading rating of the mess, took pity on the new lads and helped them to hook up their hammocks and climb into them. Like mounting a horse, there was a knack to this, and watching the "sprogs" wrestling with hammocks for the first time was always a good laugh for the experienced men, until they got bored with it. The youngsters were shown how to tie the ropes of their hammocks to hooks specially welded to the deckhead, then how to put in spreaders to stop the canvas sleeping bags closing over them like banana skins, once they were in.

After getting the hang of this – the easy part – came the seemingly impossible business of getting in. Using any suitable handhold in the deckhead, the older men heaved themselves up and swung deftly into their hammocks. As always, the new lads then had to discover just how difficult this could be. The old hands set up a makeshift scoreboard for the greatest number of attempts, the "prize" for which was the honour of being the mess cleaner for a month.

Loud cheers accompanied the new lads as they clung to the deckhead and hurled themselves at their evasive hammocks, and there were even louder cheers when they rolled out and fell to the deck. One fresh-faced lad was on his sixth attempt when Chalky called a halt to the fun. Looking like a forlorn school-boy, the rating was exhausted and had still not achieved his place to sleep when Chalky and George decided to settle him down for the night. The lights were finally put out when all of the men were safely suspended from the deckhead.

In the dim emergency lighting, the mess deck looked like the nest of a giant insect, with its restless larvae dangling and swaying from the roof. George climbed into his own hammock but he knew that he would be awake in the small hours to find at least one of the youngsters standing helplessly by his hammock after returning from a call of nature. It was the way of things, with hammocks.

HMS INFLEXIBLE, DEVONPORT DOCKYARD

At dawn the following morning, the gangways were hoisted up and stowed away and the ships were made ready for sea. Mooring cables were slipped, and the tugs pulled and nudged their clumsy charges into the open waters of the Hamoaze Estuary, where they were transformed into pictures of grace as they made their own way into Plymouth Sound. Passing Devil's Point and Drake's Island, they steamed quickly out into the Western English Channel, gathering speed and heading westwards, on a clockwise course around the British Isles. The normal course for ships heading for Rosyth was the shorter, counter-clockwise route along the English Channel and into the North Sea. The North Sea was heavily infested with German submarines now, all ships had orders to take the long way round.

At twenty-three knots, *Inflexible* and *Invincible* rounded Land's End, steamed up the Irish Sea and through the Pentland Firth into the North Sea then turned south for their base at Rosyth Dockyard. The one-thousand-mile journey was uneventful, apart from one sighting of a German periscope and a turn in the Irish Sea to avoid two loose mines bobbing dangerously along in the choppy sea. An alert lookout, high up in the superstructure of *Invincible*, spotted the mines and a Royal Marine was called to the upper deck to sink them with rifle fire.

His first shot punctured the casing of one and it sank out of sight.

After two shots at the other, it exploded. With a tremendous roar, a thick, white column of foaming seawater erupted a hundred feet in the air then fell back with a long hiss. It was the first mine George had seen explode, and it left him wondering what chance *Inflexible* had of getting through the war without hitting one. Having seen what mines could do, he took particular care to find his lifeboat station and the way to reach it quickly.

By lunchtime on October 21, having passed the Bell Rock lighthouse and the Isle of May unscathed, the ships were easing their way up the relatively calm waters of the Firth of Forth to Rosyth Dockyard. Within an hour, they were safely tied up at the dockyard, re-coaling and making ready for patrolling duty in the North Sea.

Two days later, they were back at sea, on patrol, constantly on the lookout for drifting mines and the chilling sight of a submarine periscope cutting through the grey waves like a shark's dorsal fin. *Inflexible* was one of several warships defending the coast against the occasional night bombardment by German warships and submarines. "Working-up" the crew for action was soon under way and George had to get the forward turret's crew working as a team. With very few regulars in the crew, it was not an easy task. Many of them were young and inexperienced, and it took a lot of practice and two long-range encounters with real enemy ships to get them working together properly, but the biggest bugbear the gun crews suffered was not their inexperience, it was the ship's Gunnery Officer, Lieutenant-Commander Foster. Irascible and devoid of all humour, Foster had a tongue like a rapier.

No one was able to establish any kind of rapport with him. For reasons that George never did understand, Foster had an aversion to him from the moment he clapped eyes on him. *Of all the gunnery officers in the Navy, it had to be him,* George muttered under his breath. Foster was the worst possible example of the upper class he came from. He had no time or respect for ratings. To him, sailors were peasants, to be treated more like subjects than men, and he had the knack of making them feel they were there entirely for his benefit. He was tall and lanky with sharp, sallow, features and the stark black eyes of a vulture.

Whenever George saw Foster strutting about on deck with his long, bony, claw-like hands clasped behind his back, he could only think of vultures. George's newly earned rank and modest authority meant nothing to Foster, and he resented anyone with ambition, particularly young men like George, but the main target for Foster's contempt was one of George's crew ratings called "Curly" Roberts, whose complete inability to relate to Foster brought a welter of muttering resentment and dumb insolence. Within days, a state of war existed between Roberts and Foster.

Curly was 34 and still an Ordinary Seaman after sixteen years of service. He was a great bear of a man, so wide that when he took a shower he had to sway from side to side to stay wet. He had an "old hand" attitude and a pugilistic nature. Thickly built, with a permanent scowl on his white round face, he rarely bared his irregular yellow teeth in a smile, except after downing his grog at lunchtime. This free tot of rum mixed with water traditionally dished out daily to sailors seemed to be the only thing that Roberts could find agreeable about his lot in the Navy. There was a rumour in the mess that he had once been a formidable boxer, his squashed nose being cited as evidence. George doubted it, and imagined that it had probably been flattened in a pub. The sparks flew whenever Roberts and Foster were within range of one another, and it caused crackling tension in the ship's gunnery section.

George quietly took stock of the situation and vowed wearily to stay clear of Foster, whenever possible. Meanwhile, Roberts turned into an entrenched recusant in any dealings with the gunnery officer. There can be no place in the Navy for vendettas between officers and ratings, at the best of times, but with *Inflexible* on patrol in the North Sea, the situation between Foster and Roberts was intolerable.

Germany showed initial reluctance to commit capital ships to a major sea battle, and chose instead to bombard Britain's East Coast towns and cities under cover of darkness. This did very little for Germany's war effort, but it did kill hundreds of innocent civilians and sullied the good name of the German Navy. With the best of good faith, it had to be assumed that this was done to undermine the morale of the British public or, perhaps, to score hits on Army camps: but it failed to do either.

On the other hand, the German mines sewn in hundreds around the British Isles, together with the submarines operating there did a lot of damage. They made it extremely difficult for the Navy's warships to operate in their own home waters. The toll of ships sunk by mines and torpedoes was rising steadily. There was still no solution to this problem, and it was devastating the Royal Navy.

The effectiveness of Germany's naval tactics was well and truly proven, just a matter of weeks into the war. Reluctantly, and all too late, the Admiralty was obliged to think again about the conduct of underwater warfare. Their Lordships were forced to surrender their "Old Empire" view that fast surface vessels could outrun the track of a torpedo, and were obliged to worry instead that there was still no effective way to "sweep" mines. So serious was the problem, that Admiral John Jellicoe, the Commander-in-Chief of the Grand Fleet, wrote to the Admiralty: *"It will be pure suicide taking the fleet out without sweeping, and I have nothing with which to sweep."*

WHITEHALL, LONDON
October 27, 1914

Prime Minister Asquith was maintaining his barrage of letters to Venetia Stanley, which often ran into several pages at a time, rarely missing a day. On October 27, he wrote a very long letter that began:

"My darling – you came this morning to see Violet (so I heard) and I never saw you! I was what is called busy, but if you had opened the door (why didn't you?) I should have been more than happy. However, I can't & don't complain for you were an angel yesterday. But I miss so much the least & briefest glimpse of you. I don't think you know how much..."©

That same day at around 08:45 am on October 27, 1914, *HMS Audacious*, virtually a brand new dreadnought cruiser of 23,000 tons, was on a gunnery exercise when she blundered into a German minefield off the tip of Ireland. Fortunately, she remained afloat long enough for her entire crew to be rescued and sank in the early evening. Meanwhile, the belief persisted that the might of the British and German fleets would soon meet in the North Sea for a battle of biblical proportions, for which the best ships were being kept in home waters. Unfortunately, this was where they were exposed to the greatest danger from German mines and submarines, and it left Britain's far-flung shipping lanes and naval stations to be protected by older, lesser warships.

On October 28, 1914, a signal was sent round the Fleet announcing Fisher's return as First Sea Lord to succeed Prince Louis of Battenberg. The reaction of the officers in *Inflexible* was mixed. Some thought Jacky Fisher was just the man to push the Navy forward in the war at sea. Others thought differently, and believed that Prince Louis had been an excellent First Sea Lord, who should not have been forced to resign just because of his German ancestry.

George thought it would probably make very little difference to men like him, but Roberts, who had served in the Navy when Fisher was a leading figure, thought it was the best news he had ever had. George was amazed that Roberts had it in him to admire any officer, since he had shown nothing but contempt for them so far.

Later, however, Chief Huggett cleared up his confusion by telling him that Fisher was the most famous "kick-arse" admiral in the history of the Royal Navy. Curly's admiration for Fisher suddenly made sense, and George began to look forward to seeing something of the "Fisher Effect" at his level, far down the ranks of the mighty Royal Navy.

That night, *Inflexible* and *Invincible* were on patrol with the Grand Fleet, cruising eight miles off the coast of North Yorkshire, at Robin Hood's Bay, when they were abruptly thrown into their first conflict with the German Navy. According to reports, shells were raining down on Scarborough from the sea, and *Inflexible* was ordered to investigate. Winding up to flank speed, she headed south for fourteen miles then stood eight miles off Scarborough with her lights extinguished. The crew took to *ACTION STATIONS*, and George and the rest of the gun crews closed up at their duty positions.

From the bridge and the director position in the ship's maintop, the outline of what appeared to be a small vessel could be seen against the flashes of its guns, close into the coast. As soon as it was identified as a surfaced German submarine, *Inflexible* turned towards it and moved in to close the range. There was concern on the bridge that the submarine was so close to the shore that *Inflexible's* big guns might overshoot and hit the town. The turret crews were ordered to stand down; big guns were not going to be used unless something untoward occurred. Instead, the ship's hand-operated guns on top of the turrets, smaller 12-pounders, were made ready, and *Inflexible* closed up on the German submarine. George and the others stayed inside their turret, watching through the observation hood.

The Germans seemed too engrossed in their unopposed shelling of the coast to notice *Inflexible* coming on behind them and, uncharacteristically, the German lookouts spotted nothing until she suddenly opened fire on them. The startled German gunners then swung their gun round quickly to the British ship, but she was barely visible to them. *Inflexible's* first two rounds sent spray cascading over the submarine, hampering its efforts to return fire. Now the submarine captain was caught in a dilemma. He either had to crash-dive and risk being rammed or shelled, or stay on the surface and battle it out with an armoured cruiser.

Realising what he was up against, the captain rightly chose to crash-dive. The submarine's gun was abandoned hastily, and the crew scrambled into the conning tower as quickly as they could. It immediately began to slip below the surface while *Inflexible's* guns fired as quickly as they could be re-loaded. The submarine was hit twice before she disappeared, one shell exploding on her foredeck, another on the conning tower. When *Inflexible's* searchlights were switched on, there was disappointment in the ship when it seemed that the submarine had got away but no sooner had it submerged in the foam and spray of its frantic dive, than it reappeared for a brief moment, silhouetted against the lights, with bows reared up like a whale in its last throes.

For a few seconds, the Captain of *Inflexible* thought he had forced the submarine to the surface where he could capture it. But the way its bow slid back below the surface again left no doubt that it was in serious trouble. A spontaneous cheer went up around the ship for *Inflexible's* first "kill", but as quickly as it started, it ended abruptly – dying on the lips of those men standing on the upper deck, as the awesome, sobering picture of the submarine on the sea bed came to their minds. They knew that as the sea poured in, the German submariners would be struggling for air and survival in the darkness, with no means of escape.

Inflexible cautiously inched forward to the submarine's last position and waited at the spot, searching with lights for survivors but there were none. Just air and oil mushroomed to the surface, disgorging pieces of wood, clothing, and oil. After ten minutes, which seemed like an eternity to the lookouts searching for mines and periscopes, *Inflexible* moved off towards Robin Hood's Bay to rejoin *Invincible*. Emotions in the ship were mixed, and the mood sober. For many of the crew, the sinking of the submarine had been their initiation to war, but it brought home the cold horrors of it to every man, to which they were going to have to become accustomed.

It did not take long for the men of the gunnery department of *Inflexible* to reach the conclusion that Foster's professional ineptitude was life-threatening. Had it not been for Chief Huggett's loyalty in sweeping up the pieces of Foster's near-disasters, news of his incompetence would have reached the Captain's ears. During one of his sudden and unexpected exercises for the gunners, he caused the turrets to be trained on an imaginary target while two ratings were sitting on the barrels carrying out his previous orders to reposition the tampion badges, the guns' muzzle blanks. No one knew if this happened because of his forgetfulness, or his complete disregard for the safety of his men. The ratings, of whom Roberts was one, were sitting astride the ends of the two enormous gun barrels as they began to elevate without warning.

Roberts managed to slide down his gun barrel onto the turret, narrowly avoiding having his arm trapped between the turret and the moving barrel. The other rating was on the port midships guns, and he fell to the deck and broke his arm. He was saved from going over the side only by the reaction of a startled Petty Officer who happened to be passing at the time. Although the accident was caused entirely by orders personally given by Foster, as soon as it came to light he blamed the Chief for "not being on his toes". Roberts was ready to murder Foster on the spot when he found out what had happened, and had to be restrained by his colleagues.

On a different occasion, Foster was inside one of the other

turrets, observing another of his hastily contrived loading exercises, when a shell slipped from a cradle and crushed a gunner's foot, putting him out of action for ten weeks. The story below decks was that Foster had ordered a simulated failed-hoist, manual loading of the guns, and then insisted on staying inside the crowded turret where he got in the way of the ratings manhandling the heavy shells. This time, no one else could be blamed but by the time his report reached the Captain, it claimed that the accident was the fault of "the incompetent rating himself".

After just days into the patrol, Foster's attitude and very presence in the ship had generated bitter hatred and seething discontent in the men from the Chief down. Even the most difficult men have at least one saving grace that prevents them being totally objectionable but, with Foster, the men concluded that nothing other than great distance would fit the bill. He motivated the more timid men by fear. The more spirited of them resisted and found no value in him at all, other than as a continuing topic of conversation. It was a mystery to George that he ever reached alive the rank of Lieutenant-Commander.

On Sunday October 31, 1914, three days after the submarine incident, *Invincible* and *Inflexible* were back in Rosyth, re-provisioning and re-coaling. For the crews, it meant being black from head to toe once again. Every rating and Royal Marine on board was obliged to take part in coaling. No one escaped the duty, not even the Midshipmen; scrubbed clean and back to normal when it was over, there was daytime leave for most of them to visit the local town.

George went ashore with Chalky White. They went into the first lively pub they found, shouldered their way through its bustling, noisy, smoke-filled atmosphere and ordered drinks at the bar. Standing beside the bar with a glass poised at his lips, George heard a voice calling from the back of the room. 'Wotcher, mate... got yerself a Hun sub then?' It was Sparrer, the cockney seaman from *Invincible,* he had made friends with on the train to Devonport Dockyard. He was sitting with two more sailors from *Invincible.* 'Come on over 'ere and tell us all about it, Mister Royal.'

George and his friend joined Sparrer and his mates for a noisy evening. Swapping stories during the course of the night, the names of several officers came up for discussion: Foster, in particular. Sparrer pursed his lips and drew a long breath. He had come across this officer before and what he had to say confirmed George's worst fears. There were no redeeming qualities in Foster, and no one had ever been able to understand the reason for his sour attitude to life and sailors. As if George needed one, Sparrer gave him a warning that rang in his ears for some time after... 'Watch yer back, mate. As nasty a piece o' work as you'll ever meet up with, is Mister Foster.'

Chapter Five

IN THE FALKLAND ISLANDS

Frustrated by the lack of response from the Admiralty, Admiral Cradock decided to take matters into his own hands. He had sent a signal to Whitehall to say so, which had arrived in London on the 27th:

FROM CRADOCK TO ADMIRALTY
RE ORDERS TO SEARCH FOR ENEMY AND OUR GREAT DESIRE FOR EARLY SUCCESS, CONSIDER THAT OWING TO SLOW SPEED OF CANOPUS IT IS IMPOSSIBLE TO FIND AND DESTROY ENEMY SQUADRON. HAVE THEREFORE ORDERED DEFENCE TO JOIN ME

The following day he sent another signal, relaying further information he had picked up. It took six days to reach London:

FROM CRADOCK TO ADMIRALTY
HAVE SEIZED GERMAN MAILS.
MONMOUTH, GOOD HOPE, OTRANTO COALING AT VALLEMAR. GLASGOW PATROLLING VICINITY OF CORONEL …REJOINING FLAG LATER ON. INTEND TO PROCEED NORTHWARD SECRETLY WITH SQUADRON AFTER COALING

Suddenly, the other admiral, Stoddart, halfway up the east coast of South America, now faced with the possibility of losing his flagship *Defence* to Cradock's command, sent a signal to the Admiralty on October 28, objecting to the depletion of his small force:

FROM REAR ADMIRAL STODDART TO ADMIRALTY
HAVE RECEIVED ORDERS FROM ADMIRAL CRADOCK TO SEND DEFENCE TO MONTEVIDEO… SUBMIT I MAY BE GIVEN TWO CRUISERS IN PLACE OF DEFENCE AS I DO NOT CONSIDER FORCE AT MY DISPOSAL IS SUFFICIENT

The Admiralty suddenly stepped in with a terse signal. It was a bitter blow for Cradock, and it left him fuming:

FROM ADMIRALTY TO CRADOCK
DEFENCE IS TO REMAIN ON EAST COAST UNDER ORDERS OF STODDART...

He was denied the use of *Defence*.

Unfortunately for Cradock, time had now run out and there was to be no divine intervention by Jacky Fisher because the old boy had not yet properly taken up office. Frustrated by the confusing and conflicting orders from the Admiralty, Cradock decided to go it alone with the inadequate resources at his disposal. So far, he had not experienced a full-blooded encounter with the enemy, but he did have generic and implicit faith in the historic superiority of the Royal Navy. Spurred on by that and a radio message from his cruiser *Glasgow* saying that one of von Spee's ships was now alone and detached from its squadron, there was a chance that he could slow it down, at least, until much needed reinforcements arrived.

Cradock was a courageous, impetuous man who recognised that he was the last line of defence for this remote outpost of the British Empire. He was also aware, as were all senior officers drawn from Britain's aristocracy, that personal advancement only came as a result of battles won and morale-boosting acts of courage that were certain to attract the attention of the newspapers. Taking the easy way out was therefore not an option for such an ambitious man as Cradock. His three ships could never match von Spee's German fleet on their own; they were slower and less heavily armed. He was well aware of this but felt confident that he could tackle just one lone German ship.

Belittled and frustrated now by the Admiralty's response, and harbouring a simmering, personal resentment about his situation, he ordered his fleet to sea. His decision made, he set off with his depleted fleet around Cape Horn, the southernmost tip of South America. His battleship *Canopus* – an elderly vessel with worn-out engines – followed, wheezing and wallowing in heavy seas, 250 miles behind him.

SOUTHEASTERN PACIFIC OCEAN, OFF CHILE
November 1, 1914 6:30 am

It was Jack Royal's birthday. He was forty-eight, even if he felt more like twenty-seven. Smiling to himself, he opened his cards as soon as he was awake. There was one from George and another from Emily. They instantly made him think of home. The lads of his department had made a large, humorous card that he struggled to find a place for in his tiny cabin. He wedged the cards up against the bulkhead where they had a chance of withstanding *Good Hope's* violent movements, and got on with his day.

The fluttering butterfly sensation was still there in his stomach long after breakfast, but no one would know that he was as excited as the next man about going into battle. As always, he looked calm, unfazed and totally reliable on the outside. Inside, he was concerned about the young men he was responsible for, and anxious that his department should perform professionally and efficiently. The ship was cheerful throughout, and there was an air of excited expectation. No amount of training can prepare the innermost thoughts of the men as they approach battle for the first time, but, in *Good Hope* this day, the tension was determined and positive.

11:30 am

Whipped up by fierce winds, the sea was rising, but the 4th British Cruiser Squadron pounded on at best speed, steaming north in line astern behind the flagship.

On the bridge of *Good Hope*, Cradock anxiously scanned the horizon for signs of Germans. The latest news he had received was that von Spee's squadron was anchored in the Juan Fernandez Islands, off the coast of Chile.

To take advantage of the situation, he needed to reach the area before nightfall, in spite of the weather conditions.

The dense black coal smoke pouring from *Good Hope's* four funnels carried ahead of her in the strong following wind, blowing down onto the foredeck and hanging low over the sea before rising hazily into the South Pacific sky. Ahead of the funnels, lookouts standing in the maintop position of the mast were cursing the smoke burning their eyes and throats. Following *Good Hope*, the cruiser *Monmouth* and the recently hired merchant vessel *Otranto* were pitching and rolling heavily. With every dip of their bows in the heaving blue-green sea, waves foamed white over their foredecks.

Feet astride, Cradock braced himself against the ship's vigorous movements and studied the horizon through his personal brass-ringed telescope. There was no sign of enemy ships, but he knew he was too far south of their reported position to encounter them yet.

Every inch the archetypal admiral, he had an air of isolated authority about him. His dapper-smart uniform and its wide gold sleeve bands caught the eye every time he moved, and the heavy gold braiding on the peak of his cap left no doubt about his rank, but what made him stand apart from other officers on the bridge was his commanding presence. He had the stance of a man in command, and his kindly, steel-grey eyes emanated courage, authority and experience. A silver-grey "full set" – his neatly trimmed beard served to accentuate his aquiline features and purposeful jaw.

'Orders, sir?' enquired Captain Francklin, a controlled, confident man, quite used to having the Admiral on his bridge. Cradock lowered his telescope and looked at his wristwatch.

'Maintain present course and speed, if you please, Captain... I shall be in my quarters. I think an early lunch is called for... before we sight the enemy. Signal *Monmouth* to move out to our starboard quarter. A wider search area is necessary. Maintain utmost vigilance.' He turned to his young Flag Lieutenant identified by a heavy loop of woven gold braid hanging from one shoulder of his uniform jacket. '..."Flags", let me know the moment there is a sighting.'

The officers saluted as the Captain responded. 'Very good, sir.'

As Cradock left the bridge for his quarters, below and a short distance from the bridge, the Captain turned to his First Officer. 'Number One, perhaps now would be an appropriate time for you to repair to the wardroom and take your own lunch. Please send my steward up to me. I'll have something light on the bridge today. Make sure the crew go to lunch now, in watches, and then return to their duty stations without delay.'

12:30 pm

By lunchtime, Cradock's ships were well up the coast of Chile, nearing the point where the German ship had been seen. In *Good Hope,* Jack was making his way down to the Combat Communication Centre, three decks below the water line, where men were busily preparing for battle. Apart from a few practice firings off the Falklands, many of the gunners in the four turrets had not operated big guns since their training days back home at *HMS Excellent,* and most of them were inexperienced youngsters with no battle experience at all. Being a perfectionist and immensely professional, Jack expected his division to give a good account of itself, should the need arise.

With years of experience on both sides of the fence of rank, Jack had an intuitive understanding of how to get the best out of his men. He trod the fine line between authority and empathy well, and commanded the respect of his men. He set his personal standards high, and expected everyone around him to do the same. For a moment, his thoughts drifted away to Emily. It seemed impossible that he was forty-eight. They had been together for twenty-four years! Where had the time gone? In all that time, he had only been at home with her for a fraction of it, but they were still together, even though he lived for the Navy.

He always knew it was very different for Emily. He and George were her life. She had told him so, often. There was nothing else for her. When her men were away, it was one long, hollow, lonely act of faith for her, punctuated only by letters and occasional photos from the far corners of the British Empire. She said that she felt like the injured party in a triangle of love but, as long as the other party was only the Navy, she could live with that, she had reassured him.

Never mind. He would make it up to her when he got home again but today was a big day. It was *Good Hope's* first crack at the Germans. Not only that, it was his birthday and the cooks had made him a cake. Tonight in the wardroom, he would be plied with drinks until he could take no more, and he would probably collapse in his cabin surrounded by the greetings cards from his family and friends, feeling every one of his forty-eight years. In the meantime, greetings were coming from all directions from the Captain down, as if to remind him he was no youngster anymore.

He went into the Combat Control Centre and started discussing routines with the ratings and the Midshipmen who operated the Dreyer Fire Control Table. This was an all-important piece of equipment: the heart of the gun direction system. It was here that the positions of the enemy ships were plotted in conjunction with the visual range-finding equipment located high in the ship's superstructure. When the guns were loaded and aimed, it was Jack who would fire them, on orders from the bridge.

Satisfied that everything was ready: the magazines, the bulky shells and cordite charges and the Dreyer Table operators, Jack grabbed his oilskin coat and headed for the upper deck. He braced himself against the fierce wind and stepped onto the forward deck. The sea spray peppered his oilskin like a hail of fine bullets as he made his way across the rolling, pitching, wind-torn deck to the forward gun turret. He banged on the armoured doorway, unclipped its heavy fastenings, and climbed in.

Inside, the acrid stench of vomit set him straight back on his heels. It overpowered the expected, more familiar aroma of cordite, paint and gun oil associated with gun turrets. 'Jesus!' he exclaimed. He grimaced involuntarily. He immediately saw that one of the six ratings manning the top deck of the turret looked decidedly ill. There was sick on the deck plates all around him. 'For God's sake, get that cleared up,' he snapped at John Cornish, the Leading Rating. 'And quickly! You haven't got much time. We could be at Action Stations any time now. You can't afford to be skating about in that, when we start firing.' He looked at the pale young faces peering wide-eyed from their white anti-flash hoods. They looked like a clutch of anxious seagull chicks.

'Happy birthday, sir,' they all mumbled through their hoods. He smiled and nodded his thanks.

'You, Jones.' He pointed to the ashen-faced rating standing by a gun breech, not wearing a hood. 'Where is your anti-flash hood?'

'I've just chucked up in it, sir,' Jones replied sheepishly, his face looking green. 'I feel terrible, sir.'

Jack's tone softened. He knew what it was like to be seasick.

When you feel like that, all you want is to curl up in a ball and die. 'OK, son, nip off now and get a change of clothes... and clean yourself up. Draw another hood from the store. It might just save your face in an explosion, you know. Not that I'd want to keep the one you've got right now, if I were you,' he said, making light of the youngster's abject misery. Jack had mixed feelings about these youngsters heading for their baptism of fire. He knew exactly what it was like to be cooped-up in a dimly lit turret in a heaving ship, with no view of the outside world. As the big guns fire they generate stifling heat and pressure inside a turret, and the shattering noise leaves men deaf for days.

It was an experience not easily forgotten. Smoke and the stench of burning cordite would soon fill this thick steel box of a turret, and these young lads, who looked more like schoolboys right now, would soon have to come to terms with overwhelming panic, terror and confusion. They would be oblivious to what was going on outside. Even if the ship sank, they would not realise it until the sea came gushing in through the gun breeches. The one full-time regular in this crew was Cornish. He was only twenty-two, much the same age as George. The rest of them were much younger. They were "green" reservists, attracted by the excitement of war. When the ship opened fire, Jack said to himself, they would wonder what had possessed them to volunteer.

He checked the open gun breech, and glanced along the bore of the big 9.2-inch diameter barrel at the sky beyond, checking that the muzzle blank and training liner had not been left in. He turned and spoke briskly to the crew. 'When the time comes, lads, it'll get pretty noisy in here... and busy. I want you to concentrate. Don't let the noise put you off. Remember that you're part of a team, and if any one of you lets go of his end, he will be letting the whole ship's crew down... and the Admiral. Don't forget there are twenty of your mates down below, feeding shells and charges to you. It's a team effort, and you are lucky to be the ones chosen to score the goals. When we close up on the enemy, every shell must count. The more we send their way, the less they'll send ours. There will be no time to pick your nose or scratch your arse... only time enough to do your job, as smartly as you can.' He scanned the apprehensive faces. 'And if you let me down, you'll get eight lace-holes of the Chief's boot up your backsides. Right?' he added, with a smile.

'Aye, sir,' they all mumbled.

'OK, Cornish, you can stand your crew down for some fresh air and lunch – if they need it. Close up at your positions again at one o'clock... unless *ACTION STATIONS* is called first. No one...' Jack raised an emphatic index finger, 'No one is to take longer than two minutes to close up, if *ACTION STATIONS* is piped. I want you in this turret like a bunch of startled stoats.' He nodded towards the deck plates. 'But get that mess cleaned up first. I want everything shipshape and Bristol fashion in here.'

He stepped out onto the wet, rolling deck and went away to meet the Gunnery Chief Petty Officer who had been visiting the after turret. Together they set off to complete their rounds of the crews of *Good Hope's* sixteen 6-inch midship-guns.

2:05 pm

With the squadron steaming north at 17 knots, Cradock dined alone in his quarters. A steward in a crisp white linen jacket placed a sparklingly clean soup plate in front of the Admiral, carefully turning the rim of the plate to bring its blue crest to the twelve o'clock position. Swaying against the ship's movement, he ladled hot oxtail soup into the plate, spilling some on the pristine tablecloth. He apologised profusely as he struggled with the silver tureen and ladle, and apprehension flickered in his eyes. Cradock gave him an understanding smile and picked up his spoon to savour his soup slowly and deliberately, wondering all the while what the German ship he was about to meet was doing at this precise time.

Had he known, it would have spoiled his lunch.

As fate would have it, von Spee, beyond the horizon, had decided to depart the Juan Fernandez Islands and was now heading south at 23 knots towards the British ships with all five of the warships under his command – the entire German squadron.

Having heard that the British cruiser *Glasgow* had been sighted in the area, it was an opportunity he was not prepared to pass up. Being the only British ship reported to be in the area by intelligence sources in Chile, *Glasgow* appeared to be alone but he had something else to worry about. The British battleship *Canopus*, although yet a long way away on the other side of South America, was apparently heading south towards the Falkland Islands.

It was time for him to move.

Meeting the full force of the rising head wind as they left the shelter of the islands, the German ships slackened their speed to 20 knots to take account of the waves crashing over their bows. Heavy spray showered over their foredecks and up over their bridges as they formed a line behind their flagship, *Scharnhorst*. Astern were two heavy battlecruisers and three light cruisers. Four more than Cradock was expecting.

Unlike Cradock's ships, the German warships had been together continuously for two years, under von Spee's command, and their crews shared a strong esprit de corps. There were no green reservists in the German squadron. They were all regular crews, well practised and battle experienced – worked up to a high state of readiness and as efficient as a Swiss watch. Not a week had passed without them being in action, sinking ships or attacking one allied base or another. *Gneisenau*, the cruiser immediately astern of *Scharnhorst*, held the Kaiser's personal gunnery award, and had won it several times before. Von Spee's confidence in his ships was absolute, and the only fear that haunted him was that he would not find a coaling station or a passing ship when he needed more coal.

In *Good Hope*, Admiral Cradock, deep in thought, had finished his lunch and was about to enjoy coffee when his Flag Lieutenant knocked and entered his cabin. "Flags" looked flushed and excited. 'Admiral Cradock, sir. Captain's respects… he wishes to report a sighting.' His announcement was breathless. '*Glasgow* is just re-joining the fleet and reports smoke on the horizon.' Cradock wiped his white linen napkin across his beard, with a slow, deliberate movement, rolled it up neatly and carefully threaded it into the solid silver napkin ring bearing his engraved initials.

'Very well. Tell the Captain I am on my way.' He rose casually, pausing in front of a mirror. Carefully positioning his cap on his head, he tucked his favourite telescope under his left arm, and headed for the bridge. 'What have we got, Captain?' he asked in a calm, business-like voice as he stepped onto the bridge. He focused his telescope on the horizon.

The Captain responded without taking his eyes from his binoculars. '*Glasgow* has reported funnel smoke on the horizon... one point off the starboard bow, sir, as yet, unidentified.'

Cradock turned his telescope to the right of the point of the ship's bow. The wind had risen to near-hurricane force in the past hour, and the waves rising over the ship's bow were now green and solid as the following wind shoved her nose deeper into them. In normal circumstances, funnel smoke rising high into the sky could give a ship away, long before she appeared on the horizon but, in these winds, smoke was staying low on the surface and dissipating quickly. Cradock's tone grew more impatient as he waited for a visual sighting. 'What the devil are your lookouts doing?' he asked the Captain, testily. 'Haven't you got anyone in the maintop?'

'Sir, there are three good men in the maintop,' Captain Francklin replied, calmly and patiently, 'and two closed up at the director positions. I fear the weather is against them.'

'Damned useless,' mumbled Cradock. 'We'll be taking German shells before they notice anything.'

4:20 pm

Good Hope's wireless officer sent to the bridge a report of German voices on a particular frequency then sent up a further signal from *Glasgow* confirming her earlier sighting. This was immediately followed by simultaneous reports from the ship's maintop lookouts and the director operator – *'TWO LARGE CRUISERS AND ONE SMALLER SHIP – TWO POINTS OFF THE STARBOARD BOW.'*

The hairs of every human arm and neck on the bridge stood on end. 'Aha! We've found them,' Cradock boomed, with fresh excitement in his voice. 'But rather more than we'd bargained for. Hold steady on the present course.'

The officers on the bridge continued to scan the horizon until the First Officer spotted smoke rising from the skyline. 'There, sir... off the starboard bow.'

All binoculars followed his urgently pointing finger. Cradock could just make out the grey funnels and masts of at least two ships, possibly a third, rising out of the horizon. 'What d'you make of them?' he asked.

'Four funnels apiece... definitely two German battlecruisers.' Captain Francklin responded from beneath his binoculars. 'And one light cruiser, heading south... and I think I can see other funnels... another vessel... possibly more.' He turned to his First Lieutenant. 'Number One, bring us to *ACTION STATIONS*.'

The First Lieutenant responded quickly. *'ACTION STATIONS! – ACTION STATIONS!'* The call rattled down telephone lines and voice pipes. Royal Marine bugles and bo'sun's pipes sounded the call in every corner of *Good Hope*, galvanising her crew into action. Nine hundred officers and sailors burst into feverish activity, rushing past each other along gangways and ladders between decks, to their battle positions. Hearts beat faster, and surging adrenalin widened all eyes, as the prospect of action suddenly became a reality. Shutters and cupboard doors slammed shut on the mess decks. Gun crews locked themselves into their turrets or stood behind their guns, donned their white anti-flash hoods, gloves and arm sleeves, and pushed in their earplugs.

The first shells and cordite charges rattled up the hoists into the breeches of the big guns. Below decks, watertight doorways were clipped tight. The atmosphere throughout the ship became electric. Jack Royal, in the Control Centre, took up his position by the Dreyer plotting table. At a range of 10 miles, the first firm range and bearing information was relayed down from the director operators, and Jack monitored the plotting of the targets on the table. Bearing and elevation details were dialled to the two main turrets, while the crews of the smaller guns took up their positions on the upper deck. Although the enemy was well out of range, the gunners stood to, ready for action.

Good Hope's two enormous turrets – cast boxes of armour-plated steel, eight inches thick and mounted on huge steel cylinders extending down through five decks to the bowels of the ship – rumbled into position. The big guns elevated and paused, ready and tense like a pointer on the moors.

In the chart room, Cradock bent over the charts. The Navigating

Officer was busy plotting the enemy's positions relative to *Good Hope,* and estimating range and speed. Pointing with his folded-down telescope, Cradock began to describe what he had in mind. 'We'll go about and run a parallel southerly course with them. If we turn to starboard, it will bring us that much closer.' He looked out at the sea for a moment, before returning his attention to the chart. 'If we maintain maximum speed for the sea-state, say 20 knots, that should be appropriate. Monitor our relative positions and keep station with the enemy. Where are we in respect of the Chilean coast?'

The navigator drew several lines on the chart. 'Here, sir... north of Concepción... or Coronel,' he said, naming two Chilean ports.

'Very well.' Cradock turned to his Flag Lieutenant. 'Flags, signal the squadron. I want all ships to turn and follow in line astern of us. Make it so.' The Flag Lieutenant wrote the message for the signalman, while the Captain issued orders to his bridge staff. An array of signal flags jerked up the signal mast, passing the Admiral's orders to *Monmouth, Glasgow* and *Otranto.* The squadron duly turned about slowly and formed a line behind the flagship. All guns turned with the ships, to stay directed at the Germans.

At the end of the manoeuvre, the British squadron was heading south parallel with the enemy. By then, confirmation had been received that the ships on the horizon were the German heavy cruisers *Scharnhorst,* von Spee's flagship, *Gneisenau,* another heavy cruiser of the squadron, and three light cruisers, *Nürnberg, Leipzig* and *Dresden.* Cradock and his Captain pored over the charts with the Navigating Officer and Flag Lieutenant in attendance. The tenseness of the situation showed in the Admiral's face, in spite of his efforts to look unconcerned. He had hoped for one single German ship: definitely not the five now facing him. Quite unexpectedly, he had blundered into the full might of the German South Pacific Fleet!

Cradock pensively stroked his beard as if idly petting a cat in some far-off English drawing room then slowly pulled it to a point. He straightened up from the chart table and stood erect before voicing his thoughts. 'I am afraid, gentlemen, we are heavily outgunned here. Even with the blessing of the Almighty, we have no hope of inflicting damage of any consequence on the Germans.' He paused for thought. 'However, with *Canopus* coming up from the south, our objective must now be to keep station with the Germans until she comes into range. By steaming south, we are, of course, closing the distance between *Canopus* and ourselves. The Germans will not be aware of this. As slow as the old tub is, she will outgun and outrange them when she is with us… provided we can hem them in. They will have Chile to the east… us to the west… and *Canopus* to the south. However, we shall not launch an attack until *Canopus* is within range. By then, the German gunners should have a low sun directly in their eyes …much to our advantage.'

The Captain listened intently, but there was concern in his eyes. He was thinking about *Otranto*. She was hopelessly inadequate, and had only short-range, low-calibre guns to defend herself. 'Sir. *Otranto*… she cannot possibly contribute anything to this …she will be a sitting duck for the German gunners.'

'I accept that,' Cradock snapped. 'Valid point: Flags, make a signal. Direct *Otranto* to stand west of us, out of range.' Cradock, his squadron now hopelessly outnumbered and outgunned by faster, superior German ships, could easily have chosen to retire his squadron at flank speed, in order to live to fight another day, without attracting criticism or disgrace. Half expecting him to give that very order, the Captain said nothing, but Cradock gave no thought to the option. His intention was clear: to attack, and to be in at the kill as soon as *Canopus* came into range. With the battleship's four torpedo tubes, twelve 6-inch guns, and four mighty 12-inch guns, she could certainly even the score, but only if she were there.

Cradock set his jaw and decided to keep his ships out of range, waiting patiently for the right time to attack. Having at last located this highly elusive and destructive German unit, he felt duty-bound to do whatever he could to damage it. It was now within his grasp to strike a blow for the Royal Navy, but Cradock's assumptions were seriously flawed by factors unknown to him.

Canopus was barely managing to keep up 13 knots, and it was unlikely that she would arrive before night came to transform the situation into "blind man's buff". He had also assumed that von Spee, his competent and gallant counterpart with a mission to destroy British ships wherever he found them, would be content to steam south and allow his enemy to dictate the time and terms of engagement. From intelligence radioed to him, von Spee knew that a British battleship was heading his way, and he knew where it was likely to be. Indeed, until stumbling over Cradock's squadron, his main reasons for steaming south were to meet *Canopus* and catch *Glasgow*. He also had considerable experience of the region, and this told him that at dusk, the sun would set spectacularly behind the British squadron and stop shining directly into the eyes of his gunners.

He assessed the situation carefully before making his decisions. With no desire to put his three light cruisers at risk and confident of the firepower of his two larger warships, he ordered the cruisers to move out of harm's way. Then, optimising his use of the sun, he altered course to converge with the British squadron.

7:05 pm

As von Spee had confidently predicted, with the orange sun setting behind them, the British ships stood out like black models on a practice firing range, presenting the German gunners with perfect targets. As the last rays of golden sunlight turned to orange and faded away, von Spee moved in and ordered the attack.

From Cradock's position in the fading light, the outline of the grey German ships was merging into the dark background of mainland Chile. At a distance of less than 7 miles, the German ships opened fire. Simultaneous gunflashes rippled down the sides of *Scharnhorst* and *Gneisenau* as salvos of 8.2-inch diameter shells erupted from their guns in tongues of orange flame and huge balls of smoke. The officers on the bridge of *Good Hope* were unable to hear the characteristic whistling whine of the shells above the wind, until they were raining down on them.

'OPEN FIRE! – OPEN FIRE!' The order rang down from the bridge of *Good Hope*. In the Combat Control Centre, Jack Royal slammed the mushroom-shaped red firing button by his side, and the roar of *Good Hope's* guns rumbled throughout the ship. She shuddered with their recoil. In the turrets, cordite smoke billowed out of breeches as they were snatched open. Cooling water and compressed air were sprayed into them, and they were swiftly re-

charged and re-loaded.

With ear-splitting explosions, the first two German shells plunged into *Good Hope's* upper deck. *'RELOAD! – READY!'* shouted Cornish, at the top of his voice. The ears of the turret crewmen hissed with the noise and pressure, but the men did what they had been trained to do. On the bridge, all binoculars turned to the oncoming Germans as damage control reports came in from several sections of the ship.

With the waterspouts of British shells springing up around them, *Scharnhorst* and *Gneisenau* fired again. Cradock and his men anxiously watched the flash of the broadsides they knew they were going to receive. Moments later, *Gneisenau's* shells exploded in the bow section of the other cruiser, *Monmouth,* killing a number of ratings and crippling her forward guns. Flames and smoke enveloped *Monmouth's* bridge. She slowly turned upwind towards the north, where the wind might carry the flames and smoke ahead of her. She was hit again and again, with relentless accuracy.

Jack received fresh plotting information from the director operators. Their speed and efficiency was not up to normal standards. Funnel and gun smoke was obscuring their view, the ship was pitching and rolling violently, and the enemy ships were impossible to pick out. The plotters worked frantically to provide new directions for the turrets. Before Jack could fire again, two enormous thuds echoed through the hull of *Good Hope* as German shells exploded underwater, close by. Light bulbs shattered and burst over the compartment. Glass showered down, and some lights went out. Two more shells hit *Good Hope's* superstructure with deafening explosions, rocking her from end to end.

The plotters picked themselves up off the deck, and struggled on with their duties. Jack managed to fire *Good Hope's* main guns four more times before the gun director position and a section of the bridge were blown away. Admiral Cradock, the Captain, and others on the bridge were now dead or dying.

The Combat Control Centre was inoperative. Here, and in several other sections of the ship, duty was no longer an option and an overwhelming urge to survive took over. Shells continued to plunge into the ship, and bodies and torn limbs were scattered grotesquely in pools of blood in many compartments. Fires were breaking out everywhere among buckled bulkheads and the twisted metal of the decks. Men, disorientated and wounded, with their faces blackened, were stumbling through the dense smoke, flames and wreckage, not knowing where they were, or where they were going. Some were clutching handfuls of bloody tendons where hands and arms had once been. Others were screaming with pain as their clothing burnt on their flesh.

Grabbing his Midshipman and one of his plotters, Jack made a desperate attempt to guide them towards a clear route to the upper deck, but they were forced back by intense heat, and then flung backward in the blast of another explosion. With the distance between the battling squadrons now less than 7 miles, another shell from *Scharnhorst* hissed out of the sky, straight into the base of *Good Hope's* forward turret. In a blinding, incandescent flash, Cornish and the crew of the forward turret were killed instantly. Their bodies were disintegrated and vaporised in the explosion of shells and cordite inside the turret. The flash travelled down to the base of the turret, five decks below.

Before Jack could move a muscle, a thick steel bulkhead blew inwards like a ruptured tin can as the blast came up from the base of the turret. Like a discarded puppet, he was hurled against the opposite bulkhead beside the body of one of his ratings. A fraction of a second before he lost consciousness, the ship's magazines exploded with the roar of Hell. Searing orange heat flashed through the Combat Centre, and Jack's battered body and everything else in the compartment erupted up through the ship's decks, 200 feet into the evening sky.

After taking 35 shells from the guns of *Scharnhorst*, *Good Hope* was finished. She sat low in the water with most of her superstructure blown away, incandescent from end to end. With a final rumbling hiss, she slid beneath the dark sea. The orange glow of her fiercely burning magazines was still visible in foam surging and boiling around her; long after she started her rapid descent to the bottom.

Good Hope had gone, with Admiral Cradock, Jack Royal, Cornish, and the rest of her 900 men.

It was *7:50 pm* on Jack's 48th birthday.

Gneisenau, meanwhile, was dealing *Monmouth* a similar fate.

Severely damaged, the British cruiser was listing and burning fiercely with her guns and most other equipment out of action. She was helpless. She and *Glasgow* turned slowly away from the battle scene.

Glasgow, relatively unscathed, steamed off with *Otranto* to warn *Canopus*, still over 100 miles away. There was nothing more they could do. The violence and coldness of the sea would claim anyone still alive before they could reach them.

8:55 pm

Like ravenous grey wolves gathering around a wounded stag, the German cruisers closed up on the stricken and defenceless *Monmouth*. Her engines were still running, but she had nothing left to fight with. The Germans ceased firing to allow survivors to escape, but no one abandoned the ship. Then, in what seemed to be a last defiant attempt to ram the German ships, she turned back, but they fired at her again and again, and shells poured into her at a range of 1,000 yards. Before she came within 600 yards of her tormentors, she capsized and sank, taking her entire crew of almost 800 officers and men to the bottom.

Not one man from the two British cruisers survived.

With the battle over, von Spee's squadron, hardly damaged at all, steamed away to the north, for Valparaiso. Only two German sailors had been wounded in the battle, and their injuries were minor. *Glasgow* and *Otranto* headed back to the Falkland Islands.

It was all over. The Royal Navy had been decisively defeated, for the first time in over a hundred years.

In the Falkland Islands, the Governor was at his desk when the news came in. He sat for some time, looking out over the sea, trying to take in the enormity of the disaster. His eyes were filled with disbelief and sadness. He found it hard to imagine Port Stanley without the familiar outlines of *Good Hope* and *Monmouth* anchored there, and he thought of the families who would soon be grieving in Britain. The Coronel tragedy hung over the small community like a black cloud when the news got around, and fear gripped the Islanders.

The Governor stood up and went to a wooden cabinet in the corner of his office. Unlocking it, he took out a sealed white envelope. In Cradock's neat hand, it had written on it, "To be mailed as soon as my death is confirmed." He looked at it, imagining that he could still feel the moment Cradock had handed it to him, two days before, when he left the island for the last time. A chill ran through his body as he wondered what premonition had prompted his friend to write the letter.

THE ADMIRALTY, WHITEHALL
November 3, 1914

With great irony, two signals from the Admiralty came too late. One was for Stoddart, the other for Cradock.

FROM ADMIRALTY TO STODDART
DEFENCE TO PROCEED WITH ALL POSSIBLE DISPATCH TO JOIN ADMIRAL CRADOCK ON WEST COAST OF AMERICA. ACKNOWLEDGE

FROM ADMIRALTY TO CRADOCK
DEFENCE HAS BEEN ORDERED TO JOIN YOUR FLAG, WITH ALL DISPATCH. GLASGOW SHOULD FIND OR KEEP IN TOUCH WITH THE ENEMY. YOU SHOULD KEEP IN TOUCH WITH GLASGOW CONCENTRATING THE REST OF YOUR SQUADRON INCLUDING CANOPUS

The latter would never be answered.

In Britain, news of the defeat came as a shattering blow. At the Admiralty, and in the coffee bars frequented by politicians and senior officers, the Coronel disaster became a hotly debated issue. Everywhere, the question was asked: 'Why?' Unfortunately, with Admiral Cradock and all his officers and men gone, there was no one to answer: no one to explain why he had sacrificed himself and his men tackling a vastly superior force, when the likely outcome had been both predictable and obvious. It seemed to some that this had been a foolhardy act of extreme impetuosity. To others, especially those who knew Christopher Cradock well, his actions at Coronel were simply an example of absolute British courage in the line of duty.

However much it was debated, two things remained certain – over fifteen hundred officers and men had died at Coronel, and the validity of Cradock's reasoning would never be known.

Chapter Six

THE ADMIRALTY, WHITEHALL, LONDON
Wednesday, November 4, 1914

Admiral "Jacky" Fisher sat at his desk at the Admiralty with his delicate gold-framed spectacles perched halfway down his nose. His prominent pale grey eyes were ablaze with the exasperation and anger rising inside him as he studied a long signal from what was left of the South Atlantic Fleet. It described Cradock's battle with von Spee, and listed the Navy's losses at Coronel.

Having only become the First Sea Lord again the previous Wednesday, for the second time in his career – he had hardly completed the formalities of taking office. The signal trembling in his hand had just been received. It heralded the first major problem he was going to have to deal with since his return. He read it again and again – his anger and disgust reaching new levels on each occasion. The news was a shattering, humiliating blow for the Royal Navy.

At the ripe age of seventy-three years, Fisher had lost none of his fire. He was still fit, upright, and very astute, and the expression on his rounded face was characteristically pugnacious. Even when fully relaxed, he could look as if there were objectionable smells close by; his mouth would droop at the corners and he would peer down his nose but, as he sat deep in thought, absorbing the full details of Cradock's disastrous defeat at Coronel, he had the features of a bulldog.

Christopher Cradock, it seemed, had needlessly thrown away the lives of nearly seventeen hundred gallant officers and men – and two valuable warships – simply to prove that he had been courageous but ill-equipped. Admittedly, he had given his own life, in the process but with a perfidious lack of charity, Fisher concluded that it was probably the best way for Cradock to have come out of it himself, given the decisions he had made. Had he, Fisher, been in office just a month earlier, things would have been different, he told himself. Characteristically, he elected to overlook the point that it was the very redeployment plan that he personally introduced during his previous term of office, which ultimately left Cradock with warships that were inadequate in number, firepower and speed.

Fond of citing Napoleon's axioms, Fisher made a mental note to quote, whenever an opportunity presented itself, '*Frappez vite et frappez fort*' ('Hit fast and hit hard'). This gem of wisdom – typifying his own approach to life – had clearly been ignored at Coronel, as far as he could tell, with disastrous and predictable consequences. He could see from records that his predecessor had paid little attention to Cradock's pleas for support – which is not how he would have reacted, had he still been the First Sea Lord.

It was proof enough, he thought to himself – if any were needed – that forcing him into retirement in 1909 had been an act of folly that was bound to have serious repercussions on the entire British Empire. *Those confounded idiots!* In those circumstances, had he been there, he would not have hesitated – of course – to send more ships, better ships that would have put Cradock on an equal footing with von Spee – but he had not been there, thanks to certain politicians. So now he would just have to show those particular people how much more effectively he would have dealt with the situation, had they not been so stupid as to retire him. Safely back in office with the benefit of hindsight, he relished the thought of grinding this axe in public.

He looked at the clock on the wall. It was 2:25 pm and time to leave for his appointment with Winston Churchill, the First Lord of the Admiralty. He rose and reached for his long "doeskin" uniform greatcoat with the heavy gold braid of his rank on its epaulettes. He picked up his papers, cap and black walking cane, and made his way through the corridors, across the cobbled yard of the Admiralty building, and out onto the broad and bustling pavements of Whitehall. The street was thick with traffic. Noisy taxicabs, buses and lorries crawled along the road, churning up clouds of exhaust fumes that stung his nose. Military officers in uniform and city gents in bowler hats flocked along the pavements.

Straight-backed, and with an imperious look on his face, he strode jauntily along the pavement towards Churchill's Westminster office, pleased to be back in his rightful position of importance. His indispensability having been proved to his entire satisfaction, he was now back to clear up the mess. Feeling on top of it all, he gave free rein to his expertise in walking with his cane. With a wrist-flicking, three-pace rhythm, he grounded his cane as if he were measuring precisely the distance to Churchill's office with it, and the music hall song "Burlington Bertie from Bow" would have been a fitting accompaniment to his jaunty gait.

Promenading elegantly along Whitehall, he spotted a sailor in uniform coming towards him. The man was limping, and his injured right arm was in a sling. As he drew nearer, Fisher could see the young man's mounting confusion and embarrassment at having his saluting arm in a sling while coming face to face with a senior officer – whoever he was. He stopped the terrified sailor and drew him to one side, bidding him to relax and "Stand Easy".

'Courtesy of the Hun?' Fisher asked, with a frown.

'Yes, sir... a bit of shrapnel... last week, sir.'

'Did you manage to hit back?'

'Oh yes, sir. We sunk the bug... beg pardon, sir, we sunk their ship.'

'Excellent... excellent. Well done. Where are you off to now?'

'Going to Euston Station, sir... convalescent leave.'

'But why are you walking? Didn't they give you transport?'

'Well... no, sir.'

'Wait there, lad,' said Fisher firmly, turning to the road and raising his cane to stop the world in its tracks. A taxicab pulled up immediately. 'Take this wounded hero to Euston Station right away, cabby... how much will that be?' The Admiral paid the driver and helped the stunned sailor into the taxicab. 'There you are lad, get yourself home, have a good rest, and get better soon. The Navy needs you back at sea. Tell your mother the First Sea Lord said so.' Fisher smiled warmly and waved the taxicab away.

Left open-mouthed by the experience, the wide-eyed sailor was borne away bursting to tell his story to someone. Fisher continued on his way with genuine satisfaction creasing his features. Quickening his pace to make up for lost time, and pondering why he had been summoned to the First Lord's offices, one reason stayed persistently at the top of his thoughts, churning up his self-defensive anger. He had not forgotten the bitter opposition Churchill had met with when his return to office had been announced but always the consummate politician, Churchill had handled it well – deflating critics with an impressive catalogue of the old man's strengths and past achievements.

However, the worst protagonist had not been appeased by this – Fisher's private bête noire, Admiral Sir Doveton Sturdee – Chief of the Naval War Staff and a former protégé of Admiral Lord Charles Beresford, the man who had caused his enforced retirement. Fisher hated them both equally as much, and they both hated him. Having been a member of Beresford's staff during the cataclysmic Fisher/Beresford row of 1909, Sturdee remained an ardent, anti-Fisher Beresfordite, possessed with the will to use his powerful aristocratic connections, yet again, to undermine his arch-enemy.

Before he reached his destination, Jacky's mind was made up – this appointment had to be to do with Sturdee. Not that he was overly concerned; in his sixty years of naval service, he had brushed off many a self-opinionated man like Sturdee. Nonetheless, this man was a constant source of trouble, and their obdurate pugnacity would never allow them to settle their differences amicably.

As he walked into Churchill's offices, a smartly dressed young secretary stood up and smiled. 'Good afternoon, sir. Mister Churchill is expecting you.' She opened the double mahogany doors and announced the arrival of the First Sea Lord, before spiriting away his cap, coat and cane. Churchill was seated behind a large oak desk, its inlaid red leather top covered with neat piles of documents. There was a faint aroma of past cigars and an air of authority in the functional but well-appointed room – as if important decisions were made there. Softly illuminated paintings hung on its wood-panelled walls, and a window looked out over St James's Park. A few elegant pieces of gleaming furniture were tastefully arranged around a large central rug. On the shelves of a bookcase against one wall, leather-bound volumes were neatly arranged in rows.

Churchill was wearing a black frock coat and striped grey waistcoat. At his stocky neck, a black bow tie was nestling under the wings of a stiff, white collar that seemed to be supporting his round, boyish face. He got up and welcomed Fisher with a broad smile. 'Aah, John, do come in. Thank you for coming.' His upturned palm gestured towards the leather-covered chair in front of his desk. 'Please.' Fisher sat, declining the secretary's offer of tea. With a deft sweep of his heavily gold-braided forearm, he cleared a space on Churchill's desk for his own papers. 'Damned awful business about Christopher Cradock,' Churchill began, shaking his head slowly and sitting behind his desk. 'Not something we should just take on the chin, in my view.'

'Can't afford to,' said Fisher, brusquely. Then, mindful of where he was, he smiled wanly.

'I have heard' – Churchill went on, "shushing" his way through the sibilance of his sentences – 'that Kaiser Wilhelm is positively gloating over what he calls *the complete annihilation of his grandmother's Navy!* Apparently he has awarded three hundred Iron Crosses to von Spee's men.'

Reluctant to talk about it, Fisher grunted and scowled reflectively over the desk. His relationship with Churchill was a strange one. His own career spanned sixty years of controversy and distinguished achievement, and his experience of naval matters was immense. Churchill – thirty-three years the younger, but more the senior in position – served in the Army, but had no experience of the sea at all. It was an odd alliance: an experienced politician with unquestionable negotiating skills on one side – an obdurate, cantankerous old sea dog on the other, but Churchill had always admired and supported Fisher and they shared common ground in essential areas, on which their contribution to the war could be built. While sharing the old boy's open-minded passion for innovation, he positively revelled in the blatant disgust he showed for inefficient people who minced words. Above all, he wanted to harness the Admiral's dynamism for getting things done. More than anything else, this was what prompted him to retrieve Fisher from his unwanted rose-growing retirement. Now the Great War was under way, and a very different First Lord of the Admiralty was in office at the tender age of forty. Churchill needed a new First Sea Lord, and believed that no man other than Fisher would do. So, he was back, reporting, this time, to the forward-thinking young Winston Churchill, whose support he enjoyed. The result of all this was that the two of them were getting on famously together.

'We must put a stop to Herr Spee's raids in the South Atlantic,' Churchill went on. 'If he is allowed to continue raiding our supply lines, which are vital to Britain and her war effort, we'll be in mortal danger of being cut off. No ship is safe there.' Fisher was making a special effort to be accommodating. He waited politely for Churchill to finish, but the First Lord continued delivering his points in measured, well-considered sentences, punctuated by short hesitant pauses. 'It is my considered view, John, that we should send one or two of our best ships out ...perhaps a battlecruiser or two – with larger guns? We should put an end to this German threat, once and for all.'

Fisher shifted anxiously in his chair, keen to make his own points. 'I can assure you, Winston... I have already given much thought to this.' His tone became tenser. 'Quite apart from the disruption of our supply lines that you mention, there is now another important issue at stake – the Royal Navy's international reputation – not to mention that of the Empire. It is imperative that we should achieve an immediate, decisive victory over the Germans, to put that right. The morale of the Navy must be restored immediately... and the Germans must be taught a lesson they will not forget.' Fisher was in his stride. 'Cradock was a fool to engage von Spee at Coronel. *"Frappez vite et frappez fort"* is how sea warfare should be conducted! If he wasn't in a position to subscribe to the spirit of that, he should have turned tail... or waited for other ships to arrive. Clearly he chose not to wait... probably thinking he could make a name for himself. Well, he certainly did that! He made a laughing stock out of the service. Had I been at the Admiralty, this would never have happened. I...'

Churchill cut him off. 'Yes, yes... I'm sure you are right, John, but unfortunately you were not, and Christopher obviously found himself in a very invidious position. The question is what are we going to do about it now?'

Fisher leaned forward and prodded the desktop with a finger. His eyes sparkled with venom. 'Now that I am back, you may rest assured that the Huns will live to regret their victory at Coronel. Not for long will the German Navy think it is invincible ...or that the Royal Navy has lost its ability to win battles.'

Churchill smiled. 'I am delighted to find you in such a bold frame of mind, John. You agree with my proposal, then?'

'I would have been disappointed, Winston, had you not agreed with my own proposal to take *several* of our ships to do the job!' Fisher pointed to his papers on the desk. 'I have here my strategy document, complete with orders to be signalled forthwith ...for the immediate deployment of two Grand Fleet battlecruisers from the North Sea, together with four light cruisers to the South Atlantic, with all speed.'

Churchill's delight at the old man's response crept into his grin. Already it seemed to him, his faith in the old boy was being justified. Fisher went on. 'With the balance of Cradock's squadron already there, this will create a fleet of eight warships. You should know that any one of my battlecruisers could destroy von Spee's entire squadron.'

'Excellent!' Churchill rubbed his hands. There was a glint of wily old fox in his eyes. 'Splendid, John, splendid.' A serious look flickered across Churchill's face. 'But it must be done very quickly, John... before von Spee gets into the Atlantic.' He cleared his throat, consciously preparing his next statement. 'And to command this new Atlantic Fleet, I have in mind a very capable and experienced officer.' Fisher's eyes darted a challenging, quizzical look at Churchill who was preparing a half-smile: 'Sturdee.'

The name was like a sword thrust to Fisher's heart. *'STURDEE?'* His exclamation sounded like a warship's broadside. Churchill hastened to stifle the inevitable tirade before it could erupt.

'John... John, I am well acquainted with your opinion of Sturdee. Nevertheless, he is a fine officer.'

'THE MAN IS AN IMBECILE!' Fisher made as if to rise and leave the room, but Churchill urged him to stay in his seat. If he did not establish his authority over the old boy now, the future was bleak.

'John, please ...hear me out!'

Reluctantly, Fisher sat down again, with fury in his eyes.

'This persistent running battle between the two of you... as disruptive as it is... could never be sufficient reason to cause Sturdee to step down as Chief of Naval War Staff. Yet, as you know, all the time he is there he will be a thorn in your side. Surely, you understand that I cannot permit such personal grievances ...a bitter personal feud at the highest level of the Admiralty ...to interfere with the management and direction of the Royal Navy?'

Fisher sat stony-faced. His eyes narrowed and the corners of his mouth drooped petulantly into an inverted crescent. 'But I am, sir – with the authority of your good self – the First Sea Lord. As such, I give not one jot for the opinions of an overinflated, pompous ass like Sturdee. I will not tolerate him under my feet. It is my intention to remove him from the Admiralty as quickly as possible. I... '

Brushing Fisher's words aside with a raised hand, Churchill continued. 'Nor do you have to, John. It isn't necessary. Rest assured that Sturdee holds no particular sway with me. He is, nonetheless, a competent admiral and, as such, must be afforded the degree of courtesy that befits his position.'

'Paahh!' huffed Fisher, shuffling papers, but Churchill was determined to have his say.

'With respect to your position as First Sea Lord, I am still your ally. However, if and when the Admiralty has cause to fire its political guns, I am determined that it should do so in a broadside, with no loose cannons to weaken its power. Lord Sturdee cannot be ridden over, roughshod. He could, however, be, shall we say, distracted from his battle with you.' Fisher calmed down and looked more interested in what was being said. 'In my opinion,' said Churchill with a cunning look in his eyes, 'the best way to achieve that is to give him more important things to worry about – preferably, elsewhere.'

Churchill stood up and came from behind his desk. 'It is for this very reason that I believe Sturdee should have command of this new South Atlantic Fleet, and that he should be dispatched to the Falkland Islands with all haste, tasked with the important mission of catching von Spee ...and, of course, avenging Christopher Cradock. Don't you see? Once he is out of his chair at Whitehall, and is at sea with a fleet worthy of his task and position, it will be somewhat easier to encourage him to stay at sea – away from the Admiralty ...out of range, so to speak.'

Fisher looked up at him, speechless. He sat back in his chair with the wind taken out of his sails, silently admitting to a sneaking admiration for Churchill's political mind. With neither the patience nor time to negotiate ways around obstacles such as Sturdee, the idea of removing them altogether appealed to him immensely. The two men made eye contact. Churchill was not sure which way this was going until Fisher's face slowly creased into a broad smile – one of his warm, genuine smiles.

As Churchill watched it develop, he grinned broadly. 'Excellent solution,' Fisher conceded enthusiastically. 'Excellent!'

'Splendid!' said Churchill. 'I have spoken to him ...purely, of course, on the matter of strategy for the South Atlantic. I must agree with his view that what we can expect from von Spee – with Christopher, *Good Hope* and *Monmouth* gone – is that he will waste no time in breaking out into the South Atlantic.' Fisher nodded agreement. 'And that he is bound to launch an attack on the Falkland Islands, in the process. Needless to say, this is a most important supply and coaling station for us. Should he deprive us of that, defending our supply lines in the South Atlantic would be impossible. This must not happen, John... under any circumstance.'

'Well, with no base of his own,' Fisher added, 'and our defences there weakened, he will be forced to avail himself of our coal stock there. He certainly will not venture into the South Atlantic without re-coaling somewhere and there is nowhere else to do it.'

'Precisely,' Churchill went on. 'There is not a moment to lose or he will slip through our fingers again. Sturdee must leave immediately. If he cannot reach the Falklands before von Spee, we have the awful prospect of firing our coals stock, in order to deprive the Germans of it. The only way to avoid giving such an order immediately is to give the Prime Minister a firm assurance *now* that we can get there in time and complete the task.' He went back to his seat. 'Now, John, let us get down to brass tacks. What do you have in mind?'

Briefly, they discussed Fisher's plan to dispatch the battlecruisers *Invincible* and *Inflexible* – fast, post-Dreadnought sister-ships, each carrying eight twelve-inch guns – that could outmatch the range and speed of von Spee's squadron. They would be dispatched immediately from the North Sea to Plymouth Dockyard, where they were to be provisioned and made ready with all speed. They would then head for the Falkland Islands, calling at a coaling station en route. Along the way, they would pick up the rest of the new 'South Atlantic and South Pacific Fleet' from the eastern side of South America – the three heavy cruisers, *Kent, Carnarvon,* and *Cornwall* – and the light cruiser *Bristol.* Joined by the light cruiser *Glasgow,* and the elderly battleship *Canopus* – Cradock's remaining ships in the Falklands, the new British fleet would be formidable.

With the two men in cordial agreement, Fisher returned to his desk with the daunting task of creating the new Fleet and getting it to the Falkland Islands in time. Standing between the conception of the plan and its execution, there was a mountain of logistical and administrative problems, but Churchill believed in Fisher's legendary ability to "move mountains" when he put his mind to it. Haste was the essential ingredient. If the new fleet could not reach the Falkland Islands before von Spee, all would be lost.

Fisher was bound to rise to such a challenge.

Over the next few days he worked tirelessly. Signals flew in all directions from his office. One was sent immediately to Admiral Sir John Jellicoe, Commander-in-Chief of the Grand Fleet at Rosyth, Scotland, ordering *Invincible* and *Inflexible* to leave their North Sea base and ***"PROCEED TO PLYMOUTH WITH ALL DISPATCH".*** From there, they were to sail for the Falklands on Wednesday, November 11, 1914. Objections to the impossible demands of Fisher's orders came in immediately, but revelling in his returned power, he lit fires wherever he encountered tardiness.

Wielding his authority like a tennis racket, he performed like a seasoned player under pressure – smashing problems off his baseline as quickly as they came at him.

"Jacky" was back – with a very important mission. Woe betide him who gets in Fisher's way!

Chapter Seven

GOSPORT, HAMPSHIRE
November 5, 1914 7:30 am

The telegram from the Admiralty came addressed to Mrs J Royal. The personal empathy of the clerk who had written it seemed to shine through the precisely formed, graceful characters of his copperplate handwriting. Each word was positioned precisely within the boxes printed on the form, as if his work would forever be subject to scrutiny. It read:

Mrs. J. Royal
32 St. Mark's Road
Gosport Hampshire

The Admiralty
Whitehall
London

November 5, 1914

It is with deep regret that their lordships report the loss of Lt. Jack Arthur Royal, Royal Navy, missing, presumed dead.

On November 1, 1914, the ship in which he served sank with all hands in the South Pacific Ocean as a result of enemy action.

Lieutenant Royal gallantly gave his life for his king and country.

God save the King

With Jack's smiling face looking down on her from his photo on the mantelpiece, Emily sat at her kitchen table, utterly stunned, staring at the telegram in her hand. Her body felt as cold as ice. A tingling sensation at the back of her legs quickly swarmed over every part of her body. Trembling and light-headed, she wrestled with the feeling that she was about to faint. She wanted to faint – before the awful news could penetrate the protective shell she had long since put around herself, and reach the vulnerable person inside.

She read it again, as if that might change what it was telling her. Not knowing what to expect of herself, or what to do, she put the kettle on the stove to make tea. Moving in a trance of disbelief and despair, her face was ashen and her arms and legs trembled.

She always knew this could happen one day; but she had kept the possibility hidden away in the darkest corners of her mind. Now reality was there in her hand, demanding to be faced.

Someone knocked at her front door. She went to it, still clutching the telegram, walking as if she had just aged twenty years. It was Emily's opposite neighbour, Gwen, with concern ingrained deeply in her face. 'Emily... I saw the telegr...' The words died on her lips at the sight of Emily's face. She stepped forward and threw her arms round her friend. 'Oh, Emily... who is it?'

'It's Jack. My lovely Jack, Gwen.' Her voice was flat and distant. Gwen gently ushered her into the drawing room and sat down with her arm around her shoulder. Emily cried, quietly at first, then sobbing her heart out with her body rocking in Gwen's arms.

The despair and desolation knotted like cold lead inside her came pouring out in a flood of hot tears that burnt her face. She thought of George and the pain he would feel when the news reached him. 'I have to let George know,' she managed to say, through trembling lips. 'How can I reach him? I don't know how to get in touch to tell him.'

Gwen was reassuring. 'Sshh... I'll find a way, Emily, don't you worry about it now. I'm so, so sorry, my love. I can't tell you how sorry I am.' It was an hour before Gwen felt she could leave Emily alone. She put her to bed with a stiff drink and a cup of tea then went back home for her coat and hat, and set off for the nearest Naval establishment, R.N Hospital Haslar. It took a long time to find a duty officer and explain the need to get a message to George.

After verifying the message's validity, the Lieutenant promised to get a signal to him as soon as he could.

Gwen went back to comfort Emily.

ON BOARD INFLEXIBLE IN THE NORTH SEA
November 5, 1914 11:30 am

In the mess, George was taking a break. Nearby, one of the new lads was clearing up the contents of his stomach, recently deposited on the deck. In the heavy, foam-topped waves whipped up by the cold November wind, the ship was rolling and pitching like a log.

George stared idly at the tea in the mug he was holding down firmly on the table, watching it move from side to side. His eyebrows arched as he noticed the tea climb up one side of the mug, and stay there. He sensed the change in the ship's rhythm. Having rolled to one side, she was in no hurry to come back – which could only mean that she was turning hard. He looked up and stared expectantly into space for a while, alert and ready for the call to *ACTION STATIONS* – but nothing happened. He relaxed as the ship came to an even keel, finished his tea, and went up to the upper deck, to see what was going on. On the way, he passed Chief Huggett.

'Any idea what's going on, Chief?'

'Yes, Royal, I was just coming down to tell the lads. We're leaving the North Sea now. Don't ask me why. Seems we're on our way back to dear old Devonport again, with *Invincible* ...back the way we came.'

'What?' George was puzzled. So was the Chief.

'I said don't ask me why – because I don't know. Now, hop down below and tell the rest of them.'

In the absence of an official explanation for their return to Devonport, the men were inclined to invent their own. It was not long before rumours circulated around the messdecks suggesting several possibilities, ranging from – "The war has ended," and "Devonport is under attack," to "The Germans have landed in Devon." None of the officers seemed prepared, or able, to say why there was a change of plan. The crew was unsettled by not knowing why the ship was going back, and irritation soon began to show itself. Heated arguments – particularly with "Curly" Roberts – disturbed the normally cordial atmosphere of the mess.

ROSYTH NAVAL COMMUNICATIONS OFFICE
November 5, 1914 3:05 pm

Signalman Williams, his earphones draped around his neck, was check-reading the signal concerning Leading Seaman Royal that he had just received from Haslar. A message from a medical establishment about a Leading Rating seemed to sit incongruously among the priority messages coming in from the Admiralty, one after another. The "URGENT" in-tray was already filled with priority signals about the redeployment of the Grand Fleet's ships, and even these had not been dealt with yet. Glancing at the clock above his desk, he ventured a guess that *Inflexible* would probably be well on her way through the Pentland Firth by now. Pursing his lips, he wrote "Redirect to Devonport" on the signal and placed it at the bottom of the even larger pile in the "ROUTINE" tray then went back to his desk.

DEVONPORT DOCKYARD, PLYMOUTH
November 8, 1914 9:05 am

In the early morning freshness of a clear winter's day, *Invincible* and *Inflexible* finally reached Devonport Dockyard after a slow, uneventful journey from Rosyth. The sister-ships had stayed close together for the entire trip, particularly as *Invincible* appeared to be having trouble with her engines, and had been forced to cruise at a slower speed than normal. This made the journey more risky, and a careful watch was kept for mines and submarines in the Irish Sea.

On reaching Devonport, there was an extraordinary amount of attention from the dockyard support services. The crews were staggered by the speed and zeal of the dockyard "Mateys", and the engineers and workers swarming through their ships. Equipment and machinery were checked and repaired with a speed never before witnessed by sailors in a dockyard. Mountains of coal and provisions enough for a long sea voyage waited in railway trucks on the quayside, and loading began as soon as the ships were tied up to the docks. Within thirty minutes of the first dockyard worker's arrival on board, the crews knew they were going to sail on November 11 for the South Atlantic. Where and why was still a mystery. Dockyard rumours were always rife and generally accurate enough to be relied upon, but the Admiralty – as a matter of policy, in wartime – maintained strict secrecy about the movements of its ships. Often, officers and ratings – sometimes, even captains – were told only what they needed to know to get their ships from one point to another to await further orders. Fisher's plans for *Invincible* and *Inflexible* were so sensitive that he had no intention of lifting the veil of secrecy over them until the new fleet was well into its mission. So far, everything was proceeding according to plan.

Just as all was going well, however, a major problem cropped up through the engineers' investigation of *Invincible's* poor performance. A serious defect was revealed that threatened to disrupt Fisher's battle plans completely. Some of the ship's boilers needed new firebricks, and she could not be made battle-ready without having them replaced. The head of the dockyard said that even working around the clock she would not be ready to sail out of Plymouth until November 13 at the earliest.

The Admiral Superintendent of Devonport Dockyard sent an urgent message to Fisher's office, informing him that work had begun, but delay was inevitable. Fisher's reaction, if only the Superintendent had known him better, was predictable. The instant he read the signal, the First Sea Lord burst into incandescent rage. Delay, he bellowed, would neither be inevitable nor tolerated. Signal and telephone lines between the Admiralty and Devonport Dockyard became hot with traffic, with the Superintendent and Fisher adamantly stating opposing views. In utter frustration on November 9, the Superintendent boarded the early train for London, to present his case to Fisher in person.

Two minutes after the Superintendent set foot in Fisher's office, the First Sea Lord's roaring voice and uncompromising comments could be heard above everything else in the corridors of the Admiralty. The hapless Superintendent was left with absolutely no doubt that his career would evaporate overnight if the ships did not sail, as planned, on November 11. Later that day, he was back on the train for Plymouth, with Fisher's fury still ringing in his ears.

On the afternoon of November 11, *Invincible* and *Inflexible* slipped away from Devonport Dockyard, bound for Abrolhos Rocks – midway between Salvador and Rio de Janeiro on the coast of Brazil. Aboard Admiral Sturdee's flagship *Invincible*, there were several disenchanted civilian dockyard workers from Devonport, still working frantically on her boilers with no hope of escape until the work was finished.

With the ships heading into the Atlantic, Lieutenant-Commander Foster began to assert his authority on his gun crews. Paying unwanted attention to his Chief's arrangements for training exercises for them, he announced that the crews were not physically fit enough to do their jobs properly. As the main guns had not been fired in anger for some time, he said, the crews needed intensive practice at loading and firing them.

In principle, having gunners properly worked up was not to be criticised, but this was not why the men objected. It was the intensity and severity of the training programme he forced on them that turned several of the gunners into muttering malcontents. Foster was never satisfied. He had his men assembled on the upper deck in all weathers, cutting short their breakfast every morning for a two-hour session of physical training with a Royal Marine instructor. Every day and all day, they were kept inside their turrets, carrying out exercise after exercise, until well after dark. Their loading and reaction times were as good as any in the Grand Fleet, but still he was not satisfied.

Curly Roberts, because of his bulk, found the gyrations of the physical training instructor too difficult to emulate, and it gave Foster an opportunity to pounce. Seeing Curly's ungainly efforts during "PTE" one morning, Foster ordered him out of the group, determined to make an example of him. He ordered Curly to frog-hop the length of the deck, and then do forty press-ups. As Foster looked on, strutting the deck with a sadistic sneer on his face, the anger radiating from Curly's red face was like the heat of a furnace.

On certain evenings, when the men were "off watch" and whilst recovering from a gruelling day, Foster had them piped to duty for *ACTION STATIONS* drill. Gradually, their morale sank to an all-time low. Observing the decline in their spirits and their seething resentment, the Chief convened a meeting of his four Leading

Ratings. What they had to say confirmed his worst fears. They were all decidedly fed up and aggressive, and it convinced him that he should report this to Foster in person. He needed to advise him that he was pushing the men too far. The Chief's main concern was that his gunners – the men everybody relied on to work furiously in battle – were now physically worn out beyond the point of optimum efficiency. They were, he explained, stressed, resentful and surly – and lacking motivation.

The Chief had disturbed Foster from his pink gin at the Wardroom bar, and the Gunnery Officer was furious. He made scathing comments about the "lily-livered wretches" he had been saddled with, and dismissed the Chief's concern out of hand. The Chief was accused of softness and an attempt to curry favour with the men, but he persisted until he won a concession. It was not until later that they found a maggot in the apple. Foster agreed to discontinue the morning physical training sessions, but insisted they were to close up in their turrets each day, two hours earlier. The Chief's reaction took him as close to being on a charge of insubordination as he had ever been in his entire career. He had to go back to his mess to cool off.

Late that evening, several of the more senior gunnery ratings gathered under the dim emergency lighting in the mess, talking in hushed tones about what, if anything, they could do about Foster. Roberts was one of the shadowy figures huddled around the table. After every possibility was exhausted, he suggested that the solution was for Foster to be put over the side one night. The others reacted with disbelief. At first, his idea was treated as a joke – until they saw how serious he was. 'D'you know the penalty for that?' asked one. 'That would be murder, for Christ's sake!'

Roberts gave a yellowy grin. 'No it wouldn't. I'm not talking about a murder. I'm talking about "an unfortunate accident". People do go over the side, you know. It happened in one of my ships, once. A Petty Officer fell over the guardrail in the Bay of Biscay. The ship didn't heave to ...nobody knew he'd gone overboard.'

'Christ, did you do that?' asked another.

'Naah. Course not. Nothing to do with me. It was a genuine accident, but it proves my point. Nothing happened! The PO was just reported missing. Then there was some sort of enquiry and the

Skipper had to fill in a report but that's all there was to it.' He leered at the faces around the table. The red half-light gave their faces an eerie, devilish look. 'Natural hazard, mate, natural hazard – that's what it's called.'

'Yeah, but if you pushed that bastard over the side,' another rating added, 'that wouldn't exactly be a natural hazard,would it?'

'Would have to be, wouldn't it... if nobody saw it.' Roberts looked at the pensive faces in turn. A silence descended on the group, as each man searched his soul and considered the proposal.   After several minutes, one spoke. 'Who's going to do it, then?' The others looked at him, shocked.

'I will, for one,' said Roberts, without hesitation. There was a pregnant pause.

'So would I,' said another rating who had not spoken before. They all looked at him.

'Count me in,' said another.

'Well, there you go then.' Roberts grinned as they all stared at him. 'That's three of us. We don't need anyone else.'

'Well, as much as I hate the bastard, I don't want anything to do with shoving him over the side,' said one rating, getting up to leave.

'Me neither,' said another.

Roberts shrugged. As the dissenters left the table, he added, 'The only thing you need do is keep your bloody mouths shut – or you'll have me to deal with ...all right?' His burly outline looked menacing in the dim red light. They sheepishly nodded agreement and went away to their hammocks. Roberts looked up at George, who was cocooned in his hammock. He prodded it. 'And that goes for you too, Mister Royal – right?' George peered over the edge of his hammock through half closed eyelids.

'Don't threaten me, Curly, or you'll have more trouble than you can deal with. Anyway, I wasn't listening. I was asleep when you woke me up, and I don't know what you're talking about. Now leave me be.'

Alone at the table, the three men who had committed themselves to action continued with their muttering conversation and drew matchsticks to decide who would carry it out. George decided not to interfere. It seemed to be their way of relieving their frustrations, and he felt sure that in the cold light of day not one of these men would seriously consider taking Foster's life. He fell asleep immediately and had forgotten the incident by morning.

ABROLHOS ROCKS COALING STATION COAST OF BRAZIL
November 26, 1914

The ships reached Abrolhos Rocks, joining several others that had congregated there on Fisher's orders. *Glasgow,* the surviving cruiser of Cradock's squadron, was anchored close to the armoured cruisers, *Kent, Cornwall* and *Carnarvon,* with another admiral, Rear Admiral Stoddart, on board. There was one other light cruiser, *Bristol,* and several coal-filled colliers. Re-coaling began immediately. In spite of *Inflexible's* gun crews being at the end of their tether, Foster made sure that they did not escape coaling duties.

Admiral Sturdee wasted no time in calling his senior officers to a conference on board his flagship *Invincible,* where he briefed his captains and revealed the Admiralty's orders to seek and destroy von Spee's fleet. When coaling was completed, each ship "cleared lower deck" and all ratings and non-commissioned officers, not required for essential duty, assembled on the foredecks of their respective ships, for an address by their captains.

It was a warm day with clear, bright skies. In *Inflexible,* the men – some still as filthy and black-faced as miners from coaling – stood neatly in line on the scrubbed wood-covered deck, enjoying the warmth of the sun on their backs and the spicy, earthy smell of mainland Brazil that drifted over them. Their eyes were screwed up against the bright sun sparkling and scattering on the calm sea. High spirits and anticipation caused a babble of lively chatter in the ranks.

The Executive Officer called the ship's company to attention, and Captain Phillimore walked out and stepped onto a dais in front of them. His eyes scanned the sea of faces.

'At ease, men. Can you hear me at the back?' he shouted, in time-honoured fashion.

In similar spirit, some wag at the back called out: 'Aye aye, Sir, but only when you're talking.' He smiled, as it was the best thing to do in such circumstances. Framed in the outline of the forward turret, with its gun barrels above his head, he waited for silence.

The gold leaf and red painted ship's crests on the tampion badges – the sea-blanks in the muzzles of the gun barrels – seemed to gleam with pride in the bright sunlight. The Captain cleared his throat. Like an actor on stage, he projected his cultured voice to the back row. 'I know you have all been wondering why we are here, off the coast of Brazil. I am pleased that I am now in a position to tell you. To preserve secrecy about our movements, it was not possible to tell you before and I am sorry you have been kept in the dark. 'The reason we are here is not, as some of you will be disappointed to hear, for a good run ashore.'

He paused for the expected noise of feigned, exaggerated disappointment to die down. 'We are here on a very important mission that will take us to the Falkland Islands, down towards the tip of South America, where we are to locate and take on some German warships that have been causing a great deal of trouble in the South Pacific. For those of you who didn't do geography at school, the South Pacific Ocean is just around the corner of Cape Horn, on the other side of South America.'

As the personal ribbing among the men petered out, his expression became solemn. 'I am very sorry to have to tell you that just over three weeks ago, on the first of this month, two of our cruisers on patrol off the coast of Chile were crippled by this German squadron.'

George's heart skipped a beat. 'You will be very shocked to hear that both ships... Monmouth, and Admiral Cradock's own flagship, Good Hope, went down ...sadly, with all hands.'

George felt a horse's kick in the pit of his stomach. His mind numbed and his mouth dried up. Around him, a low murmur rippled through the ranks.

Captain Phillimore went on, in lowered tones. 'I am sure many of you will have had chums in those ships – as I did – and I know you will join me in offering sympathy and sincere condolences to all the families at home who lost loved ones in that incident.'

George's memory was playing pictures of his father. He tried to grasp the significance of never seeing him again.

The Captain continued in high voice. 'When we reach the Falkland Islands, together with the ships you see alongside us now, we will be joining up with several other ships to form a fleet capable of giving the Germans a damn good hiding. There will be no time for a run ashore there. As soon as we arrive, we will be re-provisioning and putting to sea, to get on with the job. When we meet the Germans, we will deal with them in our own way. It will be our chance to avenge the loss of our ships and our gallant shipmates and I count on each one of you to give of your very best. That is all.'

The men were called to attention. The Captain stepped down and walked briskly to his day cabin. After the order to dismiss, the men dispersed in a babble of grave and emotional conversations, and went to their duty stations and mess-decks. George went to the guardrail to be alone. He steadied himself, staring into the clear water of the anchorage, trying to come to terms with the shattering news. The warm sunlight playing on the sparkling water made a bright and cheerful picture, but inside George it felt cold and dark. His father was gone, and he suddenly missed him.

Thoughts raced by, tangled and fragmented, like pictures from a demented kaleidoscope. He thought of his mother, and wondered how she would cope with it – or whether she even knew yet. What of the future now? What new responsibilities would he have to take on? He felt cheated – not ready for a changed future. He remembered how upset he had been when his grandmother died, but he soon got over that. It was her time to die, he told himself at the time. After all, she had enjoyed a long and happy life before she went – but Jack? It was nowhere near his time to die. Fathers are supposed to stay with you until they are old and grey, so that you can ask for advice, relive their experiences with them, and earn their pride. And secret dreams – what about those? In his dreams he had seen himself walking down some road as a naval officer, with his father proudly walking beside him. Now the bloody Huns had robbed him of that. Nothing could make those dreams come true now. *Nothing would ever be the same again.*

There were things he still had to tell Jack. Things he meant to say to him – but somehow never had. Did he ever really know that he was proud of him? Did he know how much he wanted to be like him? He had never told him – not out loud – and now he never would. It filled him with overwhelming regret that he never had. He still needed his father, for God's sake! Jack was the only person who completely understood about life in the Navy – and it was always his praise and approval that kept driving George to stretch himself. Now there was nothing worth struggling for – not any more. Those German bastards! They sent Jack to rot at the bottom of the sea – the cold, inaccessible sea – to be eaten by fish.

Of all the thoughts tumbling through George's mind, one persistently tugged on his sleeve of reason – the German submarine sinking in the North Sea. Was that any different? The Heinzes and Franzes dying there were probably dads – but a small voice somewhere in the darkness of his mind kept saying, *This is different. This is personal. This is Jack Royal we are talking about here – your dad.* As he stared at the horizon through a haze of anger and sadness, his conversation with his mind took a philosophical turn that surprised him. It talked about how enemy ships in the distance – seven, ten, twenty miles away – are sinister, hostile steel monsters but, when they come up close, and sink, an awful reality comes into view. They are full of people, just as real as you are.

You can see them swarming out over its belly as it rolls over, and they hurl themselves into an icy sea – like ants fleeing a kettle full of boiling water – but they are not ants – they are desperate human beings called Jack or George, Franz or Fritz. Then you suddenly get the same feeling you had as a child – after you poured the boiling water into the ants' nest... *I'm sorry, I'm sorry. I didn't really mean it. If only you weren't a nuisance!...* but by then it is too late – the damage is done: nothing personal – nobody's fault, really. *It's the war – nothing personal.* It's just that war makes people do these things to one another.

Then anger surged through, sweeping every trace of empathy out of him. *The Germans started this bloody war* – the voice said decisively – *not you. And now they have killed your father – and they will bloody well have to pay for it. You – George Royal – are going to kill Germans.* What better way was there to deal with this anger, and plug the gaping hole inside? He gripped the rail tightly and tried to swallow the hard lump in his throat. Self-consciously flicking away a tear that had dared to appear on his cheek, he heaved a great sigh,

cleared his cluttered mind, and headed for his mess. As he was about
to step from the upper deck into the ship, a rating from the Supply and
Secretariat branch came up to head him off. 'You George Royal?'
George nodded. 'My boss would like to see you. Lieutenant Parker.
He's in his office on five deck. I'll show you.'

Following reluctantly behind the S&S rating, George wondered
what else was wrong. He knew of Parker, but apart from noticing the
lieutenant looking at him in a strange way, once or twice, he had
never spoken to him or had any connection with him at all. Feeling as
low as he was, he was certainly in no mood to be discussing some
trivial stores matter with a "Pusser" – a Supply Officer. Grim-faced,
he silently followed the S&S rating through several doorways, down
through four decks, and on towards the ship's stern. They finally
arrived at a gloss-varnished wooden door with "SUPPLY OFFICER"
painted on it in gold leaf. The rating tapped on the door and opened it.
'Leading Seaman Royal, sir,' he said, before walking away. Parker
stood up.

George took off his cap and eased himself into the tiny
compartment. 'You wanted me, sir?' he said, testily.

The officer smiled and closed the door. 'Yes, Royal. Sit down,
please.' They both sat. 'Are you all right?' George looked at him,
quizzically. 'About your father, I mean?' George nodded. 'I wanted to
say how very sorry I am about your father. It must be a hell of a shock
for you.'

George looked puzzled. 'But how did you know...?'

Parker gently interrupted. 'I knew your father very well, and I am
very sad about what happened. I was told about *Good Hope* going
down just before we left Devonport, but I couldn't say anything to
you then ...we had strict orders not to. I've spoken to the Captain
about compassionate leave for you, but you'll probably understand
that he can't let you go just yet, under the circumstances.'

'That's OK, sir. I wouldn't expect him to.' George's eyes were
on the cap he was fiddling with in his lap. He wondered why Foster,
his own section officer, was not concerned with his welfare.

'Your father and I were good friends,' Parker went on,
awkwardly. 'We served together in several ships. We had some good
times together. Both promoted at the same time ...from the lower

deck, you see. Strangely enough, I've got a son in the service, too. His name is John. He's in Portsmouth Barracks right now. Jack and I used to compare notes, sometimes. When the war started we made a sort of agreement to keep an eye on each other's son, whenever we could. You know …if we happened to be serving in the same ships with either of you. Without letting you know, of course. We didn't want to embarrass either of you, or cause trouble with your messmates. We had an understanding that we would – well, you know, just keep an eye out for you.'

'That's kind, sir,' said George, not knowing what else to say.

Parker looked at him. 'Are you sure you're all right? I know it must have been a hell of a shock to find out like that. I wanted to tell you myself, privately, but the Captain insisted otherwise.' Parker was unable to read George's expression. He looked back at his desk and moved a file on it. 'Look, I'm sorry if I've embarrassed you, but if ever you want to talk to someone, or you've got something you can't deal with on your own, just come and talk to me, OK? I can't replace your dad, but I just want you to know that you are not entirely alone, that's all. Do you want to stay here for a while, on your own?'

'No…no, I'm OK, sir,' George said, quickly. 'I'm just bloody angry.' He looked down at his hands and noticed his knuckles were showing white on his tightly clenched fists. 'I want to sink every German ship afloat, right now.'

'I know, I know,' said Parker, sympathetically. 'That's very understandable. I feel just the same. You'll soon have a chance to do that – that I can guarantee.'

George had the feeling he may have seemed ungrateful, when he was really feeling quite the opposite. This meeting had come as a complete surprise, but he was pleased Parker had taken the trouble. It was good to have a link with his father, however tenuous, through someone else who had known him. 'Thank you, sir, I appreciate you making contact.' He stood up, ready to leave.

Parker looked at him. 'You know, Jack was very proud of you, believe me. All he ever wanted was for you to do well – as I am sure you will.' Life felt just a little less of a burden to George, and Parker was pleased to see it in his face. 'Take care of yourself,' he said, 'up there in your turret.'

George swallowed hard and thanked Parker for his time. He hesitated as he turned to leave. The matter of Foster's reckless management of the gun crews was on his mind.

'There was one thing... '

Parker waited for George to collect his thoughts, but George thought better of it. It was not an appropriate thing to bring up.

He smiled mechanically. 'Sorry... it's nothing, sir.'

Chapter Eight

ABROLHOS ROCKS OFF THE COAST OF BRAZIL
November 28, 1914

Admiral Sturdee's flagship *Invincible* and the other ships of his fleet slipped their moorings at dawn and steamed south in line ahead, heading for the Falkland Islands. The weather en route was fair and the fleet made good progress through the South Atlantic. In the Falklands, the battleship *Canopus* was being prepared for her role as the last line of defence for the Islands. As the old ship was so slow, Jacky Fisher had signalled his suggestion that she would serve better use as a stable gun battery if she was deliberately grounded for that purpose on the mud bottom at the mouth of Port Stanley. Her crew prepared themselves to stand alone against the inevitable German attack.

At the same time, von Spee was heading for the Falkland Islands, having successfully rounded Cape Horn on November 25th. He was taking the opportunity of a weakened Royal Naval presence in the area to break through the cordon the Allies had drawn around him, and head for home. In one final, triumphant thumb-nosing at the British, however, he was determined to stop along the way to destroy the British hilltop wireless station in the Falklands, fire the coal stocks there, and carry off the resident British Governor as a reprisal for an earlier incident. It was a dangerous and over-ambitious idea that worried his senior officers.

So alarmed were his captains that they tried to dissuade him from his ill-conceived plan but he remained resolutely determined to humiliate the British Empire with his final flourish. The Islanders imagined what was in store for them and – with only *Canopus* to defend them – lived in constant fear of attack. To give early warning of the Germans, a detachment of men from the old battleship was sent ashore to set up a lookout and communication station at the top of

Sapper Hill – the highest point in the islands. A tense atmosphere of apprehension settled over the islands as everyone watched and waited for the inevitable attack but, as the Germans rounded Cape Horn and emerged into the South Atlantic, they encountered appalling weather. Plunging through mountainous waves, they were forced to reduce speed to as little as 5 knots on occasions, and their approach to the Falklands was agonisingly slow in spite of the urgency of their mission.

From the opposite direction, Sturdee's ships were making good progress as they steamed towards the Falkland Islands. During the first three days of the southern leg of *Inflexible's* journey, Foster kept up his relentless pressure on the gun crews. Try as they might, the conspirators were unable to engineer an "unfortunate accident" for him, and a sixth sense seemed to be keeping him away from the guardrail. However, having "something on the go" kept the men's spirits up.

As the Chief was also hostile towards him now, Foster was isolated – ring-fenced by antagonistic deference, but he seemed comfortable with the situation. Then, without warning, his training programme came to an abrupt end four days from Abrolhos Rocks. The men were puzzled, because no explanation was given, but they assumed that humanity must have got the better of him, and that he was allowing them a break before meeting the enemy. Ill feeling slowly subsided, and the men got back to normal routines, thankful that the bitter episode was over – but not so the conspirators. They were still convinced that Foster's incompetence would eventually get one of them killed – probably in the thick of the next battle – and not one of them was prepared to back away from the task they had set themselves. Instead, they watched and waited for an opportunity.

Less than one day away from the Falkland Islands and in the fading light of evening on December 6, Foster ordered George and Chief Huggett to meet him on the ship's foredeck, at the forward turret. Dusk was closing in through the failing daylight when they arrived at the spot. Foster was already there, his face white with rage. Waving a hand lamp, he unclipped the turret door and pointed to the inside of it where someone had written in red paint: ***"FOSTER THE F*****G SHIT"*** under a clever caricature of himself as a large turd with long thin legs and a pointed nose. George and Chief Huggett stifled their laughter and denied all knowledge of it. Foster was screeching. 'Even if you had nothing to do with it,' he raged at George, 'you may just as well have done it yourself because I am holding you responsible. What goes on in this turret is entirely your responsibility. This disgusting, depraved insult,' he said, pointing to the work of art, 'is going to get you both into serious trouble. I intend to see someone clapped in irons for it. Do I make myself clear? You will both be charged with the offence, unless you provide me with the name of the culprit *NOW*.'

Foster's stare was cold and sinister. There was no mistaking the sadistic enjoyment he was getting from the power he had over them in this situation. He rounded on the Chief. 'You, Huggett, are not fit to carry the rank of Chief Petty Officer. You clearly have no control over these men. Some time as a rating will do you good.' George opened his mouth to speak. 'Keep silence!' Foster snapped. He glared at them, daring them to speak. 'Now. You will clean off that disgusting picture immediately, and leave no trace of it. When you have finished, you will both report to the Master at Arms. I am going to have those badges off your uniforms tonight. There is no place in the Navy for dross like you.' He put his face close to George's. 'Incompetence must run in your family, Royal.'

Hot loathing anger flashed like a bolt of lightning through George's eyes, and the knuckles of his fists turned white as he wrestled with an uncontrollable urge to smash Foster's face. For a split second, George's career in the Navy was poised on the very brink of disaster. He was ready to trade it all for one decisive lunge at his tormentor. Foster sensed it, and knew then that he had the better of him. It was a knife-edge in George's life, but he succeeded in controlling himself, and came down the right side of it. The Chief was tight-lipped, his face white with anger. It was an extraordinary situation that now seemed out of control.

Foster was completely over-reacting to a relatively minor situation – for which he could no more have them punished or reduced in rank than he could fly, but his authority meant that they had to go along with his bizarre charade. Hands clasped behind his back, he stared menacingly – daring George to strike him – but sheer willpower stopped him from giving Foster the perfect opportunity for having him locked away for striking an officer. George stood his ground and kept his eyes fixed dead ahead – regardless of where Foster placed himself. The moment of excruciating tension passed. 'You are about to discover just how much of a "shit" – as you put it – I can be.' He turned to the Chief. 'You – go to the Bo'sun's Store and get some turpentine.'

The Chief went away with his face fixed in a stony expression. Foster stood in front of George and stared challengingly. 'You will clean that off tonight, however long it takes. Then you are going down to see the Master at Arms.' The Chief, smarting badly from Foster's abuse in front of a rating, had gone away bitter and furious. He failed to return before Foster's impatience ran out. Striding impatiently along the deck towards the stern of the ship, Foster went to find him, leaving George alone on the foredeck standing rigidly to attention. Trying to calm down, George became alarmed by his own thoughts. He found himself wondering if Curly and his companions were right, and whether he should save them their trouble by shoving Foster over the side himself.

As Foster strode past the midships where the deck was narrow, a blur of movement caught the corner of George's eye. The dark shape of a rating lunged out of a doorway. Foster was thrown against the guardrail in one swift movement. There was a brief silent struggle as the officer struggled to keep his footing, but he was tipped over the rail before he knew what was happening.
Momentarily, he clung to the rail with one hand, dangling over the sea with blind terror on his face. Then he lost his grip. In a whirl of arms and legs, he dropped into the foam passing by at over 20 knots.

In the poor light, George's sight of the scuffle was fleeting and startling. It was over in an instant, and the attacker vanished as quickly as he had appeared. George could not be sure, but from what he saw, it looked like Curly Roberts! Adrenalin surged and jolted his instinct to save life, but he remained rooted to the spot. Everything honourable in his nature screamed at him to raise the alarm, yet a stronger, darker force held him back. Still furious with Foster, his anger was powerful enough to overcome his sense of duty, and it suppressed his natural instinct to raise the alarm. This time, his inner voice told him, he was going to stay right where he was – standing dutifully to attention, staring blankly ahead – just as that bastard had ordered him to do. No one else had seen him go over the side – and he was not going to see it either. He would blank it from his thoughts – his own dark secret that he would keep forever to himself. He could do that! Why should he care about the most objectionable man he had ever met?   Seconds ticked by. His pulse raced. He stiffened his back, clenched his fists, and buried his conscience. Deliberately and consciously inactive, he simply stared blindly ahead, cynically crossing the Rubicon by allowing time to pass until rescue was impossible.

In the sea, Foster surfaced in the surging foam of the ship's wake. As he struggled to stay afloat, its undertow drew him down towards the churning propellers. He swam frantically to get away from them – and out of the path of the following ship, but its sinister black shape loomed over him in the rapidly darkening sky. His struggle for life was desperate. He went under, time and time again, with cold waves breaking over his head. As the ship passed close by him, marine phosphorescence gave its bow wave a ghostly green hue. Then the next ship came by, and the next – but no one heard his cries.

By chance, an off-duty officer was standing on *Glasgow's* quarterdeck staring pensively at the sea. He was suddenly galvanised into action by what he thought was a head bobbing along in the wake. Peering hard into the darkness, he instinctively moved to raise the "MAN OVERBOARD" alarm but as he straightened up from the rail, confidence suddenly deserted him and he had second thoughts about what he had seen. Was it real, or had he imagined it? Could he justify delaying the ship's urgent mission over something he *might* have seen in the darkness? He decided that it was something he was not prepared to do. He hesitated, shrugged to himself and put the matter out of his mind.

In the icy water, Foster struggled through the waves as he watched the last ship's stern light fading into the darkness. Exhausted now, and utterly desolated, he convulsed and shivered uncontrollably as his body gave up its heat to the cold sea and his brain slowly numbed. His vacantly staring hawk-like eyes sank into his ashen, cadaverous features and his jaw chattered violently behind blue lips.

Within fifteen everlasting minutes, his energy was spent. His will to live faded away and he slipped into unconsciousness. Seconds later, his heart stopped beating and his mouth opened as if to deliberately fill his lungs with water. Alone and of no concern to anyone, his lifeless body – still clad in the gold-braided uniform of an officer – drifted silently down into the dark depths.

On board *Inflexible,* Chief Huggett returned to the foredeck and found George still standing stiffly to attention. He waited in vain for Foster to return. Then, not knowing where he had gone, he helped George clean the paint off the turret door and they both returned to their messes for the night. George looked grey-faced and lantern-jawed – as the Chief expected him to be after his confrontation with Foster. George was awake for most of the night, struggling with his conscience. However much he self-justified having ignored Foster's predicament, he still felt as much remorse as if he had pushed him overboard himself.

Curly and his co-conspirators slept peacefully and said nothing in the morning. The Chief came to the mess to announce that Foster was missing, and was embarrassed by the cheer that went up. George felt terrible. He knew he had not heard the last of Foster, but he kept the impending confrontation with the German Navy uppermost in his mind. There was no time for anything else now.

THE FALKLAND ISLANDS
December 7, 1914

When Admiral Sturdee arrived with his fleet off Port William early on the morning of December 7, he was greatly relieved to learn that the Germans had not beaten him to the islands but his relief was nothing compared to the Islanders' joy at the sight of the formidable British fleet filling their harbours. Preparations for the forthcoming battle began as soon as the ships had anchored, and they began to re-coal immediately. All hands turned to, with unprecedented enthusiasm, and worked through the night but the islands' coaling facilities were limited and each ship had to wait in turn to come alongside them. By dawn the following morning, only half of Sturdee's ships had been re-coaled.

Curly Roberts and his friends seemed to be keeping a low profile. It was impossible for George to keep the loathing out of his eyes whenever he saw Curly. Someone said that Foster might have been picked up and was probably already making his report to the Captain. They all knew that retribution would follow, when the more important business of the day had been completed. Strangely, no one looked the least guilty and no buzz went around the mess as to who might have been responsible. George was deeply troubled and had difficulty hiding it.

THE FALKLAND ISLANDS
December 8, 1914 7:50 am

By the following morning, the wind had dropped away and the sea was as calm as a millpond. Morning came bearing gifts of a light, warm breeze and a bright and sunny clear blue sky. There was no sign of the heavy weather the Germans had encountered the day before. In the German fleet, Admiral von Spee was completely unaware that Sturdee's fleet was tucked out of sight in the harbours nestling between the Falkland hills. He sent two of his cruisers, *Gneisenau* and *Nürnberg,* to shell and destroy the wireless station at the top of Sapper Hill.

As the German warships came from the south, they announced their approach with their funnel smoke spiralling high into the clear sky. *Canopus's* shore-based lookout station immediately reported the sighting to Admiral Sturdee, and a suitable reception was prepared. From her stable position on the mud of Port Stanley, hidden from German view, *Canopus* opened fire over the hills with her heavy twelve-inch guns, at a range of 6 miles. Completely taken by surprise by the shells suddenly falling around them, the German captains made off quickly, without firing a shot themselves. Most of *Canopus's* "blind" shots missed their target, but one shell at least found its mark, exploding on the deck of one of the hastily departing ships. To her credit, the elderly battleship had saved the precious wireless station, even if she could do little else.

Carefully keeping out of range, *Gneisenau* manoeuvred around the islands until her captain had a clear binocular view of Port

William. What he saw filled him with horror. Columns of smoke were now rising from the harbour, indicating the presence of several British warships with steam already up, about to come out to meet him. With great haste, *Gneisenau* ran to rejoin the German fleet, signalling the news to Admiral von Spee, who was in *Scharnhorst*, some way off to the south. When *Gneisenau* caught up, the German fleet turned en masse and steamed away to the south east, at its best speed speed. The Germans realised immediately that – unlike their previous battle with Admiral Cradock – this time they were well matched.

10:00 am

Inflexible and *Invincible* burst out of Port William at flank speed with dense black smoke pouring from their funnels. Following close behind was the rest of Sturdee's fleet. Once underway, he adjusted the speed of his ships to bring them into an orderly line for the pursuit. He detached *Bristol* to deal with some strange freighters or colliers she had spotted off Port Pleasant, and signalled *Inflexible* to steam abreast of his flagship, *Invincible,* at 20 knots. He kept *Kent, Cornwall* and *Carnarvon* in line astern of them. Some three miles ahead of *Invincible's* port bow, *Glasgow* was positioned on the left of the flagship.

In *Inflexible*, George Royal's jaw was set determinedly. He coolly put all thoughts of Foster out of his mind and concentrated on his readiness for battle. Under the watchful eye of the gunnery Chief, he was making sure that the forward turret and its crew would be ready the instant ACTION STATIONS was sounded. Although excitement was rising all around him, he was calm and focused, determined to do whatever he had to do to sink German ships.

At *11:30 am* the men were piped to lunch, as normal, and by *11:45 am* they were eating and chatting in the mess, punctuating the clatter of crockery and cutlery with their loud laughter and nervous jokes about the German Navy. No one noticed George's quietness. He was keeping his troubles to himself, and thinking only of avenging his father. With the scent of battle in their nostrils, the men were excited but incredulous that they were in a chase so soon after arriving in the Falklands.

12:30 pm

At the sight of the German ships turning and scattering, Sturdee called for full speed in order to catch them, and had the bugle call *ACTION STATIONS* sounded throughout his ships.

With the rest of his crew, George closed up in the forward turret and got ready. Gunners put on their anti-flash gear and plugged their ears. The first shells and cordite charges rattled up the shell hoists and into the guns; then the breeches slammed closed, ready for firing. With the range and elevation information coming up from the Combat Control Centre, George double-checked that the guns were on target. More than ever before, he felt like a well-oiled machine with its spring wound tight, and every ounce of his angry energy was directed at the unseen enemy in the distance.

By *12:50 pm*, the British battlecruisers were running at 25 knots, closing rapidly on the Germans and leaving the rest of the fleet trailing behind. Through the observation hood of the turret, George had a magnificent view of *Invincible* steaming at full speed beside her sister-ship – and she looked truly majestic, hissing through the calm sea at breathtaking speed, pushing aside thousands of tons of sea water as she passed. The foam curling up from the knife-edge of her bows fell in a graceful curve towards her waist and exposed the full depth of her black-painted waterline. As the sea left her stern, the massive forces at work in her propellers threw a surging, rumbling wake of bubbling white froth behind her. He knew that *Inflexible* would look the same, if only he had the same view of her.

Dense black coal smoke was pouring into the clear sky from the warships' funnels, and White Ensigns and signal flags fluttered out behind their mastheads. With their immaculate grey hulls gleaming in the bright sunlight, they conjured up a picture of the Knights of Camelot riding onto the battlefield – avenging angels. George knew he would never be more proud of being part of the Royal Navy than at that moment – whatever happened from then on. All he wanted to do was get on with it, and settle the score for his father.

Having been given the "General Chase" order earlier by Sturdee, each ship was now free to pursue and fire at will. As the trailing German ship *Leipzig* came within *Inflexible's* range, at 10 miles, the order to open fire came up from the Combat Control Centre, and the guns erupted with a thundering roar. The gun crews worked together like individual parts of a whirring clockwork motor, in spite of the smoke choking them. The noise inside the turret was shattering but the men laboured with a well-rehearsed, instinctive fluency.

For a gunner to survive in a working turret, he had to learn quickly the knack of withdrawing into an imaginary personal "shell" of detached self-preservation. He had to condition his mind to believe that he was not really there operating the guns, but that he was in a much quieter, safer place somewhere deep inside himself, operating his body by remote control. It was the way heroes described the way they carried out acts of bravery: with no apparent regard for themselves or the impossible conditions at the time. In the midst of mayhem, it is the only way to function and stay sane.

Breeches were snatched open as soon as shells left the barrels. Compressed air and cooling water was sprayed in, and new shells and cordite rammed home. When the breeches were closed and locked, the guns were ready to fire again and George shouted '*READY*' at the very top of his voice. Then came the next deafening roar and surge of pressure in the turret. The routine was repeated over and over again, as rapidly as the men could manage.

At least once the ship rocked as a German shell exploded and rattled her bones but the gunners never faltered in their work. The first few of *Inflexible*'s shells fell behind and ahead of *Leipzig*, the trailing enemy ship – she had worn-out boilers and was unable to keep up. Seeing that she would be hit at any moment, von Spee made a decision that was entirely in keeping with his honourable character. He ordered his three light cruisers, *Dresden, Leipzig*, and *Nürnberg* to scatter to safety in the south, leaving his own ship, *Scharnhorst,* and his other battlecruiser, *Gneisenau,* to face the entire British fleet alone.

Sturdee anticipated his move and sent *Glasgow, Kent* and *Cornwall* chasing after the fleeing German cruisers. *Invincible* squared up to *Gneisenau,* and *Inflexible* took on *Scharnhorst.* As the warships locked in battle and exchanged fire, funnel and gun smoke began to drift down towards the British ships, obscuring the gun director's view. By the time the smoke cleared, von Spee's battlecruisers had turned sharply and were steaming rapidly away to join his other ships on the horizon but Sturdee was determined not to lose them. The British battlecruisers wound up to maximum speed again and closed the gap.

Scharnhorst and *Gneisenau* turned to face the British ships once more while the smaller German ships made off in the hope of reaching the safety of neutral waters by nightfall.

2:55 pm

When the distance between the fleets was down to 7 miles, both sides opened fire. German shells began to reach Sturdee's ships, but their superior armour protection prevented serious damage. The same was not true of the Germans. The larger calibre British shells reached the German ships comfortably, and plunged right through their armour to explode inside with devastating effect. Sturdee made best use of the superior range of his own guns, keeping the Germans within his own range, but too far away for their guns to be effective.

As the ships jostled for position, George found himself firing first at *Scharnhorst* then at *Gneisenau*. *Invincible's* guns were also firing at both German battlecruisers. At 7 miles, it was difficult for anyone to see clearly whose shells were hitting what, but at *3:20 pm* it was clear that both German ships had been severely damaged. *Gneisenau* was taking in water and listing badly. Although gallantly fighting on, *Scharnhorst* was on fire in several places and her third funnel had been blown away.

Explosions tore through her as her shells and cordite exploded in the fierce heat of the fires raging inside her. By *4:17 pm*, she was a total wreck. Masses of dense smoke billowed around her and George could see huge orange and red fireballs glowing deep inside her hull. Her forward guns were still firing and the German flag was still flying proudly at her masthead when she finally capsized.

With nothing but gravity to hold her turrets in place, these massive structures of armoured steel, with their cast barrels and heavy machinery weighing over five hundred tons apiece, tore loose from the upturned ship. Still firmly attached to their enormous drum-like barbettes – more than four decks deep – and with more than twenty gunners and handlers trapped inside each one, they slid out of their mountings with a grinding rumble and hurtled towards the seabed with the speed of an express train.

After a moment's hesitation at the surface, *Scharnhorst* began her plunge to the bottom. Steam and air escaping from deep inside her threw up a surging mass of foam. For the gallant Admiral von Spee and his crew of almost eight hundred men, it was all over. Admiral Cradock and his men had been avenged, but few British officers and ratings at the scene took joy in it – except to give thanks that they had survived the encounter.

On the order to cease firing, the men of *Inflexible* stood in sober silence as *Scharnhorst* went down. Every man had a stark picture in his mind of what was happening to the German sailors trapped inside her. In the engine room and magazines, and everywhere below decks where sailors worked, they would be caught in pitch-black upturned compartments with the sea gushing in, fighting for dear life as she took them on their last voyage to the dark, hostile, icy world below.

The Germans dying in front of the British sailors had fought gallantly, and earned their respect but now they were gone. For once in his life, George was elated to see a ship sinking. His anger saw to that. It was a strange irony for him, and it would forever leave questions lurking in the corner of his mind. Fate, it seemed, had intervened in his life to put his father's killers under his own guns.

Cynical hatred – so often the net result of tragedy – released its grip on him. He could feel it leaving him. Although nothing would stop him missing his father, or being sad about his death, the sinking of *Scharnhorst* came as a necessary catharsis and relieved him of part of his emotional baggage. He knew he would now come to terms with Jack's death.

After waiting for some time, the British ships could wait for survivors no longer. Instead, they had to turn their attention to *Gneisenau*. She was still fighting on and firing her guns at them. The weather had changed dramatically since the day began, and the sea temperature was close to freezing. Survivors would not last long in it, and a swell was building up. *Gneisenau* fought on bravely until she also turned over and sank. It was *5:30 pm*. Of her crew of eight hundred and fifty men, less than two hundred survived and many of these died from injuries and exposure, even after being pulled from the sea. Some survivors were badly injured by albatrosses as they floated helplessly in the sea, waiting to be rescued. When all was done at the scene that could be done, the two British cruisers returned to Port William.

The three German cruisers for which von Spee had sacrificed himself: *Dresden, Nürnberg* and *Leipzig,* were now speeding south – hotly pursued by *Glasgow, Kent* and *Cornwall* – hoping to outrun the British ships until nightfall covered their escape. Of the pursuers, *Kent* was one of the ships at the back of the queue for re-coaling in the Falklands. She had not reached the front of it in time to take on fresh coal. Now she was struggling to keep up the pursuit. But so determined was her crew to catch the enemy, that the men demonstrated their absolute commitment by passing anything and everything combustible they could find on board to the stokers who were coaxing the last ounce of steam from the ship's boilers.

When all her coal was gone, all wooden fittings, furniture, and even lifeboats were ripped out, broken up and fed to the fires of her boilers. Their prodigious effort was rewarded; tenuously maintaining steam pressure, the ship kept going. Like the proverbial swan, the serenity of *Kent's* fast passage belied the frantic activity going on below the water line. By squeezing out every last knot, the British ships brought the fleeing ships in range of their guns. By nightfall, after valiantly fighting back until they could fight no more, *Leipzig* and *Nürnberg* had been reduced to fiercely burning, floating heaps of scrap iron. They both turned over and sank. Only *Dresden* – due to her superior speed – escaped into the night. The crews of the four German ships totalled over two thousand men. Of these, just two hundred were picked up as survivors. The total British losses for the entire battle were seven killed and four wounded.

When the news reached the Admiralty, Jacky Fisher's only comment about the performance of his old adversary – Sturdee – was in keeping with the ungracious attitude he displayed at times. He called the escape of *Dresden* – the only ship to get away out of five – "criminal ineptitude". However, he was pleased that justification for his long campaign to modernise the Royal Navy and its ships had finally been proved. The Falkland Islands battle was the showcase battle he intended it to be – a demonstration of the superiority of the Royal Navy, for the entire world to see. The swift and total defeat of von Spee's ships by Dreadnought-class battlecruisers was the antithesis of Cradock's defeat at Coronel. As Fisher had advocated all along, victory at sea was in the balance of speed, armour and guns. What more proof was needed?

On their return to the Falkland Islands, the British crews were exhausted but elated at the outcome of the battle. During the next two days, while the messy business of re-coaling and re-provisioning was being completed, the gunners bellowed conversations at full volume, as the continuous ringing in their ears lingered on. All lay awake in their hammocks at night, replaying vivid mental pictures of the battle. George's images included the spectre of Foster.

The men were soon back into a routine and thinking about home. George was anxious to get back to find out if his mother was coping. He felt calmer now: more at peace with himself although he was still coming to terms with some of the things that had happened lately, and one of these was seeing German sailors at close quarters. When the South Atlantic battle was over and the gun crews had stood down, he and Chalky White came face to face with some of the survivors from *Leipzig* and *Nürnberg*. They were instantly struck by how much like themselves they really were. Neither of them had seen Germans at close quarters before, and it was a surprise to see that not one of the German sailors would have been out of place around *Inflexible's* mess tables.

The prisoners looked frightened and confused, but the British sailors treated them well and made their lives as bearable as possible. Unlike the civilians at home, castigating all things German, the sailors of both navies still had much in common – the seas and ships – and thought about these rather than their differences. They had a mutual respect that people mourning loved ones at home would never understand.

Coming close to the Germans and suddenly seeing the human face behind the iron mask affected George more than he thought possible. He had never before thought of himself as a killer, but now it seemed that he was. Previously, he saw Germans only as grey monsters on the horizon. The next time he opened fire on them, he was afraid that it would somehow feel different. He would now visualise young men, just like himself, on the receiving end of his personal contribution to the war.

After living through the two most traumatic weeks of his life, home was tugging at him now. He went to see Lieutenant Parker, to ask when they would be leaving for home, and found out that *Inflexible* and *Invincible* were leaving for Plymouth within days. Once back home, both ships would be staying in Devonport for essential repairs then rejoining the Grand Fleet at Rosyth, but a few days leave was on the cards for the crews before that.

Then Foster was officially posted as "missing, presumed drowned" and a preliminary board of inquiry was held. As no witness to the incident came forward, little could be done about it. A number of ratings were called to report anything they had seen, but nothing came from this either. It came out that on the way to the Falklands, the Chief, alarmed by Foster's behaviour, took his concerns directly to a senior officer. It was an extraordinary step for a Chief, but his seniority and excellent reputation got him a serious hearing. As soon as the details were known, Foster was immediately ordered to halt his over-zealous training programme. On the investigating officer's recommendation, the Captain immediately obtained the Admiral's approval and backing to draft Foster off the ship at the earliest opportunity.

George reflected on the irony of the situation. If only Foster's attacker had known it, Foster was already on his way out of *Inflexible* but, because the Chief had taken his complaint to the Captain before the event, the officer's disappearance was highly suspicious, making a full inquiry mandatory. Curly Roberts's smug grin, never before seen in the mess, said everything about his callous satisfaction and caused Chief Huggett to say that just because an officer was unpopular, it was not justification for celebrating his death. It made George feel even worse.

The ten thousand-mile journey back to England, with a coaling stopover at Abrolhos Rocks, was expected to take about twenty-five days. It was estimated that the ships would not reach Plymouth until

January 4, which meant that the men would be spending Christmas and New Year at sea. The remedy for this was a traditional "Sod's Opera" – a bawdy entertainment show that the sailors periodically and voluntarily put on for themselves. As the point of such a show was to allow the men to let their hair down, it necessarily involved large helpings of raw navy humour – a pantomime with principals but few principles.

Preparations and scriptwriting for *Inflexible's* Sod's Opera began as soon as the ship left the Falklands. In time-honoured fashion, volunteers prepared their costumes from any materials at hand. It was not long before three "Ugly Sisters", a "Fairy Queen", and one or two other pantomime characters were in rehearsal. The sight of beefy, hairy-legged sailors – some with full beards – dressed up in costumes and getting into character was guaranteed to bring the house down and lift the most deflated of spirits. The script inevitably included foul naval language and the odd sketch that poked good-natured fun at the Captain and other ship's officers.

To George's disgust, Curly Roberts put himself forward for the part of Fairy Queen, without hesitating, but more serious matters were also in hand. The ship's Executive Officer, Commander Brown, had the task of investigating Foster's death, and he was thorough in the way he handled it. Everyone remotely connected with Foster was questioned and the circumstances of the altercation between him, the Chief and George immediately prior to his disappearance were carefully trawled for clues. Inevitably, the two of them became prime suspects.

George's stomach constantly churned with worry. As the details of Foster's last night came to light, his claim that he had seen nothing was difficult to justify. He appeared, after all, to be the last person to see Foster alive. The Chief was rightly eliminated from the investigation when the Bo'sun confirmed that he had been at his store drawing turpentine at the time of Foster's disappearance. That left George as the only real suspect and the thought depressed and scared him. Now he was trapped.

It was far too late to say what he had really seen. That would simply make him look guilty – as if he was just making up a story to get away with it. Not only that, but if he did speak up now, it would throw suspicion onto Curly Roberts. Although he *thought* he saw Curly, he was not at all certain about it. Then again, if he did admit to seeing Foster go over the side – but lied and said that no one else was involved – he would be in just as much trouble for not raising the alarm himself. He was thankful that Lieutenant Parker stepped forward as his defending officer, but he could not even tell him everything he knew. He desperately wanted to confess the truth – perhaps to Parker – but he knew that if he did, he would place the officer in an impossible position. He was doomed – and he knew it.

The situation was dire, and it hung around his neck like a ton weight. Whenever he saw Curly, he felt physically sick. Curly could see how low he was feeling, and made an effort to be appeasing and helpful but it just led to furious rows. Outright, George accused him of killing Foster, but he denied it. George would have none of it, and threatened violence. His friend Chalky White was concerned about him and gave as much support as he could.

The investigation rumbled on for days and Parker became concerned about the possible outcome for George. He spoke up for him, and privately told Commander Brown that he would stake his life on George not having committed a crime. He called the Chief who said the same but the evidence, although circumstantial, pointed at George. On the final day of the inquiry, he was marched into the Commander's office by the Master at Arms. Brown was standing behind his polished wooden desk with Parker beside it. Their expressions were stern and cold.

'Off caps.' George responded to the MAA's barked order with a snap. He stood rigidly to attention, staring at the Commander's cap. The atmosphere in the small compartment was tense and crisply formal. Brown looked him straight in the eye.

'I am extremely perplexed by this case,' he said, solemnly. 'You stand accused of the murder of a respected officer of this ship, and your situation is very grave. You were the very last person to see Lieutenant Commander Foster alive in *Inflexible*, and the circumstances of the night of December 6 have been described to me. It is very clear, Royal, that on the night in question, you of all ratings in this ship had the strongest motive and the clearest opportunity to dispose of him.' George, Parker and the MAA remained motionless.

Only Brown moved at all. He looked down at his papers then into George's eyes. 'However, I am aware of your exemplary service record, and I have received excellent character references from your defending officer and Gunnery Chief Petty Officer Huggett, but all of that would stand for nothing if positive evidence existed. However, there is none.'

Parker looked at George with a trace of encouragement in his eyes but George did not see it. He was feeling light-headed and nauseous as he stared blankly at the Commander, who continued, 'I cannot accept the premise that Lieutenant Commander Foster simply fell over the side. He was far too experienced an officer to do that. I am therefore convinced that this incident was not an accident, but a crime – an extremely serious one.' George felt his life falling to pieces. 'In view of the seriousness of the charge, I cannot dismiss it without proper investigation. In view of the lack of evidence, however, neither can I sentence you. The case is therefore suspended, pending further inquiries by the civilian authorities at our next home port of call. That will be all.'

George was in shock. Nothing in his life had been as serious as this. He was sinking deeper and deeper into a hopeless mess from which he would never emerge.

The MAA braced himself and barked orders again. 'On caps. Salute. Right turn, quick march!' George was suddenly in the gangway again, with bewilderment in his eyes. He wandered away not knowing what to do, and went up on deck for some fresh air and quiet contemplation.

Alone with Parker, Brown beckoned him to a chair, took off his cap and sat behind his desk. 'I think we can agree that young Royal probably had nothing to do with Foster's disappearance, but due process of law must be seen to have taken place – as far as that is possible at sea. The case must be handled by the police at Devonport, and I shall present the details when we arrive.'

Parker was concerned. 'What about his compassionate leave, sir? He has just lost his father.'

'Out of the question, I'm afraid. The police will probably require us to keep him in custody when the ship docks – at least until they are satisfied, one way or the other. That won't be necessary now, of course. He won't jump ship in the middle of the Atlantic, but keep your ear to the ground, Parker. Let me know if anything new turns up. I knew Jack Royal myself.' He shook his head slowly. 'There's something odd about this case that doesn't add up.'

Parker shook his head too. 'It troubles me no end. The boy had such a bright future. We can only hope that someone will come forward and prove his innocence. Any number of ratings could have attacked the Gunnery Officer. The men had such resentment for him – and he for them. It beggars belief.'

Brown looked up, puzzled. 'You do know about Foster – don't you?'

'No, sir. What is there to know?'

Brown leaned forward, elbows on his desk. 'Well, as strange as it may seem, he was once a perfectly affable chap until – incredibly – his wife humiliated him last year by running off with a bloody matelot!' Parker was stunned. 'A sailor! Can you believe it? Strange woman – from a wealthy family, too. What she was after we can only imagine. He was devastated, of course …as could be expected in those circumstances. He was a bit of an aristocrat, you know, and the disgrace must have been terrible for him. Tipped him over the edge, no doubt. He could have resigned his commission, of course, but he chose not to. Seems he wanted to stay with us.'

'To get back at ratings, I shouldn't wonder!'

'The Captain knew about him, of course, and kept an eye on the situation. But he never expected this kind of outcome.' Parker's head was shaking with disbelief. As he stood up to go, Brown added: 'Oh, and keep an eye on that young man – just in case he does something silly.'

'Very good, sir.' Parker stepped into the gangway, amazed by what he had been told.

On the evening of December 24, following re-coaling at Abrolhos Rocks, all ratings, senior ratings and officers who were not required for duty congregated noisily for the sod's opera. Very quickly, the war was forgotten and the men were rolling in laughter at the hairy fairy and the motley cast performing loudly to the strains of the Royal Marine band. In time-honoured fashion, there was dubious humour and many crude jokes and sketches about virtually every aspect of ship's life.

In one sketch, "Jolly Jack Tar" paid a visit to the ship's Medical Officer after being let loose in a notorious Far Eastern port. 'What's wrong, boy?' enquired the MO (Curly Roberts as a lieutenant with an outrageously posh accent), peering over gold-rimmed, half-moon glasses.

'Got a nasty spot, sir, right there,' said Jolly Jack, pointing to his backside. 'At the entrance to my anus, sir.'

The "MO" peered over his desk and gave the audience a camp, knowing look. 'Surely, boy... you mean the *exit from* your anus, don't you?' Loud guffaws came from the audience, particularly the officers. The real MO flushed red before dissolving into laughter.

The Captain enjoyed the show immensely, even though some of the jokes were at his expense. It was such a success that he asked for a second showing on New Year's Eve, to welcome in the New Year.

THE ENGLISH CHANNEL
January 1, 1915

Over 6,000 miles away, the German Navy celebrated the first day of the New Year in a different way. During the night of New Year's Day, the Royal Navy's battleship *Formidable* was heading west along the English Channel towards Torbay at 10 knots in company with seven other battleships and cruisers. In the full glare of the Start lighthouse, they presented a crystal clear target. It was an unmistakable opportunity for the submerged German submarine *U-24*, tracking the warships. She fired two torpedoes at the trailing ship and they both hit *Formidable*. There was a huge explosion on her starboard side at about *2:00 am*, and the sea began to pour into her engine room. Her electrical system and steam power failed immediately.

As a measure of the Admiralty's growing concern at the altered conditions of sea warfare brought about by German submarines, new instructions for such situations had been issued. Now – contrary to the traditionally accepted practice of all ships in the vicinity of a stricken vessel going to her aid, if a capital ship was attacked, all others in the area were to make off under the protection of their destroyer escorts, leaving smaller vessels to pick up survivors.

When Captain Noel Loxley of *Formidable* immediately advised other vessels by wireless that his ship had been hit, he became the first captain in the history of the Royal Navy to ensure that a long standing tradition would be disregarded, and that he would be left to his own resources.

At around *4:00 am*, when the ship was awash and about to go down, he came down to the boat deck from the bridge and ordered the crew into the sea to save themselves as best they could. Seventy of them crowded into the ship's launch, which was holed as it was launched from the sloping deck of *Formidable*. By constant bailing the launch was kept afloat and drifting until it was discovered off Berry Head by the fifty-ton Brixham smack *Provident*. The "Brixham Lords", as they were known, managed to take the half-frozen men out of the launch to safety.

The ship's pinnace, with sixty other survivors, reached Lyme Regis at about *11:00 pm* that night, but Captain Loxley and all but two hundred of the crew went down with the ship.

DEVONPORT DOCKYARD
Sunday, January 3, 1915

Due to unexpectedly favourable conditions in the Atlantic, *Inflexible* and *Invincible* arrived in Devonport Dockyard ahead of schedule. Most of the crew was stood down as soon as the ships fell into the hands of the dockyard workers. Manned only by a skeleton crew of officers and men who were not concerned about taking late leave, the ships were invaded by dockyard workers busy with essential repairs, while most of the men got ready to go home for a few days leave. For their own reasons, Curly Roberts and Chalky White volunteered to take late leave.

George was immediately escorted to the local police station for questioning. Parker stayed with him while Brown outlined the case to an inspector. At the request of the police, all leave was postponed in

Inflexible. It caused uproar in the ship, but no one was going anywhere until the Police Inspector had taken stock of the situation. Four policemen spent three days in *Inflexible,* questioning a number of people and establishing exactly where certain men were at the time Foster went missing. But nothing new came to light and the investigation seemed to lead nowhere other than to George. What little optimism he had left had gone and his spirits sank to an all-time low. When not being questioned, he sat alone, full of despondency and frustration, and nothing Parker could say made a difference.

Feelings in the ship were running high and the captain and senior officers were concerned about it. The men became angry and surly as they waited for word that they could go to their homes. There was still insufficient evidence to charge George with murder, and the police knew it but, as they were not prepared to release him, he had to stay in a cell. Captain Phillimore had strong words with the Inspector. He was adamant when he said that he was not prepared to keep his men back from leave any longer. If the Inspector insisted on doing so, he added, he would have to answer personally to the First Sea Lord, Admiral Fisher, who was aware of what was going on, and no one in his right mind would want to do that. The Inspector thought about it for a moment then agreed that leave for the men could start the following morning, but his prime suspect, he said, would remain in custody. Then, early on the morning of the fifth day, something extraordinary happened.

The ship's Master at Arms and two ratings wearing webbing belts and gaiters marched another gunnery rating to the Police station, accompanied by the Inspector. Within the hour, George was stunned when he was suddenly cleared of all suspicion, and released. He could not believe it! Suddenly, the weight of the world lifted off his shoulders and he became the real George Royal again. Dazed and on top of the world, he was escorted back to the ship by the MAA and his party, and wheeled straight into the Captain's office for the formal dismissal of all charges against him, and an apology for the anguish he had suffered.

Captain Phillimore briefly explained that Foster's murderer had now been found and that George was completely clear of any suspicion. Parker was there, smiling broadly. It was just like a dream for George. All of his troubles went in a flash. In the gangway afterwards, Parker was grinning like a Cheshire cat as he shook his hand warmly. 'I can't tell you how pleased I am that that's over,' he said. 'I knew you didn't do it – but I must admit that I was a bit worried when we couldn't find anyone who could confirm it.' He could see the bewilderment on George's face. 'Don't worry about this. There will be nothing at all on your record – I've seen to that. No harm done at all to your career. In fact, if anything, it will improve your chances of promotion. Your name will be remembered now. You'll be just like those skippers who run their ships into breakwaters – they *always* get promoted to admiral afterwards!'

George sighed and shook his head, trying to make sense of it all. 'But what really happened, sir? How did they find that other bloke?'

'Well, I think you owe that entirely to your messmates. They put the police onto him and he confessed. Go and talk to them. Frankly, it's best that I don't know what happened on that front.'

When he reached the mess, a cheer went up. Chalky was there, beaming warmly. George asked him what had been going on. He grinned and pointed to Curly Roberts. 'There's the star, mate. Without him, you'd be inside – indefinitely.' Curly gave him a casual grin and looked embarrassed. The story had to be dragged out of him.

'Well, it's a long story really. I know you thought I'd done it, and you could've easily dragged me into the frame for it – but you didn't, did you?' He looked up with a rare look of sincerity on his face. George shook his head. 'That matters to me. It made a big difference. I respected you for that. You could have easily pointed the finger at me – but you didn't.'

'But that still doesn't explain how you found out who really bumped Foster off. I knew somebody had because I saw him go over.'

'Yeah, well if you hadn't, I wouldn't have given a shit about who had shoved the bastard off the deck but we're all mates here, and once you'd been collared, we had to do something. We all knew it wasn't you, Georgie Boy, but what I did know was who that Reggie Jackson in the aft turret is. He's best mates with the bloke who's pokin' old Foster's missus – and I reckoned there had to be some connection there.' George was all ears. 'So me and Chalky 'ere 'ad a few words with 'im – sort of – down in the shell room. He soon coughed. Seems he promised his mate he'd do Foster in for 'im, if he could – and he did. Course, there's a lot more to it than that – but who cares? At least we'd found out who did it. Anyway, after our little talk he decided he would rather own up to it than go for a little swim in his hammock with a shell case for company.'

He shrugged, matter-of-factly. George's eyes widened. He was stuck for words and choked up. He slapped them both on the backs.

'I owe you – both of you,' was all he could say.

When George got his leave ticket he took the first available train home and went straight to St Mark's Road. When Emily opened the door she threw her arms around him and wept a little. To have him home, safe and sound, was the fillip she had been longing for.

He was determined to be strong for her, and he did everything possible to lift her spirits and help her over Jack's death. She was desperately pleased to have him home again but she could sense the change in him. He looked much the same; stronger and more muscular, but he was quieter and more subdued than he used to be. He said nothing about the Foster experience – he did not want to add to her worries – but he did say that he had helped to sink the ship that had sunk Jack's.

He was restless and keen to look up friends again. He took the first opportunity to see Bill and Carrie. In the town, on the way to see them, he found one of his old school friends, John Tyler, who was on sick leave from the Army. John was recovering well from a shrapnel wound in his right leg, but was still limping and walking with a stick. They sat in the nearest pub for a while, catching up on lost years. The conversation was about the war, and little else.

At first, they were slightly awkward with one another, but this soon passed. Whenever John spoke of his war in the trenches of Flanders, an unconscious stammer crept into his speech, and it was obvious that his cheerful optimism was nothing more than a fragile veneer. War in the trenches was still haunting him; more especially because he knew there was still more to come.

George remembered that John was an athlete at school: an outgoing, frantic lad with bags of self-confidence who could run and jump farther than anyone else he knew. He had just found a good position in the Portsmouth branch of a bank when the war started, and was ambitious to be a manager one day. Now, his confidence was gone, and he was hesitant and subdued, weighed down by a foreboding that he was not going to survive the war.

Seeing him made George realise that they had both changed. The innocence of their youth and the gentle ways of peacetime life had gone. In just a few months, everything they had been, and every value they used to conduct their lives by had been washed away in the mud of Flanders, or in some sea. Inconsequential things that seemed important then meant nothing now. They had grown up – very quickly. There were no steady careers or fun left to chase. Surviving the war was a career in itself, and the end of it was nowhere in sight.

As John unwound, he talked about fighting beside an Indian Army contingent in the trenches of Givenchy. 'We were in pretty high spirits when we went over there. Thought it was all going to be a bit of a laugh, especially when they took us to the front in a couple of double-decker, open-top London omnibuses. Can you imagine that? It was bizarre ...more like a bloody day's outing!' His faced clouded over. 'But when we got there ...bloody hell!' He shook his head. 'It was a nightmare, George, worse than you can imagine.'

His face went blank for a moment as his thoughts drifted. He came back without realising his mind had been on tour somewhere, and seemed surprised to find that he was with George. It made George feel uneasy. 'A bloody bizarre Christmas though,' he said, suddenly brighter. 'Hopeful, I suppose you could call it... kind of uplifting, in a way. There we were, getting the hell shot out of us – course we were giving as good as we got – when it just suddenly stopped on Christmas Day. Nobody ordered us to stop... but both sides just stopped firing as if Himself had ordered it, and everyone got out of the trenches. The lads simply declared a truce. Then our boys went into no-man's-land, bold as brass, and met the Huns halfway.'

'What the hell for?'

'Dunno, really. Just because it was Christmas Day, I suppose. The bloody Huns didn't want to be there any more than we did. Anyway, there we were, up to our arses in mud and shell holes, all linking arms and singing carols – Germans and all. Swapping fags and cigars and wine, we were. We didn't exchange anything written because we didn't have anything to write on. Then some joker produces a football, and we had a match. England versus Germany – right there in the middle of the battlefield! We won, of course, 3-2. Then we said goodbye and went back to our own trenches. Can you imagine this? I swear to you that it's true!' George puffed his cheeks in amazement and shook his head slowly. 'The next day we started shooting at each other again. Can you bloody believe it? Then a bloody mortar shell landed in my trench and killed four of my "oppos", and a piece of shrapnel shot through my arse and out the front, here.' He tapped his right thigh. 'So that was that.'

'Well, I'm glad you're OK, John.' George was struggling to find something suitable to say. 'At least you survived and got a break from it. I'm sorry you've got yourself crocked up.'

John's face clouded over and he stared into infinity again. 'Sheer bloody hell!' he said quietly. 'I never thought it would be like that, George. Bodies everywhere... having to crouch down in a muddy trench all the time, or risk getting your head shot off, but worst of all is the b-bloody noise. Day and night... shells exploding everywhere. You can't sleep, and you can't hear or think straight. I can still feel it, even now. Some of the men were so b-bloody bombed-out in their heads that they just p-put down their rifles and g-gave up.'

They sat in silence. 'It's not human,' said John, his mind drifting off again. 'The poor bastards just couldn't take any more. You couldn't b-blame them... but they got charged with d-desertion, just the same.' He began to shake. 'They were carted off somewhere... shot, I expect.'

'Christ!' George exclaimed, shaking his head. 'Poor bastards.' He was anxious to get off the subject. It was doing John no good at all to talk about it. He steered the conversation towards home and girls, and John seemed to brighten up. They finished their drinks and parted company, promising to meet up again before George's leave was up.

George went on to Bill's place. He was keen to know how life had been treating them at home. More than anything, he needed to talk to someone not caught up in the war.

Chapter Nine

Gosport January 6, 1915

Gosport was dim and gloomy. The heavy rain was coming down like stair rods. Carrie had just finished feeding Kate when the doorbell rang. She looked at the clock, wondering who could be calling at just after *6.00 pm* on a Wednesday evening. Quickly re-arranging her clothing, she went down to the door. Her face lit up when she found George Royal dripping on the doorstep. She flung her arms round his neck to hug him and plant a kiss on his lips.

'George... what a lovely surprise. I can't believe it!'

'I hope you don't mind me dropping in on you without warning. Just thought I would let you know that I'm back for a while.'

'Oh, I'm so pleased. Come in, come in. I'm afraid Bill isn't here. He's in Portsmouth on business and he won't be back for a while. He goes off to meet his business cronies quite often, but I don't think much business gets done.'

George took off his coat and shook off the rain as he climbed the staircase. He saw the crib in the drawing room and went to take a peek at Kate. 'She's grown,' he said, bending over and putting a finger in her tiny hand. 'She looks ...different.' He noticed she was wearing the little silver bracelet he and his mother had given her.

'Well, what did you expect? She's growing all the time.'

'I know, I know. How are things with you and Bill?'

'Oh, fine,' she said, breezily. Then her expression darkened as she remembered about his father. 'I didn't have much time in Devonport to tell you how sorry I was about your dad, George. Really sorry.' George shrugged.

'Thanks. It was a bit of a blow, but life goes on.'

'I never met him,' she said, going to the kitchen to put a kettle on the stove. 'Your mother was very upset. It was awful. All she got was a telegram, out of the blue.'

'No one told me at all. I heard about it very publicly when the Captain was giving a speech, one day. But I'm afraid that's how it is, these days, with the Army and the Navy. They've got so many "deceased letters" to send out, you're lucky if you get one at all.'

Gazing around the room he noticed several new ornaments, two extra houseplants and a new armchair. The apartment looked fresher and brighter than it ever had when Bill was there on his own. He looked out of the window at the grey, depressing scene outside. The rain was pouring down the road in rivulets and the gutters were filling with miniature lakes. 'How long has this awful weather been going on?' She came in from the kitchen and placed a tray of tea things on the table.

'Oh, it's been like this for days now. The worst floods in London for two hundred years, so they say. Bill is tearing his hair out. It's bad for business.' She stood in front of him, examining his face and noticing the tan that crossing the Equator twice in two months had given him. It seemed out of place on a cold, wet English January day, and made his eyes look much bluer than normal. 'It's really good to see you,' she said smiling broadly. 'Come here, let me welcome you home properly.' She put her arms around him and placed her lips squarely on his. It took him by surprise and it lingered longer than it should have done. When she felt him holding her tightly and enjoying it too much she broke away with a mischievous smile on her lips. She could see that he was embarrassed by the thrill it had given him. She poured tea and he made small talk with the taste of her still on his lips.

'What... um... has it been like? At home, I mean,' he asked awkwardly.

'Oh, it has its moments,' she said, handing him his tea. 'Very different, of course since all you good-looking men went away.' He looked up with a faintly quizzical expression. She smiled. 'But life is pretty good for us, now that I've been able to shake Bill out of his bachelor ways. He's very sweet ...he doesn't object much.' He noticed how much more attention Carrie was paying to her appearance since he first met her. She looked healthy, happy and very attractive. He had never seen her not pregnant. Her figure was back in shape and he thought she looked fabulous, particularly after his spell at sea. He wondered what it would be like to make love to her, and he kept on thinking about it until the thought excited him.

Enjoying each other and catching up on the past few weeks, their conversation roamed from the war at sea to Bill's business. All the time, George was thinking about making love to her, convincing himself that every move she made was a secret signal that she also wanted to. He carried on listening, but he was secretly wrestling with an urge to sweep her off her feet and make passionate love to her. When she went into the kitchen, he followed her, still talking. By now, he was aroused by her closeness, and the visible evidence of his feelings became difficult to hide.

Every movement she made, the way she glanced over her shoulder at him – everything about her – seemed to be telling him that she wanted him to hold her and kiss her. With his heart in his mouth, he reached for her waist, turned her towards him and pulled her into his arms in one movement. Suddenly, his lips were pressed to hers. She did not resist. Her mouth opened to his tongue and her body moulded softly into his, giving him all the encouragement he needed. His hand moved to the small of her back and pressed her body against the erection that was threatening to burst from his trousers. With her eyelids half closed, she threw her head back and gasped as his hand searched for a way under her blouse. Her hand reached for the nape of his neck, urging their lips to meet again. They were warm and open, and her hot tongue darted into his mouth and sent his pulse racing.

Suddenly, she broke away from his arms and recoiled as if she had been stung by a bee, flushed and fiery-eyed. The fleeting moment of abandon was over, as quickly as it had begun, and her self-control returned with a vengeance. 'I think you'd better go,' she said, throatily. 'I don't know what you take me for, George, but I'm not one of your girlfriends.' He stepped back immediately, stunned by her reaction. With confusion in his eyes he opened his mouth to say something about the mixed messages he was getting from her, but could not find the words. Her flashing eyes told him that he had misread the signals and, in an instant, he felt angry with himself – embarrassed by her rejection. He looked at her with a question in his eyes then shrugged and moved into the living room, unrepentant. Seconds later she followed him, blushing indignantly, and stood in the middle of the room tucking her blouse into her waistband.

'Sorry,' he said, petulantly. 'I didn't mean to offend you. I...I don't know why I did that. It must be the strain of everything.' She looked flustered and confused, her composure ruffled.

'I think you should go,' she muttered. He looked at her, still embarrassed. Suddenly he felt angry and reached for his coat.

'Fine,' he said, icily. The apartment seemed suddenly charged with the tension of their indignation. As he moved to leave, the sound of Bill returning home stopped him in his tracks. He looked at Carrie, dropped his coat over the back of a chair and sat down. Carrie hurried into the bedroom. The outside door closed noisily and Bill plodded up the stairs with heavy footfalls. As he came in shaking the rain from his coat and hat, Carrie ran to greet him. He was taken aback to find George there. They exchanged warm greetings before he went over to look at Kate.

George shot a glance at Carrie that said he wanted to leave but she was already calm and collected, as if nothing had happened.

'Beautiful, isn't she?' Bill said, unaware of their flushed cheeks. 'Just like her mum.' He took off his jacket and sat down. 'So, come on, George, what's it been like out there? Tell me what you've been doing... I want to hear all about it.'

'Well, perhaps another time, Bill. You've had a long day.'

'Nonsense, nonsense. I haven't seen you for ages and I hear you've been up to all sorts of things.'

George flashed an apologetic glance at Carrie and skated over the details of his exploits in the South Atlantic, with Bill hanging onto his every word, reliving every moment with him. If George glossed over something, he wanted more information. At the end of it, his eyes were sparkling with excitement. When their conversation turned to life at home, Bill started to tell him things he had already heard from Carrie, but he acted as if it was news. It sounded as if not much had changed while he had been away, which surprised him.

'But with all the merchant ships being sunk by submarines, surely the fruit side of your business is being hit, isn't it? From all the crates and loose oranges and bananas I've seen floating about in the sea all over the place... I expected to find none at all here at home.'

'No,' replied Bill with a grin, 'surprisingly, fruit still seems to get through... thanks to you blokes in the Navy. It gets a bit short, once in a while, but it still comes in.' He rubbed his hands together like a moneylender. 'The good news is that most of my competitors have closed up and gone off to war... especially the one-man bands. Those of us left here are doing very nicely, thank you. We're getting contracts to supply the Army camps now, and Navy ships and bases. It's very good business ...and regular. In fact, business is better now than before the war started. I really can't complain. I expect Carrie's told you about our latest developments. The partnership, I mean.'

'In fact,' Carrie said, joining the conversation in case George said the wrong thing, 'I've encouraged him to expand into the grocery business. Now that we've got contacts with all the supply officers in the area, we can increase the business that way.' George was amazed by her cool, matter-of-fact manner, considering what had happened minutes before. She sat on the arm of Bill's chair and put her arm around his shoulder. To George, it was a deliberate, calculated gesture for his benefit, to demonstrate how wrong he had been about her. She was showing him their sickening togetherness, from which he was excluded. Bill put his arm around her waist and gave it a squeeze. George felt the stab of jealous anger, and wanted to leave quickly.

'I'm convinced, George. It's the way forward for us, isn't it, sweetheart?' Bill gazed into Carrie's eyes, and she smiled back sweetly. George felt nauseous. 'We need to do *something*. Bloody income tax is going through the roof. It's being doubled, you know... going up to one shilling and sixpence in the pound ...all to pay for the war. According to the newspapers, it costs one million pounds every day now, to keep you blokes fighting out there.'

It was not the sort of detail that interested George. Business meant nothing to him. He found it boring. He shrugged, leaving a thought unvoiced that people making money at home had no right to complain about funding other people's efforts to defend the country. 'I'm afraid it'll get worse before it gets better,' George muttered, before letting the conversation peter out.

'Staying for supper?' Bill asked, after a while. 'We've got plenty of grub.'

'No thanks. It's late, and my mother's cooking for us ...don't want to let her down.' He stood up to leave.

'Well, what about one evening?' Bill persisted. 'Got a fancy girl you can bring round?' George looked at him with a wan smile.

'Give me a chance, mate, I only got back two days ago!'

'Tell you what,' Bill went on, 'come round on Saturday ...we'll get Marje round, as well... she's a bit lonely. She still hasn't got a man. Come round at about *7:00 pm* and bring a girl.' He looked at Carrie. She nodded approval, but there was a grudging, stern look in her eye. George put on his coat to leave, and went over to look at Kate. Carrie's embarrassing rejection was still burning his cheeks. He turned and smiled at Bill.

'What about you two – it's about time you got married, isn't it?' He wondered why he said that. It was a childlike thing to do, a vengeful dig at Carrie. She flushed and busied herself with the tea things. Bill shrugged and smiled.

'Dunno,' he said. 'I keep asking her, but she keeps turning me down... "When we're more settled," ...at least, I think that's what she said.' As the door closed behind George, Carrie turned to Bill with blazing eyes.

'I wish you wouldn't do that!' she said, indignantly.

'What?' he asked, in mock puzzlement.

'Tell everyone I won't marry you!' She was clearly embarrassed. 'And invite all these people round to eat. I think I've got enough to do here, with Kate and everything. I don't mind Marje coming, or George, but I'm not happy about cooking for his damned girlfriends.' Her eyes were blazing.

He smiled. 'You're just jealous, that's all,' he teased.

Her face flushed red. 'Don't be ridiculous!' She was too angry to pay much attention to his laughter.

'Anyway, I've been talking to Roy Paxman,' Bill announced quite suddenly, vigorously poking the apartment's tiny fire grate. Carrie shrugged. She had never heard of Paxman. 'You know, Paxman the grocer, in Commercial Road. Over in the city.' She shook her head. Bill looked disappointed and went on poking the fire. 'Anyway, he's one of the biggest grocers in Portsmouth,' he shouted, between rattling thrusts of the poker. 'He's got two big shops. We've been on nodding terms for years, but we only started talking properly a couple of months ago.' He stood up, put the poker down, and sat in the armchair. There was a gleam in his eyes that arrested her attention. 'He tells me that he's got military contracts... to supply groceries to the Army. The Army Service Corps, to be precise. They're the people who supply the food for the Army, wherever it goes. France, Belgium, anywhere and everywhere.'

'Lucky him!' she said, disinterested again.

'Yes. Well, he's looking to set up a partnership with someone in the fruit and veg business.' Carrie looked up, more interested. 'So, my love, to cut a long story short, we're talking about getting together and combining our businesses.' He hastened on, before she could stop him. 'See, that way we can get a share of his military contracts. We could form a partnership or a company, take on more staff, and turn both of our shops into combined grocery and greengrocery stores. What do you think of that?'

Carrie could see how pleased he was with himself. Her interest moved up a notch. She had been telling him to expand, now that so many one-man businesses had closed down since their owners had gone into the Army, but she had not thought about involving someone else. 'But would there be enough business? Where would the money come from? When I said expand, I meant here... you know, taking on new products. But this seems like a big leap into the unknown.'

'Well, Paxman and I have both got a bit put aside, and his bank is saying that it would lend us more if we needed it. But the really good bit is the "ring" we're working on.'

Carrie frowned. 'Ring... what ring?'

'A ring is, well... ' He struggled to find a place to begin. 'Look. With the possibility of military contracts, we could be dealing with much bigger volumes. What went through the shop would be only a small bit of it. Most of it would be delivered direct, straight from the suppliers into the depots, camps and ships. It saves time. As you know, that's very important with perishables. Well, if we join up with Paxman, the volumes would be even bigger.' Carrie frowned. She was giving it all of her attention but she was still confused.

'But what's that got to do with rings?'

'Ah, well. You see, with big volumes like that, you've got to go to London. Covent Garden for fruit and veg. Smithfield Market for meat and meat products. Then you can buy it all a lot cheaper. But you can't actually buy it, just like that. You have to bid for it...like an auction. You're always up against other bidders. What happens is that you make a bid then someone else bids more, then you bid more still... and so on, until someone ends up the highest bidder.'

'But do you still get it cheaper?'

'Of course I do, but not as cheaply as I could. Right now the Government is trying to control prices and, of course, all these supply officers know the sort of price they should be paying. You can't odds that. So, to make a bigger profit, you have to get the produce at a lower price in the first place.'

'But you can't do that,' said Carrie, 'unless other bidders stop bidding.'

'Exactly. That's the point of the ring. It keeps the top bid price down.'

'But where is this ring?' she asked.

'Well, the ring is not a place. It's people. Look, there are only four merchants with contracts to supply the military. The trouble is we're all bidding against each other, at the moment, and that pushes up the prices. If we all agree to a sort of "gentleman's agreement" not to outbid whoever has the turn to be the "winning" bidder, then he will get a free hand to bid a lower price, knowing that the rest of us won't try to outbid him.' Carrie was completely confused.

'But that means you only get one turn in four to make a profit... and the other three times you've got nothing to sell. So you get no profit at all. How does that make sense?'

'Aah, but the one whose turn it is to do the buying makes enough profit to pay the other three a reasonable amount of cash for not bidding at all – and he buys enough, at the lower price, for the others in the ring. *That's* the ring, you see. It's a circle of bidders who each get a turn to bid. We've been over the figures, Carrie, and they make a lot of sense. Our own retail shops will also benefit from the lower prices.'

'But it can't be legal, can it?' she asked, apprehensively. 'It sounds more like a ring of conspiracy to me!' He laughed.

'Of course it is. But it's not against the law,' he said, confidently. 'The suppliers don't want to be stuck with their perishable goods. So they *have* to sell it. Meanwhile, the Navy and the Army Service Corps will still get their fresh produce at the right prices, and we'll be making a bigger profit.'

'But someone must lose by it?' Carrie's frown deepened.

'Only the suppliers. But they are making too much, anyway!' He could tell by Carrie's expression that she was going to take some convincing. She was keen on making profit, and she had been pushing Bill to expand his business, but something about the idea of businessmen clubbing together to get the better of others bothered her. She could not take to it.

That night, lying in bed and staring into the darkness, her subconscious took off on a flight of fancy. It showed her a chain of smart grocer's shops with "Guy & Paxman" over their fronts in Portsmouth, Gosport, Fareham, Southampton, Dorchester, Brighton ...but then, in her dream, it all went wrong and Bill ended up back where he had started. In spite of Bill's continuing reassurance, Carrie remained steadfastly set against the idea of his involvement with ring dealing. Expanding the business with Roy Paxman was one thing. She was keen on expansion. It fitted nicely into her vision of a hopeful future: success, security, a house and a home for Kate – but why did he have to get himself involved with ring dealing?

Deep down, she was sure she could be more positive about settling down with Bill, if he looked as if he might be able to give her all that. But she could not keep her concerns to herself and felt that she had to give her opinion.

He explained that he could not form a partnership with Paxman and stay out of the ring at the same time. They were part of the same deal, and it was all or nothing. There was a long silence that irritated him. 'Look, Carrie, I know that you only mean well, but I can't ignore a business opportunity like this. Dammit, they won't let me do my bit in the war – what else is there for me? I've got to move forward somehow ...I need to make more of my life.'

She came over to him and put her hand on his shoulder. There was a softer, more understanding look on her face. These were sentiments like her own. 'I know, Bill, I know ...and you will one day, when the right chance comes along. I just don't think that ring dealing is that chance.' He looked at the ceiling and wondered how to put what he was thinking into words, delicately and diplomatically.

'Carrie, however much I like having you involved in my life, you have to understand that in men's business they don't welcome the opinions of women with open arms.' She recoiled as if she had been scalded. Her eyes blazed and her temper flared. She went straight for her woman's corner, and entrenched herself, angry and petulant.

'And all this time I thought you were different!' she hissed. 'I even stupidly thought that I was an important part of your life!' She turned on her heel and stomped off to the kitchen. He went after her, rushing to smooth things over.

'You are, Carrie! Of course you are. You know how much I want you to be involved. I'm not saying that's how I feel about women. I'm telling you that's how other men feel about it.' He put his arms around her, and tried to hold her close. There were several minutes of sulking silence before she calmed down enough to accept that there might be other sides to the argument.

'What men think is stupid!' she said. 'Even if *you* don't think like that. It just makes me sick!' He regretted the clumsy way he had handled it, stupidly putting his hand into the proverbial hornets' nest. He kicked himself for being so crass.

'Look,' he said. 'I know that Paxman will never bring himself to accept you as a capable businesswoman. People of that age just can't accept women in business. They're all the same. He will never discuss business with you. So I'll tell you what we'll do. I'll arrange to meet him at his home, and I'll take you along. That way you can meet him and, with a bit of luck, get him going so that you might hear enough to know there's nothing to worry about. How would that be?'

Carrie agreed.

GOSPORT
Friday, January 8, 1915

Bill, feeling remorseful about committing Carrie to another Saturday evening's entertaining, gave her a five-pound note to make up for it and told her to buy herself something nice to wear. She needed no encouragement. By Friday, her shopping expedition was planned. As if to lend support to her spree, the weather cleared up nicely and provided her with a clean, bright start to the day. After dropping Kate off for a visit with Aunt Ethel she set off briskly to the large department store in Southsea that she favoured above all other places: Biddles. Since meeting Marje, this had become her favourite place. Its fashionable, softly-scented atmosphere was like an addictive drug, and it gave Carrie the notion that mingling there with the elegant and fashion-conscious women she admired so much might rub some of their self-confidence and graces off onto her.

At the slightest opportunity, and on the flimsiest of excuses, she would be there. Sometimes it was to find something fashionable for Kate to wear. Other times, like today, it was to salve Bill's conscience. The fact that Marje – now her best friend and confidante – worked in the store was an added attraction. Her relationship with Marje was very important to her. Marje was the key to Carrie's transformation into the self-assured woman she longed to be. Marje was master of the difficult things in life: which clothes to wear with what – what was fashionable – and how real women should conduct themselves. She was always there for Carrie, and had a ready solution for any crisis – including the occasional misunderstanding with Bill and unwanted attention from men. Carrie accepted Marje's views with absolute confidence, and her admiration was so complete that – without realising it – she had adopted her idiosyncrasies and self-confident attitude, and was proudly copying her mannerisms and expressions. If Carrie could have had the big sister she always wanted she would have chosen Marje without a doubt and, in a convoluted way, Carrie's friendship and glowing admiration played no small part in her contentment to stay with Bill – and he knew it.

Arriving at Biddles, Carrie swept eagerly through its imposing front entrance in the style of the well-to-do women she so much admired, and burst into its opulent atmosphere. She gave a smile of pleasure as she savoured the now-familiar aroma of perfume and fresh new cloth that pervaded the store, and paused to absorb the murmur of conversations as fawning assistants and elegant, fur-laden ladies pored over merchandise on glass-topped counters. Brightly lit crystal chandeliers, equipped with the new electric light, hung imposingly above the shoppers from the high ceiling of the massive hall – contributing to its palatial air.

Carrie browsed at the counters for a while then climbed the broad, softly carpeted staircase to the second floor, where Marje was serving at the haberdashery counter. She smiled when she saw Carrie approaching. 'Good morning, Madam, can I help you?' she said, with mock servility. Carrie placed her handbag on the counter and smiled theatrically. 'I had better show you our latest range of silk ribbon,' said Marje in an aside. 'Or my old bag of a manager will descend like the wrath of hell. Darling, you look wonderful.'

Carrie feigned interest in the haberdashery and leaned forward. 'Tomorrow, Saturday... *7:30 pm*. Supper with George and A N Other. You won't let me down, will you? It would be unbearable without you.'

'Darling, I'll be there. What are you cooking? More importantly, what are you wearing?'

'That's one of the things I wanted to talk to you about. I need a new blouse, and Bill gave me five pounds to spend. What time do you finish?' Carrie held some ribbon up to the light. 'Can we meet and go back together?'

'Five o'clock,' said Marje, holding up different ribbon. 'I'll see you at the staff entrance. A blouse, you say? I know just the thing.'

Marje, as always, could be counted upon to come up with the ideal thing for Carrie, and sent her off to the appropriate counter to see it. Within ten minutes, she was back, looking pleased.

'Thanks, Marje, I knew I could count on you. I'll see you at the back at five.' As Carrie went to leave, Marje leaned over the counter.

'When you go to the ground floor, take a trip through the perfumery. The dark, Spanish-looking girl serving there is George Royal's new girlfriend!' Carrie was taken aback.

'New girlfriend? He's only been back five minutes.'

Marje smiled. 'Fast worker, is George. It never takes long. He thinks there's no point in finding a new girl just before his leave is up ...so he finds one at the beginning.'

'With a head as big as his, I'm surprised he can!' Carrie looked suitably disinterested, but needed no encouragement to go straight to the perfumery, where it was easy to spot the girl. She was strikingly attractive and stood out from the crowd. Carrie feigned interest in the merchandise on the counters, eyeing her furtively. The more she saw the more her cheeks flushed. The high-necked uniform dress the girl was obliged to wear took nothing away from her neat, athletic figure, and her even white teeth and sensuous mouth made Carrie feel decidedly inferior. Someone called the girl's name: it was Carla.

Typical! Carrie thought. It suited her dark-eyed, haughty sensuality that looked Italian or Spanish. Her hair was pulled back in a swathe at her neck, and it was jet-black, curly and thick. Her nails were finely manicured and quite long, and she moved with a poise and grace that made Carrie feel sick with envy. She looked hard for flaws, but there were none. Conscious of Carrie's stare, Carla came over to ask if she could be of assistance. Desperately wanting her to be servile, Carrie had an impish urge to get Carla to play the salesgirl – but her confidence suddenly deserted her. Instead, she shook her head politely and left the store, cursing Nature for inflicting upon the human race such an obvious indication of emotion as blushing, with no means of controlling it.

Strangely unsettled, she waited outside and was relieved when it was time for Biddles to close. She needed her friend's company. They met at the staff rear entrance and went to board an omnibus for the Harbour Station Ferry Terminal. On the way back to Gosport, they chattered animatedly about mundane matters until Marje finally found the moment to pop the question she was dying to ask.

'Well, what did you think of her?' she asked brightly. 'Of course, you'll get a much better look at her tomorrow. George is bound to bring her with him. Attractive, isn't she? The men all flock around her, and she is really nice when you get to know her. She's so... '

'Awful?' Carrie interrupted, feigning disgust. 'She is awful! I can't stand her!' Marje gave her a knowing, sideways glance that triggered a burst of girlish laughter. 'She's all right, I suppose,' Carrie went on, offhandedly. 'If you like that kind of thing.' Marje, whose intuition was razor-sharp, played along with Carrie's reaction.

'Look – she's probably got long black hairs on her legs and under her arms,' she whispered, raising a laugh. 'Typical continental!'

'She'll probably be as fat as a pig in a few years' time, I shouldn't wonder,' Carrie added, cynically. 'Thank goodness!'

Marje gave her a quizzical frown. 'Do I detect a teeny bit of jealousy here, darling?'

'Don't be ridiculous!'

'Aha... I'm not so sure it's that ridiculous. A handsome fellow, is our George. I could fancy him myself ... if only he'd stop going on about the Navy.' Carrie blushed all the way to her neck and changed the subject. But Marje was already on the scent of what was going on in Carrie's mind.

When Carrie reached Aunt Ethel's house and saw Kate, she scooped her up in her arms and cuddled her, and all thoughts of Carla and George went in an instant.

Saturday, January 9, 1915

As Marje predicted, George arrived at Bill's apartment with Carla on Saturday evening. There was a smugly proud grin on his face as he introduced her, and she was pleasantly surprised to see Marje's familiar face there. Later, Bill managed to get George on his own in the kitchen, where he gave him a dig in the ribs and indicated his approval. 'Got yourself a cracker there, George,' he said, with a knowing grin.

As the evening progressed, Carrie could see that Carla was every bit as attractive as she had first thought. There was absolutely nothing to criticise, apart from the fact she received too much of the men's attention. During the course of the conversation, it came out that her mother was Italian and her father was an English businessman. She had a slight foreign accent that was attractive and fascinating to the two men.

Carrie, looking radiant in her new blouse, was obviously making every effort to look her best – and succeeding magnificently. Throughout the evening, she paid only passing attention to George, and clung to Bill's side as if to demonstrate that this was where she belonged and felt most secure. Towards the end of the evening, with the men at the table, smoking, Carla and Marje helped Carrie to clear up. Alone in the kitchen with a helpful Carla, Carrie asked a few oblique questions about George, and found out that Carla had already seen him twice during the week and appeared to be very keen on him.

'He's been your friend for a while, hasn't he?' she asked Carrie.

'Quite a while... but Bill has known him longer.'

'What is he really like... is he as nice as he seems?'

'Mmm... yes... I think so.'

'But you seem hesitant... is there something wrong with him?'

'No... no, not really.'

Marje came in and picked up the thread of the conversation instantly. Carrie was embarrassed to be caught discussing George with Carla. 'I'm just telling Carla about George, Marje. I said he's really very nice – but he's a sailor, and she will have to watch out for herself. You know, a girl in every port, and that kind of thing.'

Carla looked concerned. 'What do you mean? He's not really like that, is he? I've never been out with a sailor before. Are they really like that?'

'Well, darling,' added Marje, in her all knowing way. 'The poor dears can't really help it, can they? I had a sailor boyfriend once. They go off to sea for months at a time, you know, and they get leave in foreign ports. That's when they sow their oats.'

'Their oats? What does this expression mean?'

'Sowing wild oats. You know, darling, planting their seeds! They do it wherever they can!' Carla looked baffled for a moment – then the penny dropped and she seemed quite shocked. Being a good friend to Carrie, and egged on by the look in her eye, Marje went in for the kill. 'The trouble is,' she said in tones of complete confidence, 'they do it all over the place – with goodness knows what kind of women.' Then in a stage whisper: 'And when they come home to you, you never know if they've got problems. You know – down there.' She nodded downwards. Winking secretly to Carrie, she smiled and swept out of the kitchen. Carla looked aghast.

When they finished in the kitchen and went back to the men, Carla was somewhat quieter and less vivacious. For the rest of the evening, she kept a suitable distance between herself and George – much to the amusement of Carrie and Marje. George was baffled by her sudden coolness.

From this particular evening, Carla made various excuses for not seeing George again, which ruined his leave. He spent the rest of it without female company, naïvely visiting Bill and Carrie, or at home with his mother.

Marje had seen enough to realise that her friend Carrie was in deeper emotional waters than she was prepared to admit to and, at the earliest opportunity, took Carrie aside to broach the subject in a soul-bearing chat. What came out of it was an admission from Carrie that although she loved Bill, it was not with the all-consuming passion of her dreams. It was more of an affectionate gratitude for the warmth and comfort he provided, and something she could not identify was making her hesitate about committing herself to him completely.

Marje, who had now seen her behaviour whenever George Royal was around, advised her to keep things just the way they were – for the time being. After all, she suggested, Bill was a good man, and was not pressing her to marry him, but she reminded Carrie that Bill seemed to love her and he had willingly taken her into his life, complete with Kate. 'There is no pressure for you to make such a definite commitment, darling. If you're not ready – you're not ready,' Marje said, with a simplistic clarity and a twinkle in her eye. 'It's quite understandable ...you just need to keep your options open.'

Marje always made such sense, thought Carrie. She felt reassured and the subject was put aside.

Sunday, January 10, 1915

The following afternoon, Carrie put on her best dress, coat and hat, and left Kate with Marje. She and Bill set off in the buggy to have tea with Roy Paxman and his wife, Eleanor. It was a fine crisp day, and Carrie was looking forward to the ride. The Paxmans lived somewhere on Portsdown Hill – a place she always enjoyed visiting.

Neither of them had been to the house before, and Carrie was dying to see what kind of home the Paxmans had. On the way, she passed the time describing what she thought it would be like. She had an image in her mind of a cottage surrounded by fruit and vegetables, with fruit baskets hanging outside the front door in place of flower baskets – but when they drew up outside the gates, her jaw dropped. It was a large, double-fronted house, brightly painted in plain white, with sparkling windows and a meticulously manicured garden. It stood on its own near the top of the hill, commanding an uninterrupted view of the city of Portsmouth, Gosport, Hayling Island

and the Isle of Wight – the very view Carrie had fallen in love with when she first came to Gosport. A low brick wall ran right round the spacious garden, which was full of lawns, flowerbeds and rose bushes – and there was not a fruit tree in sight.

An impressive wrought-iron gateway led to a neat, gravel driveway in which stood a gleaming, elegant Rolls Royce motorcar. It had cream bodywork and shiny metal panels over the engine. Its wheels had spokes of varnished wood and red painted rims. On the front wings, there were two big shiny electric lights, and a "Spirit of Ecstasy" mascot reached forward elegantly from the top of the gleaming radiator.

Carrie's eyes widened. 'They've got a motorcar!' she said, excitedly. 'You didn't tell me they had a motorcar.' She looked like an excited six-year-old. Bill smiled.

'Oh yes. Believe me, Roy Paxman has got it all. He knows how to get what he wants out of life, all right.' He stepped down from the buggy and hitched the horse to a railing then handed Carrie down. 'Come on, let's see what it's like inside. Just keep your ears open, and take everything in. We're going to have something like this ourselves, one day – I promise.' They crunched across the gravel and Eleanor Paxman met them at the door. She looked about fifty, well upholstered, and quite plain. Carrie thought she bore an uncanny resemblance to Mrs Trimble. Not a very inspiring woman, she thought, what the Germans call a *hausfrau,* but any similarity to the Squire's housekeeper quickly evaporated when Eleanor smiled and welcomed them. Her cultured voice made Carrie feel decidedly self-conscious.

'How nice of you to come,' she said, in sugary tones, extending her hand regally. 'Do come in.' She led them through the impressive hallway, into the drawing room. The Paxman residence was everything Carrie wanted for herself. Every piece of furniture was in the right place and looked solid, dependable, and expensive. The rooms were bright and nicely decorated, but there was a strong smell of stale cigars in the air. 'Roy is in his study. He has a large telescope, you know. He watches ship movements in the harbour... he likes to know if his imported fruit has arrived.' She laughed politely, wafted them towards a sofa and left the room to summon her husband.

Roy Paxman was nothing like Carrie's preconceived image of him. He looked scruffy in a collarless shirt, with rolled-up cuffs revealing an abundance of black hair on his arms. He was short and stocky and had a large square face dominated by thick black eyebrows. A moustache barely hid the wet lips of his tiny, mean mouth. Carrie felt his dark, penetrating eyes boring into her. He was about fifty years old, and spoke brusquely in a local Hampshire brogue. The smell of stale cigars in the house seemed to emanate from him.

'Nice to make your acquaintance,' he said to Carrie, giving her a grudging nod. He stood with his thumbs tucked into his braces. There was something about his eyes that brought a chill to the nape of her neck. She struggled not to, but she felt resentment about him before he said or did anything more. The longer she was there, the more the feeling grew. Her intuitive dislike of him crushed the initial excitement out of her, and she felt heavyhearted about being there. Carrie immediately sensed ruthlessness in him. It came from the way he spoke of himself and his business acumen before mentioning his family – implying that this was the order of their importance to him.

Eleanor sat quietly dispensing tea and biscuits, apparently immune to her husband's manner. To Carrie, Eleanor's subservient demeanour spoke volumes about the role she played in his life. Successful though he may be, Roy Paxman had doubtful qualities, Carrie decided – he was cold, calculating, and not to be trusted.

She suddenly became concerned that her softhearted, generous, caring Bill would come out of any partnership with Paxman with much less than he went into it. She kept smiling, and listening, although Paxman never once addressed any of his comments to either of the women. Carrie came to the conclusion that Eleanor was a sweet lady – far too good for a dominant braggart like Paxman – and, somewhere in the conversation, she gathered that Eleanor – who obviously came from a high-class family – had brought the founding wealth to Paxman's business. No doubt, she thought, the money would now be buried in the business: no longer Eleanor's.

While smiling and chatting to Eleanor, Carrie had one ear cocked to the men's conversation. She distinctly heard Bill hesitantly suggest that ring dealing might somehow be a bit dishonest, and she loved him for asking the question for her.

'Good God, man!' Paxman's bellow penetrated the women's conversation. 'If that's how you think, you'll never get anywhere in business! There's no law against it... and that's bloody good enough for me and it ought to be good enough for you. If you don't like the idea, there's no point in talking about partnerships. You can just stay as you are... and be put out of business by the rest of us.'

Carrie felt guilty, angry and quite sorry for Bill. She knew that he had put the question entirely for her benefit. Now he was suffering scorn as a result. She wanted to rescue him, before Paxman wore him down, and she instinctively thought of the Rolls Royce. He was bound to be desperately proud of that. It fitted her perception of him. She made a comment about the motor, just loud enough to reach him – saying how wonderful it was. His ears pricked up immediately.

'Best motor money can buy,' he shouted from the other room. 'Rolls Royce Silver Ghost...40/50-saloon limousine – nothing finer. Got it from an MP I know. He got into a spot of bother and needed cash quickly. More or less stole it off him!' He was obviously delighted to have benefitted from someone else's misfortune. Carrie looked suitably impressed, and mentioned that she had never in her life ridden in a Rolls Royce. Paxman took the bait.

'Well, we could go for a quick ride, if you like.'

'Oh yes, I would love to,' she cried, almost too enthusiastically. Bill was stunned by her brazenness, but realised what was behind it.

Paxman found it necessary to explain that his motorman, who normally drove him around in the car, did not work on Sundays, so he volunteered to drive the car and take them all for a spin – clearly keen to demonstrate his newly acquired ability to drive. Eleanor gave a sugary smile and bowed out of the excursion.

With Carrie and Bill in the back of the motor, Paxman cranked it into life and climbed in behind the wheel. They crunched serenely out of the gravel driveway and rolled grandly along the top of Portsdown Hill as far as the farthest Napoleonic fort then back to the house. Carrie immediately fell in love with it, drooling over the feel and smell of the sumptuous red leather interior and the grandness of the ride. It rescued Bill and broke the conversation nicely, so that they could bid their farewells.

Going home in the buggy afterwards, Carrie gave a lot of thought to ring dealing and the partnership idea. If anything swayed her, it would be Paxman's lovely home and the Rolls Royce – certainly not him. After the opulence of Paxman's home, returning to the apartment was a sharp letdown: an anticlimax. It suddenly felt minuscule and drab.

Carrie's appetite for the better things in life had been well and truly whetted by her visit to the house. Now she could picture Bill's business booming and booming, and she believed it could happen without Bill having to become another Paxman. Success was just a matter of hard work and good business sense. She was prepared to work hard, and she had enough business sense for the both of them – even if women were not supposed to be involved in "men's business". She and Bill could do this, she thought – and the sooner the better. The Paxman-Guy partnership and the ring dealing would go ahead with her blessing.

Bill was over the moon when she told him so.

Chapter Ten

THE ADMIRALTY WAR ROOM LONDON
Friday, January 15, 1915

In March 1913, long before the war began, Germany drew up a plan to make use of her ally, Turkey, to deplete the military strength of Britain and Russia in Europe.

The plan had three main objectives. The first was to blockade Russia's trade with the West, thus crippling her economy. The second was to seize the Suez Canal, thereby depriving Britain of her connections with Africa, India and the Far East, and the final one was to tie up British and Russian troops in other theatres of war, in order to make them unavailable for use against Germany in Europe.

Russia had only two sea trade routes to the West – the Baltic Sea in the north, and the Black Sea in the south. With the German Navy dominating the Baltic Sea, Russia's only trade route would be from the Black Sea into the Aegean Sea (and thus the Mediterranean). Unfortunately, this meant passing through the narrow Straits of the Bosphorus, part of Turkish territory. Blocking this would completely cut Russia off from the West.

Ships leaving the Black Sea had to pass through the narrow neck of the Bosphorus, which is straddled by the Turkish capital of Constantinople, into the Sea of Marmora then on through the narrow Dardanelles (the Straits formed by the Gallipoli Peninsula) into the Aegean Sea.

As soon as the war started, the Turks set about blockading and defending the Straits under the guidance of competent German officers. They laid rows of mines across the Straits and set up batteries of fourteen-inch, eleven-inch, and nine-inch Krupp guns in the ancient forts overlooking the narrow stretch of water. This done, they were in a strong position to stop ships moving between the

Mediterranean and Black Seas.

Russia's economy began to falter as soon as the Dardanelles were closed, and with Russia in severe difficulties, Britain was obliged to come to her aid. Some leaders in London argued that forcing a way through the Dardanelles to capture Constantinople was the most effective way for Britain to help her ally.

There were dissenters to the plan, and Jacky Fisher was the most vociferous of them. Having just been censured for his hotheaded suggestion that all German prisoners-of-war should be summarily executed in reprisal for the British civilians and children killed in the latest Zeppelin raids, he was particularly prickly with Winston Churchill. When all rejected his suggestion, Fisher handed in a letter of resignation but Churchill, who was becoming used to Fisher's way, assumed that the old admiral would reconsider his position after serious thought, and defused the situation in his inimitable way.

'I sympathise with your feelings of exasperation at our powerlessness to resist certain forms of attack and I presume I may take your letter simply as an expression of those feelings.'

After a moment of reflection, Fisher withdrew his resignation.

They sat at the table glowering at each other like warring bulldogs. The atmosphere of disagreement around these powerful men crackled with negative energy like a thunderstorm seeking a place to ground its lightning. 'Now to the matter of ships for the Dardanelles,' Churchill went on.

Since Fisher's return to office, the relationship between them had degenerated rapidly and communication was now terse and difficult. Both could see that the honeymoon was over, and Fisher abandoned his earlier efforts to modify his bombastic behaviour. With a pugnacious, defiant expression, he was standing firm against Churchill's latest cajoling for more dreadnoughts for his pet projects: a bombardment of Zeebrugge and an assault on the Dardanelles.

'Absolutely not,' he spat, glaring at his adversary. 'Further weakening of the Grand Fleet in the North Sea cannot be permitted.' His obduracy left Churchill frustrated and furious.

'The Dardanelles operation,' he snapped impatiently, 'must succeed. We need ships that are capable of destroying every one of the Turkish guns and forts. It is the Navy's task to make the area safe for troops to be landed. We have already seen, at Coronel, that older ships are not up to it! We must be fully capable of crushing the Turkish defences... and I have already intimated to Lord Kitchener that this will be done.'

Fisher kept punching the palm of one hand with the fist of the other as he spoke. It was his usual method of emphasising his points. 'I will not stand by and watch our superiority in the North Sea compromised! With the German High Seas Fleet concentrated there, the Grand Fleet must be kept up to strength. All that is needed for your wretched Dardanelles affair are floating gun batteries and troop carriers, not our fastest, most modern dreadnoughts. These are required for the defence of our own shores. I won't have it, Winston. Pre-dreadnoughts only can be spared – but not our best ships.' He flung his hands apart in frustration. There was a reflective pause while the men gathered their thoughts. '*Canopus* would be ideal for the task now that von Spee has been dealt with. I am prepared to order her return from the Falklands Islands.'

Churchill, hopping mad at Fisher's attitude, prodded the table with his forefinger to emphasise his own points. 'The requirement is for the forts to be silenced completely and for the Straits to be forced all the way up to Constantinople. Constantinople must be captured and occupied. That cannot be done with a mere handful of warships!'

Fisher glared across the table – his contempt for the project clear in his eyes. 'The truth of the matter is, this particular task is not achievable by any amount of ships, unless there is ground support. Only a combined effort by the Army and Navy together has any chance of succeeding. To imagine that ships alone can achieve this is utter folly!'

Churchill considered the situation, clearly angry at the stalemate. 'No,' he said brusquely. 'I do not accept your position or your attitude to this important mission. I intend to take the matter further. We can do better than this, and the Prime Minister must be informed immediately.' With no further communication between them, Churchill got up, grumpily picked up his papers and stomped towards his office.

DOWNING STREET, LONDON
January 15, 1915 3:45 pm

In drizzling rain, the chauffeured black Rolls-Royce limousine bearing Herbert Henry Asquith, the Prime Minister of His Majesty's Liberal Government, drew slowly away from his official residence at Number 10 Downing Street and nosed into the traffic of Whitehall.

In the rear seat, the Prime Minister relaxed from his formal straight-backed posture and lifted his black hat from the abundant silver hair crammed beneath it. As the limousine purred along Victoria Embankment towards Whitechapel, he glanced at the Thames. The river was in full flood: wide, grey-brown and flowing rapidly. He turned to the elegant, slim young woman beside him and smiled lovingly as he reached secretively for her hand. Venetia Stanley, the twenty-seven-year-old unmarried woman with whom he was intensely in love, self-consciously acceded to his unspoken request by placing her hand in his.

He squeezed it gently. 'My darling, you have no idea how much I've missed you these past days.' His eyes sparkled with excitement. She tilted her head forward, burying her chin in the soft fur collar of her coat. From beneath her long black eyelashes, her soulful, charcoal eyes glanced coyly at his mature pink face. It looked soft and fatherly. She looked away from his pale blue eyes.

'Mmm... yes... me too!' she murmured. He was oblivious to the lack of conviction in her voice.

'I've so much to tell you,' he whispered urgently. 'I had a meeting with the King yesterday and another with Lloyd George this morning. So much is going on... but I rather fear there will not be enough time to tell you everything before we reach that dreadful treadmill you call a hospital. Had I only known, when I was talking to Lord Knutsford the other day, what you trainee nurses go through in that place I would have told him in the plainest English what I think of his wretched system at the London Hospital. 'My poor darling,' he doted, 'you look so much thinner already... and it has only been one week since you started there. Is it really necessary for you to put yourself through so much?'

Venetia lifted her head and smiled. 'It is what I have chosen to do, Prime. I want to do something useful in the war.'

'But you will write to me, won't you... every day?'

'I will do my best,' she said, with a frown touching her smooth white forehead. 'But the training is so strenuous – it's often extremely difficult for me to find the time.' The familiar disappointed look of a small boy invaded his expression. 'But I will do my very best... I promise.'

He clasped her hand in both of his and looked adoringly into her intelligent eyes, admiring her youthful face as if he might never see it again. The fashionable hat under which her long dark hair was gathered reminded him of the new steel helmets worn by French soldiers – but he was too gentlemanly and too much in love to say so. Instead, he gazed lovingly at her, as he always did – to her complete embarrassment.

She was attractive, rather than beautiful. A nose that was not pert enough, and eyebrows that were too darkly prominent, kept her short of outstanding beauty, but he loved her aquiline features and virginal, tomboyish manner. To him, the real beauty of Venetia – which he adored – was her sharply intelligent mind, her chummy disposition, and an intellect as sharp and masculine as his own. To those in the know – colleagues and relatives alike – the relationship between Britain's 62-year-old married Prime Minister and Venetia Stanley, who shared the same age and a close friendship with his eldest daughter Violet, seemed somewhat unusual. What caused further raising of eyebrows was that the relationship had become intense on his part.

'Tell me more about the London Hospital. What is it you are learning?' he said, attentively. 'Then I will tell you what has been going on in my world. The War Council! My God, that's as much of a battlefield as the trenches! There are really difficult decisions to be made, and I very much need your opinions. You know how much I rely on you, my darling.' He looked at her with the eyes of a lovesick youth, and laughed nervously. 'You know you are the very salt of my life. Without you and your intelligent views, which you know I value most highly, I'm sure this country wouldn't be governed as well. I can only do my job properly if you advise me. But tell me first about nursing.'

She covered her embarrassment at having to go through the mundane details of her daily life, and laboriously recounted stories of imaginary wounds she had dressed, bedpans she had emptied, and her differences with Staff Nurses. He listened attentively until she ran out of things to say. Then, as was his habit, he described in detail the rantings of Cabinet colleagues, his brushes with the Opposition, and his recent meetings with the monarch and various heads of state. Glossing over only the most sensitive details, he delivered a complete account of Britain's immediate war plans and the feisty clashes between Winston Churchill, Jacky Fisher, Lloyd George and Lord Kitchener.

'Goodness!' she exclaimed, laughing nervously. 'It's a jolly good job that I'm not a German spy.' He laughed with her.

'No, not you, my darling. You know I trust you with my life. I know very well that our little secrets are safe with you.' Before he had the chance to say more, the motor gave a sudden jolt and screeched to a standstill. They were almost thrown from their seats.   Horwood, the chauffeur, slid back the glass partition behind his head. 'A small haccident, Prime Minister,' he said, craning his neck. 'An errand boy wobbled out, and I 'it the poor little blighter. I'll 'ave to go and get some 'elp for 'im. Just you stay there, sir. 'E'll be all right.' Asquith and Venetia looked anxiously out of the window. She was desperate to go to the boy, but he was already being helped to the pavement by passers-by. His injuries appeared not to be serious and he seemed to have only small cuts and grazes. A man picked up the boy's battered bicycle and dragged it to the kerb.

Asquith suddenly realised that they had stopped in Whitechapel, a short distance from the London Hospital. He turned to Venetia, who was trying to keep herself out of sight of the people gathering on the pavement. 'My dear... I hate to part like this but as we are so close to the hospital, it might be prudent for you to slip out.' He pointed to the offside door. 'Why don't you make your way around the back of the crowd... and off to the hospital, or you'll be late. I'll take care of this. It would be best not to be seen.' He glanced at his pocket watch. 'If Horwood doesn't look sharp, I'm going to be late for my wretched train.'

Venetia hesitantly agreed and moved towards the door. She really wanted to step out and use her limited medical knowledge to help the boy, but she could see the danger in the situation. This was one of "Fate's lurking submarines", which Asquith spoke of often. Being caught with him in his limousine by a passing newspaper reporter, or a campaigning suffragette, would cause great embarrassment. Reluctantly, she backed out through the door with her coat collar turned up. 'Let me know how the boy is, won't you?' she said with genuine concern in her voice. She pecked Asquith on the cheek. 'Sorry to abandon ship in the middle of it all. Till I see you again.' She gave a little wave and slipped away.

Horwood returned a few minutes later with a doctor, and the boy quickly recovered from the shock and was soon pedalling shakily down the road with a tale to tell someone. A policeman on the scene dutifully cleared the way and Horwood turned the motor around and headed back towards the West End. The traffic had already piled up in Whitechapel and Aldgate, blocking the roads. Through his rear-view mirror, Horwood noticed Asquith looking anxiously at his watch. He raised a reassuring hand and accelerated through the busy roads. Using all of his driving skills and intimate knowledge of London, he managed to skirt round the traffic to arrive at Victoria Station only five minutes behind schedule. An anxious stationmaster with a flag in one hand and a whistle in the other was holding the train for his important passenger.

With a shrill blast of the whistle, the train hissed away from the platform in a cloud of steam and smoke with Asquith settling back in his seat and reflecting on the excitement he had left behind. In the rhythmically swaying carriage, Asquith unwound and pulled out his writing case. He collected his thoughts and began to write notes – with his various pressing priorities there were many things he had to write: his next speech perhaps – comments about the last meeting of the War Council – a draft resolution? The truth would have come as a shock to any observer in this case because Asquith's first thought was always for Venetia Stanley. Although he had only just left her, he put all other priorities aside to concentrate on writing her another letter.

It began: *"My darling – this has been an afternoon of narrow shaves..."*

Such was his need that as soon as she was out of his sight, he felt compelled to write to her – once, twice, sometimes three times each day. He wrote to her while riding in motors and trains, at home, in the House, or in the middle of Cabinet and War Council meetings and his appetite for her replies was equally as avaricious and, if not satisfied, made him uncharacteristically aggressive. It was his main leisure pursuit – his hobby and relaxation. Being an intellectual with a dislike for telephones, he could dash off – with consummate ease – the most interesting and compelling of letters in minutes; and most were to his lover.

In his letters, and during his cosy limousine rides along the Embankment with her, he constantly impressed upon her that he was simply not capable of functioning properly as decision-maker without her guidance and reassurance. After years of this, during their strange "affair", he had conditioned her to believe it.

Violet Asquith understood and approved of her father's relationship with her close friend, as did all of the five children of his first marriage, because they never, for one moment, imagined that his affection for Venetia was anything other than platonic. Most people assumed this too, with few exceptions: such as one lady suffrage campaigner who had written to him the year before, calling him: *"... an old man who notoriously can't be left alone in a room with a young girl after dinner."*

Asquith's first wife, Helen, died of typhoid fever in 1891. Then in 1894, he married again – this time to Margaret (Margot) Tennant, the youngest daughter of Sir Charles Tennant, first baronet. Sadly, of the five children they had together, just two had survived infancy. These, Elizabeth and Anthony, were barely old enough to know whether their father's relationship with Venetia was "proper" or not.

Margot had been aware of her husband's infatuation all along, and she tolerated it and accommodated it with as much good grace as she could muster. Accepting his weakness for the company of attractive, intelligent young women, she seemed quite unfazed even when he held hands with them. Close friends of the Asquiths suspected that he was driven to look elsewhere for relaxation and intellectual stimulation by Margot's stressful and outspoken nature but, even to them, it seemed more than just a coincidence that his chosen companions were always women less than half his own age.

In 1908, there were as many as five such young ladies in Asquith's circle – his "little harem", as Margot playfully called it, with more than a touch of cynicism. However, by 1914 the number had dwindled to just one: his favourite, Venetia, with whom he was now deeply in love. Although some people suspected that the affair was a sexual one, no one could ever offer proof of that, and he always insisted it was simply an affectionate "meeting of minds". Even so, it had to be kept from the press and public – he was, after all, the most important statesman in the world. Britain was governing the largest empire the world had ever seen and, as its Prime Minister, he could greatly influence the decisions of the British Government and the way it went about war. Innocent though the affair may have been, justifying it to the rest of the world would have been difficult.

Asquith's career and the nation's patriotism – upon which the future of Britain now depended – were sure to suffer if his dependence upon Venetia Stanley became common knowledge. Men who were fighting in appalling conditions on the front line were hardly likely to take kindly to the fact, whether real or imagined, that a twenty-seven-year-old woman, with whom their leader was obsessed, was sharing the decisions threatening their lives.

As is often the case, there were two sides to this story. Venetia was a natural comforter with a very good mind. Unlike the men with whom Asquith was surrounded, she had clarity of thought that was untainted by political ambition. With the exception of Margot – who, like a loose cannon, was apt to slaughter friend and foe alike with friendly fire – Venetia was the only person in whom he could confide who had nothing to gain from leaking his closest thoughts to a wider audience. This is what he found so refreshing and vital about her. She was a cool, sterile dressing for his political wounds.

In peacetime, he shone as a confident and capable Prime Minister, highly respected as the leader of Government. Confronted with the difficulties of leading the country through a prolonged war, his self-confidence began to wane. It was then that he needed personal reassurance to support and confirm his decisions – a weakness that had to be kept hidden from his colleagues and opponents. Only Venetia could be entrusted with his confidences and relied upon not to stab him in the back. Moreover, the relationship had not been entirely one-sided. In her letters and during their cosy limousine rides along the Embankment together, she had at times encouraged his interest by declaring love for him.

Understandably, it was extremely flattering for a young woman to have the most powerful man in the world besotted with her, but the sheer weight of his obsessive, suffocating dependence had become more than she could take. For her own sake, she felt compelled to find a way of extricating herself from him, without breaking his heart. She wanted to remain a close friend, but needed a life of her own. However, although desperate to disentangle herself, her heart would not allow her to end the relationship. Finally, volunteering for nursing training and then service behind the lines seemed the only escape route for her. He could hardly blame her for wanting to do her bit for the war effort, and she felt confident that once out of his reach she would at last be able to establish a new life and make the break.

However, unknown to Asquith, someone else was pressing her with amorous attentions behind the scenes. It was 38-year-old Edwin Montagu, Asquith's former Private Secretary and current Financial Secretary to the Treasury. For years, he had been ardently admiring her from the sidelines of her relationship with Asquith, but she had rejected him several times before. Realising she wanted escape from Asquith, Montagu seized the moment and renewed his efforts to woo her. To his surprise and delight, she seemed less obdurate and more receptive this time. Venetia knew that Asquith dreaded losing her to another man, but this seemed the only way she would ever have the strength to break away from him. Asquith, meanwhile, was oblivious to the triangle he had become embroiled in.

What made the mixture of emotions and loyalties more explosive was that its catalyst should be none other than Montagu. However, breaking Asquith's heart for a man he considered unworthy of her – and giving up her faith in the process – would be more than he and her family could bear. Venetia was therefore carrying enough emotional baggage to cause any young woman a mental breakdown. It was singularly unfortunate for her that her great intelligence did not extend to affairs of the heart. Self-interest and forcefulness were completely absent from her nature and she was always content to drift along on the tide of life like a piece of driftwood. Now completely out of her depth in deep water, she was striking out in panic for a secure place before she drowned.

10 DOWNING STREET
January 28, 1915 10:00 am

Winston Churchill and Admiral Jacky Fisher were admitted together to the Prime Minister's room. They were barely speaking to one another, and what little cordiality they could muster was reserved solely for secretaries and staff – not extended to each other.

They were ushered into Asquith's conference room, where the War Council, of which they were key members, was to meet within the hour. They greeted him as he breezed into the room, but otherwise remained silent and sullen, standing awkwardly with their backs half towards each other. He smiled at them in turn and noted how much they resembled a pair of bookends: carved wooden bulldogs. Churchill's face looked like a thundercloud. Fisher's remained bland, apart from the characteristic droop of his mouth and his oriental manner of peering down his nose through half-closed eyelids. The wintry morning light creeping through the window drapes heightened the jaundiced tone of the "Old Malay's" complexion, lending him the image of a Siamese King. The tension between them was tangible.

'Well, gentlemen,' opened Asquith, already well aware of why they were there. 'How may I help?' They all sat. Churchill was anxious to speak first.

'Prime Minister. The First Sea Lord and I seem unable to agree a position on the Dardanelles. In fact,' he mumbled cynically to one side, 'we have difficulty in reaching an agreement about anything.' Fisher shifted uneasily in his chair and cleared his throat, but Churchill went on with a statement that sorely exercised his defective pronunciation of the letter "S". 'As you know, a telegram arrived on January 2nd from the British Ambassador in St Petersburg. It stressed, as a matter of urgency, the need for some form of direct action to be taken against the Turks, as aah... a measure to counter their advance against the Russians in the Caucasian provinces.'

'I am aware of this,' said Asquith, calmly.

'The Secretary of State for War,' Churchill continued,

"sshhssing" his way through the title, 'wrote to me immediately. Lord Kitchener asked if... aah... naval action was possible in the area, and if an operation by ships alone was feasible.' He referred to his papers. 'The First Sea Lord here has made it known that he is opposed to an assault by ships alone, and proposes that a strong military force should be landed to assist with the assault. I am given to believe by Lord Kitchener that he is very short of troops at present, and now insists that the only uncommitted division, the 29th – the very one he promised for the Dardanelles – should be left here in England, as ... ah ... reinforcements for France. I have indicated to the First Sea Lord that I would not begrudge 100,000 men of the Naval Division for the operation, but I... ah, also added that I consider Germany to be the real foe.' He glanced up at Asquith. 'In short, my position is that whilst I am uncomfortable that the Army is not available to assist with an attack on Turkey, I am prepared to consider an assault by ships alone...in the light of the shortage of military divisions. The First Sea Lord, however, is not.'

Fisher seized his chance to leap into the conversation. 'I am not one to pussyfoot over such matters, Prime Minister...' Asquith raised his eyebrows, indicating how true he knew that to be. 'It is my view that, without the benefit of a strong force of troops on the Gallipoli Peninsula – to support a Naval attack – there is little or no hope at all of forcing the Straits. Unlike the First Lord, I have intimate knowledge of this area and I can assure you that in order to reach the Black Sea, we must take Constantinople.' His hand thumping began again. *'WE CANNOT TAKE CONSTANTINOPLE WITHOUT THE ARMY, AND IT IS PREPOSTEROUS TO SUGGEST OTHERWISE!'*

Asquith and Churchill were stunned into silence by Fisher's bellowing. 'How are we to consolidate gains?' he went on. 'How are we to know if the Turks have been successful in repairing any damage we may inflict on them? If our ships enter the Sea of Marmora, past Turkish heavy guns they think they have silenced – and then the Turks repair their guns – where do you think they will be then? I can tell you – *TRAPPED!* Completely trapped. It would be an act of sheer folly. The First Lord, however – ignoring my professional advice – is quite prepared to go along with this and see us lose our precious dreadnoughts.'

Churchill moved to speak, but Fisher went on, punching his hand. 'The real problem is that this is a decision that should be left to me. After all, I am the First Sea Lord, and no one is more experienced in naval warfare than I! The First Lord, however, seems to think that all decisions concerning the Navy are his and his alone to make – and that is a situation that cannot be allowed to continue. Indeed, if it does I shall have no option but to tender my resignation!'

Asquith took a deep breath and leaned back in his chair, barely concealing the mental calculation he was making of the number of resignations Fisher had submitted to date: six, seven... no, eight!

'That is utter nonsense, John,' huffed Churchill. 'Must I remind you, sir, that it is perfectly within the bounds of my responsibility – indeed, it is my... aaah... *duty* – to make such far-reaching decisions.' Fisher looked petulant but Churchill ignored him, and continued. 'Accordingly, I have already sent a telegram to our Admiral on the spot in the Dardanelles – Vice Admiral Carden – to ascertain if he considers an attack by ships alone a possibility. I am obliged to report that Admiral Carden is willing to try some sort of naval assault. In the light of that, the Navy should undertake the task.'

Fisher's anger exploded.

'THIS SITUATION IS INTOLERABLE!' He turned towards Asquith, who was now wondering how to intervene. 'You see? This is a perfect example of my frustrations! A secret telegram from Carden that I am not given sight of, and decisions being made without reference to me... **AND I AM THE FIRST SEA LORD!'** He sat back, flushed with exhaustion and indignation, determined to fire a parting shot. 'And now he intends to give German submarines the perfect opportunity to sink our best dreadnoughts... by sending them to the Dardanelles.' He made a move to stand up, but Asquith placed a calming hand on his arm.

Fisher's pulse was racing. He tried to calm down. 'Even if I believed in the idea of a purely naval assault – which I do not – we have no suitable ships to send there. What we have are badly needed in the North Sea, where superiority over the German Navy must be maintained.' For the first time since entering the room, he graced Churchill with a furtive glance, making it obvious that he found the gesture painful. 'Yet you, sir, with absolutely no seagoing experience at all, are hell-bent on using the Navy to bombard Zeebrugge as well! Indeed, you want our best ships for the Dardanelles and Zeebrugge at the same time! Where are these extra warships to be found?' Having made his point, he directed the rest of his conversation at Asquith. 'I am absolutely opposed to stretching the Grand Fleet by diverting its ships. It will achieve nothing but the weakening of our strength in the North Sea.'

There had never been so much tension between these most senior men of the Admiralty. Fisher's face had turned from pale yellow to orange, but there was no stopping him now. 'May I remind you, sir... I agreed to return to the Admiralty on the understanding that the Navy would be in my hands. You, sir' – he pointed and glared at Churchill – 'brought me back here under false pretences. Never before, in the history of the Royal Navy, has there been so much ministerial interference in the day-to-day running of it. The situation is preposterous!'

Asquith knew the discussion was out of control. 'Gentlemen... gentlemen,' he said, holding up his hands in a soothing gesture. 'Let us discuss this calmly.' He sat back and thought for a moment, looking at Fisher. 'John, we clearly have an obligation of honour to the Russians... clearing a path through the Dardanelles for them. If it is humanly possible, we must do this to let them through from the Black Sea. Imagine, if we should succeed, it would allow them to get their much-needed wheat out and begin trading again. In turn, this would rescue their hard-pressed economy and make them more useful to us.' Fisher nodded impatiently – frustrated that Asquith should think he needed such an explanation. 'There is another aspect to the Dardanelles problem. As you know, Turkey is a bird that we have all plucked a feather from, from time to time, but now, Germany wants to eat the whole bird! We cannot permit this. Furthermore, our proposed activity there could draw the Turks away from our interests in the Suez Canal and our Persian oil pipeline. No, I am in favour of the campaign, and you should be aware of this. Delay could add to our problems. We must do something... and do it quickly.'

He leaned towards Fisher. 'Suppose Winston here was to shelve his aspirations for an assault on Zeebrugge ...just for the time being...

in return, shall we say, for more warships in the Dardanelles. Would you be prepared to go along with that?' He looked directly into Fisher's eyes, seeking a hint of compromise.

Fisher seemed a little calmer, and there was a glimmer of his old enthusiasm for a challenge in his eyes. The proposal would give him a minor victory in his dispute with Churchill, and went some way towards supporting his complaint about the First Lord's interference. After some thought, he announced his position. 'I think that might be an acceptable compromise, Prime Minister. Provided the Navy is not saddled with the task of shelling Zeebrugge, some dreadnoughts could perhaps be spared, to bolster up the pre-dreadnought fleet I have already earmarked for the Dardanelles. Our latest battleship, *Queen Elizabeth*, could be spared, for example.'

With great cunning, the old boy had casually volunteered the largest, most advanced warship the Navy had ever had. 'She would certainly be better employed in the Dardanelles than merely test-firing her guns into the sea at Gibraltar – as she is doing, at present – and would certainly give us a better chance of succeeding. But the moment we learn of German submarines in the area, she must be pulled back at once.'

The Prime Minister looked at Churchill for a response.

'Winston... How do you feel about that?'

There was a long pause while Churchill stared at the table. His expansive forehead pulsed with the thoughts tumbling behind it. 'Better than nothing, I suppose.' He looked at Asquith. 'Very well, I agree!'

Asquith stood up, signalling an end to the meeting. He was clearly pleased to have brought compromise and calmness to the proceedings. Fisher and Churchill picked up their papers and went into the lobby. As if having never had a disagreement in their lives, in no time at all they were sipping tea and discussing which ships should be sent to the Dardanelles. Asquith's expert diplomacy had apparently saved the day.

At the meeting of the War Council the same morning, the plan for a purely naval attack on the Turkish forts of the Dardanelles was supported warmly by Lord Kitchener, the Secretary of State for War, and the rest of the members. Asquith made it clear that he expected it to be known internationally through diplomatic channels that Britain had no desire whatever to savage Turkey or its people, and that the objective of its Dardanelles campaign was to open up the Straits for the Russians.

Fisher maintained a stony silence throughout the meeting, particularly when Churchill insisted on making his position a matter for the record. Although he favoured the joint naval and military operation that Kitchener was flatly opposing, he would pursue the alternative action by ships alone. It resulted in the outline of a plan for a naval assault on the Dardanelles being agreed and approved, for which detailed planning was to be undertaken immediately.

Fisher hastened away to see to it.

Chapter Eleven

DEVONPORT DOCKYARD
Monday, February 1, 1915

George ended his leave in low spirits; returning to *Inflexible* was not the thrill it had once been. After the excitement of the Falklands, the prospect of routine patrols in the North Sea hung about him like wet clothes. What made the end of this particular leave feel worse was his bruised ego. This was the first time he had ever been rejected by a girl he wanted, and he was sure that he really wanted Carla James. In the short time he had been going out with her he had begun to think she was the perfect girlfriend: attractive, intelligent, smart, interesting, and from a good family. More than that, she had definitely seemed keen on him. He wondered what had put her off. Now, the precious opportunity to get to know her better had gone.   Time had run out for George and all his colleagues in *Inflexible* and *Invincible,* as they dribbled back to their ships from different parts of the country. By *6:00 pm*, they were all aboard trying to get to grips with normal routines. The work of the dockyard "Mateys" was still going on, and the ships were a long way from being "shipshape and Bristol fashion". Compressed air hoses like endless snakes were still strewn about and tools were scattered everywhere. A strong smell of fresh paint hung in the air below decks.

Even to the most experienced men, it seemed impossible that the ships could be ready for sea in a week, but it was often like that with dockyard work. In the hands of dockyard workers, a ship could look like a complete wreck one day – then, on a decision made in some mysterious office somewhere, all the tools, hoses and equipment would suddenly disappear without warning and the ship would be casting off and heading out to sea. How this happened was one of the great mysteries of a sailor's life.

Lieutenant Commander William Johnson – the new Gunnery

Officer – came aboard to replace Foster. When he mustered the gun crews on the upper deck and introduced himself, the men were encouraged by what they saw. Their new "Guns" was young, fair-haired, blue-eyed and good-looking, and his attitude was relaxed but purposeful. Unlike Foster, he had a sense of humour and seemed ready to share a joke or two. More importantly, there was an air of warmth and practicality about him that the men sensed instantly.

After the meeting, the conversation in the mess was more light-hearted and positive than it had been for months. When Chief Huggett came in to post a notice, he felt it immediately, and left with the distinct impression that Johnson had already made his mark on them.

At the end of the week, all traces of dockyard workers had disappeared and normal routines were in place throughout the ship. She was coaled up, provisioned, and ready for anything the Germans could throw at her. Then, a dramatic change of orders came. *Invincible* was to proceed to Rosyth, as expected, but without *Inflexible*. George's ship was suddenly heading for the Mediterranean Sea instead. A loud cheer went up when this was announced, although the specific destination could not be given until she was well on the way to it.

At *7:00 am* on the morning of Monday, February 8, the two sister-ships left Devonport Dockyard in line ahead, and turned into the English Channel, heading westwards. When they reached Land's End, *Invincible* turned north for the Irish Sea and *Inflexible* turned south towards the Bay of Biscay. As they parted, sailors gathered on the upper decks, waving and cheering to the farewell "whoop – whoop" of the ships' foghorns.

Forty hours later, *Inflexible* was approaching the naval base at Gibraltar, after an uneventful journey along the coast of France, Portugal and Spain. When she approached Gibraltar she received the customary and traditional signal of challenge from the naval base: *WHAT SHIP?*

The Captain signalled his response: *HMS INFLEXIBLE* – then, in high spirits, added – *WHAT ROCK?*

As *Inflexible* nosed into the harbour, the scenery was dominated by the magnificently regal presence of the Navy's largest and most modern Dreadnought battleship, *HMS Queen Elizabeth*. Tied up at the largest dock, her decks bristled with heavy armament, including eight monstrous fifteen-inch guns. *Inflexible* looked more like a destroyer by comparison. George was dressed in his best uniform, standing on the upper deck with the rest of the "enter harbour" party lining the ship's guardrail. The proud interest with which they admired the new battleship's graceful lines and technical innovations was almost tangible.

There was no time for the crew to enjoy the sights of "The Rock" – only time enough to re-coal and re-provision the ship. As soon as this was completed, *Queen Elizabeth* led *Inflexible* into the Mediterranean Sea and they turned east for Malta.

In the bright late afternoon sunlight of February 13, the island of Malta came into view and the ships parted company. *Queen Elizabeth* kicked up her heels and continued majestically on her easterly course, while *Inflexible* steamed quietly into Grand Harbour between the impressive Fort St Elmo of Valetta on her starboard side and Fort Ricasoli on her port side. Small tugs busily heaved and nudged away until she was turned about and moored up to two giant buoys in the middle of the harbour. The towering sandstone structure of Fort St Angelo – the sixteenth century fortress of the Knights of St John that dominates Grand Harbour – cast a long shadow over her stern for the rest of the day.

The following morning, it was announced that there would be shore leave after coaling, as the ship was not expected to leave Malta for several days. On the mess decks, speculation was rife as to why the ship was in Malta. One rumour persisted above all others, supported as it was by the direction of *Queen Elizabeth's* departure; both ships would eventually be joining others in the eastern Mediterranean. For what purpose, no one would hazard a guess, but now the crew was not bothered by the uncertainty. It was warm and sunny in Malta, and Valetta was always a good "run ashore". Waiting here in uncertainty was never going to be a problem.

When George Royal came up on deck the following morning for his first glimpse of the island he knew well, he struggled to keep his eyes open against the unaccustomed brightness of the morning sun. He squinted up at the town of Valetta, tightly packed with white and cream-coloured buildings on the high ground directly overlooking the harbour. Huge fortress walls of massive, ancient facing blocks, hewn from yellow sandstone, rose like sheer cliffs from the quayside to the vantage point of Valetta's Upper Barracca Gardens – the small, sparsely treed area perched on top where the great Knights Templar once paraded.

In the brilliant sunlight shimmering across the blue water of the harbour, the view in any direction from the ship's deck was of the same pale yellow sandstone and cream and white buildings. For eyes straining against the glare, the only relief came from the few shadows falling across the face of Valetta's fortress walls. Even the vivid colours of the local boats were lost in the glare of sunlight reflecting from everything in sight. What appeared to be a flimsy structure was perched precariously against the fortress wall. It was the iron framework of the Barracca open public lift that provided access to the town from the quayside: an alternative to the road meandering the long way up the hill that George had often been obliged to take late at night.

Leading off from the main area of the harbour, natural creeks and inlets had long been made into quays and docks. In these, British and French ships of all shapes and sizes were tied up, with work and loading in progress. Ship's pinnaces and "dghajsas" – small, high-prowed, brightly painted Maltese water-taxis, propelled by single standing oarsmen and redolent of Venetian gondolas – were plying back and forth, leaving ripples to sparkle on the glassy water. To sailors who were largely unable to pronounce the name of these boats correctly, they were always known as "disos".

After living under the oppressive ceiling of cloud over Britain and the Atlantic Ocean, the clear Mediterranean sky looked more like awesome infinity. Whenever George was abroad somewhere sunny, the sky always seemed like that. The impression would only last a day or so, but it made everything more vivid and colourful while it lasted. As he stood at the guardrail, watching fish dart through the links of the mooring buoy's massive chain, a long way down, George was being pestered by locals as they paddled by in disos.

Weather-gnarled men with sun-tanned faces and flashing white teeth shouted up at him in Malti, trying to sell rides to the quay or strange, freshly caught fish. George waved. He knew what they were after but he had no idea what they were saying. To British sailors, any language other than English was a mystery, so it was no wonder that they never really understood Malti – a Phoenician-based language with Arabic modifications and English and Italian influences. Chalky White came up and joined him at the guardrail. 'Looks pretty good after winter at home, don't you think, George?' George smiled. 'Heard anything yet?' George shook his head.

'Nope... only the buzz going round the mess... no idea what's going on, but something is, for sure. I've got a feeling we'll see some action soon.' Chalky squinted at the bright stonework around the harbour.

'I've got a feeling in my water too, George... something's going on. There's lots of ammo coming on board.' Since joining the ship together, George and Chalky had become firm friends. Common interests and a similar attitude to life and the Navy had brought them closer together. The fact that they were both renowned magnets for young women had helped to cement their friendship. Chalky looked down into the clear water. 'I really fancy a bit of a splash in that, after coaling,' he said. 'There's a boat going over to that flat rock, a bit later. You coming?'

'Yeah... why not? But we're going to have to deal with this lot first.' George nodded towards a tug making for the ship, with a lighter in tow. Lighters – large flat-topped floating platforms for carrying goods – were being brought to the side of the ship, loaded with provisions and coal. It was going to be half a day's work to hoist aboard what was being delivered and take it below.

Later, with loading finished and everything and everybody scrubbed clean of the clinging, messy coal dust, the ship's boats ferried bathing parties to flat rocks a short distance away at one side of the harbour. Some of the men went for a swim; others went there just to get off the ship. In spite of the warm sun, the water was still chilly. As soon as they discovered how cold it was, George and Chalky opted out of swimming and chose to strip off and bask in the sun instead, relaxing on their towels and watching their cigarette smoke spiralling upwards in the still air.

George had a picture of Carla James in his mind. He was still wondering why she had finished with him so quickly, and he was turning over in his mind the last time he saw her at Bill's place. Something must have happened, he thought, when all three women were in the kitchen together. One of them must have said something – but what? And who would do that, anyway? Marje... Carrie?

'D'you ever get scared, George...like when we were in the Falklands, getting fired at?' The question popped the bubble of George's thoughts.

'Course I do... don't you, then?'

'Yeah, I bloody do. Banged up in the turret, I'm always expecting us to get hit. I get very scared.' He thought a bit longer. 'Can you imagine what it would be like... if a shell came right into the turret and exploded? We'd all be turned into soup.' It was obviously something Chalky had thought about before.

'That's the least of it, mate,' said George casually. 'At least you wouldn't know much about it. What I sometimes think about is what if the ship went over before we could get out. I do think about that, from time to time.'

'Best not to think about any of it really,' Chalky reflected dreamily. 'There's nowhere to hide, or run away to, is there?'

'You'd get strung up if you did, anyway.' George turned to look at him. 'D'you know they really shoot Army blokes in the trenches who are too scared to fight?' Chalky pulled a face. George was concerned about his friend. 'You're not really as bad as that though... are you?'

'Naah,' said Chalky quickly, shielding his eyes as he looked into the sky. 'It's just that we never talk about things like that in the mess, do we? Not that I really want to. I don't want everyone thinking I'm shit-scared. Everyone else – all the blokes with some time in, that is – just seem to get on with it. I've never seen any of them looking scared... ever. Sometimes, I wonder if I'm the only one that's shitting himself.'

George raised himself on one elbow and made eye contact with his friend. 'That's only their training at work, believe me. They're all frightened to death when we start firing. All of them ...including me, but once we get going, it's all right. There's no time to think about what might happen then – only what's got to happen. Anyway, you do the same... you never show how you're feeling either.'

Chalky smiled. 'Really?'

'Yeah, really!'

Chalky carried on thinking, then became serious again. 'I s'pose you're right, really. I'm never that scared that I can't do my job. My trouble is that I *know* I'm not going to get to the end of this lot. I've got this feeling, George, deep in my head... I'm definitely going to cop it before it's all over. Then I worry about my mum, and my little sister. With no dad now, what will it do to them?'

George rolled onto his back. 'What a lot of old cobblers! Nothing bad is going to happen to you, mate. Don't forget we're in the same turret, for God's sake! If anything happens to you, it'll happen to me as well... and I'm not having that. Listen, I'm not going to cop it, and neither are you – right? Think of all the girls we haven't even met yet!' George's attitude was just enough to snap Chalky out of his uncharacteristic melancholy. They laughed it off and carried on staring at the sky. After a few minutes of reflective thought, George felt the need to add something. 'The thing that does bother me, though, is not the thought of copping it, basically because I'm convinced that I'm indestructible.' He shrugged to show that he was being flippant. 'No, seriously, I don't think about that... it's the bloody awful feeling I get when I think about all the poor buggers that cop their lot when we're lobbing bloody great shells at them.' He sat upright, clasping his hands and draping his elbows over his knees. 'Did you see those German survivors in the Falklands? They were just the same as us, at the end of it all. What about all the poor bastards who went down then – not to mention the North Sea. Remember that sub we sank up there? They went down... just like my dad, with no chance of getting out. I mean, what's it all about, anyway? Who's got the bloody right to send us out there to kill people? And why do they want to send us to the bottom?'

'That's war, mate. I dunno what it's all about. Never think too much about it myself. We've just got to do what we're told and leave all the clever stuff to the admirals and politicians. We don't have a choice, do we?'

'Yes, I know. But if some admiral or politician came up to you in the street and said: "See that man over there? He's a bastard, go and kill him," you wouldn't just do it, would you?' Chalky showed that he thought not. 'But if that same admiral went back to his office and sent our skipper a signal to say we had to do it, that's just what we'd end up doing... because we'd been ordered to.'

'All part of your duty to your King and Country, old son... and you'd better get those ideas out of your mind, or you'll end up getting the chop, mate.' Chalky was bored with the line of conversation. 'Are we going ashore for a beer tonight, or what?'

'What I wonder about,' George went on, regardless, 'is who really makes all these decisions? How do they make up their minds about sending us, for instance, off to the Falklands to sink hundreds of bloody German sailors? It must be the same for them. I'll bet there wasn't one of them who was actually pleased about sinking my dad's ship. No – it's people right at the top who make decisions like that, and we go halfway round the world to carry out orders to kill people we've never even seen before!' Chalky was almost asleep, bored stiff. 'I'll bet it's someone who's never had to do it himself. Don't you think that's a bloody liberty?'

'Christ, George – put a sock in it! You think too much, if you ask me. It's war! – There's nothing you can do about it. You're in the Navy and you do what you're told... even if you're the bloody Admiral of the Fleet.'

George came back to earth again, wondering why he had drifted into such heavy thoughts. He felt glad he had talked about it – even if Chalky had not listened. He needed to put words to some of the thoughts that bothered him, from time to time. On the ship, there was never a time or place to do that. Something else was bothering George a lot, but he never spoke about it: what happened to Foster. It still preyed on his mind, even now, and he castigated himself repeatedly for not doing something to help Foster, whenever he thought about it. He had witnessed a murder being committed, and had chosen not to do anything about it. But he knew damn well that he should have. It was something he had to live with now – even if it plagued him all his life.

In the evenings, off-duty men with shore leave in Malta found nothing better to do than roam the narrow streets of Valetta and visit the abundant bars until the small hours. Some would inevitably come back on board the worse for wear but, if they were not a complete disgrace to their uniforms, the Marine on duty at the top of the gangway would usually allow the more sober ones to carry their inebriated mates to the messdecks to sleep it off. If they were too far gone, however, they were in for a night in the "brig" – as much for their own safety as anything else.

Ashore one evening, George and Chalky were wandering the streets of Valetta when they ended up in the "Queen Victoria" having a beer. A few minutes later, Curly Roberts and another gunner from one of *Inflexible's* midships turrets came in and sat with them. As the evening progressed and the beer went down, the conversation turned to the many tattoo shops lurking in Valetta's back streets. There was a debate about what the ideal tattoo should look like. To Curly's friend – who was a Scot, and naturally known as "Jock" – this very night seemed as good as any for fulfilling his ambition to have a large, intricate tattoo done on his left thigh. He already had some on his hands and arms – the standard "Mother" and "Brenda" on hearts – tattoos that sailors always regretted when a Sally or a Mary turned up later on but for the fiercely patriotic Jock, this one would be different. It was to be a picture of a large thistle, beneath which a ribbon banner would proudly proclaim, "Scotland the Brave". Jock had saved up for it, and he had been waiting to visit a foreign port where it would be cheap enough to have it done. 'Aye,' he and his belly full of beer announced suddenly, 'I hae tha money noo... sa noo's tha time!'

As substantial tattoos can be painful, the men clubbed together and Curly bought him a double "screech": a local spirit far removed from the product of a Scottish distillery and quite capable of blistering the tonsils. Jock downed it in one. 'Och aye!' His display of exaggerated Scottishness came as a hoarse whisper. 'I'll awa the noo to do tha tattoo!'

So, in high spirits, they headed for Strait Street, affectionately known as "The Gut", Valetta's infamous red-light district and boozing promenade highly favoured by sailors, but by the time they found a tattooist meeting his requirements, Jock was anaesthetised and wanted only to be left alone to sleep. It took Curly some time to get the Maltese tattooist to understand exactly what was required, and he had to resort to drawing sketches. Finally, the penny seemed to drop and the tattooist's face lit up. With unintelligible gestures, he assured Curly that he knew exactly what they were after. Satisfied with the way things were going, George, Curly and Chalky went back around the corner to the bar to wait for the work to be completed, leaving Jock unconscious on the seedy couch.

When they returned an hour later, they found him wide-awake, arguing furiously with the tattooist. The Malt looked decidedly aggressive and threatening.

The air in the dingy room was thick with Scottish and Maltese obscenities, and it took a few minutes for George and Chalky to calm them both down and find out what the problem was. Sheepishly, Jock dropped his trousers. They all leaned forward to admire the handiwork then collapsed in a fit of laughter. On Jock's thigh was correctly emblazoned: "Scotland the Brave". However, above that was a very good likeness of a pineapple.

To the confused tattooist, who had never seen a thistle in his life, the round prickly thing Curly had sketched for him could not have been anything other than a pineapple. So Jock now had the most unusual tattoo he could possibly wish for, and one to last a lifetime.

Finally pacified by his friends, Jock grudgingly compromised and parted with half the price of the work. The tattooist was also grudging in his acceptance but eventually agreed and Jock was carted back to the ship with the most unique tattoo in the Royal Navy burning inside his "breeks".

At the ship, confronted by the stiff Marine at the top of the gangway, they seemed destined for serious trouble – until they pulled down Jock's trousers and revealed the source of their hilarity. Fortunately, the Marine had a sense of humour, and they avoided a night in the ship's brig.

In Malta, the crew of *Inflexible* relaxed and an incongruous holiday atmosphere crept into the ship. There was still a war going on. But for this brief respite, it could be forgotten.

The ship was ready and waiting, poised for some development or another, but no one really knew what. 'The calm before the storm,' Chalky observed sagely – and he was not wrong because at the eastern end of the Mediterranean, a storm, of sorts, was definitely brewing.

THE DARDANELLES
February 19, 1915

Conscious that German submarines could arrive in the area at any time, Admiral Carden began his attack on the Turkish forts without delay. On the morning of February 19, the guns of the Royal Navy opened fire for the first time on the hilltop forts of Cape Helles and Kum Kale, situated on opposite sides of the mouth of the Dardanelles. Being the outposts that guarded the approaches to the Straits, these forts were destined to be initial targets.

The heavy guns of the battleships *Agamemnon* and *Queen Elizabeth* blasted away for hours, but it soon became clear that bombarding the Turkish gun batteries was going to be less effective and considerably more difficult than originally thought. Merely scoring hits on the forts was not enough to silence the Turkish guns; the guns themselves had to be hit precisely, if they were to be put out of action. They were, however, hidden – well entrenched inside the old fortifications, and the unexpectedly accurate return fire hampered the British gunners.

What made the situation worse for the British was that the Turks were using howitzer guns that were mobile, and so well hidden behind the hills that they were particularly difficult to locate and strike. The extreme accuracy required for hitting such small targets and without the benefit of continuous aerial reconnaissance was beyond the capability of guns rolling and pitching on the sea.

Command naivety and battle inexperience came to light very early in the British Fleet. In *"Aggie"* one morning, some men were standing in a group on the upper deck when the ship came under fire. As they scrambled for cover, the ship's Executive Officer came up and ordered them to "fall in aft" – meaning that they should line up formally on the after deck – where he proposed to organise them into a painting party for painting the ship's side. The order, exposing the men to direct fire, was not welcomed and the ridiculous folly came to an abrupt end only when a shell struck the ship, killing one of the Petty Officers involved. Before the order was given to raise anchor and move the ship out of range, the ship had been hit several times more. Painting the ship's side was mercifully deferred to a later date.

As other British and French warships arrived in the area, the attack was strengthened. Some of the forts appeared to have been silenced but the fact that they had stopped returning fire could not be taken as a guarantee that they were completely out of action. There was always the possibility that the crews had simply taken cover.

Bad weather then settled over the area to hamper the operation, and it was suspended for several days at a time. Progress was slow, and there was a continuous threat from the mines laid in the Straits by the Turks under the supervision of competent German Naval Officers.

Forcing the Straits by ships alone began to look like a prodigious and hazardous undertaking.

WAR COUNCIL MEETING, 10 DOWNING STREET, LONDON
February 26, 1915

With an aristocratic air and a stiffness of ingrained military discipline, Lord Kitchener, Asquith's Secretary of State for War, sat with his hands neatly clasped on the large Cabinet Room table. He looked younger than his 65 years, and a lifetime of Army service ran like an inflexible rod through his back and long neck. His formal stiffness extended to the very tips of his flamboyant but neat "handlebar" moustache of grey-flecked brown hair. An inch of crisp white shirt cuff emerging from the sleeves of his black morning coat displayed his gold regimental cuff links to advantage.

Whenever he addressed the Prime Minister, his clear, cold, porcelain-blue eyes stared from his brick red face and penetrated Asquith's relaxed aura with an unintentional hint of disdain. When he spoke, there was *gravitas* in his sermon-like delivery. 'Prime Minister, before long, the British Army will be forced to a standstill in Belgium, through no fault of its own. I am deeply concerned about the escalating shortage of ammunition, and I must ask, in particular, what is being done about increasing the supply of shells?'

The question had been asked before, and it put the Prime Minister firmly on the spot. In sharp contrast to Kitchener, Asquith's attitude to the discussion was more relaxed, as anyone could see from his well-filled morning suit, generous grey hair and soft posture. Seated at the centre of the long table, the Prime Minister passed a hand slowly over his face, from forehead to chin, as if that might wipe the burden of responsibility from it. Council members sat in silence around the table with their eyes fixed on him, waiting for him to speak. There was a long pause before he replied.

'Lord Kitchener, short of creating a new post for some dedicated Minister to watch over the production of shells – a Minister of War Contracts, perhaps? – it is difficult for me to see what more I can do. You see, the basic problem is that in our haste to build up your Army at the outbreak of war, we did so at the expense of our able-bodied, skilled and semi-skilled factory workers. Consequently, factory production has been set back, while demand has increased. Furthermore, your continued reluctance to provide accurate details of the Army's anticipated consumption of shells leaves us with no means of predicting its requirements.'

Kitchener's stare was ice-cold and unblinking. 'Prime Minister, I must reiterate the point that, with knowledge of an army's projected ammunition consumption, its strategy may be anticipated. Such information is to remain secret.' There was no sign of compromise in his tone. 'Nevertheless,' Kitchener went on, 'without shells, the Army cannot be expected to hold its own at the front. Consumption of shells is seriously exceeding supply and this will be a very lame excuse, should the German army overrun England. I have already informed General French that he has been wasting ammunition in France. He's far too extravagant. It isn't the men I mind. I can replace the men at once: but I can't replace the shells so easily.' Asquith was visibly disturbed by Kitchener's chilling choice of words, and gave a silent prayer that this competent, highly respected man was directing Britain's war machine – not the enemy's. Several Council members shifted uneasily in their seats, clearing their throats nervously.

'Rest assured, Lord Kitchener, that every effort is being made. I am currently looking to recruit women into the factories, as a means of increasing production, and I intend to do the rounds of the factories shortly to see for myself what more can be done. Now, may we move on to discuss the important matter of the Dardanelles?' Asquith referred to papers on the table before continuing. His earlier scepticism about the value of launching an attack on the Dardanelles had recently turned into great enthusiasm for it. 'I have quite warmed to the idea of this naval adventure,' he said. 'If we can slice Turkey in two – on a line from the Aegean Sea to Constantinople – by securing the Straits, the Turks will effectively be neutralised. We may then be able to accommodate the demands of the Russians. The Russians, as you know, are laying claim to the territory either side of the Straits, in order to ensure their safe use of them in the future. I have given this situation considerable thought and I am now convinced that we should go ahead with the campaign and apply ourselves to it with fortitude.'

Having been strongly advised on February 13 by Maurice Hankey, Secretary of the War Council – a person whose opinions Asquith respected highly – that the operation needed strong military support, Asquith felt free to add, 'However, it is my view that the success of the naval assault will depend upon strong military support.'

A wave of movement ran through the gathering, accompanied by mutters of: 'Hear, Hear!' To a man, the Council members warmly supported Asquith's views with the exception of Kitchener, who remained motionless with not a trace of what he was thinking in his expression. He waited for the chatter to die down.

'Gentlemen,' he said coldly, 'the situation in Europe remains uncertain. Russian resistance on the Eastern Front could collapse at any moment, leaving the Germans free to move more divisions towards the British Army on the Western Front. I have only one division at home – the 29th. These are the only professional regular soldiers not currently committed, and they have been specifically recalled from overseas garrisons and replaced by Territorials as reserves for Belgium. I will not send the 29th Division to Gallipoli until I am certain it will not be required elsewhere. For the time being, the Navy alone must deal with the Dardanelles. The 29th is to remain here.'

Kitchener's refusal to cooperate placed Asquith in a very difficult position, and it showed in his expression. As the Prime Minister, he held the ultimate power to overrule his Secretary of State for War, but to do this, as a politician with no military experience, would be political suicide for him. Such a bold step was bound to draw a strong reaction from every military man at the table, as well as their colleagues in the field. Asquith's natural tendency to acquiesce in the face of behaviour more dominant than his own now came to the fore. Everyone present could see that he was about to back away from this potential confrontation. He said nothing.

Fisher, who had been silent up to this point, stepped in and challenged Kitchener's obduracy head on, with Churchill and one or two others in support. 'But did you not intimate, Secretary, a few weeks ago, that you were about to liberate troops to support the Navy? Is that not why you are holding the 29th Division at home?'

Kitchener's cold eyes looked straight through him. He said, in a monotone, 'Circumstances have changed. Until I am sure of the situation in Europe, the 29th will not be committed to an assault on Gallipoli.' Voices rose, and conversations rattled across the table like trench warfare, with Asquith as a bystander. As the discussion raged on, he became detached and his concentration drifted away. With the trace of a smile on his lips, he closed his mind to the noisy conversation and began to make notes for another letter to Venetia Stanley that he would be writing the moment the meeting ended.

As soon as it was over he wrote her a blow-by-blow account of the debate that had raged before him, the characters involved, and the outcome. It took up a full page and was followed by two other long letters that same day.

Chapter Twelve

February, 1915

In England, the military elements of the Gallipoli assault force, depleted because of Kitchener's concern for the Western Front, assembled for its journey to the theatre of operations. From Poole, in Dorset, on February 27, and from Avonmouth on February 28, 60,000 men of the Marine Brigade of the Royal Naval Division embarked into transport ships and set out for Mudros Harbour on the Greek island of Lemnos. This was the designated springboard base for the assault, fifty miles from the mouth of the Dardanelles.

Among those embarking were two young Naval Division officers close to Asquith's heart: thirty-two-year-old Lieutenant Arthur Asquith, third and favourite son of the Prime Minister – affectionately known as "Oc" to his family – and twenty-eight-year-old Lieutenant Rupert Brooke, poet and close friend of the Asquiths.

The 30,000 regular soldiers of the 29th Division did not embark. They remained in their camp in the south of England.

The Prime Minister's wife, Margot, and his daughter, Violet, travelled to Poole to wave goodbye to Oc and Rupert Brooke, while Asquith found time to write another letter to Venetia.

In addition to the usual news bulletin, he wrote (of his son, Oc, and Rupert Brooke):

"... how lucky they are to escape Flanders & the trenches and be sent to the 'gorgeous East'... "©

In his increasingly frequent letters to Venetia, he was also revealing the depth of his obsession and the extent to which he depended on her.

His desperate attempts to convey just how much he loved her sat side by side on the pages he wrote with the details of what was going on in the House and War Council meetings.

January 12, 1915: *"...And you – my most dearly beloved, to whom every day & night, I give my best thoughts, my most intimate confidence, my unceasing devotion, my fears & my hopes, my strength & weakness, my past my present my future – you! What would it mean to you?*

I don't know – I can't think. All I know is that I am (whatever you may ever be) always – everywhere – wholly yours."

January 27, 1915: *"...If only I could even make you know where I put you – what you have become to me – how I love the thought of you – what the loss of you wd. mean to me of desolation & despair! Good night best beloved."*

February 23, 1915: *"...You will remain the mainspring of all my strength & happiness. I bless you, as I love you: you are everything in my life..."©*

Then on February 25, one of the longest sentences he ever wrote:

"...When I think of what I was 3 or even 2 years ago, and what I am now – of the incredible revolution in my inner life – of the way in which you have helped me over unspanned gulfs, of the inexhaustible wealth of delight which I enjoy in the sight of your face, the touch of your hand, the sound of your voice, your smile, your silence, the thought & the hope of you in absence, the infinitely greater charm of the actual reality over even the most sanguine and gold-misted dream: then I know that I would not 'change my state' – I won't say with Kings, the creatures & puppets of the day – but with 'Angels & Archangels and the whole Company of Heaven'.

Does it give you any happiness to know how much you have done & what you are? Your own."©

MALTA
February 28, 1915

Meanwhile, in the absence of any change in Kitchener's decision to keep the 29th Division at home, a signal was dispatched to *Inflexible* ordering her to depart Valetta for Mudros Harbour. All leave had been stopped in anticipation of orders, enabling the warship to leave Malta the same day. As a result of some softening of Fisher's initial reluctance to spare ships from home waters, other Naval warships were now on their way to the same destination. This change of heart at the Admiralty sprang from recent events in the North Sea that shifted the grounds on which Fisher's insistence that all of his dreadnoughts should remain in home waters was built. The incident in question was the first serious clash in home waters between British and German warships, which took place on January 25, 1915 and came to be known as the Battle of Dogger Bank. In this, ships of Vice Admiral Sir David Beatty's battlecruiser squadron took on the battlecruisers of Admiral Franz von Hipper's North Sea Fleet.

From German signals secretly decoded the day before, Beatty had been informed that a German Fleet would be 30 miles north of the Dogger Bank at 7:00 am on February 24, preparing to bombard Britain's East Coast towns of Scarborough and Hartlepool. Beatty, with five battlecruisers and four light cruisers, rushed to the spot from the Firth of Forth. At the designated point, he found four German battlecruisers, six light cruisers and twenty-two destroyers, which he engaged with the support of three light cruisers and thirty-five destroyers from Harwich.

The battle commenced just before *9:00 am*. By *12:13 pm*, it was over, with the Germans driven off but there was some cost on both sides. Beatty's flagship, *Lion*, suffered severe damage in the incident, but was saved. Of the German cruisers, *Blücher* was sunk and *Seydlitz* was crippled. 951 Germans went to their doom in the skirmish and of the British, 50 men were killed or wounded. Although this was not a magnificent victory for the Royal Navy, its outcome convinced the Admiralty that the Royal Navy already had established its superiority in the North Sea. As a result, "Their Lordships" felt more inclined to release at least some of the Grand Fleet's ships for the Dardanelles campaign.

A massive fleet of British and French warships could now be assembled in Mudros Harbour, where the 60,000 men of the Naval Division were heading, crowded into numerous transport ships. *Inflexible* arrived in Mudros Harbour on March 1 to join the seventeen other British battleships and cruisers already anchored there, with five battleships of the French Navy. Even the dear old battleship, *Canopus,* had wallowed through the Atlantic and Mediterranean Seas from her Falkland Islands base, to lend the support of her fifteen-inch guns.

On the evening of March 2, with *Inflexible* moored in the line of warships in Mudros Harbour, several of the ship's experienced and more senior gunnery ratings were rounded up by Chief Huggett for an address by the Gunnery Officer. The group of eight ratings, which included George Royal, Chalky White and Curly Roberts, filed into the after gun turret where Lieutenant Commander Johnson was waiting under the turret's harsh white lights. Johnson's tone at the meeting was relaxed and informal, until the reason for his talk became clear. A mixture of incredulity, excitement and tension passed across the assembled faces as he outlined his story.

After explaining the reason for the fleet being assembled in the Aegean, he described the Navy's objectives to knock out the guns and forts on the cliff tops above the Dardanelles, then force a way through the Straits and take Constantinople. The men listened to the problems the Navy had been experiencing during the previous weeks: no one could tell whether or not the guns had been knocked out until, perhaps, they suddenly opened fire again. 'Obviously, until we know that the guns themselves have been destroyed, and that they are definitely beyond repair, we just can't risk moving ships deeper into the Straits. If the Turks were to just keep their heads down for a few days, then pop up again after our ships had gone by, they would be able to cut our chaps off and completely bottle them up.' He paused, adding a touch of gravitas to the situation.

'Unfortunately, there is only one way to be absolutely sure the guns are put out of action... and that is to go ashore and physically deal with them.' He looked at their faces in turn. 'That is why I have called you here. Some chaps from the Marine Brigade have already been ashore there, trying to do this but the Turks caught up with them and they had to be pulled out... with some loss of life, I regret to say. On the 4th, they're going back again to tackle some of the other guns, after the fleet has given the forts a much bigger bashing ...but unfortunately the Marine Brigade has no "gun experts" left – men who know where to put charges where they will cause permanent damage.' He could see the apprehension in their faces, and he knew their thoughts had run ahead of him.

He quickly added the rest of what he had to say. 'The Captain has asked me to provide four ratings experienced in big guns, who are also qualified on explosives, to go ashore with the Marine Brigade and polish off the Turkish gun batteries, so that the main operation can get underway.' The men were hanging on his words. 'It's a very important and hazardous mission. I don't want to make light of it, or press people into this if I can avoid it. I would much prefer to have volunteers …ideally from unmarried men.' He looked at the young faces and smiled. He knew they were too young to be married. 'But no disgrace will come to anyone who doesn't volunteer. I can promise you that.'

'You can put me down, sir.' Curly Roberts's offer was startlingly immediate. The others looked at him in amazement. George glanced at Chalky with an obvious question in his eyes. Chalky nodded, and George spoke up.

'Leading Rating White and me, sir. We'll both go.'

'Splendid!' said Johnson, enthusiastically. His relief was visible.

'I just need one more.'

The rest of the men looked everywhere but at each other, trying to avoid eye contact. Eventually, a baby-faced, quiet young rating called Potter raised his arm self-consciously. 'Potter, sir. I'll go too.'

'Excellent! I knew I could count on you men. Right, you other chaps can go. You "raiders" – I just want to tell you that the Captain will know exactly who you are because he wants a word with you at 9:00 am tomorrow, on the bridge. After that, a Lieutenant of the Marine Brigade'll brief you, and then you'll be kitted out, ready for the expedition. Well done, lads. I'll see you in the morning.'

The volunteers returned to the mess and stayed in a huddle, chatting excitedly for the rest of the evening. The following morning the four men woke earlier than their messmates, pondering the task they had committed themselves to. But whatever their misgivings, these evaporated early during their meeting with Captain Phillimore. His spirited praise lifted their pride, and their apprehension gave way to a mixed bag of emotions: excitement, recognition and a sense of importance. When they left him, they were fired up to get on with the mission, and went eagerly on to the briefing.

As they listened to the details of their mission, they realised how important it was. Getting rid of the Turkish guns was the key to the success of the whole operation. If they could do this, they would save many warships and their crews from being sent to the bottom. It was more responsibility than any of them had ever shouldered before, and the idea of landing on enemy territory "behind the lines" was exciting and dangerous.

George was puzzled that Potter had put himself forward, and had some doubts about his reliability. Potter had never struck him as the volunteering type. Until now, he had been a timorous lad; apparently contented to stand in the corner of life watching other people get on with it. Why would someone like that put himself forward for such a dangerous assignment? In the end, George had to admit to himself that it was none of his business provided Potter did what was expected of him and did not put the rest of them at risk.

Potter, however, had a secret. Like many other young men caught up in the unquestioning rush to become men who fought for King and Country, he had a reason for pushing himself beyond the bounds of his own nature: a very personal one. This was his opportunity – and it had taken real courage to grasp it – to prove, just once in his life, that he was more of a man than the overbearing, bullying father who had made his youth a misery. Being a Naval gunner had not been enough. Only risking his life, or losing it, would free him from the stigma of his father's disdainful comments.

For George and his colleagues, the most important thing to come out of the briefing was immediate trusting respect for Cartwright. The young Lieutenant was tough and experienced, and he had led the similar mission just a few days before. His enthusiasm and courage were boundless, and his immense energy kept him in a state of perpetual momentum. The men were impressed by all of this, and were convinced that they were in safe hands.

The plan was for the four of them to land with the Brigade contingent, on the beach below the Kum Kale forts, on the southern side of the entrance to the Straits. They would land in the early afternoon: the time, according to Cartwright, when any Turkish soldier still alive would be at his lowest ebb after a morning of intense shelling. The ten Marines would carry rifles, ammunition and explosive charges. George and his colleagues would just carry rifles.

There was a steep bank to climb after they landed; it was approximately one hundred feet high and several hundred yards from their objective: the two forts. If they found the guns still intact, they would lay charges on them so that the resulting damage would be impossible to repair. The Marines were supposed to flush out any Turkish soldiers they found there, and protect *Inflexible's* group. As soon as the job was done, there would be a race to get back to the waiting cutters, and home to the ship. It all seemed simple and straightforward, and there were few questions from the men.

That afternoon, George, Chalky, Curly and Potter were kitted out with khaki uniforms, steel helmets, Lee Enfield .303 service rifles and bayonets. Afterwards, they practice-fired their rifles from the stern of the ship, and re-familiarised themselves with explosives and detonators. In the evening, they turned into their hammocks, to rest and sleep as best they could. Potter could not sleep at all: George and Chalky managed to sleep for a few hours, but Curly slept like a baby and had to be woken for breakfast.

In early morning on March 4, they were transferred to a fast destroyer that immediately steamed at full speed for Tenedos, another small island anchorage twelve miles from the landing point. When they arrived at Tenedos, at *10:30 am*, the weather was fine and the sea calm: perfect conditions for the landing. When they set off, the bombardment had already started.

As they approached the landing point the continuous rumble of the French and British naval guns grew louder and louder until it was difficult to make a voice heard above it. Through binoculars, Lieutenant Cartwright watched the flashes and smoke belching from the guns of *Canopus, Cornwallis* and *Swiftsure,* and the French warships *Suffren* and *Gaulois.* In salvos of twos and fours, shell after shell soared across the Straits and exploded in and around the Kum Kale forts. On the northern point of the Straits, the Cape Helles forts were receiving similar punishment.

Through the binoculars the scene looked chaotic. It seemed as if there were allied warships belching coal smoke and gunfire everywhere inside and outside the mouth of the Straits, both to the north and to the south. Shells poured into the Turkish gun emplacements, while Turkish near misses showered the ships with foaming white columns of seawater. To deprive the Turkish gunners of proper range and bearing information, the ships were constantly on the move. Small British trawlers, fitted out as minesweepers, were slowly moving deeper into the Straits, trying to clear the mines laid there. The sky was overcast with coal and gun smoke.

At *12:30 pm,* the guns of Kum Kale fell silent.

At *1:00 pm,* the destroyer carrying the landing party set off at high speed towards the coastline on the blind southern side of Kum Kale Point.

At *2:15 pm,* two cutters and a motor pinnace were lowered over the side, with the landing party and their equipment already on board. The cutters, tied together in a line behind the pinnace then headed for the beach. The deafening noise of the shells raining down on the Kum Kale forts stopped abruptly while, in the distance, the other bombardments rumbled on noisily.

As the boats neared the target beach, George could feel his whole body rocking with his thundering pulse. Although he was scared himself, he looked across at Chalky and gave a thumbs-up sign and an encouraging smile. Chalky managed a weak grin. Potter leaned over the side and vomited. In different circumstances, this would have prompted a cheerful but unsympathetic cheer, but today was ignored. Curly's chunky frame was sprawled out in the boat as if he was on an afternoon's picnic. Chalky's eyes were scouring the beach and cliff tops, looking for enemy troops that could start firing at them at any moment.

When the cutters were untied from the pinnaces their crews dropped their oars in the water and hauled for the beach with their oars. Cartwright shouted orders for last minute checks on weapons: loaded, with safety catches ON. Then, with a soft scraping noise, the boats grounded on the beach. The men quickly jumped over the side and waded thigh deep through the chilly sea and onto the shore. As quickly as they could, they ran to the foot of the cliffs while the boats pulled away from the beach and rowed for the ship.

So far, not a shot had been fired.

Cartwright gathered his men around him then set off up the 100-foot cliff, urging the group to follow. The cliff was more like a very steep hill, with plenty of wiry shrubs and outcrops to grab hold of, but it was difficult and exhausting to climb. The face of it was loose under foot and the dusty scree readily gave way. Cartwright peered cautiously over the top before beckoning his men over it. All breathless, they paused briefly to recover. George experienced an ominous sense of isolation as he glanced down and saw the destroyer making a creamy wake towards the horizon.

When Cartwright moved them on, George's legs began to feel like lead. His wet boots squelched as he walked, and his uniform trousers clung to his legs – cold, heavy and uncomfortable as they gathered layers of mud. He gave a thought for men in the Army who did this kind of thing all the time, and imagined that a noisy, smelly turret was going to seem like a much better place after this.

Half running, the men hurried on towards the forts along the undulating cliff top. As they came close to the forts, they could see the devastation caused by the bombardment. There were large craters in the ground – some still smouldering – and the substantial earth-covered brick fortifications of the old forts were severely damaged in places. Piles of earth and brick rubble covered most of the fort and it was difficult to pick out the entrances to the underground chambers where Turkish soldiers could be sheltering. The air tasted of dust and smoke. Suddenly, shots rang out and one of the leading Marines fell to the ground like a sack of potatoes.

The rest threw themselves into crevices and gullies, and began to return fire at the fort. Several more rifle shots came from the rubble-strewn gun emplacement. Cartwright decided to take four of his Marines in a wide, flanking arc to the side of the fort, leaving the rest to pin the Turks down with rifle fire. When he and his men suddenly ran at the fort from a different direction, firing their rifles and shouting at the tops of their voices, the startled Turks threw down their rifles and surrendered. They had had enough. Following the heavy bombardment, they were dazed and some were injured. There were just three of them, and they were terrified – believing they were being attacked by the whole British Army.

The bedraggled Turks were disarmed and taken prisoner.

Cartwright called the rest of the landing party forward and sent George and two of his Marines to search inside the fort. Cautiously they picked their way through the heaps of rubble and bricks in the darkness, half-crouching and with rifles at the ready. A Marine was left in charge of one group at the first fort, where Potter and Chalky began to work on the four huge guns. Cartwright detailed a second group to prepare to advance to the second fortification, two hundred yards farther along the top of the hill. Someone confirmed that the Marine who had been shot was dead, and Cartwright had to step in quickly to stop one of his men – bitterly angry about his friend's death – attacking the wide-eyed, desolate prisoners huddled together on the ground.

George and the two Marines finished searching inside the fort and emerged from the dark tunnel to report that no one else was alive there: the Turkish gunners were either dead, or had fled. There were four bodies, including that of an officer. Satisfied that he had secured the position, Cartwright split his second party and set off towards the second fort in two groups, approaching it from different directions. Cartwright had three men with him in one group; George and Curly were with two Marines in the other. They moved forward, running in short bursts and throwing themselves behind any mound they could find. At any moment, they expected to hear rifle fire and feel the stinging smack of hot lead. Covering the short distance seemed to take an age. Finally, the two groups were in sight of each other, close enough to make a final assault on the fort. It lay strangely silent.

With his men in position, Cartwright indicated that his group would make the final charge over the outer wall, while the others waited to be called forward. George was relieved at this decision, and he settled down to watch. Cartwright and his men checked their weapons and took a few deep breaths. Suddenly, they were up and rushing the fort, firing their weapons as they ran. When they reached the open gun emplacement, they leapt over the wall and disappeared from view. The sound of pistol and rifle fire continued for a few seconds – then stopped. There was an ominous silence.

Curly glanced at George and pulled his rifle to his chest, as if to make ready. 'What d'you think, Georgie? Looks like they've copped it. We'd better go up there and do our bit.'

'Hang on a minute, Curly, let's see what the Marines want to do.' George looked at the other two, who were staring intently at the embankment wall. Their instinct told them to wait.

After a few seconds, a uniformed arm with a pistol in hand appeared over the top of the embankment, waving slowly, followed cautiously by Cartwright's head and shoulders. 'Come on!' the senior Marine barked. 'Shift yer arses.' The group got to their feet and ran forward, jumping gratefully over the wall into the relative safety of the rubble-strewn floor of the emplacement.

'Right,' said Cartwright, his voice full of urgency, 'it's all clear here. There's nobody at home at all. You two... up there. Take my binoculars and keep an eye out down there for enemy troops coming up the road. You two keep watch over the cliff... make sure there aren't any coming up there. Royal... Roberts, show my lads where to put charges on these monsters.' He jerked a thumb at the two big guns, which seemed largely intact, in spite of shell craters and damage all around. George noticed how well the old forts had protected the guns from the concentrated shelling, and how few live shells he could find. George and Curly waited as the two Marines with explosives and wire wrapped around their bodies unloaded their heavy burdens onto the concrete floor. Under George and Curly's direction, they placed charges and detonators on the gun breeches and cradles, attached the fuses then ran the wires out of the emplacements and along the hilltop.

The lookouts scanned the countryside for signs of movement, and Cartwright urged the demolition team to speed up. But fifteen minutes painfully dragged by before the work was finished. As they were about to leave, George suddenly felt that he should get Cartwright to confirm the strange lack of live shells in the emplacement. The Lieutenant was initially irritated by George's suggestion and snapped a comment about urgency. But then he realised that George was trying to make a very significant point: the number of shells the Turks had left was in single figures. He searched the emplacement and counted only six shells. Then, with an overwhelming sense of relief, they evacuated the emplacement and ran towards the first fort.

At a safe distance, the Marine carrying the fuse generator box stopped and connected the two wires to it. On a nod from Cartwright, he cranked the handle and set off the charge. The thunderous roar of the explosion rolled across the countryside and an orange flash leapt forty feet into the air, carrying pieces of metal and brick with it. A cloud of smoke bellowed out in every direction and the men were blasted and peppered with shards of rubble and dust.

After the rubble stopped raining down, George tentatively raised his head to look around. He saw Curly staring at him with the whites of eyes gleaming in the mask of brown dust stuck to his sweaty face. A broad yellowy grin creased his urchin-like features. 'Cor, what a sight you are, Georgie-boy. If you 'ad your banjo now you could do a turn for us.' His brief moment of light-heartedness was cut short by the urgent tone of Cartwright's voice:

'Royal – Roberts... come with me.' He was already on his feet. 'We need to go in and to see if that worked.' George and Curly jumped up and the three of them ran to the smouldering, smoky ruins of the fort. One glance was enough. One of the gun barrels was completely off its newly twisted mounting, lying uselessly on its side and nose down in the rubble. The breech mechanism of the other gun had been blown clean away and was lying broken, some distance away. 'Right. Are you satisfied with that?' asked Cartwright.

'I think that's done the trick, sir.'

'Right, let's go. There's no time to lose.'

At the other fort there were four guns to deal with, and the work had not been finished. Curly settled down to help Potter, Chalky and the Marines rig the remaining charges and trail the fuse wires out of the emplacement, while Cartwright and George counted live shells – they could find only four.

Everyone was already in good spirits but the sight of a few blackened faces helped ease the nervous tension, as precious minutes ticked away. Seven more minutes passed before the charge laying was completed.

'Sir... enemy troops approaching, sir!'

The lookout's urgent and penetrating shout brought a rush of adrenalin to the situation. Cartwright jumped up and grabbed the binoculars. He went to the highest point and checked for himself. Turkish troops were approaching in force – some running along the road leading to the forts, behind two lorries loaded with soldiers.

Others were advancing in a line, over a small hill close to the landing party's escape route.

'Damn!' Cartwright muttered. 'The explosion must have alerted them. They're coming on in force. Come on, men, come on. We haven't much time.' He sent his four best men forward to a position where they could hold the escape route open, and the rest worked urgently to finish the work. By the time the fuse wires were connected up, the sound of rifle fire could be heard clearly above the constant rumble of the distant bombardment.

With an explosion much greater than the first, the guns of the west fort were wrecked. As the noise reached the Turkish troops, they fell to the ground, taking cover. The oncoming lorries pulled off the road and stopped, the drivers fearing shellfire. There was just time for George and Chalky to check the guns for damage before survival became the most urgent objective. As fast as they could, they ran back the way they had come, towards the beach. The Marines ahead of them were doing their best to keep the heads of the Turkish soldiers down, but there were too many of them. Bullets were zipping dangerously close to the running men.

It seemed like an eternity before they reached the gully in the cliff top, directly above their beach pickup point. They paused to catch their breath and set up covering fire for the last four men to withdraw from their precarious situation. Cartwright looked down, searching for boats. They were there, waiting faithfully, poised to make a run at the beach. The destroyer was several hundred yards out with guns trained on the cliff top.

The Captain and Gunnery Officer of the destroyer were anxiously watching through binoculars on the bridge, but they were powerless to help. To open fire then would have risked hitting the landing party.

On the cliff top, the exchange of rifle fire was intensifying, and the party's ammunition was nearly exhausted. With his men poised precariously on the edge of the cliff, and safety tantalisingly in sight, Cartwright made a rapid assessment of the situation. He decided that if he could put enough distance between his men and the Turks, the destroyer Captain might risk using his guns to hold them off. What he needed to do now was to get his men down onto the beach and keep the Turks at the top of the cliff, where they would be like sitting ducks for the destroyer's gunners. He had some explosive charges left, but not much wire. With luck, it would reach the beach.

He had his men dig the last charges under some rock then trail the wires down the cliff. He kept four men at the top with him to maintain fire on the approaching Turks, and sent the rest of his party down to the beach. Wasting no time, they launched themselves off the top in a desperate bid to reach the bottom. With no control over their reckless descent, they went sliding and scrabbling to the bottom in an avalanche of dust and loose rocks. Potter fell awkwardly as he landed on the beach, shattering an ankle. He writhed in agony, unable to get up again.

One of the four Marine rearguards left the top early. He came tumbling and slithering down the face of the cliff in a shower of stones and earth to land in a distorted heap at the bottom, followed by his rifle. His steel helmet came down a moment later and rolled to a standstill beside his body. He was dead. A bullet had entered his skull through his left eye and left with most of his brain through a gory hole in the back of his head. George winced as the body went still, close to where he was crouching, and felt his stomach turn.

The Marine with the detonator box hurriedly connected up the fuse wires and waited – his eyes fixed anxiously on the cliff top. To the Turks, who were some way back from the edge of the cliff, the cutters were out of sight, and they thought they had the British trapped.

Suddenly, rocks and earth cascaded down the cliff in a cloud of dust containing the three remaining men and Cartwright. As soon as they reached the bottom and scrambled to their feet, they all ran across the beach to the waiting boats, leaving the one man to fire the charge. Curly picked Potter up bodily, and ran with him over his shoulder, in a fireman's lift. The pinnace took the strain on the cutter's towline, ready to pull away as soon as the last man was safe.

The last Marine cranked the handle of the detonator generator then ran for his life across the beach. There was a mighty explosion and a section of the cliff top erupted into the air and tumbled down behind him. He and Curly were knocked off their feet by the avalanche of dust and rubble that billowed out from the foot of the cliff.

In the boats the men watched apprehensively. Slowly, the Marine and Curly got to their feet. The explosion startled the Turks and it interrupted their fire, giving the two men the chance to escape. They staggered towards the cutter, carrying Potter between them, as the others cheered them on. Curly responded with a grin – then fell headlong into the sand as shots cracked from the cliff top.

George looked on in horror as the Marine continued to drag Potter towards the boat, leaving Curly motionless on the beach. His eyes were fixed on Curly's body. He was sure he saw him move. Without pausing for thought, George jumped over the side. Before he realised what he was doing, he found himself wading back up the beach towards Curly. Rifle shots began to spatter the beach and the boats. As he reached Curly, the destroyer's guns opened up and shells pounded into the cliff top. Never was he so pleased to hear the sound of shellfire. It was something he would never forget: ultimate reinforcement.

Curly was alive, but barely conscious. As he crouched over him, George could see one bullet hole in the back of his jacket, with blood flooding from it. In a gargantuan final effort, he lifted Curly's solid, bulky body and dragged the dead weight down the beach. Two other men from the boats came to help, and together they heaved Curly into it. As the destroyer rained shells on the Turkish troops, the pinnace pulled the cutters away from the beach at its best speed and, after a few minutes, they were all safely out of range of the Turkish rifles. There was a supportive cheer from the destroyer's crew when the little flotilla of boats reached the safety of the seaward side of the ship. With the last of the landing party safely aboard, and the boats stowed on its deck, the destroyer kicked up its heels and steamed for Mudros Harbour. Dirty and bedraggled, the exhausted landing party collapsed on the upper deck of the destroyer, where mugs of tea and a tray of sandwiches were suddenly produced and passed around. The exhausted men closed their eyes and wallowed in the warmth of safety.

Some time later, Cartwright came up on deck and sat down to share his cigarettes with them. He was full of praise and genuine respect for them. 'Well done. You did a great job out there today. I'm proud of you all. We really put those bloody forts out of action... now you'll see what a difference it makes. Our chaps will be able to move up the Straits in safety now... thanks to you.' He turned to George. 'Royal, what you did on the beach there was extremely foolish... but bloody brave. I take my hat off to you. You've really got what it takes to do this kind of thing all the time.' A wide grin creased his grubby face when he saw George's expression. 'Only joking, Royal... only joking.'

His smile faded as his expression became serious. 'About those shells... I think you're right, you know. The bloody Turks are definitely running out of ammo!'

'That's what I thought, sir. They couldn't have carted them off – there wasn't time. Not only that, but they would be too heavy to move quickly.'

'But do you understand the significance of this?'

George shook his head. 'Only that they won't be able to keep up return fire.'

'Precisely! But if that's true it puts a whole new perspective on the Navy's job of forcing the Straits. It means that if you boys keep on with your bombardment, you'll soon be able to waltz up to Constantinople and take it with no resistance.' His eyes sparkled with excitement. 'I must report this as soon as we get back – and I'd like you to do the same. Christ! If we're right, it could change the whole strategy of the campaign. It's *very* significant.'

They sat on the deck of the destroyer staring reflectively into space for a while before Cartwright spoke again. 'Christ, I'm really sorry about those poor chaps we left out there. Bloody good Marines, they were – bloody fine chaps. I wish we could have brought them back, at least – but you could see yourself, there was no chance of that.' He seemed to need some moral support for losing two men. It was obviously something he genuinely felt bad about. 'But I'm really sorry about Roberts getting hit... let's hope he'll be all right. The Medical Officer's got him down below, in the sickbay. He'll have a lot to thank you for, if he wakes up.'

The journey back to Mudros Harbour was going to take nearly three hours, and exhaustion quickly got the better of the landing party. Like a litter of puppies in a basket, they fell asleep on each other in a tangle of limbs, bodies and equipment, and took no further interest in what was going on.

An hour later, George was shaken awake. It was a much-refreshed Cartwright, with a grin on his freshly scrubbed face. 'Your mate Roberts... it looks like he's going to be all right. He's asking for the stupid sod who saved him.' George grinned and woke Chalky with the news.

'He's obviously back on form already, if he's talking like that,' he said. We'd better go and see him.'

In the sick bay they found Curly sedated and only able to speak in hoarse whispers. The bullet in his back had missed the vital organs and had come out through his chest, collapsing one of his lungs. He managed a weak smile when he saw them, and beckoned George to put his ear close to his mouth. 'You stupid sod,' he croaked. 'You'll get yourself hurt doing things like that. But thank you, mate. I won't forget what you did.'

'Aah... I only did what you were doing for young Potter – and I already owed you a big one, don't forget. Anyway, we couldn't leave you there for the Turks to have their evil way with you, could we? They certainly wouldn't know what to make of you! So you'll be off to hospital now, for a good loaf. Back to "Blighty", I shouldn't wonder.' They had a few words with Potter, in the next bunk with his leg and ankle bandaged up. Although he was in a lot of pain, he had a strange little smile on his face and he chattered away like they had never heard him before. When they went back on deck, George commented to Chalky how different Potter seemed.

'Yeah, I noticed that,' Chalky mused. 'Must be some drug they've given him.'

They spent the rest of the journey back to Mudros talking about the day's mission. Chalky said it was strange but he had not felt at all afraid once they were on the beach and running. They both confessed to getting a real charge of excitement from it, and they felt proud of themselves and perhaps a bit self-satisfied. 'But I'll tell you one thing, George,' said Chalky with a twinkle in his eye, 'I don't think much of Turkey as a run ashore. I can't think why we're slogging our guts out for it.'

Chapter Thirteen

THE DARDANELLES
March 5, 1915

George relayed Cartwright's message to Johnson about the Turks being short of shells. Johnson took it seriously and immediately wrote a report for Captain Phillimore. The same day, the report was signalled to Vice Admiral Carden to be received by his Flag Lieutenant. Cartwright, meanwhile, was trying to get an appointment with the Admiral to report personally the outcome of his mission, and to impress upon him the importance of the Turkish shell shortage.

The Admiral was far too busy with more pressing matters to see Cartwright, but he did consider his news, relayed to him by the Flag Lieutenant, and the report from Captain Phillimore, and kept it in mind. However, his main area of concern this day was the enormous naval bombardment that was about to begin.

By indirect fire across the Gallipoli peninsula, the Navy's largest battleship, *Queen Elizabeth,* supported by *Inflexible* and *Prince George,* began attacking the forts of the Narrows twelve and a half miles into the Straits, with aircraft of the Naval Air Service spotting for them and guiding their fire. Heavy damage was inflicted on the Turkish gun batteries.

Queen Elizabeth, Agamemnon and *Ocean* continued the indirect attack on March 6 and 7, while several warships launched a direct attack from inside the Straits. Following this prolonged offensive, it was believed that the Turkish forts had been finally "silenced". Almost all of the ships involved in the attack were themselves hit by howitzer and other large-calibre shells – some as substantial as twelve inches – but none sustained damage that was crippling.

Only the British light cruiser *Amethyst*, covering the small vessels that were dredging the straits for mines, was badly hit. A howitzer shell plunged through her deck and exploded in her stokehold, killing twenty men and injuring several others. Although severely damaged, she survived the incident.

Then, on the night of March 8, a hitherto insignificant little Turkish vessel ventured into the Straits and unleashed a chain of events that would ultimately affect the lives of thousands, and alter the course of history. The vessel, the *Nusrat*, was a mere 380 tons – one seventieth of *Queen Elizabeth's* 27,000 tons – but the successful completion of her mission changed everything.

Unnoticed, *Nusrat* laid twenty mines inside the Straits in a three-thousand-yard string along the line of the current, in the area used in the daylight hours by the bombarding ships. The mines were set at a depth that only the keels of battleships could reach.

With the guidance of the German officers helping them, the Turks also cast a number of floating mines adrift farther up the Straits, so that they would drift down on the prevailing current to ships anchoring in the mouth of the Straits or steaming up them. When they ran out of Turkish mines, they recycled others similarly drifted down on them by the Russians, farther upstream in the Black Sea.

The efforts of the civilian dredgers to clear the Straits of mines continued but, as Fate would have it, they failed to find those sown by *Nusrat*. As all other action was suspended for ten days, on direct instructions from the War Office, no battleships entered the Straits until March 18.

Vice Admiral Carden, incapacitated by ill health, relinquished his command of the fleet and was retired to Malta on March 16, to be succeeded by Rear Admiral J M de Robeck in the local rank of Vice Admiral. Among the many threads de Robeck had to pick up during the hurried handover of command – one that slipped through his fingers – was Cartwright's report on the Turkish shell shortage. The Admiral's Flag Lieutenant glanced at it before putting it aside – making a cynical mental note that there had been no evidence of Turkish ammunition shortages during the earlier bombardment a few days ago – then dismissed it as a fantasy not worthy of the Admiral's attention.

Under de Robeck, a plan for much wider and more decisive action was hatched. It was to be executed as soon as the newly appointed Supreme Commander of the Allied Expedition in Gallipoli, General Sir Ian Hamilton, reached Tenedos from England.

On March 16, the 29th Division, finally released by Kitchener, left England in transport ships, bound for Mudros Harbour and Alexandria. In accordance with Lord Kitchener's instructions, General Hamilton, the 62-year-old Colonel of the Gordon Highlanders, hurried out from England to observe the next Naval offensive. His mission was to survey the area in readiness for the proposed landing on Gallipoli of the forces being assembled under his command.

By catching a fast train from Charing Cross Station, London, at 5:00 pm on Saturday, March 13, then boarding a 30-knot cruiser from Marseilles, Hamilton and his party arrived at Mudros Harbour on the night of Tuesday, March 16.

March 18, 1915

News was received that *Dresden,* the only German cruiser of von Spee's fleet to have fled successfully the battle of the Falkland Islands, had been caught. On March 14, near Juan Fernandez Island, the British cruisers *Glasgow* and *Kent,* and the auxiliary cruiser *Orama,* trapped her and engaged her in a brief action. After only five minutes, the German ship hauled down her colours and her crew sought safety ashore in Chile, where they were interned until the war ended. Having been set on fire in the action, the ship's magazine exploded and she went to the bottom.

There was a loud cheer from *Inflexible's* crew when the sinking of *Dresden* was announced.

That day, a mighty fleet of thirteen British battleships, including *Inflexible,* and four French battleships, left Tenedos shortly after *8:00 am* to take up their planned positions inside the Dardanelles. On board de Robeck's flagship, *Queen Mary,* General Hamilton and his party were ready to observe and make notes on the operation.

In *Inflexible,* the day started with a good breakfast, followed by Divisions and Prayers at *9:15 am.* Lieutenant Commander Johnson, "Guns" of the ship, held a meeting of his gun crews on the foredeck, and briefed them on the day's overall plan of action. This was to be a redoubled effort to knock out the Turkish forts, some twelve and a half miles along the Straits, and force a way through the Narrows past Chanak and Kilid Bahr.

After the briefing, the men collected their packed lunches from the galley and closed up for duty. George and his crew climbed into the forward turret, donned their anti-flash gear and inserted their earplugs ready for action. Missing from the crew was Curly Roberts – now on a hospital ship bound for Malta – and another seaman was being trained as a shell loader in his place.

As the ship passed the Kum Kale point, led by *"Aggie"*, George looked up at the forts where he had seen action fourteen days before. It gave him a strange feeling to be viewing them from a new perspective. On the hills, the Turkish officers in charge of the gun batteries looked down in amazement as the huge fleet came towards them; they had never seen such a gathering of warships before. Realising that they were facing an out-and-out battle, they hurried to complete their supplies and prepare themselves for the coming conflict, but their stock of ammunition was running low.

From the flashes, smoke and dull booms of howitzer fire coming from points along the hill tops, the British were aware that the Turks were still there in force, determined to defend their country to the end. Howitzers are unlike other guns. They are designed to fire shells on a much higher trajectory, so that they arrive at their targets falling almost vertically. For the ships, the upper decks were the most vulnerable parts and howitzer shells posed a very serious threat. As the ships moved farther and farther into the Straits, the waterspouts of exploding shells started to leap up all around them.

At *10:00 am*, against the growing rumble of Turkish shellfire, the ships slowed and stopped to launch the attack. Their guns were loaded and trained on the range and bearing information passed from their control positions. At *10:45 am*, Johnson relayed the order: *"FIRE"*, and *Inflexible's* guns roared into life in company with those of the other ships. Shells began to pound the forts, and the Turks returned fire that was heavy and accurate.

The bombardment of both banks of the Straits raged on for one and-a-half hours until the forts fell silent. Some of them were blazing, and it was thought that the Turkish gunners would be forced to withdraw by such a heavy attack. Now it was time for some of the attacking battleships to move forward and close up within eight thousand yards of their targets, to finish them off with greater precision. As planned, at *12.15 pm* the French battleships passed forward through the lines of British ships, and moved in closer to the forts. In *Inflexible,* the gunners worked feverishly to keep up a high rate of fire.

At *12:20 pm, Inflexible* was suddenly shaken from stem to stern by a shell exploding just behind the bridge. Somewhere behind the hilltops, out of sight, at least one of the Turkish howitzer teams now had the ship in their sights, and had found her range. Three minutes later, there were three more deafening explosions as more shells struck home. One of them landed on her starboard amidships turret, killing two gunners and wounding four. Above the ship, another shell burst, killing the lookouts and range finders. Communication to the foretop and bridge was cut off abruptly and fires broke out in the superstructure and various other parts of the ship. The Captain had no alternative. He was obliged to withdraw his ship from the action to fight the fires.

George, Chalky White and the forward turret crew emerged into the chaos raging on the deck, to lend a hand to fight fires and tend the wounded. The damaged amidships turret was completely out of action. They grabbed a hose and tackled the flames creeping out from under the damaged turret. When the fire was out and the smoke had cleared, they climbed inside it with two other seamen. This would have been Potter's place of duty, had he been fit.

Inside, it was pitch black; the only available light came through the open doorway. In the hazy gloom in the turret, they clambered over the twisted pipework to find the last two members of the crew sprawled grotesquely against the far side of the turret. Their clothing was smouldering and partly torn away by the blast. The mingled stench of cordite and burning flesh made Chalky retch. They reluctantly felt the charred and melted flesh, searching for pulses, but found none. As they manhandled the smouldering corpses through the doorway and laid them on the deck, they both kept their gazes anywhere but on the bodies. Chalky glanced nervously at George. Neither of them could hide the utter revulsion they felt. They gasped and filled their lungs with air once they were outside the turret. It was not fresh; it was smoky, but at least it did not have the smell of dead comrades in it.

'Christ... what a mess! Young Potter will wet himself when he finds out that only his daring exploits ashore saved him from dying like this.' George felt a compulsion to take one hard look at his mangled and blackened comrades. As he did, he saw something that turned his stomach over. It was the tattoo of a pineapple and "Scotland the Brave" still visible on the ragged remains of one of the legs. George went to the side of the ship and was violently sick until his eyes streamed.

The attack farther up the Straits was now being pressed home. Manoeuvring into position, the advancing French ships began their bombardment but they were subjected to severe and deadly shellfire for the whole period of their attack. When their allotted time was over, other ships moved forward to relieve them and the French battleships turned, as planned, and hastened back down the Straits at full speed to rejoin the main line of British ships.

As *Bouvet* steamed towards *Inflexible*, a muffled explosion came from inside the French ship and a sheet of orange flame erupted from her forward gun turret. She had struck one of *Nusrat's* mines. Another, much larger explosion immediately followed as one of her magazines ignited. A cloud of yellow and black smoke poured from her midships section, and she listed to starboard, lower in the water. There was no time to stop her engines, or to slow her down. With her propellers thrashing uselessly in the air, she heeled over and capsized at full speed. The crews of other ships watched helplessly as the upturned French battleship speared into the sea and disappeared below the surface. She went within ninety seconds, taking almost every member of her crew with her.

It was *2:00 pm.*

The exchange of fire between the British and Turkish guns raged on for another two hours, but a growing realisation gripped the hearts of the men who could see what was going on: events were turning against the Allies.

At *2:30 pm*, *Inflexible*, her fires extinguished and with some communication with her bridge restored, returned to the action.

Above the Straits, the air was now thick with shells hissing and whining in both directions. The sea was alive with the wash and spouts of the shells exploding around the ships, and the hilltops were hazy with the dust and smoke of exploding British shells. The scene was chaotic. It was the picture of hell that every fighting man carried at the back of his mind.

The gunners in the forward turret of *Inflexible* were exhausted. Their ears were singing with the noise of their own guns, and their eyes were watering from the stinging cordite fumes. The small oval areas of their faces left exposed by their blackened anti-flash hoods – their noses, mouths and eye sockets – were getting blacker by the minute. They were thirsty and longed to eat their packed lunches, but there was no time for that.

At *3:00 pm*, the Dreadnought *Irresistible* was badly damaged by shellfire. Her foretop was smashed to pieces and every man but one there was killed instantly. Soon after, another shell exploded on her forward bridge starting a fire. She carried on firing her twelve-inch guns, with smoke and flames still billowing from her superstructure.

In *Inflexible,* a huge thud reverberated through the hull at *3:45 pm*, as one of *Nusrat's* drifting mines exploded on her bows. To the men inside the forward turret, it felt as if the turret had been lifted bodily out of its mounting by the explosion, then slammed back down again. The dazed crew stopped firing and waited for the order to abandon ship. It was several minutes before Chief Huggett heard over the telephone line that the mine had not penetrated the hull. The men were ordered to carry on with their duties. Shaken, but still willing, they reloaded and kept firing.

At *4:09 pm*, there was another violent explosion as a second floating mine found *Inflexible's* hull, punching a jagged hole thirty feet square in her bows. Water gushed into the ship and filled twenty compartments instantly. Twenty-nine men in the flooded area fought for their lives as the sea rushed in on them. For them, there was no way out. Trapped by tightly clipped watertight doors, they drowned one by one, as what little air they had in their lungs gave out.

When the mine exploded, it lifted the ship's bows by several feet. Then, with the sea pouring in she settled lower in the water. George, Chief Huggett and one or two others were thrown onto the turret deck, but were not seriously injured. The lights went out and dust and flakes of loosened paint showered down on them. The Chief got to his feet and shouted at them to evacuate the turret and stand by for further orders. Blinking in the harsh daylight, the gunners tumbled out onto the deck and ran aft to their positions for abandoning ship.

Down below, all lighting and ventilation had failed. In the total darkness of the engine-room, where the telegraph was ringing the message from the bridge: *"Half Ahead"*, dim secondary oil lamps were lit and the engineers carried on. The ship, with her bows low in the water and listing to starboard, made for the entrance to the Straits and away from the action.

At *4:13 pm*, another floating mine struck the other stricken ship, *Irresistible,* exploding in a huge fountain of spray and a deafening roar. She immediately began to dip her bows into the sea and list to starboard. The forty men trapped inside her were already dead before the ship headed for shallow water to beach herself.

Around both ships the scene was chaotic. Men were swimming frantically and clinging to floating debris. Drifting tables and chairs and pieces of loose equipment surrounded the ship's cutters laden with survivors. Braving the continuous cascade of Turkish shells, two British destroyers deftly came alongside the sinking ships and took off their helpless crews.

With no sign of its imminent arrival, a Turkish shell suddenly exploded in the middle of *Irresistible's* quarterdeck where the men had been ordered to wait patiently to be rescued. Although several were killed or injured, there was no panic. The men continued to wait quietly, as best they could. One entire watch of the crews of *Inflexible* and *Irresistible* – half their total complement – was taken off by the destroyers. A decision had been made somewhere that the rest of the men would remain on board to try to get the ships safely to Mudros Harbour. George was thankful to find himself on a destroyer, once again, heading for safety. He looked back at his "home", not knowing if she would survive the night.

At *6:05 pm*, the signal flags *"GENERAL RECALL"* were hoisted, ordering a complete withdrawal of the fleet from the ill-fated expedition. All battleships turned to withdraw, covered by the long-range heavy bombardment of *Queen Elizabeth,* but at *6:30 pm*, the battleship *Ocean* struck a floating mine.

Within minutes she was listing heavily and sending out distress signals. Although holed herself, she took *Irresistible* in tow and limped towards Tenedos. The badly damaged fleet headed for Mudros Harbour with its tail between its legs, counting the cost.

The most serious losses were in the French fleet. *Bouvet* had gone down early in the bombardment. *Gaulois,* another battleship, was so badly damaged that only beaching saved her from sinking and *Charlemagne* was badly damaged by shellfire.

For the British, the losses seemed catastrophic: *Ocean* and *Irresistible* were both mined and slowly settling in the water. *Agamemnon* and *Albion* were severely damaged by shellfire. *Inflexible* had been mined twice and badly damaged by shell-fire.

Ocean and *Irresistible* did not survive. In the night, the last men had to be taken off, and both ships slowly went to the bottom in deep water.

LONDON
March 18, 1915

As shells flew thick and fast in the chaos of the Dardanelles, love letters were flying thick and fast in London to mark the gathering storm in the Prime Minister's personal life.

At the London Hospital, Venetia Stanley wrote a short letter to Edwin Montagu, which she had begun with a *"Dearest"* salutation. In her letter, she described the pleasure she had had from spending the previous day with him, and stated how much she wanted to receive letters from him.

Recently, new warmth had entered their relationship and their letters were now more affectionate than ever before. Montagu was now even bold enough to begin his letters to her with *"My very dearest"*, and he was greatly encouraged by the warmth and recognition she now bestowed upon him. At last, there seemed to be light at the end of the tunnel of his love. The same day, a long handwritten letter to Venetia from Asquith described his day in great detail. After recalling what happened at the dinner and Bridge evening he had shared with guests the night before, he went on to describe his recent hour-long conversation with the King and the details of his morning meeting with Lord Kitchener.

During this meeting, he recalled, Kitchener had said how distressed he was by the *"way in which our men had expended their ammunition, particularly shells, last week"©*. He wrote that Kitchener had also shown him "a very interesting telegram" from Ian Hamilton, who was already in the Dardanelles. It concluded that the Admiralty had been "over-sanguine" as to what they could do by ships alone, adding that the Turks and Germans had been able to repair their fortifications every night. Furthermore, this telegram suggested, both coasts of the Straits bristled with howitzers and larger guns in concealed emplacements, and the channel was sown with complicated and constantly renewed minefields. Asquith ended his letter to Venetia: *"I never loved or needed you more"©*.

THE DARDANELLES
Sunday, March 21, 1915

In the Dardanelles, a very difficult decision was taxing the Supreme Commander of the Gallipoli campaign.

Lord Kitchener's instructions to Sir Ian Hamilton had been explicit: a landing on Gallipoli by the Army was not to be undertaken until all of the forces placed at Hamilton's disposal had been assembled and properly prepared. Even then, the attack was not to be launched until the Navy had successfully demolished the Turkish gun batteries commanding the Straits.

Following the disastrous bombardment of March 18, Hamilton and de Robeck now faced far-reaching decisions that, in the normal course of events, should have been the War Council's responsibility to make. Should there be a further attempt by the Navy alone to force a passage through the Straits? Should the next attempt be a combined effort by the Army and the Navy? If the Army was to land, how and where was this to happen?

Having himself committed the Navy to forcing the Straits, Churchill, in London, was as keen as ever that the Navy should see it through. Kitchener was expecting to see a more decisive result from the Navy before committing his one remaining Army division.

Meanwhile, First Sea Lord Jacky Fisher continued to express his serious misgivings about a purely naval assault. Everything now hinged upon the new Supreme Commander's decision.

Hamilton's "scientific survey" of the campaign area, upon which crucial decisions involving tens of thousands of men now had to be made, was an amazingly flimsy document. In the absence of proper reconnaissance, it was put together from what he had seen through his binoculars from the bridge of *Queen Mary*, and the only maps he had brought from England with him: the travel maps of the 1908 Baedeker Guide to Constantinople and Asia Minor.

Based on a binocular view of the beaches, and information from his holiday guide book, Hamilton's three day "survey" seemed hardly adequate for the momentous decisions he was about to make. From the Allies' perspective, the events of March 18 presented a bleak picture of the Navy's ability to force the Straits by itself – unless appalling losses were to be accepted. On the single day of action so far, 650 men had been lost, together with three capital ships sunk and four seriously damaged. On the other hand, three fully crewed replacement ships were on their way and, apart from the appalling and tragic loss of the French battleship *Bouvet* with 600 of her men, in terms of men – by far the greatest asset – the Royal Navy had only lost fifty in the action.

Convinced that a further unassisted attack by the Navy would not succeed, de Robeck telegraphed Churchill on March 21 to report that he intended not to launch a further bombardment until the Army was ready to land troops. This was expected to be mid-April.

General Hamilton had realised that the lack of suitable beaches in the area meant that he could not risk a piecemeal assault. Instead, he believed, his only chance of success was to fling the whole of his available forces ashore at once, and to make feint landings elsewhere at the same time. Unfortunately, the embarkation of his troops in transports had not been carried out with this in mind, and a complete reorganisation was needed. As the facilities at Mudros were inadequate for this purpose, he decided to put his entire Army ashore at the Egyptian base of Alexandria, in order to regroup and plan for the landings. As if to provide justification for the delay, bad weather then settled over the area.

Asquith and Churchill, Asquith's advisor in such matters, were both dismayed by de Robeck's decision not to launch more attacks until the Army was ready. Churchill, with great prescience, wanted to force another attack. He, in particular, was convinced that one more immediate attack by the Navy would do the job. He was now very concerned – having personally committed the Navy to this action – that if it was seen to fail, his reputation and political career would suffer a disastrous setback. Additionally, he feared that the Conservatives in opposition could be expected to seize it as a means of forcing him out of office in revenge for deserting their party for the Liberals some years earlier.

As much as they wanted to, neither Churchill nor Asquith could force de Robeck to undertake another attack when it was his formally reported decision not to do so. De Robeck was, after all, the "Admiral on the Spot" and interference with the decision of an officer in this position was unprecedented, and would certainly have resulted in Jacky Fisher's immediate resignation. The result was that there was no second attack by the Navy and all action was suspended until mid-April. Asquith and Churchill were left frustrated.

Churchill, who was apt to give nicknames to certain people in his conversations with friends – particularly those who disappointed him – began to refer to de Robeck as "Admiral Rowback".

By a quirk of Fate, Churchill's instinct to attack once more had been right. If one more attack had been made immediately it would have surely succeeded because, as the British and French Fleets were aborting their bombardment on the evening of March 18, the Turks were on the brink of running out of ammunition, shells in particular, and their resistance was close to collapse. For their mobile howitzers – the guns inflicting the most damage on warships – they had few shells left, and could do nothing about their shortage. Additionally, their forts and gun batteries were severely damaged.

On March 18, the Allies therefore came within hours – if not minutes – of breaking the back of Turkish resistance and forcing a passage through the Straits. The Russians had picked up radio intelligence to this effect, some days earlier and, as a gesture of goodwill towards Churchill, had passed the information to him but he was unable to convince de Robeck of its validity.

Although Churchill was right to believe that one more immediate attack would have brought success, he did not have the authority to order it. Control over the decisions about to be made was unfortunately not his to exercise.

MUDROS HARBOUR
March 23, 1915

Although badly crippled, *Inflexible* succeeded in reaching Tenedos, where she anchored in shallow water. An inspection revealed huge damage to her hull. Temporary repairs were carried out, and she limped slowly off to Mudros to have a cofferdam placed over the gaping hole. This watertight "patch repair" permitted the flooded compartments to be pumped dry, and preparations were made to escort her on a slow journey to Malta for further temporary repairs.

For George and his *Inflexible* shipmates, the battle was over for the time being. After a few days of further hardship being accommodated in a makeshift, tented Army camp on the sandy slopes overlooking Mudros Harbour, they were allowed back on the ship for one last chance to recover what was left of their personal effects and uniforms, before she set off for Malta.

George was lucky. His mess deck had been untouched by shells and mines, and he was able to retrieve all his kit but many of the men had lost everything; all they owned had either been blown away or submerged in seawater.

The men were downhearted about losing their ship. It had been their home, and now they were to be sent back without her, not knowing what was in store for them – apart from the inevitable period of "survivor's" leave. The officers had been given makeshift accommodation on several other ships anchored in the harbour, and routine organisation went by the board.

The wounded men were transferred to hospital ships, and the dead were committed to the sea. A memorial service on the foredeck of the flagship was arranged for Sunday March 28. For this, Lieutenant Commander Johnson sent small sealed envelopes to George and Chalky, the day before. The notes told them to dress as smartly as the remains of their kit would permit, and to stand in the front rank of the crews of *Queen Elizabeth* and *Inflexible* when they massed for the service. A citation about their Turkish exploit was to be read out.

After the service on Sunday morning, the Executive Officer of the flagship stepped forward and read out the citation:

"On March 4, 1915, a most hazardous cutting-out expedition was carried out by men of the Royal Naval Brigade and the Royal Navy, on Turkish fortifications at Kum Kale.

With supreme courage, and in the best tradition of the Royal Navy, Leading Seamen George Royal and Arthur White, and Able Seamen John Roberts and Edward Potter volunteered to accompany and assist the men of the Naval Brigade in an effort to destroy enemy gun emplacements.

The fact that the operation was a complete success was in no small part due to the expert knowledge, skill and bravery brought to the task by the men of this small Royal Naval contingent.

I commend them most highly, and have the utmost pleasure in announcing the accelerated promotion of Roberts and Potter to the rank of Leading Seaman, and Royal and White to Petty Officer.

Their promotion is to be confirmed by Captain Phillimore at the Captain's Table at 9:00 am, March 29, 1915.

Signed this twenty-fourth day of March, 1915 Vice Admiral J.M. de Robeck, Royal Navy."

When caps were raised for the traditional "three cheers", George found a lump in his throat that he could not swallow. He felt extremely proud, and would have given anything to have his father there, watching his first moment of recognition.

The following day, the promotions were confirmed for George and Chalky. Lieutenant Commander Johnson who, with Cartwright, had put forward the recommendations, shook their hands warmly. Lieutenant Parker, the Supply Officer who had befriended George, was at the Table with one of his own ratings. Afterwards, he found George and offered his congratulations. He was full of praise for him and said with great sincerity, 'Your father would have been extremely proud of you.' It made George feel that Jack was not that far away after all.

Trained crews in the Royal Navy have always been more highly valued than the ships they sail in. Being sorely needed now, every experienced sailor stranded in Mudros without a ship was sent home as soon as transport was available. In groups – some large, some small – the men were given passage in any ships returning home.

On Thursday, April 1, George and Chalky, with their new Petty Officers' "crossed-anchor" badges roughly but proudly sewn to the arms of their tunics, were visiting the makeshift transit control office, searching for their own names on the notice board. This would tell them when, and by what means, they were going home – but they were not on any list. Puzzled, they brought this to the attention of the Writer behind the desk.   He shuffled papers and scanned his lists, but all he could find against their names was "Special Complement". It meant as little to him as it did to them. He went away to speak to the Master at Arms.

While he was absent, George turned the page round to see if he could make any sense of "Special Complement" – but he could not. However, Chalky could never resist ribbing his friend. 'I always knew I was special, George... but if they've got you on the same list as me, there must be something wrong.'

'Ha bloody ha,' replied George.

The Writer returned to his desk. 'Well, gentlemen, "Special Complement" means that you belong to a Lieutenant Cartwright of the Naval Brigade. Here are your discharge papers from your old ship,' he looked at his list, '*Inflexible,* wasn't it? And your authorisation for detachment to Lieutenant Cartwright.'

George and Chalky wandered out of the tent thoroughly confused. 'What the hell is this?' said Chalky, scratching his head.

George read on. 'It says here that the "SC", as we are now known, has its headquarters in Tent 32A. Let's go and find it.'

The pair walked up and down the rows of tents until they got their bearings, but there was no Tent 32A. Finally, a passing sailor pointed out a small hut to them, standing on its own, behind Tent 32. The door was open. Inside, Cartwright was sitting at a homemade desk, studying a hand drawn map of the Turkish coastline. He had two men in Marine uniforms with him.

He was genuinely pleased to see them. 'Ah, my two new Petty Officers. Come in, chaps, come in. Nice to see you again.' He noticed the confused look on their faces. 'Have you been briefed?'

'Briefed, sir?' said George, puzzled. 'We haven't been told anything!' A look of frustration passed over Cartwright's face.

'Oh, for God's sake! You should have been briefed on this little unit of mine – "SC", and you should have signed a form volunteering for it. I thought you would jump at the chance.'

George explained that none of this had happened, and they had no idea what they were in for. Cartwright went into detail. Admiral de Robeck had recently agreed with Cartwright's suggestion that there was a temporary need for a small unit of men, led by a Naval Brigade Officer, to carry out certain operations falling into the gap between the Army's and the Navy's responsibilities. This had arisen because of the extraordinary level of cooperation that would be required for a very big combined forces operation now being planned. All the men of the unit had been hand-picked, and were volunteers.

Because George and Chalky had acquitted themselves so well in their recent attachment to Cartwright, he said he assumed they would be pleased to be part of the new unit. So, weren't they? Anxious to get home for some leave and for their Petty Officers' training course, George and Chalky wanted to know how long the attachment would be. About four weeks, they were told, then it would be over and they could go home. They thought about it for a few moments, looked at one another then signed up as "volunteers".

Cartwright was pleased and introduced them to two other members of the unit, the Marines with him. Over the following days, they were kitted out with special outfits with the letters "SC" stitched into the shoulders of their tunics, rifles, knives, torches, packs and other equipment, and they did some arduous field training together – frequently in the middle of the night.

A drill instructor brushed up their handling of their weapons, and endeavoured to knock the "sloppiness" out of them. The man's back was a straight line from the back of his peaked cap to the heel of his boots, and the yardstick he tucked under his arm as he strutted about formed a perfect parallel with the ground he walked on. When looking anywhere above their navels from beneath the near vertical peak of his cap, his head tipped backwards, presenting a substantial military moustache like a yard broom. Years of shouting orders had given him a gruff, grating voice, and he spoke in monosyllabic barks.

He made a particularly large issue out of the order "Fix Bayonets" – the simple business of pulling the weapon from a waistband scabbard and fixing it to the rifle barrel. 'Rieeght, men,' he barked. 'The order "Fix Bayonets". This is a two-part order – "Fix" and "Bayonets". On the order "Fix", you do nothin'… waaiitforit… you *waits*… savvy? But when I shouts "Bayonets" you whips 'em aaht an' whops 'em on.'

They learnt the Turkish and German equivalent of field phrases such as *"Halt. Friend or foe?"* and *"Halt, or I shoot!"* but Chalky found both languages difficult to grasp – the German in particular. Then, on one of the unit's night exercises, Cartwright was slinking about in the darkness in a mock attack on a compound guarded by Chalky and George, when Chalky spotted a dark outline near the fencing. He pointed his rifle at it and bellowed the challenge he believed he had been taught. *"Halt, oder Ich scheiss!"* There was a moment of stunned silence – then loud laughter from Cartwright.

It was one of those moments, which seem to crop up in times of tension, when a mildly funny incident inexplicably strikes a chord in someone's sense of humour, sparking off disproportionate, uncontrollable, infectious laughter.

On this occasion, Cartwright's belly laugh had him weak-kneed and helpless as he staggered from the gloom, unable to explain the cause of it but so infectious was his laughter that George and Chalky were brought to their knees without knowing what they were laughing at. It was some time before he explained that, to a German, there was a world of difference between the word *"schiess"* and *"scheiss"* – however similar they sounded to an Englishman.

Chalky never did remember which word he should use but Cartwright said it probably would not matter. He said he was sure that a genuine German soldier challenged with: *"Halt, or I shit!"* was going to be too helpless with laughter to pose any real threat.

Chapter Fourteen

LONDON
April 1915

At home, the Prime Minister and the Government were troubled. Under the excellent leadership and statesmanship of Prime Minister Asquith, the Liberal Government had handled the early stages of Britain's involvement in the war with considerable skill and efficiency but his was a peacetime Government, unused to the demands of a full-blooded war. By the spring of 1915 its shortcomings were becoming obvious.

There was also a dawning realisation that the war would not be over in a matter of months, as originally thought, but could instead turn into a long and bitter struggle – a war of attrition – for which no preparation or contingency plan had been made. The strain of carrying the war forward, in terms of managing and providing manpower, production and finance, threatened to be much greater than anyone had anticipated.

After the first eight months, there were signs that all was not well with Asquith's Government, plagued as it was by mounting difficulties. Up to this point, the Opposition and the newspapers, in a show of solidarity for the good of the country, had made a conscious effort not to attack the Government. Now, however, confidence waned. With the tide of discontent at the high water mark, the newspapers and the Opposition went on the offensive.

The most persistent problem nagging Asquith was the matter of munitions. Production, particularly of shells, was falling well behind the demands being made by the Army and Navy. Many of the country's skilled and semi-skilled workers had been recruited into the fighting forces, leaving munitions factories short of skilled manpower. Meanwhile, the simplest solution of turning over more factories to munitions production while recruiting and training more men and women to replace missing workers was thwarted by trade union obduracy.

Unions, fearing profiteering by employers, blocked the Government's most obvious means of dealing with the shortages. Excessive drinking by factory and shipyard workers, which was put down to increased pressure and higher wages, was also impacting production. So serious was the drink problem that Lloyd George, Asquith's Chancellor of the Exchequer, said in a speech at Bangor on February 28, 1915: "Drink is doing more damage... than all the German submarines put together." There was no easy solution to this problem either.

Local prohibition was bound to cause working-class resentment and another possibility – a State monopoly of the drink trade was considered to be politically unacceptable. Lloyd George then attempted to apply his favourite method of control by increasing taxes on drink, but this had to be withdrawn quickly. Even when the King and Lord Kitchener "signed the pledge" for the duration of the war as an example to ordinary people, it did nothing to ease the problem.

Finally, a Liquor Traffic Central Control Board was set up, and this had special powers to control the sale of alcohol in the vicinity of any centre of production considered important to the supply of munitions. Then the Government was accused of using the drink problem as an excuse for its inability to organise the supply of munitions. At this point the newspapers decided to enter the fray.

They began to attribute failures of the Army in the field – and there were several of these setbacks – to the shortages of shells, and Asquith was labelled "a wait and see leader" incapable of organising properly the production of munitions. The criticisms were only partly justifiable. Unlike Germany, which had been preparing for this war for forty years, Britain had been drawn into it at much shorter notice, and was expecting it to last only a matter of weeks. Consequently, in organising supplies for her own forces, Britain was now struggling to catch up with Germany.

In the meantime, Asquith had been trying for some time to draw Italy into the war on the side of the Allies, in a move that was expected to bring the war to a swifter conclusion and enhance his standing, but Italy was being difficult, demanding, indecisive and downright slippery. A breakthrough in negotiations – which would have silenced Asquith's critics – was nowhere in sight.

To add to his problems, crippling friction and disruptive disagreements had become commonplace in the corridors of Whitehall. Kitchener and Lloyd George were in open conflict. Kitchener and some of his senior field officers were at loggerheads and the atmosphere between Fisher and Churchill could be cut with a knife. Eventually, a positive solution to the munitions problem was put forward by Edwin Montagu.

He proposed that the Government itself should take over control of armaments factories, with Lloyd George leading a Special Army Contracts Directorate. Lloyd George agreed, but on condition that he would have absolute control over it. Kitchener flatly refused to allow this to happen, believing that knowledge of the Army's projected armaments requirements, by which the nature and strategy of his forces could be predicted, was too sensitive to be entrusted to politicians and non-military officials. To Asquith it seemed that every silver lining had a black cloud attached to it.

Then Greece promised to tip the balance of power in favour of the Allies with its offer of several divisions of troops to support the Gallipoli landing. The Greeks, sensing that Constantinople and Gallipoli – which they had long yearned for – might be the potential spoils of the campaign, were desperate to be part of it. Asquith was delighted but along came another black cloud: Russia.

As Asquith was heralding the support of the Greek Army, the Russians, wanting the Straits for themselves, rejected the very idea that Greece might one day occupy Turkish territory, and the idea was nipped in the bud before it could take root. So, whichever way Asquith turned, there were problems and setbacks – relief for which could only come from his beloved confidante, Venetia Stanley, but, much to his consternation, she was preoccupied with her nursing training and had become much less available to him. Signs of his desperate need for her, and the pressures he was experiencing, leapt from the pages of his letters. In March 1915, he wrote to her:

"... My love for you has grown day by day & month by month & (now) year by year: till it absorbs and inspires all my life. I could not

if I would, and I would not if I could, arrest its flow, or limit its extent, or lower by a single degree its intensity, or make it a less sovereign & dominating factor in my thoughts & purposes & hopes. It has rescued me (little as anyone but you knows it) from sterility, impotence, despair. It enables me in the daily stress of almost intolerable burdens & anxieties to see visions & dream dreams... "©

Meanwhile, in the eastern Mediterranean, a massive reorganisation of the Gallipoli forces was underway.

THE PORT OF ALEXANDRIA EGYPT
April 7, 1915

Troops from all parts of the French Republic, New Zealand, Australia and India had been brought to Alexandria to join forces with the British regulars assembled under General Sir Ian Hamilton for the assault on Gallipoli. The busy Egyptian port was bustling with activity and clogged with the impedimenta of an army on the move. In the dry warm air, there was a pervading cacophony of ropes straining in squeaky pulleys, the groaning and clanking of cranes, the chuffing of trains, and the bellowed orders of NCOs and officers in charge.

Transport ships lined the docks, with cranes and hoists working feverishly to load the equipment and stores being piled up on the docksides. The hundreds of horses and braying mules, tethered in long, snaking lines and waiting patiently to be embarked, added their own smells to the dusty, hazy air hanging over the docks. In tented camps outside the city, thousands of troops were living and training in the desert sand, preparing for the forthcoming expedition. Their spirits were high and a strong camaraderie was developing between men drawn from vastly different parts of the world. For many of them, it was their first encounter with foreigners and colonials. New Zealanders and Australians trained with Gurkhas and Indian as well as French and British troops in a spirit of cooperation not seen before.

In the command tent of the combined forces, Hamilton, a wiry, brittle-looking man in his late sixties, stood with his arms akimbo among members of his staff, surveying a makeshift map of the Gallipoli Peninsula. As he leaned forward to pore over it, his delicate hands darted furtively across the document like the paws of a dormouse. With a satisfied expression, he stood erect and rounded off his conversation with his French counterpart, General d'Amade.

Their battle plans for the landings were now complete, and the detailed arrangements for shipping the combined forces to Gallipoli were well in hand. Donning his uniform topi, which seemed at least one size too big for him, he positioned its chinstrap with military precision between his lower lip and the point of his chin, bristled up his neat, white moustache and pulled his tunic jacket straight under his Sam Brown belt. General d'Amade straightened his pillbox cap and followed Hamilton out of the command tent, into the sun and sand. The entente cordiale between Britain and France was never more evident than between these military gentlemen. Their mutual respect positively shone through their body language.

With everything in place, it was time for Hamilton and his General Staff to leave for the island of Lemnos, fifty miles south west of the Dardanelles, confident that their forces would follow them to the island in good order. They were off to finalise plans with Vice Admiral de Robeck for throwing this most eclectic of armies ashore at Gallipoli.

For the crews of the Royal Naval warships in Mudros Harbour, things had been quiet since the aborted attack of March 18. The more severely damaged ships had already left the harbour. The bulk of the troops had been sent to Alexandria. There was little to do but wait. The atmosphere was relaxed enough for occasional boat trips to be organised to take picnic and swimming parties to the island.

To ensure that the Allies maintained their control of the entrance to the Dardanelles, two battleships at a time had been keeping up a daily routine of shelling the Turkish forts. When it was discovered that the Turks were using the lighthouse at Cape Helles as an observation post, it was swiftly dealt with. With Naval Air Corps aircraft spotting for them, the Navy's warships brought the lighthouse down.

Everything was now ready: poised for the arrival of the combined military forces from Alexandria and Mudros. The mighty enterprise was gaining momentum.

GOSPORT
Friday, April 9

At home in Gosport, a much smaller enterprise was also gaining momentum – Bill Guy's new partnership with Roy Paxman was going well. His shop in Gosport, now repainted and fitted out as a branch of the "Paxman & Guy" chain of two shops, was attracting more customers since he began supplying groceries as well as fruit and vegetables. Paxman's bull-like approach to business and his knack of mixing with the right people brought an increasing number of orders from the Army Service Corps and naval dockyards.

As anticipated, the partnership's ring-dealing activities began to boost Bill's profits, and it started to look as if hanging on to Paxman's coat tails was the best business move Bill had ever made. With his confidence soaring in line with his burgeoning profits, it was not long before plans were made to take on more staff and delivery vehicle but with the supply of able-bodied men and machinery drained by the war effort, it was difficult to find either.

For some time, Carrie had been agitating for Paxman and Bill to come to terms with the idea of filling the gap by employing able-bodied women instead, but try as she might, she could not shake Paxman out of his prejudiced, chauvinistic attitude towards working women, and her views were dismissed as soon as she uttered them.

It infuriated her. She had shown that she was already an indispensable part of Bill's business and he had no doubt that she could have run it on her own. She remained frustrated that no one would acknowledge the fact. Many women felt a strong urge to help the war effort in some way or another. They clearly could not serve on the front line, but were willing to do anything to satisfy their need to help. Social life had generally been killed off by the war and, frustrated by a lack of useful work opportunities, women at home began to form charity organisations and daytime clubs, to do whatever they could to support the troops and the families they had left behind. By now, most married women with children already had lost husbands and sons to the fields of Belgium, or the depths of the ocean.

Marje had been put onto part-time hours in her job at Biddles, as the luxury and clothing trades fell away. To pass her time usefully she had joined a woman's volunteer organisation working at Haslar Hospital. There, she helped to pack medical supplies for ships and the many small hospitals now set up in the former Big Houses. Carrie, caught up in the feverish frustration of women who wanted to do something for the war effort, joined the organisation as well and worked with Marje whenever she could. She enjoyed the contact with other active women and listening to their views.

Bill's reluctance to stand up to Paxman was straining his relationship with Carrie. Whenever she put forward ideas for the business, he would readily agree with them. Then, when he came face to face with Paxman, he would waver and wilt. He seemed embarrassed to be seen standing alone among men, arguing the case for women and she instinctively knew that he would be no help at all in getting employment for women in areas other than in their accepted roles as cleaners, clerks and secretaries. 'I can't understand why men are so... so... obstinate,' Carrie railed at him one evening, with her green eyes blazing. 'You men obviously think the war is some kind of private club!'

She was infuriated by his lack of reaction. 'You can see for yourself that there are no men left in the country to do these jobs. Yet you'd rather go without, than employ some women. I can't understand it. There are many women desperate to do something useful, with their men being away. I know... I talk to them. Many would willingly work, if only men would let them do something. *And they can do any job equally as well as any man.*'

'Oh, can they?' There was a definite Paxmanlike arrogance in Bill's tone these days. 'What about delivering coal, then... and sweeping chimneys. Would women do that?'

His uncharacteristic cockiness shocked her; from him, she at least expected a sympathetic ear. 'Yes, they damn well would. In fact, now that you mention it, I know a woman chimney sweep who comes into the shop – one of your *own* customers.'

'Rubbish!'

'It's not rubbish! If you're here the next time she comes in, I'll show you. Better still, I'll get her to come round and clean your chimney for you.' Bill noticed that she unconsciously used the word "your" when she was angry, and sensed a mild sea change in her attitude to him. He backed away from the subject and promised to talk to Paxman about it again, but she knew that he was just pacifying her. Carrie was beginning to see flaws in Bill's character she had not noticed before, and it seemed like the sharp end of a wedge poised to come between them.

It unsettled her, as Marje found out one day when Carrie was talking about her emotional confusion. 'Do you think working with Paxman has influenced Bill?' she asked with a frown.

'I must say that I've noticed a bit of a change in him myself recently but I thought it was just because he's so busy. Are you sure you're not being a bit too sensitive about it, darling?'

'No... I'm not. He has changed. Things are definitely different now. He's always away on business, and he's more interested in that than he is in Kate and me.'

'But surely he's only doing what you wanted him to do... expand, I mean. You must be fair. If you want material things, like the Paxmans, he's got to work as hard and take on more responsibilities. You're going to have to put up with him being distracted, now and again.'

'I wouldn't mind if that was all it was. But there's more to it than that. It's as if Kate and I don't exist sometimes. When Bill comes in now it's all "Roy this" and "Roy that", until bedtime. Then he's always tired. We never...you know...do things anymore. Instead of growing more like a family, we seem to be leading separate lives under the same roof. I feel more like a housekeeper, and I've already had my share of that. It's not what I was expecting.'

'It sounds exactly like the average family situation to me, darling' said Marje, reflecting on her own childhood. 'I don't quite know what you expect out of life.' She could see the pain in Carrie's eyes. 'Darling, are you quite sure you aren't looking for trouble?'

Carrie's eyes narrowed. 'What's that supposed to mean? What trouble?' There was a knowing look in Marje's eye.

'I've been thinking, darling. You could be deliberately leaving the door open for something to come in and threaten your relationship with Bill... inviting it in, perhaps, to test the strength of your own commitment.' Marje's observation stung Carrie, but it struck at the truth like a perfectly flighted arrow. Marje was right, as she was apt to be. Carrie was now deeply involved with every aspect of Bill's life, and he with hers, but something about their relationship was not quite right. She was no longer as sublimely happy as she had been initially, and it gnawed at her constantly, making things worse; and she did not know what to do about it but if she did not have Bill, where would she go... and what would she do?

Elsewhere, Venetia Stanley's emotions were in a similar state of confusion.

WALMER CASTLE, KENT
April 12, 1915

On the weekend of April 10, there was a tense atmosphere at Walmer Castle, the impressive residence on temporary loan to the Asquiths. Venetia Stanley and Montagu had both been invited to spend the weekend with the Asquiths, but the bizarre *ménage á quatre* proved too much for Venetia. With both Montagu and Asquith pursuing her favours, she fell ill and went to bed early. Montagu was very frustrated and accused her of deliberately avoiding him after previously leading him on. A tiff developed between them that took several days to settle.

In different rooms during the weekend with Margot at large in the house, both Montagu and Asquith were busy writing letters to Venetia. Eventually, Margot sat down and began to write a letter of her own – to Asquith, her husband. Finally unsettled by the intensity of her husband's dependence on Venetia, Margot sent him her touching letter on their return to 10 Downing Street on April 13. In it, she revealed her concerns about the depth of his feelings for Venetia, and intimated that she felt somewhat ousted from her position as his wife. He immediately wrote a tender response, reassuring her that his feelings for Venetia could never replace or surpass his love for his dear wife.

Oblivious to Montagu's own feelings and eternal hopes for marriage to Venetia, Margot sent her husband's letter to Montagu, by way of interest, in order to enlist his support in getting Venetia married off to someone – anyone, but the relationship between Montagu and Venetia was already scaling new heights of mutuality, and Venetia's frustration with her seemingly hopeless predicament between Montagu and Asquith was boiling over.

On Sunday, April 18, she wrote to Montagu: *"My darling... What can I say to you after this short time that you've been gone. That I want you back fearfully. Yes I do...*

*(T)his Sunday has made it very difficult to go on writing to the P.M. as tho' nothing had happened. Darling, what am I to do? Obviously what I ought to do would be to try to carry on as I've been doing, you've both been fairly happy under that regime... Then again when to tell him... Why can't I marry you and yet go on making him happy, but you'd neither of you think that fun... I am so perplexed and wretched, I want so much to be happy and yet not to make anyone else unhappy. You made everything seem so simple, but now you are gone it's as mangled as ever... Darling I **think** I love you Venetia"©*

Then on April 19, Asquith stumbled headlong into the biggest political blunder of his long career as Prime Minister. It concerned the supply of munitions, and came in his speech to munitions workers during his visit to a Newcastle factory. Prior to this, newspapers and the Opposition had been busy making much of the Government's difficulties over the supply of shells. People all over the country knew very well that British generals on the Western Front had been calling, constantly and continuously, for more shells than could be supplied. It was common knowledge.

Asquith was naturally keen to avoid alienating the workers with negative comments, and wanted to impart an upbeat message when he addressed them. By way of assisting him in this task, Kitchener supplied him with some carefully worded positive information for his speech.

It was an assurance that General French at the Western Front had confirmed that he already had adequate shells for his next forward movement against the German Army.

Simply that ...but for reasons known only to himself – an over-zealous attempt to motivate the workers, it seemed – Asquith blew this useful titbit of military information out of all proportion. In his speech, he intimated that there was no shortage of ammunition at all, and there never had been one. He referred to newspaper statements suggesting that the operations of the British Expeditionary Force were being crippled by the Government's failure to provide the necessary ammunition. He said: *'There is not a word of truth in that statement.'*

The newspapers seized on his blunder immediately, and depicted him as a Prime Minister out of touch with the facts of war production and the problems of the British Expeditionary Force. They added that what he had said in Newcastle completely contradicted what other members of the Cabinet had been saying. It was tantamount to an accusation of lying, and it left him wide open to attack and criticism from all sides.

In Venetia's world, things were coming to a head. Her emotions were in turmoil, swinging from anger to tenderness for Asquith then back again.

She agonised over when and how to tell him about her intention to break away and marry Montagu. Her letters to Montagu were now more frequent and more urgent. In her letter of April 20, her anguish was clear, and there were hints of unintended emotional blackmail by Asquith:

"My darling... What a fool I've been haven't I... I feel so ungrateful to him & yet at times I resent very bitterly that he should stand in the way. And yet I know you are right & that it wd be almost impossible for me to go to him & say 'In spite of the fact that you've again and again told me that if I were to marry life would have nothing left to offer you, I am going to marry Edwin.' How could he have been so cruel as to say that to me? But I must see you, he has no claim on me has he?"©

Some weeks before she had tried to give Asquith strong hints that she might be on the brink of accepting someone's marriage proposal but, by skilfully manipulating her emotions – out of desperation, rather than malevolence – he drove her back into her shell and destroyed the courage she had found to tell him the truth.

Unable to face the awful reality of life without her, he chose to simply step over the hints he had been given, selfishly telling her how desperate it would make him if she were to marry.

April 23, 1915

Rupert Brooke, poet and personal friend of the Asquith family – in transit with the Naval Brigade to Gallipoli in a transport ship – developed septicaemia after being bitten by a mosquito. He was transferred to a French hospital ship where he died on April 23. He was buried the same day on the Greek Island of Skiros. The news shook the Asquiths and broke Violet Asquith's heart, shattering cruelly her secret, unrequited love for him.

GALLIPOLI
April 24, 1915

In the Aegean, the huge military and naval force aimed at Turkey was ready and poised for the landing at Gallipoli. The assault had been planned for daybreak on Sunday, April 25, 1915. The ultimate objectives were to secure the peninsula and eliminate the Turkish guns stopping the Navy in its tracks then force on with the Navy, to Constantinople but both inside the Straits and on the Aegean coast, the shoreline of the peninsula was formidable.

For the best part, precipitous cliffs fell directly into the sea – or left a beach only eight or ten yards wide, at best. This rendered most of it either impregnable or extremely unsuited to landing troops and their equipment from the sea. Hamilton therefore confined his planning to the few beaches that offered some chance for the troops to land and move inland with their heavy artillery and vast amounts of supporting stores and equipment.

Strategically, the ideal landing points would have been at either side of the narrow neck of the peninsula, where a rapid link-up from both sides would have annexed the peninsula quickly. However, there were no suitable beaches there. Instead, the main landings were necessarily focused on the southernmost tip of the peninsula, where there were occasional stretches of beach with cliffs only fifty to one hundred feet high. The regulars of the British 29th Division were destined to land here but this would leave them with the whole length of the peninsula to cover before they could reach any point of strategic importance. The Australian and New Zealanders – the "Anzacs" – were to land at Gaba Tepe and Suvla Bay, some 14 and 20 miles north along the Aegean coast of the peninsula. The French were to make temporary landings at Kum Kale, on the opposite side of the Straits, as a diversion. They would then be withdrawn to join up with the 29th Division.

Unfortunately, the initial Naval bombardment of March 18 had alerted the Turks to the potential threat of invasion, and the five weeks delay since then had given them ample time to prepare defences and reinforce their troops. They were determined to defend their country to the bitter end and, with the help of their German comrades, intended do this ferociously.

At *10.00 pm* on April 24, the invasion force set out. The troops were transferred from their transports to warships that would carry them within sight of the peninsula. As there were no ships capable of putting them directly on the beaches, they were to be rowed ashore in cutters and whalers – the Navy's small wooden boats. The arrangements for landing were cumbersome and fraught with danger.

Once the battleships got close enough to the coast, troops would transfer to the cutters and whalers for the actual landings. Steam pinnaces, behind each of which a string of six or eight boats would be tied, were to tow the boats as close to shore as possible. The boats would then be cast off and rowed onto the beaches by sailors but for "V" beach, something special was planned.

"V" was the one landing site of several on the tip of the peninsula that had been chosen for landing the heaviest equipment and guns. Admiral de Robeck had given his agreement that an old but substantial collier, *River Clyde*, could be deliberately run onto the beach, to provide a permanent landing pier and clearing station for future supplies. When she grounded, two thousand Dublin Fusiliers would be crammed inside her. For this experiment, *River Clyde* – dubbed with some irony "the Ship of Troy" – was specially converted and given extra armoured protection for her sides and bridge. To allow the fusiliers to disembark quickly, it was intended that a string of lighters would be secured as a floating bridge between the collier and the beach. To speed up the construction of this floating bridge of lighters, an anchor point for the lines from the ship was needed on the beach, to which the lighters could be tied.

As gunfire was expected as soon as the Turks realised that a landing was taking place, a decision had been made to have the anchor point and lines already in place on the beach before the ship came in. This task had fallen to Lieutenant Cartwright and his "Special Complement" unit. His orders were to land a small group on the beach in the darkness prior to the landing, to find or make a suitable anchor point before *River Clyde* arrived on "V" beach. Immediately after the landing was successfully completed, he and his unit would return to *Implacable*.

Because of his past experience, and by his very nature, Cartwright was the best officer for the job – not that he could resist such a challenge in any event.

Chapter Fifteen

THE DARDANELLES
April 25, 1915

At *1.30 am* on April 25, with *Implacable* as close to the coast as her captain dared go, the landing boats were lowered and the troops began to climb into them. *River Clyde* was close by.

With the commotion of loading and assembling the strings of cutters and whalers going on at one side of the ship, Cartwright, George, Chalky and the two Marines, John Beckworth and Tom Pearse, loaded their equipment into their own cutter at the other side. There was a lot to carry: an ammunition box, food, water, long wooden stays, coils and spools of rope, and a strange board that looked like two mess table tops joined together with hinges, folded in two with a rope carrying handle on the hinged side.

On being handed this, Chalky had to comment. 'Now I know what the Special Complement's job is – we're off to wallpaper the Sultan's palace walls!' Then, in tow by a steam pinnace commanded by a youthful Midshipman, the landing party left the security of the darkened ship's side towering above them and headed across the choppy, pitch-black sea towards the faint lights at the tip of the peninsula. Their hearts were in their mouths.

Shortly after *2.00 am*, the Midshipman, his eyes well accustomed to the darkness by now, skilfully picked out "V" beach from the black, craggy outline of the coastline silhouetted against the faintest hint of dawn in the sky. Cartwright knew this coastline better than anyone and already had his binoculars trained on the landing area. The crew of the pinnace slowed down to pull the cutter in towards their stern, and Cartwright told the Midshipman he was ready to let go and head for the beach. Cartwright was muttering that they were so close to the shore that he was concerned about the pinnace's engine being heard by lookouts on the beach.

The Midshipman realised that once the cutter was cast adrift, Cartwright's men would find it impossible to row against the strong tide running past the point of Cape Helles. He was not, he said, going to jeopardise the operation and place their lives at risk through any shortcoming on his part, and he told the Lieutenant he was going to take him a bit farther along the beach. Cartwright objected, and there was a bizarre disagreement between them that wasted precious minutes. The Midshipman was respectful to the senior officer, but he reminded Cartwright that until his cutter reached the beach, the responsibility of getting it there was the Royal Navy's. He was adamant that, of those present as they drifted around in the darkness under the noses of the Turks, he was the senior representative of the Navy and was therefore in charge at that moment!

Cartwright protested, and was on the point of untying the line himself, but he knew that the Midshipman was technically correct. To avoid wasting any more time, he conceded, but felt angry and frustrated all the same. With the party anxiously waiting in the boat, and Cartwright cursing quietly in the darkness, they steamed blithely on past their landing point before the Midshipman would give his crew the order to cast off the cutter. As the pinnace turned and passed them in the darkness, they could just make out the Midshipman's cheery wave as he headed back to the ship.

As soon as the landing party put their oars in the water and began to row for the beach, they appreciated just how accurate the Midshipman's judgement had been. Borne on a three-knot current, they were almost past the beach before they could reach it. Cartwright was quick to admit his error and vowed to apologise to the ruffled "Middie", back on the ship. Manic heaves on the oars finally brought them to the beach and there was great relief when the wooden keel finally grounded on the sandy shore.

The two Marines quickly leapt over the side and waded up the beach, silently melting into the background gloom followed by Cartwright. George and Chalky stumbled onto the beach and did their best to secure the cutter, then unload it. As they finished, they felt cold fear closing in around them. The other three had disappeared, and they were suddenly alone in enemy territory, in darkness. Having had strict orders to be absolutely silent on the beach, they just stood there in the gloom beside the pile of equipment, with their hearts pounding frantically, wondering if their last day was dawning. They could see the dark blurred outline of the ships, well out to sea but apart from the swishing and hissing of the waves gently caressing the beach, and the soft warm breeze, they were in complete isolation.

It was *2.30 am.*

Cartwright, John and Tom suddenly appeared out of nowhere, much to the relief of George and Chalky. They were breathless, but pleased with the results of their reconnaissance. 'There's no one on the beach,' Cartwright explained, in an urgent, hoarse whisper. 'But we can see plenty of activity on the ridge…up there, where the lights flash occasionally, by the fortifications. I'm afraid our lads are in for a pasting when they land, but there's nothing we can do about it. We can't signal them or send a message, and the landing is too far underway to change anything. All we can do is get on with what we came here to do, and take cover before it gets light.'

He turned to the Marines. 'Beckworth, Pearse, give a hand to move the boat... we need to get it to the far end of the beach and hide it behind a ridge or something. Then I want you two to get out of sight up there, under cover to watch out for Turks.' They did their best to hide the large cutter then returned to the opposite end of the short stretch of beach. 'The ship will come in at this end,' Cartwright explained. 'To act as a kind of jetty. Now we need to find a solid place for attaching the main cable when she comes in. There's not much here, but I think we're in luck. Over there is a big volcanic rock that should do. Have we got rope and stays?'

George looked at the pile of equipment they had brought. 'Yes, sir, enough for a tripod… and we've got the pulley blocks.'

'Good! Let's get them all over there then.'

The dawn light was creeping in – too rapidly for their liking – and they had to move quickly. With all they had brought with them heaped by the rock, they set to work. They lashed the stays firmly together to form a tripod, and bedded it down on firm ground in front of the rock. Then they suspended the pulley block from the lashings on the stays, and secured the whole arrangement to the rock. Chalky passed the rope through the pulley and coiled it onto a spool, ready to run out. It was secure and solid enough for attaching the ship's line when it was eventually thrown to them.

'Right,' said Cartwright, satisfied that their mission was completed. 'I'm going to put this flashlight on top of our tripod, to guide the ship in. With a bit of luck, she should end up right there.' He indicated a point just above the waterline. 'Now let's take cover... but bring the spare equipment with you: especially the board.'

The only cover on the beach was a sandy gulley. They concealed themselves in this, as best they could. It was several feet deep in places and ran in a haphazard line for some way along the length of the beach, providing good cover. They settled down in a deep part, twenty yards away from the tripod, and hoped that the Turks would not spot it when daylight came up. Cartwright turned to George and Chalky. 'Now the board. You're probably wondering what that's for?' Chalky grinned and looked at it.

'Well, just a bit. I thought maybe we were going to have a picnic and a game of cards, sir.'

Cartwright picked it up proudly. 'That, I've learnt from experience,' he said, displaying it in the gloom, 'could save your life. I got the "chippies" to make it up for me.' He untied the rope and unfolded the board, flat on the ground. The whole of the inside of one flap was painted with the Union Jack; the other was painted beige. He pulled the hinged edge up to form a triangular shape of it, and tied rope between the two sides to stop them spreading. 'You see, when our troops come charging onto the beach, they will be pretty wound up to shoot first and ask questions later, and they'll fire at anything that looks human, including us – in spite of the fact that they should have been warned that we are here. When you suddenly arrive on enemy territory, like this, it's easy to get carried away and forget everything you have been told ...except to kill everything and anything that moves. But one thing you'd never do is fire at the Union Jack.' He placed the contraption on the seaward side of George, with the flag side facing the sea. 'There,' he said. 'Perhaps we won't get shot by our own lads now. All you have to do, Royal, is make sure it doesn't get knocked over.'

George quietly appreciated Cartwright's eccentricity. Although a bullet would have passed clean through the board, it gave him a warm feeling to be behind it. The painted Union Jack suddenly seemed like a piece of armour-plated steel. From their position on the beach, they watched the ships and kept an eye on the Turks at the same time. They broke open the ammunition box and shared out rounds for the rifles they were all carrying, and opened their food rations and water. They had barely finished their makeshift breakfast when the first real half-light of dawn came over the hills and transformed the scenery. Black shadowy outlines of the night that had seemed threatening were gradually transformed into harmless, mundane objects of the day.

As the scene took shape, George could barely believe the precariousness of their position. Apart from the gulley they were in – which was fortunately quite long – the beach was otherwise completely exposed. With their backs to the sea, they faced a semicircle of hills. On these, to their right, the fort of Sedd-el-Bahr was perched like an imposing ancient ruin. Although the massive guns of the fort had long been put out of action by constant Naval bombardments, the demolished fortifications provided a mass of masonry for sharpshooters and guns to be concealed.

Cartwright scoured the hills and the battered fort with his binoculars. 'Good God!' he said, not taking his gaze from the eyepieces. 'The Turks are dug in everywhere. That fort is alive with them.' Just then, the heavy rumble of ships' guns opening up some distance away on another landing site shattered the eerie silence. It signalled *Implacable* and her two accompanying destroyers to open fire on the hills behind Cartwright's group. They cowered as shells hissed over their heads and pounded into the Turkish emplacements.

The noise of the exploding shells was deafening. George shouted to Chalky. 'Christ! Now you know what it's like on the receiving end!'

'Bloody murder!' he called back. 'Bloody good job they've got the range.' Shells kept pouring into the hills and the fort, which was just a few hundred yards beyond them. Cartwright and his men made the best use of the cover they had found. For now, at least, the attention of the Turks was on the ships firing at them, and they had not spotted the tripod or the men on the beach. The landing party was totally exposed to any shell falling short of its target, and George caught himself muttering a prayer through tightly clenched teeth as he tried to melt into the sand. He clung to thoughts of better times and willed the ships' gunners not to make mistakes. It felt like the end of the world had arrived, right there and then.

From somewhere inside the fort, there were several loud thuds as howitzer shells hurtled out to sea. Two destroyers were moving slowly towards the beach, towing behind them strings of steam pinnaces, whalers and cutters loaded with troops. It was the advance party of three companies of the Dublin Fusiliers, part of the 29th Division on which so much depended. The destroyers kept up their fire. Farther out to sea, *Implacable* suddenly stopped firing as the approaching destroyers reached a predetermined point, close in to the shore. There, they stopped to let go of their strings of boats, and provided covering fire for the painfully slow journey of the troops to the beach. The sides of the heavily laden wooden boats – their "gunwales" were nearly awash. It was almost fully daylight now, and the Turks had a clear view of the whole operation, as did Cartwright and his men. The steam pinnaces towed the boats as far as they could, then left them to make their own way the final fifty yards. The sailors rowed frantically towards the beach, into a murderous hail of Turkish lead.

Cartwright felt he had to do something. Although it would be an inadequate, futile contribution, he ordered his men to fire at any Turkish troops they could see clearly. By now, there were several coming down the beach from both sides, firing rifles as they came. At every advance, they threw themselves into the sand to take better aim. The landing party opened fire in both directions. Until then, the Turks had not noticed them, but now they were fired on with a vengeance but as Cartwright occupied the only cover on the beach, and the Turkish soldiers were more exposed, it gave his men the advantage.

Three times George took aim and fired at the crouching figures. Each time, he saw his target buckle at the knees and slump into the sand. For a moment, the startled Turks seemed like sitting ducks. Caught in their own struggle to survive, Cartwright's group needed no encouragement to shoot as many Turks as they could but before long, their limited ammunition was exhausted. With just a few reserve rounds left, they could do no more than keep low and wait for whatever Fate had in store for them. Then, quite unexpectedly, their spirits were lifted. The Turks withdrew and retreated back along the beach. Cartwright and his little group began to feel they had made a difference, however small. They felt good about it but the fire from the elevated, entrenched Turkish positions farther up the hill continued mercilessly and although Cartwright's team was no longer immediately threatened by the Turkish attempt to overrun it, George watched helplessly as the disembarking fusiliers, trying to get ashore from their boats, were cut to pieces. One after the other, they fell dead into the sea or backwards into the boats. One of the boats, hit by a shell, simply disappeared complete with its crew and cargo of fusiliers. Another arrived at the beach with only two men alive. The rest of the boats came in with most men dead or wounded before they could ever set foot on the beach.

Eventually, what survivors there were scrambled up the beach and made for Cartwright's board. It was like a magnet for the British troops – a welcome sight in such a hostile place. As the gulley was the only cover on the beach, it quickly became the centre of the skirmish with most of the surviving fusiliers huddled inside it.

George found himself wedged between two of them. They were young: about the same age as him, breathless and wide-eyed with fear and battle excitement. Their eyes stared into the distance with their nerves on a knife-edge. When their commanding officer led them forward in an advance, they were so single-minded they did not hesitate for a moment. A display of real guts, George's inner voice told him: a desperately close, naked, personal commitment – not the remote, long distance battles he and Chalky fought from inside an armoured turret.

Within yards of the gulley, the officer and one of the fusiliers fell dead in the sand and the other was down, wounded in the leg. Without waiting for orders, George and Chalky crawled across the sand and dragged him to safety. Back in the gulley, they dressed his wound as best they could and gave him a cigarette. Their act of compassion made them feel better, surrounded as they were by hundreds of other dead and dying men they could do nothing for, but it did little to dispel the growing anger, remorse and sense of futility they experienced at the sight of the brutal carnage on "V" beach. Boatloads of troops continued to reach the beach, only to suffer a similar fate.

Gradually, however, the number of survivors increased enough to mount an offensive to push the Turks back. The Turks fought fiercely, but under the continuous fire of the ships and the spirited charges of the fusiliers, hundreds of them were also killed or wounded. Eventually, they fell back to the maze of trenches and barbed wire enclosures in the hills.

At sea, *River Clyde* was making her move. Escorted by a destroyer, the converted collier with two thousand Dublin Fusiliers between her decks picked up speed and headed directly for Cartwright's marker. Behind her, she was towing two lighters for constructing the bridge to the beach. For Cartwright and his men – mere spectators on the beach – the large, undamaged vessel steaming at speed for the beach was a vision of fantasy. The hairs on George's body bristled and he felt the strangest of tingling sensations at the nape of his neck. This was something extraordinary; something that should not happen – a sight he would never see again in his life: a perfectly sound ship steaming at speed towards land to beach herself – a ship in the act of suicide – before his very eyes.

Often, when he was idly staring into the sea from his speeding ship, he had tried to imagine such a scene and wondered what it would be like. What would happen to all the energy of thousands of tons of metal travelling at speed, if it rammed a solid rock, or a dock wall? Now he was going to see for himself and he wondered ... would *River Clyde* thunder up the beach and reach their hiding place? He shuddered at the thought.

With waves curling up from her grey bow, she drew closer and closer until she loomed large in the surreal scene. The destroyer turned away, anxious not to run aground itself, and *River Clyde* came on alone. She had a determined look, as if she were gritting her teeth and bracing herself to mount the beach but her final arrival was a shattering anticlimax. There was no explosion of energy, no great crash. She simply rose slightly in the water and came to a gentle, uneventful standstill a long way from the shore. Far from reaching George, or Cartwright's estimate, the ship stopped short a hundred yards from the water's edge – far too short to be of any use.

It was *10.00 am* on Sunday morning.

The Turks were taken aback by this extraordinary manoeuvre and stopped firing for several minutes. The group on the beach stared in disbelief, each man with the same question in his mind. 'What now?' She was too far out for the troops to land on the beach, even with a bridge of lighters. It seemed that either *River Clyde's* captain had not been able to bring himself to beach his ship at her best speed, or he had kept her speed down to reduce the impact on his passengers. Alternatively, someone had made a monumental error of judgement about the shallowness of the shoreline seabed at "V" beach. Whatever the cause, there was no turning back. The ship was stuck fast on an unnoticed sandbank in the wrong place.

Cartwright stared at the ship with frustration and disbelief in his eyes. 'Marvellous! There's nothing quite like seeing a plan coming together as nicely as that,' he muttered darkly. Suddenly, Turkish rifle and machine-gun fire started up again, raking the ship and the beach. The foreshore erupted in a storm of flying sand and water.

Cartwright was desperately scouring his mind for a sensible plan of action for the hopeless situation, but to venture out into the hail of lead now sweeping the exposed beach, would have been an act of certain suicide. His only comment was filled with despondency.

'Jesus Christ!'

There seemed nothing more appropriate to say. He looked at the faces around him. In their eyes, their expectations of him were clear. 'Right!' he said, as positively as he could. 'There's only one thing for it. We'll have to take our line to the ship. It's the only way they'll ever secure the lighters!' Hearts sank at the prospect, but they knew he was right. 'White, Royal, you're both sailors... you must be good swimmers. You take one end of the spool each and run like hell with it, into the sea. We'll come after you, in case one of you goes down, and we'll join you in the water then we'll all swim the line to the ship's side. OK?'

George had an overwhelming urge to say: 'No, it's not OK, you bloody maniac!' But under the influence of his sense of duty, the words came out as: 'Right, sir.' He could not believe his own crass acceptance of what now looked like an invitation to commit suicide but as he prepared himself for it, a millisecond burst of introspective activity in his mind shut out the sounds and realism of what was going on around him.

There were probably three reasons why people act bravely in

circumstances such as these. Firstly, they choose to be brave to avoid being found wanting by their colleagues. Secondly, the sudden call on their courage shuts down their natural sense of self-preservation and thirdly, they do not pause to consider the consequences of what they are doing. That was it! At last, he had an answer to one of the most confusing questions to have come out of his experiences of the past six months. He could do all three of these things – so now it would be easy to be brave.

When his mind handed back his consciousness to him, it came as a jolt. The cacophony of the shellfire, rattling machine guns, shouting voices and screams of pain on the beach returned abruptly, startling him with its loudness. He was confused for a moment and wondered if he had been unconscious for a while but his mental excursion had only taken a split second, and nobody had noticed. Chalky was only at the point of wishing him good luck and preparing for their dash. George no longer felt afraid but the experience left him wondering if he was going off his head.

Before he had time to think, it was time to go. They discarded their rifles and kit, drew a deep breath, and ran barefoot to the tripod as fast as they could. They grabbed the ends of the spool and ran down the beach with it, paying out the rope as they went. When they reached the water, they plunged in and struggled out into deeper water. The spool of rope was heavy and its lack of buoyancy took them by surprise. In the water, it felt extremely cumbersome. They struggled to move it towards the ship and quickly reached the point of going down with it just as the others arrived to give much needed help. Although the Turks were not specifically aiming at them, bullets were sputtering the water close by. The sea was foul and bloody, and full of debris and bodies.

Working as a team, the five men gathered enough bits of floating wood to keep them afloat with their burden of rope. Like a raft made up of limbs and pieces of wood held together by sheer willpower, they slowly kicked their way towards the ship with their burden. As they reached it, a square steel door in its side creaked open and sailors threw out a scrambling net. It spilled out of the doorway and trailed down into the water. Exhausted, they clung to it gratefully, waiting for someone to take the rope from them. Two sailors climbed down and took the rope ends from the exhausted men, then returned to help them up.

Farther along the beach, a Turkish machine-gunner was framing the climbing men in his sights. What he saw was an opportunity not to be missed. He pressed the trigger, but his Maxim gun misfired and jammed. He hastily cleared the faulty round, re-cocked and fired again. This time his weapon worked perfectly. It rattled and spat a sputtering trail across the water and up the side of *River Clyde*.

As a sailor helped Chalky off the scrambling net, they each took two rounds of Maxim fire. The sailor staggered back through the doorway, fatally injured. Chalky stiffened and let go of the net, falling backwards without a sound. With a puzzled expression fixed on his face and his eyes staring a question at the sky, he landed spread-eagled in the sea and floated momentarily. Before anyone could reach him, he sank slowly out of sight and the sea closed over him. He drifted down to the sandy seabed.

The burst of Maxim fire rattled and ricocheted off the steel plates of the ship's side, and George felt a heavy crack on the top of his head. He tightened his grip on the net, and clung on. His eyes clamped tight involuntarily, and all he could see was a jumble of brilliant diamonds dancing on a sea of black velvet. He thought something heavy had fallen on him, but he could not tell what it was. Something told him to keep hanging on until someone came for him, while a warm sensation ran down his neck. He could hear voices somewhere in the distance, and he felt hands pulling at him, trying to drag him down. *Hold on, hang on,* he was telling himself – *don't give in, and don't let them drag you down!* But his grip finally gave way and someone prised his fingers off the net. He felt himself getting lighter and lighter as his resistance weakened. When he could hang on no more, he gave in to a desperate weariness crawling over his body and let the warm feeling closing in around him carry his body away.

On the ship, willing hands helped Cartwright, John and Tom carry George to the makeshift sickbay. It had been an effort to get him off the net, and he had lost a lot of blood. It was oozing through his hair and down his back, but he was alive. How seriously he was wounded, no one could tell. As a doctor examined his wounds, George lapsed in and out of consciousness. He briefly surfaced and looked up at the serious faces looking down at him. He saw Cartwright, John and Tom, but no Chalky. Before he could ask, he slipped into a deep unconsciousness.

With their new rope link to the beach in place, the crew of *River Clyde* carried on, as planned. They heaved the lighters from the stern of the ship and ran them out in front of her. Although continuously under fire, the ship's Commander, two Midshipmen and two sailors slid into the water and stayed there for an hour, securing the lighters to the line that now ran from the ship to the beach. One Able Seaman was shot and killed and another was seriously injured by Maxim fire. A Midshipman wounded in the head had to be rescued. Finally, the lighters were secured but the gap between them was still too great for the heavily laden troops to jump across.

Even so, the disembarkation went ahead. The fusiliers poured out across the lighters and attempted to wade ashore, but the water was too deep and the Turkish gunfire too relentless. Soon, the lighters were heaped with dead fusiliers and more were drowning in the sea. Finally, the attempt to land them had to be abandoned until it could be done under the cover of darkness. On the beach, where the gunfire was still murderous, the surviving troops clung to the cover of the gulley

By now, all their boats had either been holed or completely destroyed and *River Clyde* was stranded well out of their reach, raked by Turkish howitzer fire. There was nothing anyone could do except to hold on and wait for darkness. Being stuck fast, the ship was a perfect target for the Turkish gunners. Four shells struck her reinforced plates but, mercifully, did not penetrate far enough to explode between her decks. The British ships farther out at sea continued to beat down the Turkish fire with their guns but the situation was now stalemated – a veritable nightmare.

The ship was still full of soldiers, crammed into a space that was intended to accommodate them for only a few hours. Facilities were limited and the holds stank of body odour and the vomit of fear but it provided a safe haven from the hurricane of lead that raged all day outside. Hearts were heavy when word got around that five hundred of the first thousand fusiliers disembarked between *10:00* and *11:00 am* that day were already dead.

John and Tom sat in a corner with Cartwright, deep in silent thought. For once, Cartwright had no cheery word for anyone and they all experienced the same sense of despair and desolation at what they had been through that day. Losing Chalky and, perhaps, George was the worst possible outcome for Cartwright. Under cover of darkness that night, another lighter was brought to the beach, and Cartwright and his two remaining men worked with the ship's crew to secure it to the raft of lighters. With this in place, the gap to the beach was closed.

Before daylight, the disembarkation of the remaining fusiliers went ahead in the dark with greater success. There was little Turkish fire, and almost all of the troops reached the beach safely. George, according to the doctor on board, was lucky. A bullet had deeply creased his skull, but had passed on by. A skull fracture was suspected, but there was no way to establish the extent of the damage. With his head heavily bandaged, sedated with morphine, he continued to drift in and out of consciousness, not knowing where he was, or why. All he knew was that he had a pain in his head that was unbearable.

Later in the day, reinforcements arrived in the form of the French company withdrawn from their temporary landing on the other side of the Straits. Now they were allocated to join the 29th Division at "V" beach. Together with other regulars of the 29th, they landed, adding new strength to the operation. The following day, more troops were landed and the Turks were pushed back more forcibly. The foreshore had finally been secured and was now free of all but sporadic rifle and Maxim fire, the battle having moved into the hills. Stores, heavy guns, horses, mules, ammunition and water supplies streamed through the landing pier and distribution centre that, as intended, *River Clyde* had become. Having given help and assistance wherever they could, Cartwright and his men had made their contribution.

After three days there they were exhausted and very relieved when a boat was arranged to take them back to *Implacable*. They wanted to take George with them, away from the front line so that he would receive better medical attention, but a doctor convinced them that he would be better off on the hospital ship that was due to take all the wounded away later that day. Reluctantly, they went back to the battleship without him.

As they left the beachhead, yet more troops and equipment were being landed: more heavy guns, additional mules, horses, ammunition and supplies. The invasion of Gallipoli seemed firmly under way on "V" beach.

At the other four landing sites there was a very different story. On some, troops had been landed with very little initial resistance, only to be engaged in fierce fighting later. On others, men were mown down as if with a scythe as they came ashore and it was only the courage of the following waves of troops that permitted footholds to be gained. On other beaches, errors of navigation had placed men on impregnable beaches where they died uselessly and pitifully, in thousands.

By now, all the invasion beaches had become congested with the detritus of war as if some enormous vessel had been shipwrecked on the coast. Stranded boats, rafts, stores, tents, troops and bodies were abandoned everywhere and, in the sea, upturned topis were floating like jellyfish among the bodies and debris. Farther inland, battles, many hand-to-hand, raged day and night as every inch of land was determinedly fought over: sometimes taken, lost and retaken in a single hour. The resistance of the Turks was fierce and unrelenting, and their troops – supported and guided by German officers and regulars – always retained the supreme advantage of elevated, well-prepared positions.

For the Allies, this was like Hell on Earth.

Chapter Sixteen

PORTSMOUTH
Saturday, May 1, 1915

The meeting of the Women's Social & Political Union – now known as the Women's Union in deference to a non-activist agreement signed on the outbreak of war, was well attended. The Portsmouth Guildhall meeting room was filled with women of all shapes and sizes from every social level, and it opened Carrie's eyes. Glancing at her face, Marje could tell from her look of wide-eyed wonderment that it had been a good idea to invite her.

Carrie suddenly discovered such commonality of purpose there – with more women than she believed possible – that she was now bursting with a belief that women deserved to be recognised. She hung on every word of the visiting speaker, and felt more than eager to be involved in the massive Suffrage Rally planned for July in London. 'I thought you'd be interested,' Marje shouted, as ear-splitting applause brought the meeting to a close.

Carrie's eyes were sparkling. 'I can't wait!' They filed out into the bright sunlight of the Guildhall Square, past the two ranks of stony-faced policemen at the doorway warily scanning the flocking women for any hint of militant behaviour, and headed for the Portsmouth Ferry terminal. 'It's so exciting! I had no idea so many felt the same.' Marje smiled.

'You wait till the rally. People are coming from all over the country for it.' She looked reflective for a moment. 'I think Christobel Pankhurst is so brave – risking herself like that. She's still on licence under the "Cat & Mouse Act" you know.'

'What d'you mean?'

Marje smiled. 'I think you've got a lot to catch up on before you can call yourself a *Suffragette.*'

'I'm not really sure I want to. All I want is to see more women being offered jobs and more responsibility. "Suffragette" sounds more like *martyr* to me – and I don't want to be one of those …and I don't want a licence from that cat and mouse thing.'

'Suffragette, martyr – they're one and the same thing, darling, if you're a true believer like Christobel Pankhurst. It was her mother, Emmeline, who founded the movement years ago, you know. But Christobel and her sister Sylvia more or less carry the flag now.'

'But who's the cat and who's the mouse?'

Marje laughed and looked at Carrie as if she were an inquisitive child. 'Two years ago, Emmeline Pankhurst and some of her followers planted some bombs…'

Carrie looked alarmed. 'Bombs?'

'Yes – one in Kew Gardens and another in Lloyd George's new golf villa at Walton Heath …it was completely demolished – all in the cause of votes for women. Anyway, they got caught and tried at Epsom Court, and were sentenced to prison but inside, they all refused to eat and caused the Government no end of embarrassment. So a new Law was passed – the "Prisoners, Temporary Discharge for Health Act 1913" it was called. It meant that anyone who refused to eat in prison was sent home under special licence. Then, if they misbehaved once again, they were put straight back into prison. It was the Government's way of playing "cat and mouse" with them.'

'Good God! I never knew things like that went on in this country.' Carrie gave her friend a sideways glance. 'Anyway, how d'you know so much about it?'

Marje gave a wry smile. 'I nearly came a cropper myself once. Not with bombs, I hasten to add – but in a demonstration. I got arrested, so I had to learn about these things. Fortunately, I got off. But that's what I was saying about Christobel… she's been arrested once, and could be sent to prison if she gets arrested again.'

Carrie was amazed at her friend's hidden depths, and began to see her in a new light. When they reached the ferry terminal they stood at the quayside for a while, watching a warship leaving harbour with its flags flying in the sunlight and its crew lining the guardrails. A wistful look came into Carrie's eyes. 'I wonder how poor George is getting on. I hope he's all right. Do you ever think about him?'

'Yes, of course I do. But not in the same way as you – I suspect.'

Carrie smiled and gave her a playful slap on the arm.

They were just about to move away when a scruffy woman with unruly, dirty hair and unwashed hands shuffled towards them. She was carrying a basket with a filthy cloth over it. Marje saw her coming and turned to Carrie. 'Don't look now, but we're about to be asked for money – a "Gippo".' As Carrie turned, the woman suddenly drew her hand out of the basket and threw a handful of foul-smelling grey mud. It splattered over Carrie's hat and face. Before she could move, the woman threw another, then another – covering Carrie's jacket and skirt and splashing Marje's clothes.

'There you are, *Lady bleedin'Muck*,' the woman hissed with her mouth curled into a snarl. ' 'Ave some more, ya stuck-up bitch – I got plenty.' She threw another handful of filth then hurried away across the road, into a side street. Carrie gasped and put up her hand to her face, looking aghast at her clothes. There were tears of anguish in her eyes when she saw the extent of the damage and realised how she looked.

She stood open-mouthed and speechless, her arms held away from her body, trying to catch her breath – a picture of dejection. Marje tried to help clean her face and clothes, feeling desperately sorry for her. Taking no account of the mud going onto her own clothes, she put her arms around Carrie and hugged her. 'Oh darling, how awful! What an evil bitch – that woman ought to be locked up! She must be the mother of one of those "mudlarks" and that's that foul stuff from the bottom of the harbour.' She tried to rub it off with her handkerchief, but it simply spread. Carrie was shocked.

Several people stopped to help and sympathise, and all she could say, over and over was, 'Why? Why me? What did I do?'

'It's your clothes, dear,' said one of the woman helpers, in a cold, flat, knowing voice. Carrie had a strange feeling when she looked into the woman's eyes. There was cold sympathy in them, but no empathy. 'They're too fine. If I were you, I'd put all my best things away until the war was over. No sense in rubbing all our noses in what you've got is there? Anyway, this lot is certainly ruined. You won't get that stain out – and it will always smell, you know.' With that, she walked off leaving Carrie stunned and deeply reflective.

As they hurried home, Carrie began to notice for the first time that other women, including Marje, were all dressed simply. Everywhere she looked, she saw plain, dark clothes with hardly a trace of elegance. She could hardly believe it. All the time she had been dressing to look chic, everyone else had been dressing down for the war. It was something that had completely passed her by – as if she had been living in a different world, with blinkers on.

'Is that what all that was about?' she asked, looking pained and puzzled. 'Am I really overdressed, Marje? Tell me the truth.'

Marje looked uneasy. 'Darling, I didn't want to stop you in your tracks. You wanted to improve the way you looked, and it's not my place to say anything ...but, ...well, people *are* trying to look a bit sober, these days. It's all the bad news people get every day and the economy measures going on. Even families with tons of money dress more economically these days. Haven't you noticed? I really thought you knew.' She could tell immediately from Carrie's expression that she had not, and was now feeling belittled and diminished by the sudden realisation.

Carrie soon got over her little drama, and she learned from the experience. From then on, her best clothes were put away and reserved for very special occasions only, and she conformed to everyone else's subdued, wartime dress sense – although it went against the grain with her. The woman was right about the mud. The stain and the smell would not come out and the clothes always reminded her of Portsmouth Harbour. On the other side of the Atlantic, a more sinister drama was about to begin a few days later.

NEW YORK
May 1, 1915

On the morning of Saturday, May 1, 1915, an ominous warning to the world from Germany appeared in American newspapers. It took the form of an advertisement posted by the German Embassy in Washington, which gave formal notice by the Imperial German Government that any vessel flying the flag of Great Britain or any of her allies was liable to destruction. The advertisement further warned travellers that if they sailed into the war zone, they would do so at their own risk. It seemed no coincidence to observers that Britain's giant, four-funnelled passenger liner, Cunard's *Lusitania*, was scheduled to leave New York the same day, bound for Liverpool.

In command of *Lusitania* for her crossing to England was Captain W T Turner, and on board were 1957 people – a crew of 700 and 1257 passengers. Of these, 944 were British and Canadian, 159 were American, and the remainder were of seventeen other nationalities. The ship was a large, instantly recognisable unarmed symbol of Britain's dominance of the Atlantic passenger routes. She was 785 feet long and 88 feet broad, and had a gross tonnage of 31,550. In ordinary conditions she could make 25 knots, but tended to steam at 21 knots in wartime. By May 7, Lusitania was in Britain's coastal waters in clear weather, eight and a half miles off the Old Head of Kinsale on the south coast of Ireland, going at the reduced speed of 18 knots.

Unknown to Captain Turner and the Royal Navy, beneath the calm surface of the sea a lurking German submarine was stealthily stalking his ship, preparing to launch an attack. At 2:30 pm, without warning, the submarine launched a single torpedo at the great liner, and its commander settled back to watch the result through his periscope.

On the bridge of *Lusitania*, Second Officer Hefford was standing on the starboard side, scanning the sea, when his attention was attracted to something moving in the water. Suddenly, he called out, 'Here's a torpedo.' The cry brought Captain Turner rushing from the other side of the bridge and together they watched helplessly as the wake of the torpedo drew a ruler-straight milky line directly to the side of their ship. As the torpedo hit the thin plates of the ship's side, there was an explosion in the area between the rear two funnels that threw up a cloud of smoke and steam from a gaping hole below the waterline of her starboard side. Immediately after the initial explosion there was a further dull thud inside the ship.

Captain Turner gave immediate orders for the lifeboats to be lowered to the guardrails, and for all women and children to be put into them first. Ringing the order down to the engine room to "stop ship", he found that the engines were out of commission and incapable of stopping her. Correctly deciding that it was not safe to lower the lifeboats into the water until the ship's speed was right off, he waited for her to slow before giving the final order. But the momentum of the enormous liner carried her on and she was still underway several minutes later when she began to heel over to starboard and go down by the bow.

At crazy angles, the dangling lifeboats filled with women and children were lowered to the water as the crew tried frantically to get the passengers away. Some of the davits holding the lifeboats broke under the strain and several boats capsized – tipping women, children and infants in arms into the sea. With many passengers and members of the crew still on board, the ship began her headfirst plunge to the bottom of the Irish Sea.

Captain Turner remained on the bridge until the sea gushed in and washed him away. Twenty minutes after the first explosion, the great liner had gone, leaving hundreds of people dying in a sea foaming with her death throes and littered with debris, dead bodies, and overloaded lifeboats.

Still submerged, the German submarine slipped silently away. Of *Lusitania's* total of passengers, 785 were lost and 472 saved. When she went down, 124 Americans perished with 59 of the 90 children, and 35 of the 39 infants on board. Among those saved was Captain Turner. When the news broke, it caused outrage throughout the world, demonstrating as it did Germany's intention not to differentiate between ships of war and unarmed unescorted passenger ships.

The German authorities justified the sinking by claiming that *Lusitania* had been carrying ammunition for which the British had used the passengers as a cover. The second explosion, Germany said, was evidence enough of the presence of explosives on board the ship, but the British and American Governments hotly denied this, and accused Germany of callous butchery.

The sinking of *Lusitania* and the loss of its American passengers was an act Germany would come to regret, because it lit a fire in the belly of America and sowed seeds of doubt about the wisdom of her neutral stance in the war.

When the news of *Lusitania's* sinking reached England, the anger of British citizens erupted and they spilled onto the streets in a series of riots. German restaurants and shops all over the country were wrecked and looted. In London's East End, troops had to be called out to deal with the rioting and looting of German homes and businesses there. In the aftermath, all Germans and Austrians in Britain were interned for their own protection, and any family with an alien as a member of the household had to obtain a permit. A child, overhearing its parents discussing the safety of her German governess, asked anxiously *'Oh, mummy, must we kill poor Fräulein?'*

After the *Lusitania* outrage, all Germans and aliens in Britain became objects of vilification, and spy mania swept the country. Spies were spotted everywhere. But a large number of "sightings" reported by ordinary citizens were merely figments of their imagination. In spite of this, MI5, the spy-catching department of Britain's Secret Service Bureau, which had been tracking a number of known German agents, both male and female, arrested a number of them and had them shot as spies. Only the females were spared.

Any non-British governess or foreign domestic staff, even if they had been in the service of British families until they were old, came under suspicion and their names became a burden both to them and their employers.

People were accused of spying for various reasons – because they "looked odd", or were "whispering", or because they had "names or voices like Germans".

As hysteria and hatred for all things German grew, a spate of name changing was sparked in Britain. The Bernstein family changed its name to Curzon, Steineke changed to Stanley, and Stohwasser became Stowe – and so on.

Even British soldiers who just happened to have foreign-sounding names were obliged to change them – in spite of the obvious fact that they were actively fighting against Germany.

When the King later abolished all German titles in the British Royal Family and adopted the Windsor family name, there was widespread relief at this popular move.

Whatever respect the British still had for Germans after the declaration of war seemed to evaporate with the sinking of *Lusitania*.

PORTSMOUTH
Sunday, May 9, 1915

A crowd of eight young men – some essential workers not required for war service, some unfit or unwilling to enlist – finished drinking at the Nelson Tavern and, worse for drink, spilled noisily out of the public bar to pause on the corner of Nile Street and Unicorn Road. At the dockyard's Unicorn Gates – an impressive, towering arched gateway of stone set in the high walls – several smartly dressed uniformed sailors wearing white belts and gaiters, with rifles at their shoulders, were on guard duty.

In the Nelson Tavern, the rowdy conversation had been mostly about "German bastards" and the sinking of *Lusitania* two days before. This, and the beer consumed, stoked up a disproportionate, over-zealous patriotism. To the annoyance and embarrassment of the sailors saddled with guarding the gates within hailing distance, the drunken men waved and shouted words of encouragement before shambling noisily up Nile Street – a straight, narrow cobbled street of continuous terraced houses. As the men ambled along the street, alarmed residents twitched their lace curtains and peered out anxiously. One or two of the more stalwart housewives enjoying a quiet afternoon opened their doors and hurled abuse at them.

Fanny Ward – a resident well known for her forceful opinions – flung open her front door and stepped menacingly onto the pavement. Hands on hips, she confronted the crowd in her Sunday-best pinafore. The men stopped and stared at her. Her rounded face was flushed red and her eyes blazed angrily. With the two large warts sprouting small tufts of hair on her hooked nose, and two front teeth missing, she was not a pretty sight. 'Ain't you bleeders got nuffink better to do than ruin every uvver bugger's day awf?' enquired the delightful Mrs Ward, stridently.

The men shuffled into a group around her, muttering words of dubious advice – but she was not concerned. 'Sod off, yer old bag,' said one. 'Yeah, 'op on yer broomstick an' piss awf!' said another.

One man, who appeared to be their natural leader and spokesman, stepped forward calling for quiet with his raised arms and faced up to Fanny Ward. 'Listen, missus,' he said, through his clenched teeth, 'we got no quarrel wi' you. We're off up the road to give them bastard Germans in Charlotte Street a bit o' what for, that's all. We're not goin' to stand by and let them lot drown our wimmin an' kids... even if you are. You're British, incha? You ought to do the same.' Fanny stared at him while the men waited to see what she would do next.

With a husband wounded in the front line somewhere in Europe, and a sailor son on the high seas in the Navy, the idea of getting one back on Germany had a certain appeal for Fanny Ward. 'Right!' she said, her top lip curling back to reveal the rest of her yellow teeth. 'I'm gonna do just that. You 'ang on there while I get me bag.' Jaws dropped as she disappeared into her tiny house. Seconds later, she returned carrying a canvas bag. 'Right, let's go!' she said, enthusiastically, as if it was her place to take charge.

There was a babble of approval from the astonished men, and they surged up the road towards Charlotte Street, where there was a German delicatessen and an Austrian baker's shop. Along the way, the men picked up all the missiles they could find – bricks, stones and pieces of wood – and their anger mounted as they went. By the time they reached Stimfel's delicatessen, the mood of the crowd was explosive and it wasted no time smashing the shopfront to pieces.

Charlotte Street was already littered and malodorous with the remnants of Saturday's stall market. Pieces of rotting fruit and vegetables, paper and packing case debris, were strewn all over the cobbled roadway. Within seconds, the shattered glass of Stimfel's shop front was added to the mess. The sheer vandalism of it was like a drug to the crowd, which was growing by the minute. Men were egging each other on in a blind craving for the wanton destruction of "enemy property". With the delicatessen wrecked, they moved along the road to Bachus's baker's shop. When they found this heavily shuttered, their frustration reached fever pitch. From the depths of her canvas bag, Fanny Ward materialised the "chopper" that she used for firewood, and attacked the shutters with it.

'Go on, gal,' encouraged the crowd, 'get stuck in,' but the metal shutters would not give way, not even to Fanny's chopper, and a sense of frustration and anticlimax swept the crowd on, to find something else to vent its anger on. Someone spotted a branch of the grocery shop of Paxman & Guy.

'There's anuvver bleedin' 'un bastard,' he screamed. 'Go on, let 'im 'ave it!'

'No!' Fanny tried to shout, ''e ain't German... 'e's local,' but she was shouted down by men hungry for revenge or satisfaction – they knew not what. All they could think of was smashing something: anything.

'Sounds bloody German to me,' said one, 'an' that's good enough.' That was all it took. He hurled a large stone, and the big shop window crashed to the pavement in a cascade of splinters and shards of glass. In no time at all, Roy Paxman's pride and joy was in ruins. When there were no more shops left with remotely German names, the crowd ran out of steam, fell quiet, and gradually dispersed.

With their anger vented, the ordinary people who had briefly become animals went back to their ordinary lives, leaving Charlotte Street resembling a battleground. For a while, it had been a battleground – for the misguided emotions of deeply frustrated people.

WHITEHALL, LONDON

Among Asquith's gathering black clouds a silver lining shone through in April as some positive news came to lift the Prime Minister's flagging spirits. At last, a breakthrough had been achieved in the negotiations with Italy. To his great relief, the Treaty of London was finally signed on April 26, pledging Italy to "enter the field" on the side of the Allies within one month. It was a significant occasion, but not significant enough to outweigh the rest of his political problems and new concerns in his personal life.

For some time, he had been feeling uneasy and troubled by his relationship with Venetia Stanley. She appeared to be too busy to see much of him, and her letters had become sparse and infrequent. Now she seemed set on going to France at the end of her training, to nurse troops in a military hospital there. To no avail, he tried to dissuade her. Then a date they were both dreading for entirely different reasons loomed large on their calendars: Monday, May 10.

Asquith was dreading it. It was the day his lover was due to leave

England for the military hospital at Wimereux, near Boulogne. That she was leaving London to be where he could not reach her readily depressed him and occupied much of his thought. Venetia was dreading it because she now had to face up to telling him that she intended to marry Edwin Montagu. For her, the chance to get away from London made this the right time to bring his preoccupation with her to an end – finally and completely.

She intended to announce this devastating news when she reached Wimereux. There she could write to him without fear of his close attention and immediate access, and, in the meantime, all she had to do was keep him at bay. An invitation from the Churchills to stay with them over the weekend prior to her departure fitted the bill perfectly. She was, after all, the first cousin of Clementine, Winston's wife, and she had every reason to spend her last weekend with them at their Hoe Farm residence, near Godalming.

Unfortunately, she fell ill there and developed a fever during the weekend and had to postpone her departure for Wimereux. She returned to her London home to rest, with her plans in disarray. She could not bring herself to give Asquith news that would shatter him whilst she was still within reach of him, but she could no longer delay telling him about her intention to marry Montagu for fear that he would hear the news from someone in the know.

On Tuesday, May 11, when Asquith heard that she was ill and had postponed her departure, he immediately called at her home to see her. He was told that she was suffering from a mystery illness, and that he could not see her, so he wrote to her instead, wishing her a speedy recovery from her headache and depression – suspecting, but not knowing, what had caused it.

Then, on May 12, his world fell apart. He received a letter written from her sick bed the day before. With this, she ended their relationship, completely and irrevocably, and informed him that she was going to marry Edwin Montagu.

Asquith was devastated.

He did not know which way to turn, or how to console himself. Lost was the love of his life, his ally and confidante: gone to marry the unattractive Jew they had both mocked in earlier times. His heart was broken ...his dream ended and his life shattered. That same day he sent her short, moving note, revealing how distraught he felt:

"Most Loved – As you know well, this breaks my heart.
I couldn't bear to come and see you.
I can only pray God to bless you – and help me.

Yours."©

Surrounded by mounting difficulties, and now losing the one person he had always relied upon for advice and counsel, his will to fight deserted him but his troubles were just beginning.

The Dardanelles campaign now seemed doomed to failure and had already cost Churchill the confidence of his own Party. Now the Conservatives, whom Churchill had deserted in favour of the Liberal Party years before, saw the opportunity for revenge. With pressure mounting for the ousting of Churchill and confidence in the Government badly shaken, Asquith felt beleaguered, emotionally shattered, and close to the end of his tether. His enthusiasm for matters of the day and his ability to act decisively seemed to fade away with his fanciful dreams for a happy ending with Venetia.

Another black cloud then arrived to darken his gloom. On May 13, the entire Italian Government – the very men who had signed the Treaty of London two weeks previously, tendered their resignations. At a stroke, the one moment of brightness he had experienced in recent times vanished. On the same day, there was other disturbing news in London. The Royal Navy's battleship *Goliath* had been lost in the Dardanelles with five hundred of her crew. Travelling slowly by nature of her duty to cover the Allies' eastern flank she had been an easy target for a torpedo.

At the Admiralty, senior officers took little note of the fact that a Turkish destroyer, not a submarine, had fired the torpedo. For them, the threat of German U-boats in the area had become a reality. Then, from Europe came further bad news. There had been another military setback at Aubers Ridge. It resulted in a serious blow to the well-being of Asquith's Government and the press began to bare its teeth. On May 14, the leader in the morning's *Times* newspaper directly attributed the failure of the Aubers Ridge offensive of May 9 to the shell shortages created by the Government's failure to properly organise the output of munitions. At the War Council meeting on the same day its members were told that the situation in the Dardanelles was dire and that Hamilton's troops were pinned down at two minor bridgeheads on the Gallipoli Peninsula with no hope of an early breakthrough. A similar situation existed on the Western Front.

Then, on May 15, no lesser person than Britain's own First Sea Lord Jacky Fisher pushed the Government over the brink, dramatically and finally. In one final, cataclysmic disagreement with Winston Churchill – over naval reinforcements for the Dardanelles campaign – Fisher tendered his very last resignation and, quite literally, went into hiding. On his departure, he wrote to the Leader of the Opposition, Bonar Law, indicating what he had done.

It was the straw that broke the camel's back. It sent a signal to the newspapers and the Opposition that the Government was in a state of divisive disorder: an opportunity not to be missed.

A serious drama was in the offing.

PRIME MINISTER'S STUDY, 10 DOWNING ST., LONDON
Monday, May 17, 1915

The Prime Minister sat quietly at his desk, staring vacantly out of the window at the grey skies above Whitehall. He seemed not to notice when David Lloyd George rapped the door and came in to see him. His visitor waited silently for a few moments, looking at him. Asquith's shoulders were visibly borne down by his recent ministerial and emotional disasters and the sparkle had left his eyes. They looked dull, tired, and red-rimmed, and his ample silver hair was more unkempt than usual.

'Henry?' Lloyd George had to call for his attention.

'Henry?' Asquith turned slowly, revealing the true extent of his weariness. 'Bonar Law will be here in a minute, Henry,' said Lloyd George, as softly as his gravelly Welsh voice would permit. He wanted to show empathy. After all, he was in a similar position himself – in a relationship with a young woman, Frances Stevenson, whose parents had made a gallant effort, weeks before, to put an end to the affair but, right now, he was anxious to get on with the very serious and important matters at hand. 'He's going to want answers now that Fisher has done a bunk. What are you going to do?'

Asquith stared blankly for a moment, summoning his concentration. 'We shall just have to see what is on his mind then, shan't we?' Not blessed with boundless patience, Lloyd George was becoming tetchy. He stepped forward snappily and dropped his compact stocky frame into a chair in front of the desk, and leaned forward, earnestly.

'For God's sake, man... you know damn fine what's on his mind! We've got our backs to the wall. The Government is in disarray. The First Sea Lord has done a bunk. The Dardanelles campaign is in a bloody mess – and the Opposition's got all the ammunition it needs to bring us down now. We're facing a vote of "No Confidence"!'

Asquith turned and stared out of the window. 'We'll have to buy him off somehow.' The Prime Minister's matter-of-fact manner stretched the feisty Welshman's patience to the limit.

'Buy him off?' His voice rose several decibels. 'Buy him off? What the hell can you buy him off with? The best you've got to offer is a coalition!'

'That is the last thing I want to do, David. There must be another way.'

'There is no other way, Henry... believe me. He's already been to see me. I'm sorry, but there is no other way. The sooner you agree terms for a shared government the better it will be for the Liberals... and the country.' There was a long pause as Asquith gazed up at the sky outside, gathering his thoughts.

'What do you think it will cost us?' he said quietly.

'Well... I suppose, for a start, you will have to offer members of the Opposition a number of positions of high office in the new government... the details for that will have to be worked out with Bonar Law... and an influential position for Bonar himself. You should stay as Prime Minister, and I will relinquish the Treasury and offer myself to the munitions problem. You must demonstrate that all Parties are represented and have a real say in the future conduct of the war.' Lloyd George's forehead creased in a frown as he went on. 'But one thing is certain... Winston must go.'

The Prime Minister was taken aback. He leaned back in his chair. He did not want this to happen, and he lacked the ruthlessness to oust an old friend from office – especially one as promising as Churchill, whose energy and drive he had always admired. He was distinctly ill at ease with the idea of dismissing him. 'No, I don't think that will be necessary,' he said, offhandedly. 'I intend to keep Winston in office. I'll do my best to keep him at the Admiralty, where he can continue to deal with the Dardanelles situation.'

Lloyd George's ire rose and flushed his cheeks red. 'Live in the real world, Henry! It will not work. Winston must go. The Tories want his head on a plate. He's even lost the confidence of some of our own members... he's seen as reckless and damaging. We have to distance ourselves from him, if we are to survive this.'

Sharp knuckles rapped the door and it swept open. A secretary announced and admitted the Right Honourable Mr Bonar Law – a dapper, youthful man with a neat walrus moustache that covered his entire mouth. Asquith stood up and all three exchanged routine formalities. 'Welcome, Bonar, please take a seat.' The Prime Minister welcomed him with a forced smile. Bonar Law sat down.

'I am sorry to be visiting you in such critical circumstances, Prime Minister,' he said in a cultured Scots accent blurred by faint Canadian undertones. 'We need to discuss a number of issues that are causing concern amongst Opposition members.' He took papers from his valise. Asquith sat back in his chair, summoning up an attentive expression. 'The three main issues concerning us,' Bonar began, 'are firstly: public anger in the newspapers that the Government has not properly organised the supply of munitions – which we have debated on a number of occasions – and secondly: the Dardanelles situation. As you know, it is my personal view that this is a disaster from which we should withdraw immediately – before we lose more ships and troops, and find ourselves incapable of withdrawing with anything left.'

He braced himself for his main proposal.

'Finally, we feel the time has come for an all-party government to run the war effort. Clearly, the scale and nature of this conflict is much greater than any of us envisioned at the outset. Whilst there is universal praise that the present Government, under your excellent leadership, Prime Minister, has acquitted itself with great honour and fortitude, there are serious concerns about the future. From here on, managing the war effort is likely to be a massive and difficult task which we feel could only be handled properly by a coalition of all interested parties.' Asquith and Lloyd George looked at one another without speaking. Bonar Law looked for a response to his well-prepared diatribe.

'And would a reconstruction to include all Parties receive the full cooperation of the Opposition?' Asquith asked, tentatively.

'Yes, indeed. But ah, yes,' Bonar Law continued, looking a trifle uneasy, 'there is the matter of Winston Churchill's involvement. The Tories insist that they will not submit their willing cooperation unless Winston is removed from office immediately. He must be distanced from any position of power.'

'But Winston is such a fine and capable man.' Asquith's objection was driven by genuine concern. 'Only he has the knowledge and ability to bring the Dardanelles campaign to a successful conclusion.'

Bonar Law was firm. 'I am afraid there can be no cooperation whilst Winston remains in a position of influence.' Asquith looked deep into his eyes and saw nothing but sincerity there. This was fact: it was no political bluff. There was an awkward silence.

Eventually, Lloyd George rose and extended an arm to Asquith's shoulder, drawing him to the far corner of the room and away from Bonar Law. Their heads went together and they talked in urgent, hushed tones. Lloyd George was clasping Asquith's shoulder with one hand and forcing home his points with expressive gestures of the other. Finally, Asquith's head dropped in a gesture that indicated his surrender to the arguments. They returned to their seats.

'Very well,' Asquith said solemnly, with a resigned, weary gesture. 'We will invite certain members of the Opposition to join with us in a reconstruction of the Government... but it must be understood that this will be for the duration of the war only.'

'Of course, Prime Minister.' Bonar Law was visibly relieved. 'I will now put the case and seek the cooperation of all parties concerned.' He gathered up his documents and stood up to leave. 'I am sure you are making the right decision. It is in the interest of us all that both Parties should combine and share their varied talents to bring this destructive war to a successful conclusion.' With that, he nodded to Asquith and left the room, followed by Lloyd George.

Asquith sat in silence. A small tear glistened onto his cheek. With no one to share the burden of his grief and despair, he felt utterly desolate. He drew paper from the ream on the corner of his desk and began to do what he had secretly vowed he would never do again. He wrote to Venetia Stanley. He wanted her to know how forlorn he was without her, and how deep the despair he was feeling at that moment. He told her that no matter how hellish some of his days had been since the war began, whatever his trials and troubles, she had been the one person in the world to whom he could always turn. She was the only one who would always heal and inspire him, and was now no longer there for him, at a time when he was on the brink of such astounding, earth-shaking decisions, which he would not have taken without her counsel. This would be the most bitter memory of his life.

He carefully folded the letter without reading it. It was his practice never to re-read what he had written. Then he sat back in his chair and gazed at the sky with darkness in his heart. He had lost everything he cared about. If only Venetia would miraculously appear in his room to say what a terrible mistake she had made! With a sharp knock, the door swung open. He turned towards it expectantly – happiness leaping to his eyes, but it was not his beloved Venetia, and the flash of light in his eyes went out as quickly as it had come. His excitement crumbled.

It was Churchill bustling into the room – preoccupied and failing to notice Asquith's despondency. He was excited and had good news to deliver. 'Prime Minister,' he began, 'I am very pleased to tell you that we have nothing at all to fear from the Tories... or their...aah criticisms. I have here all the documents I need to demonstrate once and for all the validity of our actions. We can justify, without question, what we are doing in the Dardanelles, and calls for my resignation will count for nothing in the House when I produce these.' His eyes twinkled as he patted the pile of papers under his arm. 'Furthermore, you will be pleased to hear that I now have a very fitting replacement for Lord Fisher. Together, we will achieve the campaign objectives and bring about a successful conclusion to it. We can silence the Tories once and for all.'

Asquith stared blankly, hearing what was being said but not

listening. When Churchill paused, waiting for a reaction, Asquith looked into his eyes and said vaguely, 'No, this will not do. I have decided to form a national government with a coalition with the Unionists, and a very much larger reconstruction will be required.'

Churchill was completely stunned. He opened his mouth to speak, but Asquith cut him off with a simple sentence that shot through his heart like a knife. 'What are we to do for you?' he asked. Churchill was dumbfounded. This told him more succinctly than any other seven words could ever do that his career at the Admiralty was at an end. His heart sank like a cold stone tossed into a bottomless ocean. No matter how much he pleaded to be left in office to finish the job in hand, it was made clear that his time was over. He was being ousted from his beloved Admiralty; and his entire political career was ending there and then.

He was heartbroken: devastated beyond words.

Within days, the Government was reconstructed and Churchill was reduced to the office of Chancellor of the Duchy of Lancaster: an honorary position without power or duty. Shunted into this political siding, he was now to be excluded from influencing the outcome of the Dardanelles campaign; a cause he had made his own. Yet he was genuinely convinced that in his hand he had the means to snatch success from the jaws of that particular disaster. Filled with utter frustration and burning anger at Asquith's betrayal, he descended into the depths of depression.

Meanwhile, Asquith sent his official letter of invitation to the leader of the Opposition. In it, he said:

"After long and careful consideration I have definitely come to the conclusion that the conduct of the war to a successful and decisive issue cannot be effectively carried on except by a Cabinet which represents all parties in the State... I am therefore in a position to invite you and those who are associated with you to join forces in a combined administration in which I should also ask the leaders of the Irish and Labour parties to participate..."

Bonar Law initially had some difficulty persuading the Tories of the Unionist Party to accept a coalition. He explained to them that there were no alternatives. It was not possible to elect a proper new

Government without an election, and an election while the country was in the thick of war was unthinkable. In the end he succeeded, and replied to Asquith:

"...We have now communicated your views and your invitation to our colleagues, and we shall be glad to cooperate with you in your endeavour to form a National Government."

In due course, a New Cabinet was formed. It consisted of 12 Liberals, 8 Unionists, 1 Labour member and Lord Kitchener. Meanwhile, the struggle in Gallipoli continued.

THE DARDANELLES
May 25, 1915

In the Aegean Sea, off the northern landing beaches of Gallipoli, the British battleship *Triumph* was on duty covering the flank of the Anzac forces when she fell prey to a German submarine. Shortly after being hit by a torpedo, she sank. Two days later, inside the Dardanelles, the same German U-boat sank the battleship *Majestic*, on similar duties. The Navy's losses were becoming unacceptable, and it was clear that many more ships would be sunk if something were not done about German submarines.

The Admiralty's response was to withdraw *Queen Elizabeth* from the Dardanelles campaign and return her, together with the rest of the most modern warships involved, to the Grand Fleet in the North Sea. As they left, Admiral de Robeck was obliged to transfer his flag from ship to ship.

With some irony, the arrival of German submarines in the Dardanelles achieved much more than the sinking of two British battleships. At a single stroke, it achieved an immediate reduction in the Royal Navy's presence there. Hastily vacating its position of absolute dominance in the area, the Navy left a much-depleted force of older, slower warships to support the campaign. It signalled the turning point in Britain's efforts to force the Straits, and a perceived failure for which Churchill was forever to be blamed.

During the five weeks following the April 25 landings, territory was painfully gained by the troops in push after push, but progress was pitifully slow. The advantage was always with the defenders. Now, once again, the fierce resistance of the Turks pinned the Allies down, and the prospect of siege warfare loomed.

Countless acts of bravery and heroism that beggar belief occurred daily in the Allies' lines, in every area of the conflict. But these had a great cost, and were to little advantage. The advances were short-lived, and were dearly paid for in the blood of soldiers falling in thousands on both sides.

Already, the total losses of the Turco-German forces in the peninsula were estimated to be not less than 55,000. The Allies' casualties, both Naval and military, had reached 38,686 men. These figures already exceeded by 480 the total killed, wounded, and missing for the whole of the earlier Boer War.

For the Allies, the Gallipoli campaign was not going at all well.

Chapter Seventeen

After being wounded on April 25, George Royal was transferred to a hospital ship anchored off the Greek Island of Imbros. There it was confirmed that he had sustained a fractured skull from the Turkish machine-gun bullet that had glanced off his head. For three days after the incident, he was never fully conscious. He was heavily sedated and drifted from unconsciousness to semi-consciousness in a jumble of mental images and waves of pain, not knowing at all where he was or what had happened.

Beneath his turban of bandages there was an ugly, seeping wound in his scalp. Had he been conscious, his vanity would have caused him to care about all of his hair being shaved off; but he knew nothing of this. All around him the previously empty bunks were rapidly filling with injured soldiers and sailors. Some of the patients had relatively minor injuries but there were many with appalling wounds from the chaotic battles raging all along the coastline and foreshore of the Gallipoli Peninsula.

George's severely concussed brain swelled rapidly coming under pressure as it reached the limit of its allotted place in his skull. His condition deteriorated, causing alarm. On the third day, he slipped into a coma. Overworked doctors shook their heads turning their attention to the more hopeful cases. When the hospital ship had as many patients as it could cope with, it was relieved by another and left the Aegean Sea for the Mediterranean island of Malta.

Caring for George was a thankless task for the nurses. He had no control over his inert body, and he had to be kept alive with whatever liquids they could put into him, but they persisted and he continued to survive. Then, at *11:30 pm* on May 6, he rewarded them in the only way he could: his eyes briefly flickered open for the first time in twelve days. By the time the ship reached Valetta Harbour four days later, the medical staff was altogether more optimistic about his chance of ultimately making a full recovery.

His pain was devastating and it was only with regular doses of medicinal morphine that he got through each day. Eventually, the doctors seemed concerned that George was becoming addicted to it and decided to stop giving it to him the moment he left the ship.

BIGHI NAVAL HOSPITAL, MALTA
May 10, 1915

In the 19th Century Naval Hospital in Malta, George discovered that he would have to learn to deal with his pain himself – and get along without the opium to which he had become accustomed. The starchy matron of the orderly, pristine ward where he was sent had no sympathy with that aspect of his suffering. For her, duty meant getting him fit enough to return to his own duty, and exactly that would happen in her ward. She coldly told him to get a grip on himself, and then virtually ordered him to get well quickly.

She wanted him transferred home, as he surely would be, as soon as he was fit to travel. She kept her true feelings, if she had any left, well hidden by a sternly casehardened, matronly manner and let him know that he would not stay in Bighi for ever, cluttering up her ward and using beds that were needed for more deserving cases.

Gradually, the pain in his head subsided, and he began to take more notice of his surroundings. In spite of the large fans whooshing day and night from their long stalks fixed to the high ceiling, the air in the ward was hot from a sun blasting down every day on the sandstone building. Bighi Hospital was situated just behind Fort Ricasoli, overlooking Valetta Harbour. With the windows open wide, familiar smells and sounds of naval activity reached the ward and George spent his days picturing what was going on out there. Then one day, a Petty Officer recovering from a minor wound came in to tell him that he had also been on *River Clyde* during the fateful landing. At last, George had met someone who could fill in the blanks of his memories of that day and he was shattered by the news that his friend Chalky White had been killed there. His spirits crashed and he was left in a deeply reflective, melancholy mood for which the PO got an icy blast from the matron and was sent on his way.

New patients arrived regularly from various parts of the Mediterranean and Aegean areas, bringing news of battles and casualties. In the hospital the patients were better informed about what was going on in the area than people at home were. Reports were depressing and it seemed that nothing was going right for the Navy or the Army – particularly in the Gallipoli campaign. For George, it made his personal efforts there seem even more futile.

During his time in Bighi Hospital, George kept digging into the dark corners of his mind and retrieving sketchy images of what had happened to him and his friends. The more he tried, the more he remembered. It was as if the clout to his head had revitalised his mind. Mental pictures seemed more vivid than ever before, and he was able to recall and relive almost any incident at will but now, things that had been challenging and exciting at the time seemed to have a very different slant as he lay in the calmness of the ward staring at the fans gyrating above him.

The thought that dominated his thinking was the futility of it all – the impermanence war brought with it: the destruction, maiming and death he had witnessed. Bitterness festered in the core of his mind and images kept popping up of ships sinking and men struggling desperately to survive, Germans he had killed, and the young Turkish soldiers he had personally shot on the beaches of their own homeland.

It was not what he expected when he joined the Navy. There was no talk of war then – just images of a comradely, thrilling life his father brought back from exciting, sunny, far-off parts of the world. How could he have known what was to come? He was young and naïve then, with no conception of warfare or any idea that its horrors would reach out and consume him. His lonely, personal reflections depressed him and left him low. There was no one left he could discuss these things with: no one to share his personal burdens.

Deep down, George knew he would always carry out the duties he had taken on when he joined the Navy and he was not afraid of dying, but now he wanted to shed the responsibility for killing human beings, whoever they might be, or whatever they might have done. However, he knew that he would be forced to do it again, all too soon, and the prospect filled him with disgust and apprehension.   One thought kept screaming in his head – *I don't want to do this any more,* but there was no way out of this situation. He knew that too. All he could do was re-bury these disturbing thoughts somewhere at the back of his mind, where they had insidiously taken root. He forced his troubled mind away from the horrors of war and onto the task of conjuring up pleasant images – of home, his mother, and Carla James but, when he managed to do this, he always seemed to end up thinking about Carrie and Bill.

He could picture Carrie's face more easily than his mother's, or Carla's. Why? What really was the relationship between Carrie and Bill? They could get married, if they wanted to – but they had not. Did they have a permanent relationship – or was it a convenient, temporary thing that would come apart one day? Why, also, was he thinking about Carrie more often than he cared to admit? The one thing that speeded up his recovery – both physical and mental – was being well enough to be wheeled outside for part of each day, where he had a good view of the harbour and its activities. It gave him the feeling that he would soon be back to sea, and normality – or, better still, home. Then a visit from another patient took him by surprise.

It was Curly Roberts, who had also been at the hospital for some time, not knowing about George's injury and admission to the hospital. Curly was recovering well and back on his feet but there was a question hanging over his fitness to continue service in the Navy.

'I don't know anything else but the Navy,' Curly kept saying. 'I can't imagine life in "Civvy Street". I reckon I'll have to get a transfer to another branch, if they'll wear it. Maybe I could join the Supply Branch and become a "Pusser's Mate" or something.'

George felt sorry for him. One way or another, their lives seemed destined to be wrecked or ruined by the war.

On July 10, George had the best news he had had in ages. Matron came into the ward and told him he would be going home to Haslar Hospital on the next available ship. He could not wait. He was sick of being in bed, doing nothing, and he longed to be as far from the dark shadows of Gallipoli as he could get. At least at home, in familiar surroundings, he thought – his mind would be on other things, and the war would just be a remote and distant thing that he could let pass by for a while but for certain other people at home a lot was happening, in a variety of ways.

DOWNING STREET LONDON

Storming off in a rage in the way that he had, Jacky Fisher caused uproar in London. When the King was informed that the First Sea Lord had resigned in the middle of war, he was outraged, and suggested that if Fisher did not return to his duties immediately, he should be hung from a yardarm for deserting his post but he went into hiding and no amount of coaxing by Winston Churchill or Asquith could get him to return. Eventually, Admiral Sir H Jackson succeeded him as First Sea Lord.

The Germans rejoiced in the changes in Britain's government, and called it "another sign of Britain's hopeless confusion", but Maximilian Harden, a German publicist, had somewhat more respect for Britain's abilities than that. He immediately distanced himself from the official view and, with uncanny perception, wrote:

"England is awakening, and will not sleep again, save in death."

As everyone feared, the change in Government caused problems. At first, there seemed to be no great improvement in the management of the war effort, and Kitchener persisted with his strong belief that all military efforts should be concentrated upon the Western Front. Lloyd George, meanwhile, favoured attacking the enemy in other, wider areas – namely, an Eastern Front. Disagreement and controversy in the Government continued to hinder its progress, and there were further setbacks as new Cabinet members took time to familiarise themselves with their new jobs, and catch up with aspects of the war in which they had hitherto not been involved.

As they bedded themselves into their new roles, there was a gloomy period of inaction, lightened only by one amusing story from Gallipoli. It transpired that the Turks were completely nonplussed by the multi-coloured nature of the forces facing them in Gallipoli and their greatest surprise came at the Anzac's beach when the Maoris landed to join the New Zealanders there. Some of these – although better educated than many of their colleagues – were full-blooded Maoris who cherished the warlike traditions of their ancestors. Shortly after their arrival in Gallipoli, they performed their blood-curdling war-dance less than 100 yards from the Turkish trenches, leading one Constantinople newspaper to report: *"THUS, FOR THE*

FIRST TIME IN ALL HISTORY, THE DARDANELLES HAVE HAD TO BE DEFENDED FROM ATTACK BY CANNIBALS!"

Under David Lloyd George, a new Ministry of Munitions generated feverish activity throughout the country, speeding up contracts and creating new centres of production. The task was immense, and he put the full extent of it into perspective when he announced one day that while Germany was turning out 250,000 shells a day – mostly high explosive ones – Britain had been producing a mere 2,500 a day. "We trusted too much to the old firms without seeking new sources of supply" – he explained – "this, and the changed conditions of modern warfare."

Bonar Law, in his new role as Secretary of State for the Colonies, later inaugurated a new Inventions Board to assist the Admiralty in encouraging scientific effort in all aspects of naval warfare. It had a Central Committee, to which Jacky Fisher was invited as its new President. Having exhausted all efforts to find an alternative way back to power, he accepted the invitation.

While all this was going on, Asquith remained in deep despair about losing Venetia, and took to writing his woes to her closest sister, Sylvia Henley. Sylvia provided whatever comfort she could, but was no substitute for the real thing.

In a moment of utter desperation at her silence, he wrote to Venetia at midnight on May 14: *"This is too terrible. No Hell can be so bad. Cannot you send me one word? Only one word?"*©

She responded, and this gave him enough encouragement to write several more letters to her, but it was clear that nothing was going to change her mind. They had an emotional meeting on May 23, as she was about to leave England for Wimereux. Afterwards, Venetia was moved to write to Montagu, to tell him that she could not pretend that Asquith's unhappiness did not affect her deeply:

"How could it not? For three years he has been to me the most wonderful friend & companion, and to see him just now made wretched by me is, and should be if I pretend to any heart at all, a real sorrow."©

Then in June 1915, the lovelorn Asquith made a visit to the Western Front himself. On his way back, he called at Boulogne on June 3 and met Venetia there. It was then that she finally convinced him that nothing was going to dissuade her from marrying Edwin Montagu but she implored him not to let it destroy their friendship. On his return to London on June 11, he wrote a long, conciliatory letter in which he reaffirmed his love for her and implored her to give him time to come to terms with his feelings.

In the Montagu and Stanley families, Venetia's intended conversion from Christianity and her proposed marriage to Montagu were causing consternation and argument. In the meantime she alarmed Montagu by announcing that she was enjoying her new nursing life in Wimereux so much that she was considering staying on. It immediately indicated to Montagu that she would probably use this as an excuse to procrastinate about her conversion of faith. He was horrified, and crossed the Channel immediately to persuade her to come home.

In the wider conflict there was a period of relative inactivity. While German submarines continued to carry out sporadic attacks on small freighters and towns on the East Coast of England, the superiority of the Royal Navy in the North Sea was well established. The war at sea calmed down to a level of routine exercises and patrolling, and a strange lull descended upon it. The attempts of the German Navy to break out of the ports where it was bottled up became feebler and the Royal Navy's attention turned to recreational sport and leisure activities at its main base in Scapa Flow. The military struggle in Europe continued, but this too entered a phase of stagnation, as the lines moved back and forth with very little progress either way.

In the Dardanelles, battleships that were doing very little were gradually withdrawn to Mudros Harbour, where the crews enjoyed a break from action. Ashore in Gallipoli, after some desperate assaults and counter-assaults in July, the campaign settled into the bloody and bitter monotony of trench warfare but General Hamilton was busy. He was making plans to mount a supreme effort from the Anzac and Sulva Bay bridgeheads the following month.

Apart from the effort of holding their existing positions and carrying out the odd skirmish on land and sea, it seemed that enemies everywhere had temporarily run out of steam, and were taking a breather before renewing their efforts.

July, 1915

By July, Britain's resources were now sorely taxed by her involvement in too many theatres of war – Europe, Gallipoli, Egypt, Mesopotamia and Africa. She had the additional task of providing reserves and garrisons for the defence of the United Kingdom and outlying parts of the Empire.

The Government's duties to the nation and its allies were many and varied. Not only did it have to provide an adequate supply of troops and equipment to various theatres of war, turn out an inexhaustible supply of munitions and maintain freedom of the seas, it also needed to keep essential industries going to maintain a worldwide credit. Men in dockyards and factories were already working seven days a week and overtime to do this, falling asleep whenever they knocked off work.

Meanwhile, German submarines were inflicting serious damage upon Britain's economy by crippling imports. People at home were forced to tighten their belts severely. It meant hunger, blackouts, coal shortages and the curtailment of fuel and light. A further War Loan campaign had to be launched.

On Saturday July 17, in pouring rain, the rally organised by suffrage societies paraded the streets of London carrying banners proclaiming "WE DEMAND THE RIGHT TO SERVE". Carrie and Marje were there – eyes shining with belief – chanting along with the crowd of 30,000 women. It was a milestone in the movement's history, and it demonstrated how strongly women felt that they should be employed in order to free more men for the Army.

Lloyd George received their deputation and it brought about change. *"The first thing to do was to get rid of the prejudice of trade unionists and the conservatism of businessmen"*, he said (in respect of employing women).

Later, he confirmed that 50,000 women aged 14 to middle age, were already working in munitions factories – 12 hours a day, 7 days a week, for 32 shillings a week. They had proved, he said, to be two and a half times more productive than men. It resulted in a Board of Trade Registry being instituted for organising women volunteers.

By the end of July, 1915, women volunteer munitions workers were being enrolled in thousands. Sixteen new "national factories" had been set up by the end of the month, together with a new Volunteer Women's Police Force and a new entry scheme for employing women on railways.

For Asquith, who had been against the suffrage movement all along, it was a depressing event – but not as depressing as another that took place on Monday, July 26. Having carried through her conversion of faith, Venetia Stanley finally married Edwin Montagu on this day, in the house of Lord Swaythling, Edwin's brother.

For Carrie, the Government's new attitude towards women seemed like the beginning of the end of men's prejudice in business, and one in the eye for men like Paxman. She was overjoyed that she had, in some small way, made her contribution to that.

GOSPORT
Thursday, July 29, 1915

Alone in the apartment with Kate sleeping peacefully, Carrie cleared the table and settled down to the task of reconciling the day's takings. For some inexplicable reason it had not been a great day in the shop and it hardly seemed worthwhile keeping it open for the last twenty minutes of opening hours but in case of a last minute rush she left her promising new assistant, Maude, in charge of it so that she could concentrate on the books. The young but bright Maude represented the first and only concession Carrie had won in her struggle to get Paxman & Guy to employ women but she was confident that there would be more to come.

With a deep sigh, she gave the ledger and the cash box on the table a look of reluctance, leaned back in her chair and stared at the window. Momentarily, her thoughts drifted onto other things: her life in general, and the evening she was about to spend on her own, once again. A sad weariness came to her eyes and faded their usual bright green hue. The price of success was proving greater than she had bargained for. Right now, it hardly seemed worth it. She had expected – and was willingly prepared – for hard work but the true cost now coming to light was unexpectedly high: Bill out night after night on business and, for her, night after night at home alone with only her thoughts and Kate for company. She forced herself to concentrate on the job she knew she had to do.

'Yoo-hoo …Miss, are you there?' It was Maude, calling up the stairway.

'Sshh! Kate's asleep, Maude. What's the matter?'

Maude came up looking excited. 'Sorry, Miss, there's a gentleman in the shop asking to see you. He says his name is Paxman …like our shop, Miss.' Maude leaned forward, confidentially. 'He's got a great big motor outside... real posh it is.'

Carrie could hardly believe that Roy Paxman would drop in at the shop without notice; but it was possible. *What the hell for?* she wondered. 'All right, Maude, go back down and tell him I won't be a moment.' She went to the mirror and checked her hair, peeped at Kate, and crept down the stairs with puzzlement on her face. As soon as she entered the shop, she could see it was Paxman. She smiled as best she could although there was no smile in return.

'Ah, there you are. I just fancied a trip over here to take a look at the new branch and see how you're doing. I'd like a word in private.' Carrie was flustered and tried to think of a single valid reason for Paxman needing a word with her. He must have known Bill was away. She smiled and showed him up to the apartment.   Before she could ask him to sit down, he took off his hat and dropped into the armchair. He made no effort to hide his look of disdain as his gaze quickly swept the room. 'I'll make tea.' Carrie was keen to get the meeting over with. He grunted, following her movements with cold, staring eyes. She filled the kettle and came back to sit at the table. 'Just doing some bookkeeping,' she said nervously, with a half-smile. 'We're doing very well, as it happens.'

'Good, good. Pleased to hear it.' There was an awkward pause. Carrie looked at him and smiled, but he just stared at her. He seemed to be wondering how to phrase whatever it was he had to say. 'I've been informed that you took part in that bloody silly women's suffragette fiasco in London a week or so ago,' he said, with all the subtlety of an avalanche.

Carrie's body stiffened. She could sense what was coming. She stood up quickly and went to the kitchen. 'I did as a matter of fact,' she said as she moved away. 'Is that a problem?'

He struggled out of the armchair and followed her. 'Yes, my girl, it is! It's not good for my business.'

Carrie hated being called that, and she despised his tone. She also noted how he still referred to the partnership as "my business". 'How on earth could the Women's Union affect our business?'

'I've got a reputation in these parts. Every businessman from here to London knows me…and they know exactly where they stands wi' me. It's the basis on which I do business. Everyone knows that never in a thousand years would I allow women to muck about wi' my business…or theirs. Men know I wouldn't do business wi' them if they allowed women into their businesses.' Carrie stared at the kitchen wall with her back to him, biting her tongue. She had no choice. 'And you've been feedin' your young feller wi' a load of rubbish about women being employed in my shops – like that little tart you've got down there now.'

He came closer, trapping her against the sink. She winced at the stale odour of cigars and the alcoholic fumes coming from his mean little mouth. From the corner of her eyes she could see that he was unsteady on his feet, and was desperate to get away from him. Picking up a tray full of tea things, she determinedly squeezed past his bulky frame and moved into the lounge, putting as much distance between them as possible. She felt more secure there but he came after her. 'I'll not have that,' he boomed, returning to the middle of the room. There was angry contempt in his dark eyes. 'There's a place for women… and it's not in men's jobs and men's business, d'you understand me?'

She froze in his glare but her own anger rose and goaded her into fighting back. She had had enough, and the time for niceties was over. 'It's the attitude of men like you, Mister Paxman, that thousands of women like me have been struggling to change. You're out of date…

prehistoric, if you ask me! I've got every right to speak my mind and it's time you listened. Women are every bit as good as men – especially when there's a war on.'

He stepped forward, unsteadily. 'Look, my girl, if you want to stay around here with Bill Guy, you'd better learn to stay at home where you belong and keep your trap shut about women's rights. Keep your views to yourself or it'll be the worse for you. Women haven't got rights, d'you understand me? No rights at all…'cept what men give 'em.' He moved forward, menacingly. His anger frightened her, and she stepped back but before she realised what he was doing, his big hand gripped her arm like a steel vice. 'Let me tell you something, girlie. I know where you came from, and what you are. Around here, I know everything – and no young servant girl with a bastard is goin' to get under my feet. You'll either keep your mouth shut, or pack your bags and move on and find a man somewhere else to get your claws into. That shouldn't be too difficult for you. You've done it before, and by the looks of you, you could do it again.'

He suddenly took another step forward, putting his face close to hers. His closeness was repulsive. 'So, we 'ad to 'ave this little chat, you see. At least you know now. If you want to stay here, keep away from things that don't concern you.' His large hand, covered in black hairs, tightened its grip and hurt her. It prevented her from her pulling away. A sneer twitched his wet lips and his eyes rolled lazily, momentarily out of control. 'It would pay you to remember… I've got you in the palm of my hand,' he slurred, raising his other hand and closing it slowly into a fist in front of her face. 'I could squeeze the life out of you any time I liked.' He searched her eyes for signs of fear then sneered when all he saw was defiance. 'I like girls wi' a bit of spirit… in the proper place.'

He studied her features for a moment, with a strange look coming to his eyes. 'You know, I think we would get along if only you came to your senses. I'm not an unreasonable man to people I like. It might pay you to be nice to me.' Carrie arched her back to keep her face away from his. There was no mistaking what he was saying. As she felt his other hand on the small of her back, pressing her body to his, panic swept through her and she struggled to free herself but she could not break away from his powerful grip.

With a deliberate movement he released his grip on her arm, placed his hand on her breast and squeezed it painfully – all the while grinning drunkenly. The more she struggled, the more he squeezed. 'Let me go. Let me go, you bastard!'

'Oh, quite the lady, aren't we? Got 'onour to protect now, eh? That's not what I've heard!' He tried to shift his grip to go further. She writhed and struggled with all her might. 'Come on now, come on. You know how to use it to get what you want, don't you? It's never been a problem before. D'you think I'm not good enough, or something?'

Carrie fought like a cornered tigress but he was too strong for her. She wanted to scream but she knew no one would hear and she was afraid of scaring Kate to death. Her eyes flashed anger and contempt. In desperation, she spat in his face. Very little came out; fear had left her mouth bone dry, but it was enough. It was a gesture of defiance and it broke his grip. As he stepped back, wiping his face in disgust, she stamped hard on his foot and ran into the bedroom. Shutting the door firmly she leant against it, her heart beating wildly.

'You bitch. You filthy little bitch!' Paxman doubled up, clutching his foot. She stood with her back to the door with her eyes wide with fear and her pulse racing. He came to the door and tried to get in but she put all the weight she had against it. 'I'll not forget this, you little vixen,' he hissed through the door. Then he gave up trying and busied himself with straightening his tie and jacket. 'You just remember what I said and if you even think about telling 'im about any of this, I swear there will be such trouble for the pair of you, you'll wish you were dead. Mark my words!'

Kate woke up, frightened, and began to scream. Carrie picked her up and cuddled her. 'Everything all right, Miss Carrie?' It was Maude at the top of the stairs, sounding concerned. Carrie could not have been more pleased that she had given her a job. Paxman grabbed his hat and glared as he brushed past her on his way out.

'You get back to the job you're paid for, and mind your business.' He clumped unsteadily and noisily down the stairs, and was gone.

'It's all right, Miss Carrie, Mister Paxman has gone now.'

Carrie emerged tentatively from her room, carrying Kate. 'Thank you, Maude, thank you. It's all right. Just Kate having a nightmare, that's all.'

'Oh, all right, Miss.' Maude looked unconvinced, but went back to the shop. Carrie settled Kate down and sat at the table. Her hands were trembling and her mind raced. Her heart was beating as if about to burst. She could not believe what had just happened. As she thought about it, she made up her mind to tell Bill, come what may.

That night, she stayed up late with her thoughts in turmoil waiting for him to come home. When he arrived at 11:45 pm, he said he was tired and could not concentrate on what she was telling him.

He found it all too much to absorb and told her to leave it till the morning when she was less hysterical. It would probably seem like nothing then, he said.

Carrie was livid and hardly slept at all that night.

In the morning she tackled him again. At first he did not believe her story, suggesting that she had had some kind of bad dream. Eventually, when he had no choice but to believe her, he insisted on playing it down.

She was furious. What she expected was that he would be enraged, furious, and indignantly defensive of her – then rush to Paxman to have it out with him but instead, he seemed evasive, excusing of Paxman, and obviously reluctant to even mention it to him. She was disgusted with his response. Suddenly, she could see that he had become Paxman's trembling lapdog, and it filled her with revulsion.

The incident left her brooding about Paxman's influence on their lives and his grip on Bill. How was it going to affect the business and their future together? She had never felt so isolated and alone. Bill's insouciance left a scar on their relationship that would be irreparable and her disgust for Paxman was overwhelming. Her hopes for a secure future were shattered: an illusion that had just vanished in an instant. For days, she went around feeling sick with worry and burning to get even with Paxman one way or another, and determined to make some changes.

In distant parts, the Commander of the Gallipoli forces was also set on making some changes.

GALLIPOLI
Friday, August 6, 1915

Hamilton's plans for a renewed attack on Chunuk Bair began in darkness, on the night of August 6.

The 9th Army Corps landed at Suvla Bay to add strength to the forces pinned down there and other new forces were coming in from Mitylene, 120 miles away from the area into which all the scattered detachments were eventually to be concentrated. The ultimate objective of this grand assault was to make a deep and decisive thrust inland in order to gain control of the Peninsula at its narrowest point and cut the bulk of the Turkish Army off from its supply and communications route to Constantinople.

From the very beginning, the attack was ill fated and marred by mistakes and disasters. By coincidence – as bizarre as it was unlucky for the British – the Turkish Army had also been preparing to launch a decisive attack on the British. When allied troops reached the Turkish trenches, they found them packed with soldiers who would put up ferocious resistance to drive them back.

The new attack gained Hamilton little and cost thousands more lives. Its objective was never achieved, and it resulted in yet more trench warfare and stagnation.

Chapter Eighteen

PORTSMOUTH DOCKYARD
Saturday, August 7, 1915

The hospital ship bringing George and hundreds of other wounded soldiers and sailors back home nosed gently into Portsmouth Harbour in bright sunlight at *11:30 am*. For the first glimpse of the Solent and the dockyard, those capable of standing, like George, gathered at the guardrails to bask in the sights and sounds of home.

As the ship passed Gosport, there were women waving and cheering on both sides of the harbour mouth, and George wondered if Emily was there. She was not, but that was only because no one at home had any idea what time the ship was due to arrive. These were just passers-by, expressing relief that unlike some who would never be home again, one ship full of wounded was at last safely home. Ships in the harbour sounded their foghorns and crowds of dockyard workers cheered spontaneously and patriotically, warming the hearts of those who could hear them.

It took many hours to offload the wounded and send them off to hospitals. By late afternoon, George and several other sailors, Petty Officers and Chief Petty Officers were being checked into Haslar Hospital at Gosport. For George, the situation was perfect. If he had to be in hospital at all, the Navy could not have chosen a better place for him. The following day, Emily, Carrie and Bill came to see him together, and the emotions and conversation flowed. It made his head spin, and he ended the day with a headache.

George thought Carrie looked fabulous, and he was more pleased than he should have been to see her again. In stark contrast to Emily's old black clothes – ones that George could distinctly remember from years ago – Carrie was wearing her best for him. She looked prosperous, fashionable and colourful, and he noticed the admiring glances she was attracting in the ward.

Being well enough to be classified as "walking wounded", George was no longer confined to his bed. It gave Emily an opportunity to give him several tearful hugs. It embarrassed him, but cheered Emily's spirits more than anything else had done since she first had news that he was injured. He could see the long past months of anxiety and worry deep in her eyes, and he was pleased to see it begin to fade away. There was so much to talk about, so much catching up to do.

George persuaded the nurses to exchange his turban of bandages for a more simple dressing just in time for the visit, and Carrie kept telling him how good he looked, and promised to visit him often. Now that she and Marje were doing part-time work in the same hospital, she could do that several times a week, she told him. Bill seemed pleased to see him again and made chummy comments about his hair, the nurses, and anything else he could make light of, but he looked uneasy. 'Sorry, George. Can't stand these places. They give me the creeps. I always think I'm going to catch something and end up in here myself.'

George felt that he could live with that. He was just pleased to be home. It was better than he had imagined, being with the people he had missed. All thoughts of the war faded into the background now that he was back. After "lights out" that night, he found it difficult to sleep. The day was still going around in his mind. From what he could see, everything and everybody appeared exactly as he had left them. It was as if time had stood still here, while his life had been racing by but there was something different, for anyone perceptive enough to notice it. The warmth and respect that had once positively glowed between Carrie and Bill had gone.

Individually they reacted to people as they had always done, but between the two of them, communication seemed tired and strained. Bill's comment could not pass into the conversation without a challenge from Carrie. Even when she was not contradicting him, she avoided eye contact with him. George guessed that their private conversations had become verbal tugs of war. For the entire time she was there, she was bubbly and excited to see him but she said very little to Bill. It saddened him to see that all was not well with his friends, in spite of their efforts to hide it.

The next time Carrie came to see him, she brought Marje who had not changed a bit. She was as lively and cynical as ever, and in her company instead of Bill's, Carrie's face lit up as they sat in the grounds chatting. George was hoping that a chance to speak to Marje on her own for a moment would come naturally but eventually he had to resort to asking Carrie to fetch him a glass of water.

'Everything all right between those two?' he asked as casually as he could, as soon as Carrie was out of earshot.

'Yes, darling, of course,' Marje beamed. 'Why do you ask?'

'Oh, nothing really… I just thought I felt a bit of stress there.'

Marje gave him an odd smile that told him he was not imagining the problem. 'No, they're fine …just fine. Carrie is going through a difficult time. That's all.'

He wanted to know more, but seeing Carrie coming back, Marje firmly shut the door on the conversation and changed the subject.

At the end of the week, the ward had a visit from an ebullient Chief Petty Officer Physical Training Instructor, whose job was to resurrect patients and restore their fitness for duty. He had the physique of a fully wound spring and bounded about like a playful puppy. When he returned to make a formal introduction of his programme, he strutted the floor, point-toed, looking like a gymnast on the point of starting a competitive gymnastic routine. George took to him immediately, and resolved to take the opportunity to restore his debilitated muscles. He was keen to be fit again.

The road to fitness was necessarily a hard one, but he discovered along the way a keenness for running and exercising with the weights and machines in the Chief PTI's physiotherapy gymnasium. Lieutenant Parker, who had been appointed to Portsmouth barracks after the loss of *Inflexible*, came to see him with the news that George had been awarded a "Mentioned in Dispatches" medal for his exploits in the Dardanelles. It was a great honour, signified by a miniature insignia of an oak leaf attached in bronze to the ribbon of what would be his first medal: the Dardanelles campaign medal, when it was eventually struck. George was pleased with it, although Parker said that, in comparison to the Victoria Cross he believed George deserved, it was a derisory award.

In hospital, there was neither the time nor the privacy to discuss personal matters properly, but he was compelled to confide in Parker how much his role as a gunner now preyed on his mind. Parker listened and was obviously concerned. He leaned forward in his chair and lowered his voice. 'Don't talk about this with anyone else,' he said, with a frown creasing his forehead. 'People don't understand sentiments like this. We're at war …and there is nothing any of us can do but see it through to the end.' He glanced around, before continuing. 'This is not the place to be talking like this. Keep it to yourself until you're out of here. Come and see me then. We'll talk it through.' George was thrown by Parker's reaction, but accepted the advice. If Parker could do something for him, he would see him as soon as possible.

Carrie was as good as her word. Befriending the pleasant and cooperative Nursing Sister, she obtained special permission to visit George outside normal visiting hours, whenever she left her work at the hospital. Seeing her frequently and feeling his fitness returning brightened up the rest of his stay in hospital. Her visits were the highlight of the week. They swapped stories about their lives and became engrossed in a growing enjoyment of each other.

Her disenchantment with Bill slowly filtered into their conversations and, reluctantly, she confessed that she felt lonely and completely trapped by her circumstances. She was pleased to learn that George was a good and sympathetic listener. Until then, she had seen him only as a self-absorbed talker. She flirted with him, quite obviously, and he basked in it. Her natural tactility led to warm and personal touches that became meaningful for both of them.

Emily, Marje and other people came to see him, but it was Carrie's next visit that always excited him and kept his eyes glued to his wristwatch. He was thrilled every time he saw her, and could not stop thinking about her. As weeks went by, he became convinced that she was really made for him. Before he knew what had happened, he had fallen in love for the first time. If this serious, gut-wrenching feeling whenever she left him was not love, he was never going to experience it in his whole lifetime. He could not take his eyes off her when she was there, and he could not think of anything else when she was not. When he was alone, his mind took to wandering off to an imaginary future where they were always together, loving one another and wanting nothing more. Then reality would blunder in and drive his thoughts into uncomfortable corners.   In spite of what he wanted for himself, did Carrie feel the same? How would he ever know? There was too the question of Bill; even if things were not exactly perfect between them, she belonged to him – his own best friend. Even in his most fanciful dream, where a magic wand would make that all right, she still seemed to want more out of life than he could afford to give and there was Kate to consider as well. He cursed being stuck with the modest pay of a humble Petty Officer, and realised, deep down, that he would never be able to provide for all three of them – not to mention a home. In any event, to have Carrie for himself would mean taking her away from Bill. Could he be that much of a rat?

George had never been so disturbed by a woman before, and knew that he was sailing in uncharted waters. Yet he wanted her badly, not just for now but for all time. An overwhelming compulsion to be with her dominated his thoughts and he had to know if she felt the same, in spite of being afraid of the answer.

HASLAR HOSPITAL, GOSPORT
Friday, September 10, 1915

George was finally discharged from Haslar for sick leave on Friday, September 10. The wonderful times alone with Carrie had ended, never to be repeated. What chance would there be ever to see her alone again? He cursed all the opportunities he had missed to let her know what he really felt for her.

On the walk home he immediately noticed the real changes the war had brought to his hometown. In spite of the late summer sunlight, it looked gloomier than he remembered. Everywhere he looked there was an increased presence of khaki uniforms and military equipment, against an even larger backdrop of battleship grey. Most striking was the dark drabness of civilian clothes. Carrie had told him about this. Colourful, fashionable clothes had gone by the board... flushed away by the constant stream of letters bearing dreaded news to wives and mothers, and the desperate need to use hard-pressed earnings for things more essential.

Like everything else around him, it made him think of Carrie; how special she was, standing out from the crowd the way she did. It also had him trying to estimate just how much he would have to earn to keep her happy. Trying to banish negativity from his mind, he gave a thought for the Chief PTI who had put the spring back in his step, and made up his mind to enjoy his leave. The next thing coming up was his Petty Officer's course in Portsmouth Barracks and he intended to make best use of this chance to move a step up the ladder and one step closer to Carrie's expectations.

He spent the next Sunday afternoon with Bill and Carrie, talking about old times and his experiences in the Dardanelles. Being with her was what he wanted most, and his secret longing for her made him resent Bill's company. Pangs of jealousy and a feeling that he was being treacherous made him uneasy. A knot in his chest that he had not felt before kept making him sigh, but it would not go away. Face to face with Bill – not just a mental picture that he could easily brush aside – his fantasies of sharing his life with Carrie faded away.

Carrie was trying hard to be pleasant to Bill, but she could not hide her coolness. She was unhappy and clearly a different person to the one George had left behind. Bill struggled to extract warmth from her but there was none, and her body language said that she was there with him simply because she owed it to him. How sad it was to see two people like this, thought George. How different it would be if he were in Bill's shoes, but he was not. This was their personal problem and he ought not to interfere. Although it made his heart ache, he decided to back away from Carrie and stay clear of the black chasm opening up between her and Bill.

This was something new for George. Sentimentality had never held him back from any woman before but this was very different. He was too close to both of them, and felt too much for Carrie. For the first time since he had known Bill, he was relieved to leave the apartment. He made his excuses and stood up to go home.

When he went to kiss Carrie goodbye, she did something that took him completely off guard. She secretively pressed a tightly folded piece of paper into his hand. He closed his hand quickly, made his farewells, and left. It began to burn the palm of his hand, and he could not wait to look at it. Out of sight, he snatched it open and read:

Dearest George,

What wonderful times we had these past weeks. Are you sorry they had to end? I am. If you want to see me again, please be here tomorrow evening at eight o'clock. I'll be alone.

With the tingle of anticipation running up his spine, he read it several times on the way home. What did it mean? Was she proposing an affair? He had very little sleep on Sunday night. Carrie's note kept flicking through his mind. This would be his last chance to tell her what he felt about her – although he knew that he had to say that he was not going to do anything about it. It stayed in the forefront of his mind – a mixture of apprehension, excitement and regret.

Brushing aside Emily's encouragement to stay at home with her on Monday evening, he made excuses and set off to meet Carrie, arriving at the front of the shop far too early. Killing time, he walked up and down the street looking aimlessly in shop windows. Feeling guilty and self-conscious, he decided to wait at the back entrance, where every passing man in a suit and hat resembled Bill and seemed to stare knowingly. In the last echoes of the town clock as it struck eight o'clock, he knocked on the door and waited impatiently, heart in mouth. The sight of her at the doorway took his breath away. He had never seen her hair down before. Freshly washed and tumbling onto her shoulders in a golden cascade, it framed her face like an ornate gilt picture frame. It shone in the late sunlight of the autumn evening, making the pale green of her eyes translucent. He hesitated, transfixed, until she hastened him in and closed the door.

Once in the apartment, he felt self-conscious and furtive about being alone with her in Bill's apartment. Uncharacteristically, his poise deserted him and he seemed clumsy and awkward. He was burdened with so many emotions he had to share with her – sincere, serious things that he really wanted her to know – but the starting point always eluded him. They talked instead about how warm it was and how well they looked to each other. His strained expression seemed to amuse Carrie, and she decided to make him a cup of tea, to relax him. When she went to the kitchen, he sat on the edge of the armchair, telling himself not to waste this chance to speak his mind.

It seemed an age before Carrie came back, poured the tea and sat down on the sofa opposite him. 'Carrie/George – Sorry!' Their words tumbled over each other and stopped abruptly. They looked at one another and laughed. 'Go on, you first,' she urged.

He concentrated shyly on his hands and looked uncomfortable. 'Carrie, this is very difficult for me to say.' He looked serious, and wrung his hands. She began to wonder what was coming. 'I know you didn't like me, at first …as a matter of fact, I didn't take to you then, either …but I really like you now.'

'I'm glad, George.' In the presence of his awkwardness, Carrie seemed even more controlled and serene. 'Go on – tell me more. A girl likes to know these things.'

He glanced up, wishing that he did not have to. 'Trouble is…things have changed. Everything's different now.'

'What do you mean, George: *different?*'

He shifted uneasily in his seat, realising what a mess he was making of it. 'Well, when you were coming to see me in hospital, I aah…' His words trailed off as Carrie crossed her legs. He had not realised that she was wearing a housecoat. It fell open at the knee, revealing a leg every bit as shapely as he imagined it would be.

'Yes?'

'Look…I know I shouldn't say this… I don't have the right, and all that… but I just can't help it.' He stared open-mouthed for an instant. 'Carrie, I think I love you.' The words came out in a rush, and he seemed shocked to hear them. He looked into her eyes, expecting to find ridicule but there was none. There was a long, silent pause as she gazed at his face. Frowning, she stood up and reached out for his hands, drawing him to his feet to face her.

'George, I'm very glad you told me that. I suspected as much, but I didn't know. Now I have something to tell you: I don't think that I love you.' Dismay suddenly flashed in his eyes and his heart missed a beat. 'No, George,' she said slowly and deliberately. 'I don't *think* I love you …I *know* that I do!' Her teasing had been brief and fleeting, and stopped as soon as she saw his pained expression.

It took a moment for her words to sink in.

'Are you sure?' he said, incredulously. '*Really?*'

'Really – certainly – definitely – absolutely!'

A wide, silly smile suddenly lit up his face. In an instant, there was nothing but exhilaration in his sparkling blue eyes. Throwing his arms around her, he eagerly pressed his lips to hers. For several minutes they kissed and caressed feverishly, frantically searching for an expression of the sheer joy of finding one another. Their kisses became more passionate and their touches more intimate. Hardly pausing for breath, they became lost in the heady urgency of precious lost moments. Soon, their discarded clothes were lying haphazardly on the floor and they were hurrying towards nature's own expression of love – purposely put there for moments like this.

Their urgent need completely overwhelmed any feelings of guilt they may have had. In one swift movement, George lifted her onto the edge of the table and gently pushed her backwards. She did not resist. She laid back, ignoring the ornaments she was knocking to the floor as he moved closer. Small gasps and moans of pleasure escaped from her parted lips as the table creaked with the pulse of their passion, and tiny beads of perspiration began to form on his forehead. He gripped her waist and held it firmly as her body arched and writhed beneath him, and she gave a loud moan as an explosion of pleasure surged up from her toes and filled every part of her body. Her nails dug into his flesh as months of pent-up passion and frustration drove him towards his own moment of golden fulfilment. Suddenly, he groaned and arched his back, and his love erupted inside her as if to fill her whole body.

After a few moments, he drew her gently into an embrace and felt the fire of her skin on his. Sweat trickled down his chest in a tiny rivulet and meandered between her breasts. Only when he was softly whispering words of love to her did he notice her sobbing quietly against his shoulder. He pulled back to look at her face, but she quickly turned away to hide the tears. 'Carrie, my love – what's wrong?'

'Nothing, darling, nothing…I'm so happy.' With her face wet with tears, she kissed away his quizzical frown. 'You mustn't mind me, George. It's just that I'm happy. No one has ever made me feel like that before – no one. You won't understand. It's a "woman" thing. For once, I've found someone for myself… someone *I've* chosen for myself. Someone who loves *me*... and someone who can make me feel like that.' He gently lifted her tear-streaked face to look into her eyes. She tried to explain...'Until now, every time I've been with a man it's been for a reason. Because I imagined I had to, or because giving in might just make my life better. But this time it's different and I'm happy, really happy!' She flung her arms round his neck and kissed him.

'Carrie. I want to tell you something. It's the same for me. I know it seems sudden, but the truth is, what I feel for you started a long time ago... from the moment I met you. It's just that I didn't realise it. That bang on the head made me realise a lot of things but that doesn't matter now anyway. Right or wrong, I'm all yours now. Nothing will ever change that. I will never leave you. Whatever happens to us from now on, we'll always be together – I promise.'

She saw the love in his eyes, and her tears welled up again.

'My God! Look at where we are!' he said suddenly, trying to cheer her up. The table had moved to one side of the lounge and the floor was littered with clothes and ornaments. She laughed.

'Powerful man!'

'Only because of you, my love.'

'What a mess! We must tidy up a bit and calm down. We need to talk about what we are going to do. We've got a much bigger mess than this to deal with now.'

They got dressed and put the room back in order, then settled together on the sofa. Entwined in George's arms, Carrie felt contented and happy. George's stumbling self-conscious uncertainty was gone forever – as if it had never existed. They were one now, in heart and mind, and they were basking in the warm glow it gave them. Before they could really be together, there were problems to overcome, but feeling alone and unloved would not be one of them. The difficulties ahead would be easy to deal with now, he told her, and decisions would be easy now that they had each other. They decided not to tell Bill or anyone else until George's Petty Officer's course was over. After that, they would know where he was going to be sent next and would have a better idea how and where to set up home together. In the meantime, their plans would be a secret and they would steal time together whenever Bill was away, no matter how wrong it might be.

That night, George went home with the scent and sensation of her still on his skin, feeling happier than he had ever been in his life. Elation overcame his feelings of guilt and buried them forever.

On Monday, September 20, George began his course in Portsmouth barracks and the Gunnery School at *HMS Excellent*, a shore-based naval establishment on Whale Island, a small island in Portsmouth Harbour built by convicts from the dredging of the dockyard in the 1800s. It had not escaped George's attention that no lesser person than Admiral Jacky Fisher had served there twice himself on his way to the top. George settled down to it enthusiastically.

Once in the full uniform of a Petty Officer, he began to notice, with some enjoyment and satisfaction, that his new rank brought respect and a feeling of importance. Although this was just the first rung in a long ladder it felt secure and ready to support any effort he might make to climb higher. During the day, he was fully occupied by course lessons, learning about duties of Chief and Petty Officers, and the leadership of men. At night, he was free to think of his future with Carrie and Kate, and to see them whenever possible.

Emily sensed that George had found a relationship with yet another "young lady" and, in spite of his reluctance to talk about it, she was pleased to see him happy again. She was glad there was someone special enough to get him back into the swing of things but never in a thousand years would Emily have guessed who was responsible and that was fortunate for him.

Carrie and George made love and talked about the future at every available opportunity, drawing back the curtains of their pasts and eagerly learning about one another. With an assurance that what was past was past, she explained how she had come by Kate. Here she exercised a woman's prerogative to juggle with the truth – just a bit – for the sake of self-confidence, and gave him the same story she had given Bill. She got the same reaction: indignant anger at the Farleighs. He wanted to know who Kate's father was, but she would not say. Whoever he was he was to remain a mysterious "*very* important person".

When she told him about her experience with Paxman he was furious and was ready to go and see him immediately. It was just the reaction she expected of "her man", and it filled her with loving pride to see it but she had to make him see that if he did confront Paxman, he would give the game away. Knowledge of their affair was something Paxman would enjoy using to his advantage. She would have loved it if George had given him a good hiding but she had to restrain him. Paxman's behaviour was something they had to live with, for the time being.

Having explained how she became pregnant with Kate, she let him into the secret of her allowance for Kate's upkeep, and it set him thinking more positively about his ability to support all three of them but apprehension about making ends meet still lurked secretly in his mind. Carrie's allowance for Kate was almost enough to pay the entire rent on a house that would be large enough for them, but there were other costs to worry about: clothes, furniture, food, light and heat. Above all else, he wanted everything to be right when they eventually came together as a family, and a thought that troubled him was that he might fall short of Carrie's expectations.

Against George's advice, Carrie confided in Marje about what had happened and their plans for the future. For once, Marje had no witty or reassuring comments to make. She loved Carrie and was very fond of George, but Bill was a long-standing friend, and she could not hide her sympathy for him and his situation. She told Carrie that she was uncomfortable and embarrassed to be party to what was going on behind his back, particularly as she had already accepted them as a married couple, more or less. Carrie was surprised by Marje's reaction. It unsettled her and, for Carrie's sake, it worried George too. The relaxed, happy relationship they always enjoyed with Marje was replaced by a feeling of unease, and it affected all three of them. When he found Carrie in tears about it, his fragile happiness suddenly became grounded in cold realism.

Time was running out. He would soon be back at sea, and still had nowhere for them to live, and he had a secret fear that Marje's coolness could give Carrie second thoughts about their future plans. George found that he had less to smile about and more to worry over. Not being a man to fall at the first hurdle, or leave problems unresolved, he thought of nothing else but ways to keep Carrie happy. Then, during a course lesson on the Navy's pay structure, he realised what he had to do. More money and greater security was the answer, and the only way to get them was through promotion. He had to push for accelerated promotion and a higher income – consciously and unashamedly.

In the meantime, he would ask Emily for help. That is what mothers are for – to help their children in times of crisis. She had a spare room, and she could not refuse him. Then his problems would be solved. Unfortunately, George was still not sufficiently worldly-wise to know that life does not always respond positively to positive thought alone.

THE ROYAL FAMILY HOME ST MARK'S ROAD, GOSPORT
Thursday, October 14, 1915

Sitting opposite one another at the kitchen table, George and Emily had the most serious argument they had ever had. In spite of his desperation, she would not give in. 'No, George – NO!' She was genuinely shocked and hurt that he could expect her to take another man's "wife" and child into her home. The picture of her perfect son that she always cherished was ruined the moment he asked. 'Have you gone mad? Whatever are you thinking? I'm ashamed that a son of mine would even think of doin' such a thing...or expect me to get involved.' He was frustrated and angry by her response.

'But this kind of thing happens all the time these days. Anyway, they're not married – you know that. What's happening between them is not our fault. Carrie was already very unhappy, and we know that we can be happy together, because we love each other.'

'Love? What do you know about that? You're far too young to talk like that. You don't know the meaning. That's not love. That's ... it's ...it's getting your oats from another man's wife, that's what it is. It's not right, George! It's disgusting, and I wish you'd never told me. I don't want anything to do with it. What about Bill? He's your best friend, isn't he? How could you do something like that to your best friend?'

He looked down at the table, wearily. After all he had been through, to her he was still a child to be chastised and corrected. Even now, she could not look at him and see an adult – yet in the Navy, he was considered old enough to die. 'You're so young, George,' she said, in a calmer tone. 'You haven't really lived yet. The last thing you need right now is a family and a baby. I know Kate's very sweet, but God knows whose child she is. Son, the best thing you can do is go back to sea and forget all about it, and wait till you find a nice young lady of your own who hasn't…you know, got herself into trouble already.'

He shook his head despairingly. He began to realise that in spite of his mother's outward acceptance and friendliness towards Carrie, there must have been sinister thoughts buried in her mind, and they were coming out now. His anger flashed in his eyes. 'Nothing you say will change how I feel about Carrie. I'm old enough to make up my own mind now and you'll just have to get used to it.'

'I'll do nothing of the sort! If you're determined to make a fool of yourself, and shame me, I'll certainly not help you do that.' She could not ignore the anguish and desperation in his eyes. For a moment, she could see the little boy she knew and loved – petulant and cross and looking hurt so soon after his recent experiences. It wrenched her heart and made her want to give in. She could see that he was grasping at what he thought was happiness but she knew it would be best for him in the long run if she stood her ground. 'That girl is not for you, son. Can't you see what she's up to? She only went to live in sin with Bill Guy because she was in trouble. Everybody knows that. He represented safety for her, that's all. When she did that she made a commitment. Now she's found out she's bitten off more than she can chew, so all she wants to do is find a way out of it – and that's you.'

Emily regretted it as soon as she said it. It was not what she believed. It was simply a weapon, found too easily. She bit her lip. She wanted to take it back immediately but the damage had been done and it showed in George's face.

A cold realisation that she had gone too far gripped her heart: she was going to lose him. His eyes blazed, and he looked furious enough to hit her. She half hoped he would but George controlled himself. His gaze dropped and he heaved a deep sigh of bitter frustration and regret. His demeanour softened, but a resigned flatness in his voice chilled her to the bone.

'I'm not going to listen to any more. We've got nothing more to say to each other. I know what I have to do. I'm going to be with Carrie. We'll just have to cope on our own. I'm going… and I won't be back.' The words fell into her lap like paving stone. She could feel the weight in the pit of her stomach. As she reached out for him, he stood up to go.

'Don't, son … don't go!'

'I'm going. I'm going back to the barracks. I'll stay there until I sort something out. I can't stay here.' He picked her hand off his arm and flung it from him as if it were something repulsive. 'Don't touch me!' He stamped up the staircase, gathered his things into his service suitcase, and went to the door. Emily was sobbing quietly at the kitchen table when he turned and paused briefly. They stared at one another, both dreading that there would be no way back from this, but neither would speak. The door slammed with a bang, startling her. An icy chill ran down her spine.

While George strode purposefully down the street, Emily gazed forlornly at the photos of her son and dead husband, and howled pitifully at the kitchen walls. The floodgates behind which she kept her emotions in check had never properly closed after Jack's death. Since then, her feelings had seemed like a river in flood: contained, but always on the brink of bursting through. She realised that she had lost her son, as surely as if he too had been drowned at sea, and life was never going to be the same again. Her self-control gave way and tears surged up from the depths of her heart to pour out onto the kitchen table. She sobbed for George and for Jack, and the pain the war had brought to wives and mothers everywhere.

There seemed no end to it.

The men in Gallipoli and their wives and mothers at home were experiencing similar feelings.

GALLIPOLI
October, 1915

The campaign was in stalemate. Some territory had been gained, but it was pitifully little to show for five hard months of bitter slogging battles and appalling losses.

In the Suvla Bay area, the Anzacs had secured a strip of coastal land some 2 miles wide and 8 miles long. At Cape Helles, in the south, British troops had succeeded in occupying only 4 miles of the tip of the peninsula, and they were now embroiled in continuous, vicious, hand-to-hand trench fighting in an effort to hold their positions. To add to their difficulties, 30,000 Allied troops were laid low at any one time during the summer months, weakened by dysentery, and there was a constant shortage of water at the front. So dire was the situation in this waterless land that some wounded and fallen soldiers – left for dead among the countless bodies lying in the dusty scrub-land – survived only by crawling from body to body to drain the last dregs from their dead colleagues' water bottles.

In London a question hung like a spectre over the campaign and the advisability of continuing with it, and there were calls for a complete evacuation of Gallipoli. By telegraph, Lord Kitchener discussed the alternatives with General Sir Ian Hamilton. On October 11, he called for an estimate of the likely losses should there be an evacuation, and Hamilton responded that such a step was unthinkable. Four days later, Hamilton was recalled to London and replaced. General Sir Charles Munro succeeded him in command on the grounds that "His Majesty's Government desired a fresh, unbiased opinion from a responsible Commander".

Dejected, Hamilton left the area six days later.

Soon after arriving in Gallipoli, Munro became totally convinced that evacuation was the only course open to the Allies. He wasted no time reporting his findings to Kitchener, noting in his dispatches that the position of the Allied troops "presented a military situation unique in history". He observed that just the merest fringe of the coastline had been secured but these beaches and piers on which the troops depended for supplies were constantly exposed to enemy shellfire. He reported that the Turks dominated the Allied entrenchments completely, and there were no suitable artillery positions for the invading forces. Communications, he added, were insecure and depended entirely upon weather conditions, and no means existed for concealing and deploying fresh troops, because the Turks enjoyed full powers of observation and strong artillery positions. In short, the British situation amounted to a catalogue of every possible military defect from which there was no hope of advance and in which a large number of troops were locked up to no military advantage.

When Kitchener received Munro's telegraph, he decided to go there to see for himself.

Chapter Nineteen

GOSPORT
Saturday, October 16, 1915

George was frustrated to find that Bill was not going to be away at all for his last weekend in Gosport. The only way he could see Carrie was to meet her somewhere out in the open. As arranged, he went to the park shelter, hoping that she had been able to make a suitable excuse for taking Kate for a walk. A chilly wind gusted through the trees. He turned up his coat collar as rain began to fall.

In the almost deserted park he sat alone on the bench and watched the bad weather sweeping across the grey waters of The Solent. The wind struggled to lift the wet brown leaves from the path, but succeeded only in driving rain into the wooden shelter. Its tired, glossy, dark green paint – the paint with which all local councils seemed to armour-plate their assets – gave off the smell of his short childhood.

He recalled clearly the games of "chase" and "hide and seek" he used to play there and, with guilty pleasure, found his name scratched in it. The two remaining children playing in the rain were dragged home, protesting, by their mother.

Carrie came down the path ten minutes late, with one hand holding down her hat and the other on a new pushchair from Biddles. She seemed apprehensive and flustered as she fussed over Kate's well-being. A broad smile chased the weary look from George's face, which lit up at the sight of her. He jumped up to give her a kiss, but she bent over to attend to Kate and his gesture came to nothing. 'Sorry about this,' he mumbled, gesturing at the weather. 'It would have to do this on our last weekend, wouldn't it?'

Without replying, she glanced around to see if they were alone then sat down beside him. He leaned forward to see Kate, buried somewhere under a canopy. When he looked back at Carrie, her face looked pale and stern. He broke the bad news about his row with Emily, expecting Carrie to be upset that he had still not arranged accommodation. He was surprised when she said nothing, and misread her expression.

'Dearest, I'm sorry that I have to go away but cheer up! I'll be back on leave before you know it. It's a blow that my mother won't cooperate, but we'll soon find a room for you somewhere. I'll send all the money I can. It'll be all right, you'll see.' He gave her a reassuring, oversized smile but she remained stony-faced. In the poor light, her green eyes looked grey and dull. She drew a deep breath.

'It's not that, George. It's other things.'

'What things?'

Well, it's us really.'

'What d'you mean…us?'

'I mean, what we have been doing… and what we're planning to do.' His suspicions were aroused in an instant. Transfixed, he waited for the bad news he sensed was coming. 'I've been giving it a lot of thought… believe me and, to cut a long story short… I… I just can't do it, George.' His face fell and his pulse began to race. She kept her gaze on the horizon, determined to avoid what might be in his eyes. 'I'm very sorry, George, I really am. I just got muddled up.' Still avoiding his face, her attention was fixed on the pushchair. It was the latest model and her fine hands gently wiped away spots of rain from the handle as she fondled it lovingly. 'I thought it was what I wanted, George but it isn't and it's wrong. I can't do that to Bill. However difficult the situation is with him, I can't just leave him.'

'But, Carrie, we've already made promises to one another. And what we've done, we've done… we can't go back and undo it!'

'I know, I know – and I feel terrible that we have, but that doesn't make it right, does it? It's… it's sinful.'

'Sinful? It's not a sin to be happy, Carrie! He doesn't love you but I do. You're not married to him, are you? You have a right to be happy…and you do love me, don't you?'

Close to tears, she looked down at the ground. 'Yes,' she said in a little voice. 'I do, but that's not all there is to life.' She turned and looked into his eyes for the first time since arriving. They were full of shock and disbelief, and the pain of betrayal.

'But it is, Carrie. It's the most important thing. I've seen it with my mother and father. It's the only thing that matters. Whatever happened to them, they always had each other…they were together. That's why they stayed happy…because they loved one another.'

Tears were streaming down her cheeks. She hated every second of what she was doing to him. 'I want more than that, George. I can't stand being poor. I've been poor; and I've seen what real life is like. I can't go back to wondering where the next penny is coming from. I've only got one life, and I won't waste it on being poor.' She straightened her back and wiped her eyes, anxious to bring the conversation to a close. George felt the stab of finality and moved to put his arm around her. She gently shrugged it off and stood up.

'But Carrie… please! You can't do this to me. I love you. What am I going to do? I thought you loved me. I trusted you. For God's sake…if I can't trust you, I'll never be able to trust anyone.'

The words went through her heart like a hot knife, but she was determined not to weaken – she had to see it through. She bit her lip and held back her tears. 'I do love you, George… I do but that's just weakness getting the better of me… a moment of passion that we should never have allowed to happen. I will always love you, but I can't go with you. I have to stay. I'm sorry… really sorry.'

She grabbed the pushchair and hurried off through the wind and rain, clutching her hat with one hand. Tears were pouring down her cheeks and she never looked back.

George's shoulders slumped. He bent forward and put his head in his hands. A feeling of desolation, despair and emptiness tore at his stomach. He was ashamed to feel tears welling in his eyes but he could not fight them off. Burying his face in his hands, he began to sob like a child. From somewhere deep inside, all the tears as yet unshed for Chalky White, his father, his mother, and all of his secret fears came with a vengeance. They poured through his fingers and fell with the rain onto the cold concrete floor of the desolate shelter.

When there was nothing left inside him, he got up feeling empty, bitter, and utterly lost, and made his way back to Portsmouth barracks. For the next forty-eight hours he stayed inside a shell of personal isolation and spoke to no one. He was devastated, and could only find consolation in going back to sea.

PLYMOUTH DOCKYARD
Monday, October 18, 1915

With his desolation hidden behind a thin veneer of well-being, George joined his next ship, *HMS Argyll*, determined to pick up the pieces of his life. His new ship was one of the Navy's largest battlecruisers of the "Improved County" class. In 1913, she had been the leading gunnery ship of the Atlantic Fleet. After a major refit at Plymouth Dockyard, she was off to join the 3rd Cruiser Squadron of the Grand Fleet, at Rosyth, Scotland. With the German Navy bottled up in its home ports, the North Sea was as quiet as any place could be in the Navy – not that George cared where he was, as long as it was at sea and away from home.

Initially, the ship seemed cramped compared to *Inflexible*, due to her age and pre-Dreadnought design but at least his hammock days were over. During the refit, new bunks had been fitted to the senior ratings' messes and, for the first time since he had been going to sea, he had a proper bed to sleep in. He remembered Admiral Jacky Fisher, whose hand was sure to have been in this innovation somewhere in the past.

Conditions on board were all too memorable. The familiar "Dockies" were frantically working everywhere, with their tools, pipes and pots of paint strewn about the decks. The refit had overrun its allotted time and there was urgency in the air once more. At least the POs' mess had been finished. It was small but pristinely cosy; not at all like the ratings' large messes he'd known. When he met the other POs, he was immediately given a new nickname: "Flash", because of a streak of silver hair mysteriously marking his recent head wound. Getting back into the swing of life on board was exactly what he needed. It helped take his mind off Carrie, if only a little. He longed for the day they would cast off and get to sea.

October 25, 1915 10:00 am

The weather was truly foul. A gusting wind, close to gale force, was driving heavy squalls of rain in from across the English Channel one after another. The streets of Plymouth were deserted and it seemed that people who could avoid going out in it had the good sense to stay indoors. Standing just inside one of *Argyll's* doorways, George looked out across the open water of the dockyard, with a grimace fixed to his face. The downpour dappled the surface of the sea, which was churned up by the wind, and the water streaming down the ship's superstructure was flying past the doorway horizontally.

A passing rating stopped beside him. 'Pretty grim, eh, Petty Officer? What do you reckon – think we'll still sail in this?'

'Yep, I'm afraid so. There's no choice. In peacetime, it might be different,' he said, sagely. 'But in wartime, the Navy stops at nothing. We'll leave all right.' He stepped through a watertight hatchway and clanged down the steep metal steps to join his colleagues in the mess below. Several looked up at the rattle of his feet on the ladder. Being a Petty Officer was still a novelty to George, and he had not yet shaken off the feeling that whenever he went into the POs' mess, he had done so by mistake.

In *Argyll,* he was by far the youngest of them. Although one or two were friendly, a few of the older men were initially grudging in their acceptance of him. Stan Kenny was one of the friendly ones, and George liked him instantly. Stan – in his forties and a Petty Officer for many years – had obviously been "passed over" for promotion. In spite of that, he had a sunny disposition and still had a sparkle in his eyes, particularly after his lunchtime "tot" of the navy's finest rum. 'Still blowing a hooligan up there, George?'

George nodded. 'Enough to swamp a battleship but we'll be all right.' Stan had quickly taken to George. He quietly admired youngsters who got on but having not known George in better times, he took his tight-lipped and quiet manner to be normal.

'Of course we will, we've got to go clockwise around the coast anyway. Once we turn north past the Bristol Channel, it'll calm down a bit, you'll see. We'll be running before the wind then, and this old tub will cope with anything.'

On the bridge, Captain James C Tancred was discussing the ship's course to Rosyth with his First Lieutenant and the Navigating Officer, noting the navigational hazards to be passed. He frowned as he looked out at the weather. 'In normal circumstances – considering this is *Argyll's* first day out after a major refit I would have enjoyed the option of delaying our departure for better weather. But we are behind schedule and we have to be on station in the North Sea by Thursday. We must leave on time. Apparently, the Third Cruiser Squadron cannot do without us.' He turned to the Navigating Officer. 'The submarine threat to the East prevails. So, as always, we shall take the western route. I am assured by the Chief that the ship will have steam by *1500 hours*. We'll cast off and be on our way at *15:15.*' He glanced at the bridge clock and left for his sea cabin.

The Navigating Officer began to plot a chart of the British Isles, making due allowance for the ferocious wind and the anticipated drift. There were adequate lighthouses at the natural hazards along the ship's course, and they were manned but to deprive enemy ships, particularly submarines, of navigational aids and stationary targets, most of them were not showing light during the war, except by special request. *Argyll's* course was past the Lizard Point into the Irish Sea, up through the Scottish channel known as The Minch, past the Outer Hebrides then on through the Pentland Firth that separates The Orkneys from mainland Scotland.

The Navigator identified the lighthouses to be passed during the hours of darkness and noted which of them could be turned on by signalled requests. He made a list of these for the Captain and passed it to Midshipman Evans, a young officer assigned to bridge duties. He then prepared a detailed course for the Captain.

On time at *15:15, Argyll's* lines were cast off and she slipped away from the quayside. An hour later she was steaming out of Plymouth Sound into heavy seas in the English Channel. By the time she had passed Lizard Point, Wolf Rock, Land's End and the Isles of Scilly there were many grey-green faces among the younger ratings and officers, and a powerful smell of fresh vomit pervaded the decks below. With the gun crews on standby, George had nothing to do. He sat in the POs' mess feeling queasier than he had for years.

'Always look on the bright side,' bubbled Stan. 'The good thing about rough weather is that you don't have to worry about submarines. They can't cope with seas like this. They have to stay down below.' The older man was feeling fine, but he noticed that George was about to have his first-ever bout of seasickness. He went to his locker, pulled a small spirit bottle from its depths, and thrust it into George's hand. 'There you go, mate. Get some of that down you.' George unscrewed the top and sniffed the contents. It was Navy rum – Petty Officer's issue and much neater than the familiar ratings' "grog" he was used to. 'Go on, have a good swig. That'll sort you out in no time. I always stash a drop for times like this.'

Reluctantly, George swigged. It took his breath away. 'Great. Thanks,' he croaked, with his vocal chords anaesthetised. Within seconds, the spirit hit his stomach like pieces of burning coal and he began to feel better.

October 26, 1915

At 16 knots, the ship pounded on through the night. By daybreak on the 26th she was abreast the mouth of the Bristol Channel, heading northwards into the Irish Sea. Unhindered by submarines, she pressed on and, 24 hours later, was pitching sickeningly through The Sea of the Hebrides.

With each downward plunge into the chasm of a trough, the sea seemed to defy gravity and all the known rules of fluid mechanics. Menacing hills of frothing water would rise up to tower over her superstructure in every direction. Seconds later, she would be on top of one of them, poised momentarily with her screws thrashing uselessly in the air, before plunging 60 feet into the depths of the next watery valley with a rattling, creaking shudder. Working below decks with no visual references, the hardiest of seamen were feeling the effects but trying not to show it.

During the afternoon of Wednesday, October 27, *Argyll* rounded Cape Wrath and, later that night, she cleared the Pentland Firth before turning southwards in the North Sea for the final leg of her journey.

THURSDAY, OCTOBER 28, 1915

Although it seemed impossible at the time, in the early morning hours of October 28 the weather worsened along the East Coast of Scotland. Farther south, between the small Scottish towns of Arbroath and Carnoustie, a three-masted, 2,211-ton steel sailing barque by the name of *Hoche* – owned by Societe Nouvelle d'Armement of Nantes – was sheltering close inshore. In ballast and under tow between Ipswich and Leith when the storm came on, she had been left to ride out the storm at anchor.

The captain, his wife and the crew were up all night in fear of their lives as they watched huge waves crashing over their ship with the noise of thunder. Huddled beside her husband in the wheelhouse, the captain's wife sat in her black fur coat, petrified and shivering with the intense cold.

In *Argyll* – a warship of 10,850 tons and one of the Navy's largest – the crew had no fear that she would founder in foul weather. For them, it simply made the journey extremely uncomfortable. She pounded on through the night, still making 16 knots to reach the Isle of May before daylight, in order to avoid the attention of German submarines.

Just before midnight on the 27th, Captain Tancred, referring to the navigator's list of lighthouses, had authorised a signal to be sent to the Admiral Commanding Coast of Scotland, at Rosyth. It requested the Bell Rock light to be lit to guide *Argyll* past the Inchcape Rock – the last natural hazard the ship had to contend with before turning into the calmer waters of the Firth of Forth.

The Inchcape Rock, or Bell Rock, is a 2,000-foot reef of jagged sandstone that lurks just below the surface at high water. It is situated 11 miles off the coast of Angus, at the mouth of the Firth of Tay.

Completely isolated from the coastline, Fate seems to have put it there for no purpose other than to catch unwary seamen. With great regularity, ships of all kinds impaled themselves on the treacherous rock throughout history until a lighthouse was built there in 1811 by the grandfather of the great Robert Louis Stevenson; Robert Stevenson.

Well aware of its dangers, *Argyll's* Navigating Officer plotted a course to pass the Bell Rock by eight and a half miles, a margin that he and the Captain considered adequate.

Tancred then retired to his cabin to rest, leaving the First Lieutenant in command of the bridge, assisted by Evans.

ROSYTH NAVAL BASE
October 28, 1915 12:30 Am

With *Argyll's* signal in his hand, the Duty Officer grimaced as he considered his dilemma. There was no radio or telephone link with the keepers of the Bell Rock lighthouse, and no signalling lamp would carry far through the rain and fog. The only means of communicating with them was by voice from a boat.

Being a reasonable man, the prospect of sending men out in conditions that he could only imagine, made him extremely uneasy, but there was no other way. Reluctantly, he ordered a motor torpedo boat to put to sea.

1:50 am

Making best speed through the 30 miles of choppy, dark, windswept waters of the Forth, the torpedo boat finally reached the mouth of the estuary, to be met by a wall of angry waves churned up by the gale-force winds. The young Lieutenant in command immediately realised that his boat would be swamped if it ventured farther, so he was obliged to turn back. He radioed Rosyth at once to send a larger vessel to carry the message to the Bell Rock keepers.

When the Rosyth Duty Officer received the message, he signalled the battleship *Queen Mary* – on patrol close to the Forth – requesting her assistance. In the calm of his office, his heart sank at *2:17 am* when he received *Queen Mary's* reply.

"REGRET THAT OWING TO HEAVY SEA I AM UNABLE TO COMMUNICATE WITH BELL ROCK LIGHT"

This was the best the Navy's largest, newest and most advanced battleship could offer – and it was not enough.

Despondently, he passed his hand over his worried brow and sat back in his chair wondering what to do next. After a few minutes of contemplation, he realised there was nothing else he could do without endangering lives. Putting aside an innate concern for duty left undone, he abandoned his efforts and turned to other matters with a clear conscience.

ABOARD HOCHE
October 28, 1915 2:30 Am

In the steel barque *Hoche* further along the cost, the wheelhouse door suddenly crashed open, startling the captain and his wife. With rain and seawater pouring from his oilskins, a crewman hurtled in shouting hysterically that there were cracks in the forward section of the hold. The constant snatching of the anchor chain was tearing the ship apart, he shrieked, and the sea was pouring in.

Before the captain could react, another thirty-foot wave rolled over the ship with a deafening roar, shattering the wheelhouse windows with its weight. The anchor, embedded into rocks on the seabed, held fast as the ship strained against it. Under the enormous tensile forces in the anchor chain, the ship's bow section ripped away from her hull with an agonised screech of tearing tortured metal. Still attached to the seabed by the anchor chain, the bow section fell straight to the bottom.

In the next instant, the sea engulfed the barque and dragged it to the seabed with everybody on board still inside.

HMS ARGYLL
4:15 am

The First Lieutenant struggled off the bridge to answer a call of nature, leaving Evans alone to strain his eyes into the darkness ahead. The oncoming waves breaking solidly over the ship's bow were spattering the bridge windows with foam and obscuring his view. All he could see was fog, darkness and squalls of heavy rain.

Down below, all off-duty men were sleeping fitfully. George, having helped Stan to dispense with his saved-up rum, was sleeping peacefully in spite of being thrown from side to side in his bunk.

Men in the engine room, working with one hand firmly on the safety rails, kept the ship's two massive screws turning, thrusting *Argyll* through the storm. Like the slow rising of theatre curtains, the dense squall enveloping the ship began to lift. Evans narrowed his eyes and leaned forward at the bridge windows. Suddenly, he turned from the windows and bellowed at helmsman to spin the wheel. In the gloom ahead he could see a white shape taller than *Argyll* with the sea foaming at its feet. Seconds later, the port lookout hailed: "SAILING SHIP AHEAD!"

He was mistaken. This was no sailing ship. What he had taken for a large spread of sail was the towering white granite structure of a lighthouse – and the ship was heading straight for it.

A deep rumble ran through *Argyll* as the steering engine raced to put the rudders hard over, and it brought the First Lieutenant running to the bridge. Captain Tancred, who had also heard the report, arrived on the bridge seconds later, expecting a collision.

'What is she doing?' he asked, breathlessly.

'It isn't a sailing ship, Sir,' replied Evans, with contrived British coolness. 'It's the Bell Rock lighthouse.'

'FULL SPEED ASTERN!' barked Tancred.

Together, the officers – utterly helpless as the lighthouse drew closer and closer – waited anxiously for the ship to slow. Then, with a sickening lurch, then another, Argyll stranded her full 450foot length on the rocks, two ships' lengths from the base of the lighthouse. Below, there was an explosion of activity. Men tumbled out of bunks and hammocks and scrambled into whatever clothes they could find. Believing the ship had been torpedoed, they rushed up on deck to assemble for lifeboats. George and the other POs ran up to take charge.

On the bridge, Tancred was calling for damage reports from departmental officers and heard that the hull was pierced in one of the stokeholds. Fuel oil had escaped to start a serious fire. Men ran out the fire hoses and brought it under control quickly. As yet, there were no casualties but the worst news was that *Argyll* was now stuck fast at the top of high water, and there was no hope that she would ever be refloated.

Tancred sent frantic signals:

"URGENT – ARGYLL ASHORE ON BELL ROCK. SHIP BADLY DAMAGED. AFRAID WILL RIP HER BOTTOM AS TIDE FALLS. APPEARS THERE IS NO HOPE OF SAVING SHIP."

His signals sparked frantic activity ashore. The Broughty Ferry and St Andrews lifeboats, six destroyers and several tugs struggled in the teeth of the gale to reach the stranded warship.

On the upper deck of *Argyll,* waves were crashing over the men assembled there, and they were in constant danger of being washed away by the foaming turbulence around them. As the tide began to turn, the ship's full weight bore down on the rocks. There was a loud grinding noise below decks as the ship settled firmly onto the seabed – where she was sure to break up. The two "A" frames supporting her propeller shafts tore away from her stern, leaving her two massive propellers – complete with sections of their shafts – lying on the bottom beneath her hull. Now, with no means of propulsion, she was doomed.

In their helpless situation, the 655 officers and men of *Argyll* were poised on the brink of disaster. They could only wait for someone to tackle the impossible task of plucking them off. If the ship slid into deep water now, she was sure to sink. If she remained on the rocks, there was every chance she would break up around them. Petty Officers and Chiefs were organising their men into orderly groups, sheltering wherever they could in the lee of the ship's superstructure and trying to make sense of the situation. Orders had to be shouted at the tops of voices in order to be heard above the screaming wind.

Stan struggled over beside George. 'Bloody ridiculous,' he bellowed in George's ear. 'We'll be sitting ducks for torpedoes when dawn breaks – if she lasts that long.' He pointed at the lighthouse. 'Seems crazy... there's safety over there. What's wrong with the bloody keepers? They could do something. At least if we could get her tied up to that she wouldn't drift away.' George nodded. He was thinking that falling into the sea right now might not be such a bad idea. It would put an end to his personal torment once and for all. 'And look – the wind is carrying everything over to their bloody front door. I reckon if we fell in there's a chance we'd get washed over there. We could knock 'em up, couldn't we?'

George shrugged off Stan's flippant comments. No one could survive the waves thundering over the base of the lighthouse: some were climbing halfway up to its lantern room but it concentrated his mind on the danger they were in. He shouted to Stan. 'What if we tied a line to a float ...a wooden grating, or something, and floated it over there? Better than waiting to drown!'

'Yeah – good idea. But it would be useless unless there was someone to get hold of it – and those buggers are asleep.'

George nodded agreement and gave up the idea.

Inside the lighthouse, Principal Keeper John Henderson was entirely unaware of the drama going on outside. His two assistants, Colin McCormack and Donald Macdonald, were still fast asleep. All night the granite tower had been swaying and reverberating with the wind and waves beating against it, and they could hear little else. Quite used to storms, they had shuttered their tiny windows firmly and were sitting the storm out in lonely isolation. As was his custom, Henderson opened one of the shutters at *5:45 am*, just as dawn struggled through the heavy clouds racing overhead. Peering into the storm, he immediately saw the big warship on their doorstep.

He thought his eyes were deceiving him. Then he ducked down, instinctively, and immediately woke the others. 'Come an' sae this,' he said, breathlessly. 'It's a bloody Hun battleship...oot there on tha rocks!' McCormack and Macdonald leapt out of bed and peered cautiously over the windowsill.

'God Almighty! Ya cannae see th' deck for sailors. But that's nae German, Johnny – it's wannae oors.' They all looked again and saw that the ship was British – stranded, and in grave peril. Henderson immediately clambered the long circular staircase to the lantern room, to try to communicate with the crew. The others opened their doorway 30 feet above the crashing waves and took in the full horror of the scene on their doorstep. They realised instantly – and with a great deal of apprehension – that they were the only hope of rescue for the men clinging desperately to life out there.

News that the keepers were up and about went round Argyll in a flash. It was then that George and Stan decided to try floating a line over to the Bell Rock. They set some ratings to work and within fifteen minutes they had a strong rope, long enough to reach the lighthouse, tied to an empty oil drum. Securing the other end to one of the ship's steel mooring hawsers they threw the barrel into the sea then watched anxiously as it washed slowly towards the rocks – and past them. After several attempts – hauling it back each time – they succeeded in landing the drum at the foot of the lighthouse.

The keepers managed to snag the rope in a grapnel hook then began to haul it in through their doorway. The three men made a prodigious effort to drag the heavy hawser across the seabed, but it repeatedly got caught between rocks. With the hawser only halfway to the lighthouse, news suddenly came down to the crew that two destroyers, *Hornet* and *Jackal*, were fast approaching. The hopeless task of getting the hawser to the lighthouse had to be abandoned. Frantically waved hand signals told the keepers that *Argyll* was going to haul back on her hawser, and they thankfully gave up their exhausting efforts.

As the ship's crew hauled back, the rope skittered across the keepers' floor like a startled snake, snagging McCormack's foot in a loop. He fell to the floor and struggled to free himself, but the relentless jerking on the rope dragged him kicking and screaming towards the open doorway. Henderson and Macdonald fell on the rope and heaved back to save him. Unaware of the drama unfolding inside the lighthouse, *Argyll's* crew pulled harder, and a bizarre tug-of-war took place in these strange circumstances but at the Navy's end of the rope there was more muscle-power and the keepers could see that they were about to lose their colleague, hopelessly tangled in the rope as he was.

Henderson flung his arms around McCormack's chest and braced his feet against the doorway. As he clung on desperately, Macdonald rushed to find a knife to hack through the rope. At the last possible moment, when it seemed that nothing could prevent McCormack falling to his death on the rocks the rope went slack and the three keepers tumbled back to the safety of the lighthouse floor.

6:30 am

By now, the storm had eased and the wind had lost some of the intensity of its ferocity. All *Argyll's* lifeboats had been lowered successfully into waves that were still heavy and high. Beside *Hornet*, clear of the rocks, were some of the men already rescued. The rest waited anxiously on *Argyll's* stern.

Jackal turned to bring her stern to *Argyll's*. It was a dangerous manoeuvre, calling for great seamanship from her Captain. Too close, and she would also run aground on the rocks. Too far away, and the men could not be reached. Several times, she moved in, only to be forced away again. Finally, she came close enough.

Rising and falling vertically like a demented lift, *Jackal's* stern bumped and ground against *Argyll's*. Each time they came level, men jumped. The gap between them seemed like the gaping jaws of a sea monster willing them to fall inside but, on the other side, the outstretched arms of *Jackal's* crewmen waited to drag them to safety – if only they would jump.

The senior ratings and officers left last. When George's turn came, he waited with Stan and four other men for the destroyer's stern to come near. Just as George jumped, the gap widened unexpectedly and he lost his footing. Falling between the two ships, he grasped a rope hanging from the destroyer's stern with one hand, and hung on as the ship lurched away and downwards. A crewman was trying desperately to lift him up, but the weight was too much for him. In a sudden flash of foreboding, George could clearly see what was about to happen.

Dangling helplessly with the sea washing over him, the two ships were about to rise again and grind against one another – with him between. He was about to be crushed. Nothing he could do could stop it. Everything began to happen in slow motion. He felt no panic. With bizarre cynicism, his mind remained focused as it ran over some cold thoughts... *let go and just drift away – would anyone care? Why hang on to get crushed and mangled, then drown anyway? Does it matter if I live or die here? What a ridiculous way to go!* ...

Fate intervened. One of *Jackal's* men shared George's glimpse of impending disaster and was quick-witted enough to act on it. He stepped forward and released some slack in the rope. It let George float away out of danger. As George fought for breath in the waves rolling over him, the crewman then hauled back on the rope with two of his colleagues to bring George to the side of the ship.

After what seemed an eternity, he was heaved up onto the deck, where he spluttered and coughed the North Sea out of his lungs. Wet, cold, wide-eyed and exhausted, George got to his feet to thank his rescuers, and was rewarded with a big grin on a familiar face.

'Well, bugger me if it ain't Mister Royal!' George could not believe his eyes. It was "Sparrer" from *Invincible*. 'Good to see yer, mate. Cor, fancy gettin' yerself shipwrecked! Wot was the navigatin' officer's excuse this time?' He put on a posh officer's voice: ' *"These must be new rocks we're on"*, I s'pose? Anyway, can't stop now – got to save some 'uvver poor buggers. I'll see yer in a mo.'

With that, Sparrer went back to his duties.

George was taken below with the last of the rescued men, where towels, dry clothes and another tot of rum made him feel human again. He spent some time with Sparrer and promised him a drink one evening then by *12:30 pm* was back with *Argyll's* officers and ratings, safely ashore at Rosyth. Every man was rescued and the only injury sustained during the entire incident was the nasty rope burn on Colin McCormack's leg.

Officers and ratings required elsewhere were given a few days rest, and then dispersed to ships. Some, including George, were sent home on leave by train to await new drafting orders. He had lost everything he owned: all his kit, his money and all his personal possessions. It seemed appropriate that it should happen this way, he thought, losing everything he cared about in one hit and he promised himself that it would mark a completely new beginning in his life.

German intelligence and the morale of the British public were used as justification for burying the embarrassing accident and keeping it from the press. The British public at large never heard about it and as there was no inquiry, no one was ever blamed for losing one of Jacky Fisher's ships. Someone, somewhere would have paid dearly had he still been in office, but he wasn't.

Once back in Portsmouth barracks, George was issued with a new uniform and granted three days leave, which he declined. He decided to spend the time in and around the barracks without going home. He could not face the risk of bumping into Carrie in the street somewhere. It would hurt too much, and would set him back again. When he could stop thinking about her, he felt more buoyant but when she crept insidiously into his mind – more often than he wished – he crashed into the depths of despondency again. As for Emily, he did not wish to see her either. Had it not been for her unwillingness to help him, he would still have Carrie, he said to himself. He had nothing to say to her.

In a fog of self-pity, he made up his mind that it would be better all round if he just kept to himself until he could go back to sea again. He would leave them all guessing – not that anyone would care where he was but, for all his determination, he twice found himself wandering furtively around in Gosport, gazing up at Carrie's window in the hope of catching a glimpse of her. He saw nothing, not even Marje, who walked by and noticed him standing outside the shop one evening, staring at Bill's apartment window.

Chapter Twenty

PORTSMOUTH
Thursday, November 4, 1915

When the new motion picture "The Tramp" came to the Portsmouth Rialto – a picture house known locally as the "fleapit", Marje was desperate to see it. It starred Charlie Chaplin as a hapless tramp, and she was told that it was hilarious. Working beside Carrie at the next packing session at Haslar Hospital, she tentatively suggested they should see it together. It was a clear indication to Carrie that she wanted to patch up their differences over Carrie's infidelity now that it was over, and Carrie eagerly agreed. Carrie chose a Thursday because, she explained, this was Bill's regular Masonic Lodge meeting night, and Aunt Ethel would have Kate to stay.

Linking arms on the way to Portsmouth that evening, and pleased to be friends again, the two of them chattered like schoolgirls making up after a tiff. They were both keen to have a good time, and carefully avoided talking about George. 'I've always wanted to know,' said Marje, mischievously. 'What exactly do Masons do at their meetings?'

'God alone knows ... but it's very secret, whatever it is. I know that women are not allowed to join. Heaven knows what goes on. They won't even let other men know until they are in it themselves ... and Bill won't say a word about it.' Marje gave a shiver.

'Sounds positively sinister, darling. How do you put up with it?'

'I don't have anything to do with it. It's just another man's game, as far as I'm concerned. It's all stupid secret rituals and funny handshakes. Oh, and they wear funny little aprons, for God's sake! I know, because I saw Bill's once. I mean, how could anyone – except a man, of course – take that seriously?'

'But they do, don't they? I've been told that all the most prominent men are in it. It's some kind of "brotherhood". A bit like this new Ku-Klux-Klan thing in America.'

'Well, not exactly. They're not against black people, or anything like that. I think it's more of a secret way of doing business.'

Marje leaned forward in quiet confidence. 'I was told once that they all dress up in peculiar clothes and do a funny dance around a dead chicken ...and part of the ritual is to kiss its bottom! Ugh!' She shrieked with laughter, drawing glances from people in the street.

In high spirits, they arrived at the picture house and bought their sixpenny tickets then settled into the uncomfortable seats of the auditorium. Carrie suddenly dissolved in convulsive laughter – the unstoppable kind that can follow a time of stress.

'What is it, darling?' Marje was immediately infected by Carrie's laughter and was anxious not to be left out of the joke – whatever it was. 'What is it?' she pleaded, as Carrie dabbed her eyes.

'It's… it's just that I suddenly had this vision that while we're sitting here, Bill is dancing around somewhere in a pinafore, kissing a chicken's bottom!' They were still giggling when the lights went out, and it took a loud "shush" from the audience to stop them.

The black and silver images flickered silently across the screen. An elderly woman, whose hands and face glowed eerily in a solitary puddle of yellow light, jangled notes out of a battered piano at the front. Glancing up at the screen, she did her best to create pathos and heighten the golden moments of hilarity and drama of Charlie Chaplin's performance. For forty minutes, Marje and Carrie laughed and cried together in the dark, stuffy, malodorous atmosphere, completely lost to the fantasy world of Hollywood.

When the film ended they left with smiles on their lips and tears in their eyes, shuffling out with the smiling crowd. Outside, wet pavements and falling rain brought them abruptly back to reality. Huddled under Marje's ever-handy umbrella, they picked a way through the crowd sheltering under the frontage of the Rialto. Suddenly, without speaking, Marje unceremoniously bundled her friend into the darkness of an adjacent shop entrance.

'What are you doing?' Carrie's laughter died on her lips as she caught Marje's icy stare. Following it to the roadway, she saw a couple waiting for an approaching taxicab. Their arms were linked tightly and their bodies seemed moulded together.

Carrie's jaw dropped. With eyes like green saucers, she stared in disbelief. It was Bill and Carla James! Transfixed, she watched silently as the couple got into the taxicab. The intimacy of their body language and the obvious affection of their laughter and glances shocked her. Her mouth stayed open as the taxicab sped northwards, in the opposite direction to the Gosport ferry. Her hands were trembling and she could feel her pulse racing at her temples. 'That was…'

'Yes, darling, I'm afraid it was …without a doubt.'

Carrie was stunned, unable to talk. Marje found a taxicab to take them to the ferry, and led her to it. All the way home, they talked angrily and indignantly about it and Carrie struggled to come to terms with what they had seen.

'I can't say that I'm not shocked,' Carrie said, still dazed, 'because I am but I suppose I can't exactly blame him either.'

Her forgiving tone annoyed Marje. 'Yes, you bloody well can, darling. He's a bastard! He doesn't know anything about you and George at all. For all he knows, he's being unfaithful to you. I can't believe it. Seeing that bitch behind your back! He's a pig, and I'll never forgive him.' She looked at Carrie. 'You won't forgive him, will you, darling?' One look at Carrie told her otherwise.

'I don't know what I feel, really,' Carrie said quietly, staring vacantly. 'I'm still dazed. It's all so confusing. I feel hurt and betrayed, angry, belittled but guilty, sad, relieved – all at once. There could be some simple explanation, of course.'

'Oh, for God's sake, Carrie. You could see from that exactly what was going on. The man is obviously…well, he's doing more than just holding her hand. Even I can see that! There's no other explanation. The only good thing about it is that you know about it now. If you handle it carefully, you'll be able to get out of that awful situation and go off with a clear conscience, if that's what you want.' Marje pulled a face as she had another thought. 'Oh my God – George! If only you'd known. Oh, Carrie – I'm so sorry.'

Carrie's eyelids dropped momentarily. She shrugged and forced a thin smile. 'Too late for that, I'm afraid. I sent him back to sea with a broken heart. He'll never forgive me. It's all over now. Anyway, I finished with him for entirely different reasons. I know I've done the right thing.'

Marje was not so sure any more, and her expression said so. They both stared silently into space, thinking. Marje came back to today's problem. 'The only thing I want to know now is how long this has been going on. I'm going to find out! Tomorrow, I'll ask some discreet questions. I'll soon know, believe me.' Without noticing the time passing, they were at Carrie's door. Marje gave her friend an affectionate hug. 'Try not to let the cat out of the bag until I have found out something, darling. It's best to have plenty of ammunition before you hit back. I'll let you know as soon as I've got it. Try not to think about George too much. Be as polite as you can to Bill – and be asleep when he gets in.' With that, she left for home.

Carrie stood in the dark alone with her thoughts, watching her friend's flashlight flicker off down the street but as much as she tried not to, that night, Carrie did spend time thinking about Bill, Carla and George. She just could not help it. The future suddenly looked grim. She missed George terribly. Next to Kate, she wanted him more than anything and rejecting him had been the hardest thing she had ever done. Instead of getting over him, she loved him even more, but he was gone. She could do nothing about that now. It was over. She had seen to that.

Tears trickled silently down her cheeks as she thought how cruel and unjust life could be. She had happiness in her grasp with George, but she had thrown it away. She'd had to do it. However much love there was between them, it would have been ruined in the end, she told herself – unless there was security too. Living on a shoestring was all right for some people, but not for her. She knew herself too well to pretend that money did not matter.

Now all she had left was a partner who was betraying her.

She buried her head in her pillow and sobbed until there were no tears left but within minutes, George was back in her mind. Finding out about Carla changed everything. If George was only there now, she could tell him that she loved him dearly and that money did not matter so much after all. They could manage with what they had. Being together and not losing one another – those were the most important things – but how could she tell him if she was not completely convinced herself? Would a lack of money ruin everything? Her head began to spin and spin until she was totally incapable of separating fact from fiction; what she felt and what she really wanted out of life – which was the most important? Anyway, he was gone for good now. He would never forgive her for what she had done to him so there was no point in getting into a state about it.

Now she had a reason to end her relationship with Bill, and that is what she should do but then what? Where would she go? How could he betray her and Kate like this – especially when she had sacrificed her own happiness to stay with him? It hardly seemed to matter that she had strayed off the path herself because she had put that right of her own free will. Would Bill, she wondered, do the same for her if she confronted him with his own indiscretions? What a mess! She and George, Carla and Bill – four adults exchanging partners behind each other's backs, and not knowing. How bizarre. How sad! She had to get out of the situation.

She needed no more proof to end it: just the courage to do so. I'm very good at ending things, she told herself, cynically. Whatever the outcome, I must do it – and now, rather than later but what if she had made a mistake? What if there was some perfectly reasonable excuse for him being there with Carla? She felt ridiculous thinking it, but perhaps Bill's Masonic activities might have something to do with that. She quickly dismissed the thought, knowing that she was just making excuses for him.

As Marje had urged her to do, she buried her feelings and carried on as if she knew nothing, and waited for the right time.

Sunday, November 7, 1915

Using her contacts, Marje eventually got to the truth. When she told Carrie that Bill had begun seeing Carla soon after she came to his apartment with George, Carrie was visibly shocked and became dismayed then extremely angry. Suddenly, like a penny falling in a slot machine, everything dropped into place. It was all connected with Bill's late nights, his business trips away and the beginning of all those evenings and nights she had been alone in the apartment. It matched the change in his behaviour towards her. It all came together in Carrie's mind in a sudden flash of obviousness-in-hindsight. She had been betrayed! That is where his cold indifference had come from: not Paxman, or business! And how well it worked. She had ended up feeling lonely and unloved, angry and frustrated; and it was that that had turned her fascination with George into an irresistible urge.

Whose fault was it after all – if anybody's? She talked for hours with Marje, and admitted that mischievously causing Carla to finish with George was a spiteful and selfish thing to do. It had backfired badly on her. 'I think not,' said Marje, with a tone of confident reassurance designed to make her feel better. 'Bill obviously took a shine to Carla the moment he saw her. I noticed it, and I'm surprised you didn't. He stepped in with Carla the moment he knew he could. If she had really wanted George – and Bill had let her know that he was definitely happy with you, he would never have stood a chance with her. Darling, you have nothing to reproach yourself for.'

Carrie thought hard, while Marje watched her quizzically.

'Does it matter now anyway?' Marje asked. 'He obviously wants her, but he probably feels guilty – as indeed he should but now that you know all about it you can end this bloody charade and send them both packing. The thing I'm sad about is George. If only we'd known about the happy lovers before you sent him away, you might have felt differently. I feel bad that I influenced your feelings, and I can't forgive myself, but how was I to know?'

Annoyance flashed through Carrie's eyes. 'Marje! How many times do I have to tell you? I finished with George because it wasn't right. There are other, more important things in life.'

Her friend pulled a matronly face. 'Like money, you mean?'

Carrie flushed indignantly. '*Security!* Not money.'

The confrontation with Bill that evening was not the explosive, distressing occasion it could have been. At first, he denied having an affair. He shouted angrily that it was a ridiculous thing to say and how dare she fling accusations at him? His defensive anger told her all she needed to know but ultimately, faced with facts as undeniable as the colour of his eyes, he began to squirm. He called her a liar, then – after she pressed him harder – admitted everything, flippantly, and then justified it as a short, out-of-character "fling" caused by pressures at work. Thirty minutes of heated conversation later and he was describing Carla's charms and admitting that he had not been able to resist them. His tactless excuses infuriated Carrie but she could see the truth in his eyes: he was in love with the woman. When he began to tell her that his love for her was entirely different, she could not take any more. She broke down and sobbed – furious with herself for letting him see what he had done to her.

He tried to convince her of how wretched, sad and sorry he felt about letting her down, but failed to say that he was prepared to end the affair so that they could begin again: not that she wanted him to. Somewhere along the way, their relationship had turned into a friendship – it was obvious, but now that there was Carla, even that would be destroyed if it lingered on. There was no alternative; Carrie knew she had to leave quickly. She ended it, there and then.

Bill's remorse seemed to be genuine and she had to stop herself feeling sorry for him. Remembering how good he had been to take her in at a time of crisis, she wanted to make things easy, so she lied and told him that she had somewhere to live and that she would easily cope on her own. He could get on with his new relationship, she told him, with no more guilt: she would move out quickly to clear the way for it.

He was so relieved to have everything out in the open that he forgot to ask where she was going – and she did not say.

The following day, she had a long talk with Aunt Ethel.

GOSPORT
Wednesday, November 10, 1915

In a final farewell tinged with happiness, relief, tears of gratitude and regret, Carrie and Bill parted amicably. Carrie took a taxicab to Aunt Ethel's house, with Kate and her possessions, and settled into the tiny spare bedroom that would be her home until something better came along. Ethel was pleased to be of help, and quietly enjoyed the thought of having Kate more permanently in her otherwise lonely life. After unpacking – and not finding enough space for all their clothes – Carrie pushed her half-filled suitcases under the bed and put Kate in a crib beside her then climbed between her own crisp, chilly white sheets. As soon as her head touched the pillow, her mind began to fork through the events of the past days and weeks, examining each one in detail.

Homeless and with no male companion again, dependent upon her aunt's charity and with a child to bring up alone, the future looked bleak and doubts about the forthright decisions she had made were gripping her heart painfully. If only she had not turned George away! They would probably have been very happy together. Poor but happy: but how could she be happy and poor at the same time? Surely, she could have money *and* a man who loved her? Yes, of course but all that and a man *she* could love – that may never happen! She fell asleep with the vision of her future obfuscated by unanswerable questions.

LONDON

For Lord Kitchener, the war felt much the same. After visiting the troops in all areas and bases of Gallipoli, and discussing the situation with the senior officers present, he returned to London to gain support for a complete withdrawal from the area.

His fear was that this could not be done without further huge losses. The eclectic Army in Gallipoli, totalling more than 90,000 troops from Great Britain, Ireland, France, Australia, New Zealand, Newfoundland, French West Africa and India, with 4,500 animals, 1,700 vehicles and 200 guns, had to be withdrawn from under the noses of Turks less than a hundred yards away in places. Achieving this called for an unprecedented level of cooperation between the Army and Royal Navy.

GALLIPOLI
December, 1915

It was the new Commander, General Munro, who had the task of planning the withdrawal, and he immediately surprised everyone by electing not to employ diversionary action. The only feint he intended was a daring one, implicit in his insistence that life in the trenches should go on as normal – including a continuation of routine attacks on the Turks. The withdrawal would begin in the northern zones.

Covered by rearguard action, troops in the most forward trenches of Suvla and Anzac withdrew quietly for the safety of their transports on December 19. The remaining troops, equipment, stores and animals were moved out successfully and embarked in transport ships, in the darkness of the next ten consecutive nights. The operation was carried out so efficiently that it took the Turks by surprise and only three men were wounded.

Now came the more difficult task of withdrawing the southern forces, which would take place after Christmas.

In the trenches of Europe, this particular Christmas, there would be no friendly football match in No Man's Land between British and German troops. The naivety and innocence of 1914 – the first Christmas of the war – had gone. Anger and hatred had replaced innocence. In Britain, there could be no forgiveness for the "German atrocities" of 1915 – only horror and dismay. The sinking of unarmed hospital and passenger ships deeply offended the British sense of "fair play", as did civilian deaths – including those of women and children, caused by the indiscriminate shelling of East Coast cities, the haphazard Zeppelin bombing of innocent civilians and the October execution of the British nurse Edith Cavell. "Britishness" could no longer be afforded.

Fighting continued wherever the war was being waged, with no dramatic changes in its general ebb and flow. The new German Fokker monoplane was causing consternation in the air above the trenches of Europe, and the Russians were preparing a new offensive on their front.

The war at sea was concerned mainly with submarine and mine activity, and at Scapa Flow and Rosyth – respectively, the bases of the Grand Fleet and the 3rd Cruiser Squadron – the accent was once again on relaxation and recreational activities. Apart from occasional exercises in the North Sea, there was little for battleships and cruisers to do.

At home, more women were being employed to release men for

the war, and they now had jobs in munitions and aeroplane factories, railways, omnibuses and trams, offices, the Post Office, and as Voluntary Aid Detachments (VADs) ambulance drivers and nurses.

Nightclubs were now a feature of wartime life. By Christmas 1915, Soho had become the centre for London nightclubs, and boasted 150 – of which many were said to be places of ill repute capable of duping servicemen out of their meagre earnings. It had also become a burgeoning shopping centre.

Food was in even shorter supply and average prices had doubled since 1914. Eggs were now a luxury. Sugar, wheat, and cotton were scarce, and there was growing concern that prices were being inflated by profiteering. The Government began to look more seriously into this problem and the practice of ring dealing among wholesalers. A Food Controller was appointed to stamp it out.

The demand for able men for active service was outstripping the supply of volunteers; the committee debating this reached the conclusion that it would be necessary to introduce conscription early in 1915.

Because of the escalating cost of the war, a doubling of Income Tax, to 3s 0d in the pound, was imminent.

People were cursing the war for blackouts. Enforced economy of fuel and power and the threat of aeroplane and Zeppelin raids had set the country back fifty years in terms of lighting the streets, making them hazardous places after dark.

GOSPORT
Wednesday, December 22, 1915

Carrie returned from a pensive stroll in the park with Kate, wondering if she would ever again be able to walk past that shelter without thinking of George. Aunt Ethel came to the door to whisper that there was a man waiting to see her; a Mister Briggs. With a quizzical frown, she went into the front room to see what he wanted.

Briggs was an elderly man in a creased formal suit. A bowler hat rested on his knees, which were clenched tightly together, and a stiff shirt collar hung loosely around his scrawny neck. He struggled to his feet as Carrie came in. 'Miss Palmer... Miss Carrie Palmer?' She nodded. 'Miss Palmer, I... I am sorry to call on you unannounced. My name is Briggs, and I'm a solicitor's clerk from Springer & Callow in Commercial Road, Portsmouth.'

He paused as if he had forgotten what he came for.

'Yes – what can I do for you?'

'Aah...I have, aah, been trying to locate you for some time – on the instructions of Mister Springer, that is of course... on a matter of great importance.' Curiosity caused Carrie's heart to flutter wildly.

'On what matter precisely?'

Briggs looked flustered and embarrassed. 'I'm afraid I don't know,' he admitted. 'I merely have instructions to find you to give you this.' He handed her a crisp envelope. She opened it with apprehensive haste. It explained nothing, but invited her to the offices of Springer & Callow, at her earliest convenience, to discuss – as Briggs had said – a matter of great importance. She was confused by it, and told him so. 'I'm sorry, Miss Palmer. I have only been told that it could be to your advantage.' He dragged out a pocketbook and consulted a calendar in it. 'When shall I say you will come? With Christmas and The New Year upon us, and the 3rd of January being the first Monday of 1916...'

'The 4th,' said Carrie, arbitrarily, keen to avoid appearing too eager.

'Fine.'

His pencil crawled over the page. 'What time would suit you?'

'Ten-thirty.'

'Ten-thirty am on the 4th of January it shall be, Miss Palmer. Thank you. A Merry Christmas to you.' He shuffled out.

Tensely curious, Carrie watched him through the window. Outside the house, Briggs donned his bowler with a "duty-well-done" pat of his hand, and strode off. Hastily reading the letter again, she noticed that it asked her to produce birth certificates for herself and Kate on her visit to Springer & Callow. The more she thought about it, the more agitated she became. The only reason she could imagine for this – and one she dared not think about too deeply – concerned the tenuous but undeniable bloodline connection between Kate and the Farleighs. It made her feel sick.

In almost all theatres of war, there was a respectful lull in fighting during the days of Christmas, but new vigour would be applied immediately afterwards. At home, it was a more sober season than usual, and people had to use their meagre resources to celebrate it as best they could. Carrie faced Christmas with some trepidation, having been unable to eat properly since last seeing George. She knew from the fit of her clothes that she was losing weight, and the constant knot of apprehension in her stomach was making all food look like some kind of poison. Carrie, Ethel and Kate spent the time quietly together, trying desperately to feel like a family. Carrie forced herself to eat in spite of her reluctance, regretting it the following day when she felt sick.

Bill showered Carla with Christmas presents. No one around him knew that problems had developed between himself and Roy Paxman, and that government officials had been showing unwelcome interest in the activities of the "ring". Higher Income Taxes and shortages of food products were beginning to depress their fortunes. The profits of the three Portsmouth branches of Paxman & Guy were also suffering from misdirected anti-German feelings and constant damage being done by naive demonstrators.

As the wrecking and looting of shops could not be attributed to Acts of God or the War, insurance companies refused to pay out. More and more, the partnership was obliged to rely upon its wholesale business with military establishments, but officials had given a clear and sinister warning – suppliers involved in ring dealing would soon be forced out of Government contracts, and possibly arrested. The dream was fading and Paxman was worried by the bank loan he had secured on his home.

George was determined to confine himself to Portsmouth barracks for the Christmas period, and volunteered for duty but in a last-minute fit of loneliness and remorse, he went home to visit his mother, and they succeeded in patching up most of their differences.

Emily was ready to do almost anything to restore her relationship with her son, and listened eagerly when he told her that his affair with Carrie was over.

Taking care not to put her foot into anything she would

afterwards regret, she was sympathetic – especially when she learned that his love for Carrie had stemmed from betrayal by Bill and Carla. It gave Emily the perfect excuse to be the mother George needed.

'Oh, George, if only you'd told me that the poor girl was being treated so shamefully, of course I would have welcomed her and her little girl here!'

George stared in wonderment as she said it, shaking his head in frustration then shrugging off the irony as a piece of history.

THE SOUTHERN ZONE OF GALLIPOLI
January, 1916

In Gallipoli, a more significant piece of history was taking shape.

It was realised that the task of plucking the British and French armies from the southern zone at Helles would be fraught with danger and had the potential for heavy losses.

It was expected that the Turks, as soon as they realised that they were alone in the north, would rush their artillery and troops from Suvla to the south, in anticipation of further British withdrawals from there. Every part of the southern area was exposed to Turkish shellfire and, in the Straits, there was the continuing threat of German submarine attacks.

After a Christmas of frantic planning, the evacuation of the tip of the Gallipoli Peninsula began on the night of January 1, 1916. It was to be an orderly and gradual withdrawal over several nights, and tension was high.

At home, also in a state of tension, Carrie set out to find out what was behind the mysterious invitation of the solicitors, Springer & Callow.

PORTSMOUTH
Tuesday, January 4, 1916

After what seemed a long wait in the solicitor's waiting room, a starchy female secretary showed Carrie into the senior partner's office. The woman placed documents on the leather-topped desk and swished out. Bewildered, Carrie glanced nervously around the room, noting the yards of book spines crammed into bookshelves and documents tied with red ribbon on the desk. The room had the leathery, dusty, papery smell of a schoolroom. She sat down cautiously on the edge of a leather-bound chair. Wondering what she was doing there and feeling sick again, she realised how tense this meeting was making her feel.

After a few minutes, a kindly looking man with a fixed, yellowy smile came in proffering a limp, bony hand. She took it and thought how much he resembled her old schoolmaster: a slight stoop, hooked nose, gold-rimmed spectacles, and an abundance of gold watch chain dangling from his waistcoat pockets. He went behind his desk.

'Springer,' he said, as an afterthought – rather obviously, Carrie thought. 'You must be…' he bent forward, looking down his nose at the documents on his desk, 'Miss Carrie Palmer… is that correct?' His knees cracked as he sat down behind the desk. 'And did you bring along your birth certificate today – and that of the child?'

'Yes, I did.' Carrie drew them from her handbag and offered them to him with a trembling hand. He studied them in silence then handed them back with a smile.

'Thank you. Now, would you mind telling me if you have ever been in service, Miss Palmer?' Carrie's fear suddenly turned into a flush of anger. She resented being interrogated without explanation, and she imagined how Marje would handle the situation.

'Mister Springer, I have no idea why I am here or, frankly, what business it is of yours if I have been in service.' It worked. Springer was visibly alarmed that he may have overstepped the mark and annoyed her. He smiled profusely and held up his claw-like hands in a gesture of surrender.

'I'm so sorry, Miss Palmer. Rest assured that there are valid reasons for my asking, and it could be to your advantage to answer my questions. The reasons will become apparent soon. All in good time, Miss Palmer, all in good time.' She noticed his tendency to give a slight sniff at the end of every other sentence.

Still slightly ruffled, she decided to go along with his game of mystery – after all, she was otherwise not going to find out what this was all about. She answered his questions and told him about Farleigh

Manor. He asked the names of the Squire and his son, and she confirmed them. Visibly reassured by her answers, Springer dropped his interrogatory manner for one of smiling subservience.

'I am sorry, Miss Palmer, but it was necessary for me to establish, beyond doubt, that we have the correct Miss Palmer before disclosing our instructions. You do understand, of course?' Carrie did not, but she nodded. He pulled a crisp, sealed envelope from the document on his desk and, with a sober smile, handed it to her then stood up to leave the room. 'I shall return in a few minutes. In the meantime, please be good enough to read this. It will, no doubt, explain why I have asked you to come here today.'

Frowning, she accepted the envelope and watched it tremble in her hand. Her heart beat faster as she hastened to see what was in it. It was addressed to her by name in a neat handwriting that she did not recognise and was marked "Strictly Private & Confidential". Mystified, she tore it open and looked quickly to the end of the letter. It was from Edward Farleigh!

Confused, she went to the beginning and saw the crest of Farleigh Manor. It was dated July 15, 1915. She read on:

"My dearest Carrie,
If you are now reading this, it can mean only one thing. I am lying dead somewhere in some foreign field. In that case, the deepest regrets I take with me are that I have never seen our child and that I shall never see your fabulous face again."

Carrie bit her lip and looked up, fully expecting to find Edward standing there. She could picture him clearly. Tears welled in her eyes and a cold hand gripped her heart. The pit of her stomach felt like a huge void. She read on a few minutes later, but it was through a mist of tears.

"...A thousand times I have regretted losing you, and cursed the manner of our parting. Every night since then I have prayed that I wd find you back at the manor, and that things wd be as they were before. So deep is what I feel for you still that had I survived this wretched war, I know that I wd not have rested until I found you again. I want

so much to tell you that I have never stopped loving you with all my heart and that it was only out of respect for my father's wishes that I have kept my distance since you left – as wretched as that has made me.

But as you read this now, you will understand that I can no longer do these things for myself. I now hope and pray that you will accept this letter as my faithful and truthful ambassador."

With her heart in shreds, Carrie was forced to stop reading. She was unable to see the words for tears. Sobbing quietly, she stood up and went to the window, clutching a handkerchief to her eyes. Behind her, the door gently opened slightly then closed quietly again. Struggling to control her tears, she read on…

"You must be wondering now, after all said to the contrary, how I came to be in the line of fire at all. Therein lies a story, my love, and you will find it strange, as do I, that the heart, once set firm on a matter, should be so fickle as to soften with love or harden in the heat of angry regret.

You see, my dear father, who was all I had after you left, insisted on going to America to visit a dying friend. Fate wd have it that when he returned to England, he shd sail on the Lusitania and perish with other poor souls who went down with it.

I cannot express how very sad this made me. Neither can I explain how angry I have become with the way of this war. Nothing now is as it was. Everything is changed: my objection to serving in the war, in particular. Now, I discover, I have a fervent need to do so. Accordingly, I have secured a commission in the Army.

After training, I shall be serving the cause in Belgium, where I intend full well to avenge my father's death one hundredfold and more. However, I am mindful that shd I fall in battle, no one will be left in the Farleigh line: save, of course, for the baby boy or girl that I trust was safely delivered of you, and whom I know to be truly yours and mine.

As there is no one left alive who could claim to be of Farleigh blood, no cousin or other descendant, however remote, other than our child, I have instructed Solicitors that, on my death, all that is now mine, having been passed to me on my father's untimely death, shall be the child's: the Manor, the estate, and all moneys, incomes and properties therein. Your child – our child – is now the sole source of the blood of my family, and is therefore deserving of all the assets of its ancestors.

I now wish to do in death that which I could not do in life: that is to take care of you and ours. I once made you a promise that you would one day have the position and status that you crave for. Please forgive the circumstances in which I now fulfil that promise. I no longer have choices.

The Solicitors will explain everything to you. You and the child are well provided for. It was my dream that I would be there to love and care for you both. But better this way than not at all.
Know that I will love you for all time.
Edward"

Stunned, Carrie sat down with tears streaming down her face. Her head was bowed, and her heart was aching. She felt empty inside. The door opened quietly and the receptionist came to her and put an arm around her shoulders to comfort her. 'There, there, my dear,' she said softly. 'I know what you are going through. Mister Springer and I lost our eldest son eight weeks ago. We know exactly how devastating it is. Let me make you a nice cup of tea.'

Carrie nodded and thanked her; surprised by her initial misimpression of the woman and realising now that she was Springer's wife. On her return, she sat and talked until Carrie recovered from the awful news, and Springer came back offering sympathy and a few comforting words before slipping back into business.

'Obviously, I have not seen Squire Farleigh's letter, but I have been given an overall picture of the circumstances with my instructions. Not now, of course, but when you are ready to discuss the administration of the will and the Farleigh Estate please telephone my wife to make an appointment. We are working in conjunction with the firm of Abbott, Ruxley & Small, in Dorchester, to carry out Squire Farleigh's wishes. Little can be done at this stage. Probate has to be dealt with before the estate is administered. In the meantime, we must discuss precisely what is to be done with it.'

Carrie looked at him, blankly. He smiled. 'You will need advice on how to proceed – which we shall be pleased to offer – and I am sure you will need time to think about your inheritance. In basic terms, there is a very generous provision for yourself in the sum of £10,000. You are also to be joint Trustee with Abbott Ruxley of your daughter's substantial inheritance. You could, of course, move to the Manor and manage the estate yourself. Alternatively, it could be let or managed professionally until your daughter reaches the age of twenty-one. The net income of such action would naturally accumulate to the benefit of your daughter but from it the Trustees could possibly agree to providing further income for the maintenance of your daughter, should this prove necessary.'

He could see in Carrie's eyes that he should go no further at this point. She looked pale and bewildered. Behind her, Mrs Springer was glaring reproachfully at her husband, and he suddenly looked nervous. 'But all in good time,' he said. 'All in good time.' He sniffed and shuffled his papers then leaned forward in confidence. 'This will all take time to deal with, Miss Palmer. However, I have arranged for a bank to make you an advance against your inheritance – on advantageous terms, of course. Mrs Springer will give you details and the necessary documents on your way out. You may draw on the account as soon as you wish. But I won't keep you any longer. I am sure this has been a most stressful and bewildering experience for you.'

Carrie's head was still spinning when Mrs Springer gently showed her out. Remembering hardly anything, other than Edward's death, she wandered aimlessly through Portsmouth, staring blankly at a world that was strangely different now. It felt like a dream. To reassure herself that it was not, she read Edward's letter again and looked at the bank's letter of authority. Her legs felt weak as the significance of her new situation gripped her. The key to everything she had ever wanted, or ever could want, was there in her hand, but with it had come an unexpected burden of responsibility and sadness, and the guilt that she knew she would also have to live with.   Buried in the deepest corner of her heart, from where they could never, ever, be exhumed were secrets of her relationships with Edward and

Thomas Farleigh that would surely haunt her for the rest of her life. She had an irresistible compulsion to see Farleigh Manor once more, but knew she would never be able to live there. Neither would she be able to stay there again, even for one night, for fear that the Farleighs ghosts would confront her with truths and take back all that Edward had left her.

Poor Teddy! She had been very fond of him.

What she needed now, more than anything, was Marje's reassuring company. Still in shock, she went to the staff entrance of Biddles and waited, anxiously turning over in her mind how she could explain away why she and Kate had been left the entire Farleigh estate. She desperately wanted to confide in Marje, but even she could not be told the truth: not everything – but what could she say? The more secrets and lies she hid, the more that would have to follow.

When Marje suddenly appeared, Carrie had still not decided what to tell her. So she made it up as she went along, and said that as there were no Farleighs left after Edward's death, and rather than leave the estate to the Inland Revenue, he had left it to her because she was his father's favourite employee. Marje frowned at this and wondered why, in that case, had she been dismissed? But that, explained Carrie, was after the will had been drawn up – which no one had thought to change before Edward was killed!

Marje was incredulous, but felt obliged not to question her dear friend's explanation. In any event, her sheer delight on Carrie's behalf overshadowed everything else, and the unsatisfied questions left in Marje's mind paled into insignificance against the brilliant happiness and utter joy they shared over Carrie's new wealth and position. Carrie decided not to mention that the real Mistress of Farleigh Manor was, of course, Kate. At Carrie's insistence, Marje swore on her mother's life that she would not tell a soul about Carrie's inheritance until she herself chose to disclose it.

Bursting with curiosity about the scene of the many stories she had heard from her friend, Marje jumped at Carrie's invitation to accompany her and Kate on a day's visit to Farleigh Manor – and to help her decide what to do with it. Together, they went to the bank that afternoon to arrange Carrie's new account. There, the fawning attention of the manager finally crystallised for Carrie the awesome reality of her situation. Suddenly, she was independently wealthy – a real woman of means who could have anything she wanted, within reason, including a white house of her own on top of Portsdown Hill!

When she reached home, she swept Kate off her feet and hugged and hugged her until she could feel her happiness permeating into the little body wrapped in her arms. 'I know you don't understand all these things, my pet,' she murmured into the bewildered child's ear. 'But trust Mummy…everything's all right. Everything is going to be fine from now on…you'll see.'

Chapter Twenty-one

FARLEIGH MANOR
Thursday, January 6, 1916

It did not take long for Carrie to arrange a visit to Farleigh Manor. Using her new bank account, she drew out enough money to take her there in the luxury of a chauffeur-driven hired motorcar, with Marje and Kate. As the motorcar finally crunched along the gravel driveway to the front door, Marje gasped at the magnificence of the impressive house. An agent of Abbot Ruxley, the Dorchester solicitors, was waiting patiently to show them round. Carrie explained that she knew the property well, and there was no need for him to accompany them to every room, but he did.

The dustsheets covering all the furniture gave the place a cold, eerie look – a feeling of finality and of times past. The rooms were icy cold and Carrie gave a slight shiver as she stood in the drawing room. Memories of teasing Edward there came flooding back; and the awful row he and his father had had that was heard throughout the house. In her mind, the dining room still echoed with Jacky Fisher's booming voice and images of the glittering tables she waited on. Her tiny bedroom was smaller than she remembered, and the big kitchen was dark and empty – silently emanating scenes that only she could see.

Marje's chattering and boisterous exclamations echoed through each room they visited, but Carrie hardly noticed. She was busy with her thoughts – no more so than in the bedrooms where a wistful look came to her eye as, lovingly, she passed a hand over the ornately carved mahogany bedstead.

Thomas's limousine – the very one that had carried her into exile – still glistened and gleamed as it stood silently in the garage with nowhere to go. Edward's horse, Prince, whinnied in the stable. She opened the door and went to him and nuzzled into his neck, inhaling the smell of him. Then she held up Kate to stroke his shiny soft coat.

The man from Abbott Ruxley told her that Mrs Trimble, the housekeeper who had made her life a misery, and Sally Parsons, the scullery maid, had retired and left, but the stable boy, Bob Heritage, and Thomas's faithful old driver, Stan, had been kept on to look after the horses, the motorcar, and any maintenance that had to be done.

As they walked from room to room everything was stirring Carrie's memory and conscience. When the tour was over and they were back in the kitchen clouds suddenly gathered in Carrie's eyes. She leaned to Marje to whisper. 'Would you be a pet and take Kate for a little play while I take a walk around by myself? I just need a little bit of time on my own.'

Recognising the look on Carrie's face, Marje held out her arms and took Kate without questioning the plea. 'Come on, sweetheart, let's go and see that nice horsie again, shall we?' She turned to the man from Abbott Ruxley. 'Mr...?' She inquired, rather grandly.

'Ross,' he said quickly.

'Right, Mr Ross, would you be so kind? The stables, please.' Marje was enjoying being the lady of the manor for a few minutes.

Carrie stood, trance-like, inside a vast bubble of awakening memories. She was in the large kitchen where much of her life was still embedded, and she stood there looking at the big pine table, scrubbed white. She ran her hand slowly over its smooth surface, wondering how many times she had been forced to scrub it by Mrs T and recalling one time when she was fulfilled on it and another when she had to sit there in some discomfort. How all that had changed now! What was the turning point? The sights and odours embedded in the fabric of the room carried her back to a time when it was busy – filled with laughter and the Dorset brogue of the manor's bustling domestic staff.

It was suddenly November 1913 again and Carrie could see herself sitting at the table as clearly as if she were looking in a mirror. 'Sit there, you liddle bitch!' The sound of Mrs T's screeching still seemed to be filling the room and echoing across the granite flagstones. The occasion was Mrs Trimble's discovery of Carrie laughing and chatting animatedly with Edward Farleigh in the courtyard. She loomed over Carrie with her plump arms akimbo.

'Just what do you think you'm playin' at, you liddle tart?' she shrieked, giving Carrie's face a loud slap that snapped her head to one side. Carrie's hand flew instinctively to her stinging cheek. Mrs Trimble's normally soft Dorset burr became harsh and hard when she was angry. She leaned forward and prodded Carrie's chest with a thick finger. 'I know egsackly what you'm up to, my girl... swingin' your 'ips around in front of Master Edward whenever he's around. You'm leadin' 'im on, as much as you can. I've been watchin' you. You'm nothin' but a schemin' liddle bitch!'

Her words flew at Carrie like a swarm of angry wasps, accompanied by some of the tiny flecks of white spittle gathering at the corners of her mouth. 'Squire Thomas is goin' to 'ear about this, young lady, and you'll be out in the street as quick as a flash... mark my words. I'm goin' to tell 'im...oh yes... as soon as he gets back tomorrow.' Carrie's eyes, burning like a trapped tigress's, were flashing angry defiance. There was a long pause as they stared silently at each other with their eyes locked combatively.

Eventually, old Mrs Trimble's tired, faded, blue eyes flickered and succumbed to Carrie's intense, penetrating stare. It was a significant moment for Carrie. It sent her confidence surging. She knew Mrs Trimble would not go so far as telling the Squire. Even if she did, he was sure to pay little attention, because everybody knew that he had a soft spot for her. In fact, everyone at the manor knew that the Squire regarded Carrie as the most likely successor to the old housekeeper, when the time came for her to retire but in spite of being in his favour, Carrie could not afford to lose her job – not yet.

With well-practised control, Carrie quickly dispensed with her defiant anger and lowered her eyes submissively. In an instant, she transformed herself into a helpless child, complete with soft expression and welling tears. 'I... I wasn't doing anything wrong, Mrs Trimble,' she said in a small voice, sobbing quietly. 'Honest! I like Master Edward, that's all. We get on well. I didn't mean to do any harm, Mrs Trimble.'

'Well, you 'ave... and the Squire is sure to tell you 'imself... in no uncertain terms. I doan' know who the 'ell you think you are,' said Mrs Trimble, her stance and tone still threatening, 'but there's no place for you 'ere. Your mother would turn in 'er grave, rest 'er soul, if she saw you makin' up to Master Edward the way you do. You'm a servant! You can never equal the likes of Master Edward... 'owever 'ard you try.'

'I know that,' said Carrie, lowering her shrewdly repentant gaze to the hands wringing in her lap. 'I just wanted to be his friend.'

'Well, you can't be, and that's that! It's not your place to be. Your job is to look after the Squire and Master Edward when you'm told to, like the rest of us, and mind your place, *THAT'S ALL*. You stay away from Master Edward, d'you 'ear?'

'Yes, Mrs Trimble. I will... I will.' Carrie's reassurance was eager. Sally Parsons continued making Edward's tea then pointedly put the teapot and milk jug down with a bang on the bare wooden table.

Gathering a napkin, china and cutlery from the high pine dresser at the back of the kitchen, Carrie laid a tray in respectful silence. With an occasional angry glance, Mrs Trimble busied herself with bustling in and out of the large, well-stocked pantry-room. 'Now go and take Master Edward 'is tea, and come straight out again. D'you 'ear? I've got work for you to do.' Mrs Trimble's fury had dissolved into plain, old-fashioned anger by now.

Carrie demurely wiped the tears from her cheeks and picked up the tray. 'Yes, Mrs Trimble... thank you, Mrs Trimble,' she said, almost curtseying before walking out into the corridor. As soon as the door had closed behind her, she turned, pulled a face and poked her tongue out at it before hurrying along the oak-panelled corridor.

Out of Mrs Trimble's sight, she paused at a wall mirror and placed the tray on the table under it. Tucking away the loose strands of hair that were hanging like fronds from her limp, damp linen bonnet, she leaned towards the mirror and examined her burning cheek. Slapping and rubbing the other one briskly with the palm of her hand to even up the colour of her face she reddened her lips by scraping them under her even white teeth. Satisfied with her makeshift repairs, she squared her shoulders and carried on her way.

At the door of the drawing room she knocked sharply and swept in, smiling seductively. The log fire crackling in the large stone fireplace gave the spacious airy room the smell and atmosphere of homely warmth. Edward was sitting on a velvet-covered *chaise longue*, warming himself by the fire.

Although Carrie had long since mastered the art of gliding through the manor as if she was mounted on castors, this was not how she moved when Edward was present. Entirely aware of her shapely body and in control of every part of it, her hips now rolled provocatively and her legs swished audibly against her long black skirt as she cruised across the large oriental rug. Placing the tray on a low table beside Edward, she bent over pertly and poured his tea, just how he liked it.

A smile teased his lips as his eyes traced the outline of her body. When she stood up to draw away, his hand closed over hers. He slowly pulled her down and pressed his lips to hers. 'Tonight,' he whispered in her ear. 'My room tonight...when Mrs "T" is asleep. Father won't be back until the morning.'

Carrie straightened up and placed a casual hand on his shoulder. 'Oh... I don't know, Teddy. That old bat's on the warpath now. She's just given me a roasting. She saw us in the courtyard, you know. She went mad out there in the kitchen. Threatened to tell your father! I just don't know... it's too risky.'

Edward put his arm around her slim waist and gazed up at her. 'Nonsense!' he said, softly. 'It's the chance we've been waiting for. God, I want you,' he said, softly. 'Please!'

Carrie disentangled herself from his arms and looked into his irresistible clear brown eyes – soft and appealing as a basset hound's. She ran her fingers through his dark wavy hair. 'We'll see,' she said, gently. 'We'll see.' With a disappointed look, Edward watched her every movement as she left the room. At the door she turned and beamed a broad, impish smile. 'All right, then,' she said, smiling provocatively. The door closed behind her before he could react. Hiding her smug smile as best she could, she went back to her duties and left Edward to stew in his desperate excitement.

Meanwhile, in the kitchen Carrie was keeping her thoughts to herself as she dealt willingly with the stream of orders Mrs Trimble flung at her. She smiled to herself and worked mechanically, with her mind on different things. Nothing that the old housekeeper did to her now mattered anymore. She would not have to put up with it for much longer. The end was in sight. It had been a long time coming, but things were going to be different from now on, *very* different.

The estate that had been the seat of the Farleigh family for generations was impressive. Rolling away from the neat front lawns of the manor's forecourt, it sprawled endlessly across thousands of acres of Dorset farmland, to the hilltop copses on the horizon. It was the most significant and noticeable estate in the county. At this precise moment, Carrie felt more in touch with it than she had ever been. The nine years she had been living there seemed like a lifetime, yet she could picture the day her mother had brought her to it, hand in-hand, for the very first time.

As a 14-year-old, she had been wide-eyed and bewildered by the size and splendour of it, and had cried herself to sleep when her mother left her there. She could never question what was happening then. All she knew was that it was "best for her", and that her mother had been overjoyed and proud to settle her there in the service of the Squire but, as the years drifted by, Carrie began to long for more. By the time she was 20, a feeling that she was lost in a cul-de-sac overwhelmed her. She felt trapped in a dead end and became desperate to find a way out. She wanted to tell her mother that the thought of being a lowly servant all her life was eating away at her spirit, but never had the courage, until it was too late. Just as she found strength to speak her mind and tell her mother of her fears, she lost her. Typhoid came to the village and took both her parents.

That was when she fell into the depths of despair. It seemed like some kind of punishment, to be left isolated and alone and irrevocably buried in a lifetime of service. It was Fate's revenge for her daring to want a better life. At the funeral, she stood white-faced and tearful by the grave feeling utterly diminished and robbed of her spirit. When she returned to the manor that day, stark images of the funeral kept returning to haunt her.

All she could think about was the uneventful and mundane existence her parents had lived out in the village, and the vastly different life she witnessed every day at the manor. Her parents' lives and the twenty-five years they had been together seemed to count for nothing. In all that time, they had seen the sea only twice, had never once strayed beyond the county's boundaries, or owned anything other than the clothes they stood up in. Life seemed so cruel, so unjust. Something snapped inside Carrie that day. She made up her mind that she would rather do anything than end up in the same little village cemetery with nothing to show for her life. There just had to be more to life than that, and she was going to find it.

She made herself a solemn promise. She did not know how, but she was determined to find a way of leaving the manor and finding a better life than her parents had had. However, she had to face facts; only one person in the world was going to break life's burdensome cycle for Carrie Palmer, and that was Carrie Palmer.

At the moment of realisation, a new force seemed to surge through her, firing her will to change things. Her wistful longing suddenly crystallised into a single burning ambition to move onwards and upwards, and she was transformed from victim to achiever overnight. It was as if a light had come on in Carrie's life. Once it had, the transformation was complete. She knew exactly what she wanted and was filled with hope for the future but there was a problem. Her new attitude brought her into immediate conflict with the Squire's starchy old housekeeper.

There was never a place for ambition and fanciful dreams in Mrs Trimble's world. Unlike Carrie, she had been both proud and grateful to remain entrenched in the employment of the Farleigh family all her life. So should Carrie be, she muttered often. Service was a way of life. It was a worthy profession, a fulfilling dedication, and no self-respecting girl could ask for more, she said, repeatedly. Nor should disrespectful girls, with heads filled with "modern rubbish" be allowed to dream of elevating themselves above their station. 'You'm what you are, and that's *IT!* No sense at all tryin' to change things,' she would say, brushing aside all hopes and aspirations with a wave of her podgy arm.

Carrie's continuing belief that life is what you make of it attracted nothing but mistrust and anger from the old housekeeper; and a battle of wills. 'Too ambitious for your own good you are, my girl. It'll be the end of you. Mark my words.' Carrie became sick of hearing it, and the more determined Mrs Trimble became to knock some sense into her, the more Carrie longed for what she could see every day: a grand house, fine furniture, horses, money, and status – in fact, everything the Farleighs had. 'Why shouldn't I?' she petulantly asked herself, 'I'm worthy of it.'

Edward was the Squire's only son. He had reached adulthood side by side with Carrie. Although they watched each other from opposite sides of a huge social gulf, there was a playful, bantering bond between them, which Mrs Trimble could neither tolerate nor understand. The housekeeper's disapproval, however, served only to strengthen their friendship.

When Carrie became a woman, she did so with a sensuous beauty for which most women of class would willingly give their eyeteeth. It unsettled Mrs Trimble and put her on edge. Carrie practised and practised in front of her mirror until the look was perfected. With this developed sensuous glance and a coy flash of her stunning eyes she could, if she wished, draw a man to her side from the other side of a crowded room.

Edward was never short of women. There were plenty. His father saw to that. Family lineage was on Thomas Farleigh's mind from the moment he lost his wife Madeline in a riding accident. Edward had no siblings, neither did he, and the future of the Farleigh family attached itself to Edward by the fine and fragile thread of expectation. Nothing would ever be certain until he married and fathered a child but try as he might, Edward could not find love with the young women his father constantly paired him. In spite of this, he remained resolute that he would never marry without true love.

Carrie's knowledge of the manor and its occupants was deep and intimate. She knew all the secrets and nuances of their lives. Although the manor house was large and grand, there was no place to hide from a determinedly prying servant. She knew every creak of every door and floorboard, and overheard conversations and observed things never meant for her. She knew very well that Edward had tried to please his father by falling in love with one of his "suitable" young ladies, and aware that he had failed miserably. She also knew that what he expected of a woman was not to be found in any daughter of his father's friends. She knew because she had secretly watched him trying. She had seen him fumbling through their impenetrable clothing in search of it, and seen him deflated by their self-conscious, inane, girlish giggling. She understood exactly what he was looking for. It was unashamed sexual enjoyment, and the complete surrender of an equally passionate partner. That would bring him to his knees, and Carrie knew the way.

The more she thought about it, the more excited she became. In her dreams, they were made for each other. It took a giant leap of faith, but she could picture herself as the wife of the future Squire. She knew how to behave. She had watched fine ladies and knew exactly what they did. Anyway, no one would dare to criticise her if she were the lady of the manor. She and Edward would live happily ever after and make enough babies to guarantee the Farleigh name forever. It could happen, if she wanted it – and how she wanted it!

It would only take Edward to fall in love with her, and all her dreams would come true. Was that so impossible?

It had to be handled carefully. There must be no obvious rush. It had to happen gradually; unobtrusively, naturally, as if it were something that Edward discovered for himself, and could not resist. It would begin with her dazzling smiles that he said he adored. And it did. Then came the occasional brush in passing. When he seemed to enjoy that, she found reasons constantly to reach up for something. Tucking her long blonde hair into her servant's cap would do: anything to show off her shapely body.

When she sensed that his interest had become something more than childish friendship, she responded immediately. She could tell from his glances that he really wanted her, but sensed that his upbringing held him back. She had to help him find the courage to burst through the social barriers and sweep her off her feet, with no thought of turning back. Her teasing got bolder; she allowed him to touch intimate places and feel the warmth of her bare flesh. When she finally allowed him to hold her breasts, his hands trembled with excitement. It took weeks of teasing and tantalising, but now he was ready. His resolve had finally cracked, and he was a wreck – she knew that – lying helpless and awake at night, thinking of nothing else but making love to her. Now it was time he should!

Outside that night – that very first night she had gone to him – it was cold and wintry. Fine, powdery snow fell heavily, shrouding the estate in a white mantle and gathering on the statues and balustrades in the forecourt. With its elegant façade picked out in fine brush strokes of snow, the graceful Regency manor house sat like a giant *choux* pastry dusted with icing sugar as the cold night closed in around it. Inside, the log fires were crackling in ornate stone fireplaces, warming the main rooms.

Sitting by the fire in the drawing room, Edward's impatient longing was getting the better of him. Willing the hours away and listening to gramophone records, his thoughts of Carrie made time stand still as he tried desperately to force his mind onto something else. His restless gaze wandered over the room and settled on the portrait of his mother, above the fireplace. He wondered what she would say if she knew about Carrie and what she would do if she knew what he was feeling right now. Quite often, he could feel his mother's presence in this particular room.

His father seemed incapable of letting go of her completely, and it showed more in the drawing room than in any other part of the house. Everything there was evidence of Madeline's fine taste. Elegant pieces of furniture graced the room, and pictures and ornaments complemented each other and were perfectly arranged. Nothing had been changed in the room since she died, ten years before. He remembered the awful shock of being called from the classroom as a 16-year-old boy, to be told that his mother had had an accident. That was it – she was gone, and he never saw her again. Mrs Trimble ran the household after that.

Thomas never really got over it. He simply plunged into a depression. When he recovered from that, he buried himself in the management of the estate and entertaining friends at the manor. Edward was quietly proud of him. Maturely charming and good-looking, he was now 52 but looked much younger. Being immensely wealthy, he had attracted flirtatious attention from several widows and wives over the years, but he had never discovered a lady matching up to his beloved Madeline.

Politics and current affairs bored Edward but of late he had been obliged to take an interest. There was a lot of talk about trouble brewing in Europe and the possibility of a military conflict. Taking a more active role at his father's social table now, he was often drawn into discussions about such matters. Among Thomas's friends were several eminent politicians and military men, all members of the London Masonic Lodge of which Thomas had become a key and active member since Madeline's death. For Edward, it was interesting but strange to be seated at dinner next to important people he had only read about: luminaries like Brigadier-General Seely MP, Lord Beresford, or the former First Sea Lord of the Royal Navy, retired Admiral "Jacky" Fisher.

Although this was entertaining, he also had to suffer overbearing encouragement to join the Navy or the Army, but his experience on the sidelines of these social occasions had already convinced him that Britain's military forces were led entirely by old dinosaurs in a constant state of bickering disagreement, with hardly a good word for one another. He shuddered at the thought of serving under such people, and was not afraid to let his father know it.

Later that evening, with the business of the day over, Sally Parsons went home to her little cottage in Puddletown, the local village, while Mrs Trimble finished cruising through the manor carrying out her evening rituals. Filling her stoneware hot-water bottle, she went to bed, leaving Carrie alone in the kitchen with the silverware to clean. The house was quiet at last. Edward put away his gramophone records and went to his bedroom.

When her chores were finished, Carrie packed the silver away and scrubbed her hands at the sink then filled her hot-water bottle and a large wash jug with hot water. Lighting a new candle, she finally put out the kitchen lights and carried the jug up to her bedroom. In her tiny room next to Mrs Trimble's, she stripped off and stood in a washbowl filled with hot water and washed herself from head to toe with some Castile soap Edward had given her on her birthday. Fresh and glowing in a clean nightdress, she climbed into her bed. The meagre warmth of her hot-water bottle slowly seeped up through her body, and she began to wonder when she could count on Mrs Trimble being sound asleep. There was no danger that she would fall asleep herself; her heart was pounding so loudly that she was sure Mrs Trimble would hear it.

Thirty long minutes later, the steady rhythm of the old housekeeper's snoring was rasping through the walls. With her pulse beating in her ears, Carrie slid out of bed, put on her dressing gown and slippers, and lit the candle again. Knowing exactly which creaking floorboards to avoid, she carefully picked her way along the chilly corridor, down the servants' stairs, into the hall. She paused in the darkness with blood pulsing ferociously through her veins. A feeling of apprehension and vulnerability swept over her. Her impulse was to turn back for the safety of her bed but something stronger urged her on. She hurried up the main staircase with doubt and fear running their icy fingers down her spine.

At Edward's door she hesitated for a moment, unsure if she should knock or call out, or if he had perhaps fallen asleep. Then the door opened and suddenly he was there. She threw herself into his arms, and he drew her into his warm room, locking the door behind them. Now she was safe. In the glowing, flickering light of the bedroom fire, his open mouth closed over hers. He hastily undid her gowns. Startled by his eagerness, she grasped his hands – then released them and let the gowns fall to the floor. He stood back, feasting his eyes on every feature of her face and every curve and mound of her sensuous body. He gently ran his fingers through her hair. He had not seen it down before, at its full length. She felt vulnerable and self-conscious. 'My God, Carrie,' he breathed, 'you're beautiful. You don't know how much I've longed for this.'

He kissed her soft, warm mouth passionately. His hands and lips felt like fire on her body and she could feel his hardness pressing against her. He sank to his knees, his hot mouth wandering eagerly over her breasts and her smooth white stomach. She threw her head back, writhing and grasping at the hair at the back of his head.

'Teddy... Teddy,' she whispered, 'come to the bed ... please.' She pulled him towards the large bed, tugging the cord of his pyjamas. They climbed onto the soft mattress, naked at last. Pulling his body onto hers, she let the warmth of her nakedness soak into his skin. Suddenly, he launched his body at her, clumsily and far too eagerly, but she gently restrained him and spoke softly in his ear. 'Gently, Teddy..., gently. Don't rush, my love.' She put her arms around him, moulding her body to his and pressing her breasts against his chest. Her soft lips traced a delicately gentle line down his neck and over his shoulder.

As the heat of her body flowed into his, she sensed that he was wrestling with an uncontrollable urge to plunge into her with one frantic, animal thrust. But she held him and made him wait. 'Oh God,

Carrie.' His voice was dry and cracked, and his eyes rolled as he drifted through a haze of anguished, expectant ecstasy.

Slowly and deliberately, she began to move her body under his, gyrating against his solid erection until she was sure that his self-control was about to break under the strain of his excitement. As his body tensed, she opened her thighs and drew him to where he ached to be. He raised himself and struggled ineptly to penetrate her, and she winced with the pain of his clumsy lunges. She had to calm his eagerness and reach down to help him. Then, with a long moan, he was suddenly inside her body. The unaccustomed presence within her made her wince.

With his self-control dissolving, he began to jerk rapidly but she resisted, and slowed his impatient movements into long, deliberate rhythmic thrusts. She could see from his expression that he was already lost in a mist of ecstasy. He was moaning quietly and gasping as he gave in to overpowering urges. His thrusts became faster, deeper, more animal. Then, with a hoarse groan escaping from his dry throat, he arched his body and his hot passion surged deep inside her.

Shuddering involuntarily for a few moments, his body softened and sank gently onto hers. His breathing was heavy and his skin was on fire. When she kissed him, his lips were cold, drained of blood. She wound her arms around his hot back and urged him to stay inside her, but he could not. After a few minutes, he slid away. Still aroused and unsatisfied, she felt happy and contented to be where she was.

'I love you, Carrie.' His voice was a dry whisper, buried in his pillow. 'I'll never let you go.'

'Sshh, Teddy, you don't know what you're saying. Best not talk like that. What would your father say... me being what I am?'

He raised his head to look into her eyes. 'I don't bloody care what my father thinks. You're mine now, and we'll be married … I promise.' He moved to her side, resting his weary head on her warm bare shoulder. She ran her fingers through his rich brown hair and watched the glow of firelight flickering on the ornate ceiling, a contented smile on her throbbing lips. Edward lost all sense of time and slid into the deep sleep of utterly spent passion. Making love to Carrie was more deeply satisfying than he had ever thought possible, and it left him convinced that he was experiencing the true love that he had been seeking. Carrie knew that and her mission was nearing completion. They lay together, cocooned in the warm softness of his bed, alone with their thoughts.

As the night merged into the morning hours, the contented smile was still lingering on Carrie's lips when exhaustion threatened to overwhelm her. Reluctantly, she chose to leave the warmth of Edward's bed before she had to give into it. As she moved, he stirred briefly, murmuring words of love. She smiled and kissed him, and went back along the chilly corridors to her own cold bed.

That night Edward dreamt about her and nothing else. When he woke in the morning, he longed to see her fabulous face again, and ached for the closeness of her body. He was sure that he was in love, and convinced that he had found the perfect wife. His experience that night placed Carrie above every woman he had ever known. She was everything he had ever dreamed a woman could be – loving, yielding and welcoming, uninhibited, and unashamed of her own passion. There was no doubt in his mind that he was going to spend the rest of his life with her and, from that moment, he was hopelessly in love and desperate to be with her all the time.

He was sublimely happy, with only one care in the world. It was the matter of telling his father that he had fallen in love with a servant, his own servant, and that he was going to marry her. He put off doing it, time and time again. Now was not the time, he said, with Mrs Trimble making threats.

Mrs Trimble chose not to inform the Squire of her concerns, after all. Carrie was especially discreet: kept out of her way, and got on with her work. It seemed to Mrs Trimble that she had at last heeded the warnings she had been given, and was finally turning over a new leaf.

During the coming months, Edward's love became intense and obsessive, and thoughts of Carrie dominated his mind day and night. Although opportunities for making love did not come easily, he managed to find times when they could be alone together. They made frantic, passionate love many times, with an abandon that exceeded his wildest dreams. Their love was exciting, uninhibited and just as he always imagined it would be with the right woman. They stole moments of intimacy in little-used rooms of the manor, in a barn, in a bathroom, and in Thomas's garaged car. With playful recklessness, they once did it on the kitchen table in the dead of night.

Carrie controlled the relationship, and Edward was besotted enough to follow wherever she led. She was the most important part of his life and he could not do without her. He promised her everything, when the time became appropriate. She would give up being a servant then, he promised, and would take her rightful place beside him.

Meanwhile, Mrs Trimble's sixth sense continued to nag, but she saw nothing to justify outright suspicion. She maintained a cool distance between herself and Carrie, and said very little other than to give orders, sure that if there really were things to know, she would find them, sooner or later. Edward kept up a show of socialising in his circle, but quietly and coolly kept all women at bay.

Thomas noticed this, and started to worry secretly about the sexuality of his son. For such a man as the Squire, with high hopes invested in Edward, the prospect of having an only son who was not "normal" was too appalling to contemplate. He could never bring himself to discuss his concerns with anyone, until one day over a sherry he falteringly put them to the family doctor. Doctor Harvey laughed and reassured him. 'Edward? Good God, man. He's perfectly normal! As fine a specimen of manhood as one could wish to carry the Farleigh family name.'

The Squire was reassured, but not entirely convinced.

Then one day in March 1914, Carrie fell ill and was unable to leave her room until after breakfast. Two days later it happened again; then it was every day for the next two weeks. Mrs Trimble, with a knowing expression that she could barely hide, feigned concerns for Carrie's welfare and persuaded the Squire to call in Doctor Harvey. When the doctor announced his diagnosis, all Carrie's dreams came crashing down.

She was pregnant!

Thomas was stunned when the doctor told him. His face turned grey and he slumped into a chair, staring vacantly into space.

Mrs Trimble fluttered about in a quandary. She was not sure how to react. She was clearly furious, but did not know which way to turn.

Angry that the "deceitful and brazen liddle bitch" had succeeded in putting one over her, she was consumed by a fear that this was going to bring the Farleighs all the trouble she had seen coming. Sick with worry that a rift could now tear Thomas and Edward apart on one hand, on the other she was bubbling with glee that Carrie's comeuppance was just around the corner.

Fortunately for Edward, he was away for the day.

Thomas summoned Mrs Trimble and Sally Parsons to his study in turn to find out who Carrie had been seeing. Hesitating over her conflicting loyalties and claiming that she was loathe to point the finger, Mrs Trimble immediately cited Edward and voiced strong suspicions that "poor young Master Edward" had fallen victim to the "outrageous flirtin' of that graspin' trollop Carrie". Sally confirmed every word. After ten minutes of the Squire's considerate but persistent questioning, Carrie broke down and confessed to her affair with Edward. Thomas was devastated, and reacted swiftly and decisively. When Carrie left the Squire, she ran into the hall, white-faced and in tears, and went straight to her room to pack up her belongings, ready to leave Farleigh Manor in the morning.

Mrs Trimble was delighted, but was puzzled by Thomas's reaction. What she had hoped for was that he would fly into a rage and evict Carrie on the spot, that night. Instead, he seemed more preoccupied and concerned than angry. He sat alone, waiting for Edward to return from his daylong excursion to Dorchester market.

When Edward finally arrived, Thomas bustled him into the drawing room and the two men were locked in heated conversation for the best part of the evening. Their raised voices could be heard clearly through the sturdy doors, especially by Mrs Trimble, who found a lot to busy herself with outside in the hall that evening. Carrie could hear it from the gallery outside her room.

Edward admitted that he was Carrie's lover, but furiously defended her, and his behaviour. The two men paced the floor of the drawing room, manoeuvring around the furniture and confronting one another like matador and bull. 'Love? Marriage?' Thomas bellowed. 'Don't be such a bloody fool! What do you know of love? As for marriage, it is out of the question, d'you hear! I won't hear of it. The girl is a servant, for God's sake.'

'But you don't understand,' Edward shouted. 'That doesn't matter to me. I am going to marry her... and things will have to change around here. I just don't care what people think!'

'Don't be ridiculous, you young idiot!' Thomas was fuming. His steel-grey eyes blazed and his face was contorted with fury. Edward was angry at being treated like a youth. 'Don't imagine, for one moment, that I will stand by and allow you to do that! It would ruin your entire life. Such a marriage is impossible. We'd be humiliated and unwelcome in our own circles. I won't have it.' It was easy to imagine him flinging his arms wide, gesturing utter despair then spinning on Edward. 'Consider this, Edward. I will not allow you to remain here, if you stay with that girl. I'll disown you if you go against me... believe me. You will be cut off immediately, without hesitation. 'What then? No money, no income, and nowhere to live. How would you survive then... eh?'

Edward's silence told its own story, but he was still pleading his case. Thomas raged on. 'I could understand you wanting to bed the girl. God knows she's attractive enough... and that does happen in some houses, but when it does, it's just for lust – not love. Do you understand the difference?'

'Of course I do. Don't be ridiculous.'

'I sometimes wonder. Look at you now. A poor fool besotted with a maid! You could have had her without all that emotional rubbish. But to think of marrying the girl... and having babies? That is entirely out of the question. When you eventually marry, my boy, it will be to a lady... someone of equal standing. The blood of the Farleigh family is not going to be carried forward by some servant girl – not in my lifetime.'

The emotional charge behind Edward's argument began to weaken as one by one his objections were crushed by his father's fury. 'It is done,' said Thomas, with a tone and gesture of absolute finality. 'Over. She leaves first thing in the morning. It is the only way out of this mess. I have already given her thirty pounds, and I have assured her of an allowance of forty shillings a week for the next five years, provided she leaves this area immediately and has the child well away from this family. That is as much as a married artisan is paid... and a more than generous amount to raise a child on.'

'But where is she to go?' Edward's concern was real and earnest.

'Frankly, I don't care. I understand she has a cousin or an aunt in the Portsmouth area, and will probably go there. 'You can banish any thought of following her, Edward. I have extracted a firm undertaking from her... under threat of her allowance being stopped, that she will never reveal that she became pregnant under this roof. She is never to voice an opinion as to the father of the child... or to see you again.'

'Opinion?' Edward looked confused. 'The poor girl doesn't have to speculate about that, does she? I am the father of her child, and I am not afraid to admit it. This was entirely my doing.' His resolve staged a minor comeback. 'And I intend to stand by her.'

'Speculation is exactly what it would be,' retorted Thomas. 'I am sure of it...and I forbid you to lay claim to the child. You will never say anything about this unfortunate episode, d'you hear?'

Edward's honour seemed to be getting stretched to the limit. 'How many times do I have to tell you, Father, the child is mine. There can be no doubt. I can't believe this. All of my life, the one thing I have always been sure of was your honesty, integrity, and fairness ...until now. What happened, happened because I wanted it to happen. I made promises to Carrie. She is the innocent in all this. How can you, of all people, put the blame onto her... then banish her, without pity or conscience?'

Thomas drew a deep breath and spoke slowly and quietly. 'Because, Edward... I know, for a fact, that...' his voice faltered momentarily, 'that the girl has, er... Edward, I'm sorry. I did not want you to know this, but there has been someone else. Someone else has been with the girl, and the child may not be yours. By that I mean you could never be certain that it is. I'm sorry. That is why she must go. She could never be trusted.'

With anguish plainly in his voice Edward came back at his father. 'I don't believe you! How could you know this, before me? This is a ploy, isn't it? If it is true, who the hell is the man?' he demanded, 'WHO?' Thomas became defensive.

'I am afraid I can't tell you that. Just accept that it is the truth.' He strode for the door. Enraged, Edward followed him.

'You can't tell me, because it isn't true... is it?'

'It is.' Thomas paused as he reached for the handle of the door, anxious to leave the room.

'Then tell me who it is, for God's sake. Otherwise, how can I believe you?' Thomas hesitated at the closed double doors with his back to Edward, handles in his hands. He turned his face to Edward's pained gaze.

'Edward, it is true. I wanted to protect you from this.' Thomas searched for words and looked into his son's eyes. 'Edward, the child could equally as well be mine!' With that, he opened the doors and swept into the hall. The words struck Edward like a thunderbolt. Completely crushed and speechless, he stared in stunned disbelief as the doors swung quietly together in his father's wake.

'This cannot be,' he said quietly to the closing doors. When his senses returned abruptly, he rushed after Thomas and found him in his study, staring vacantly out of the window. He demanded an explanation and stood open-mouthed as Thomas revealed the details of Carrie's promiscuity. He admitted, painfully and falteringly, that knowing nothing of Edward's involvement, he had encouraged Carrie into his own bed in a single moment of frustration and loneliness. She had hesitated, he said, but had not refused.

Edward saw red. He was extremely angry with his father for using his position to pressure Carrie into his arms, but furious with her for betraying his love. With all of his dreams tumbling around him, his ire turned on Carrie. Consumed by a maelstrom of emotional confusion, the pain of his anger, self-pity, embarrassment and disillusion tore through him all at once. He was left in pieces, sullen and vengeful. With his emotions in shreds, he went to his room clutching a bottle of his father's Chivas Regal, and locked himself in.

'Carrie… CARRIE!'

Marje's anxious voice carried up the stairwell and onto the galleried landing outside Carrie's old room. When Carrie abruptly came to and snapped out of the deep well of memories she had been wallowing in, she found herself slumped on the landing floor with her face wet with tears and pressed, childlike, against the balustrade. She was softly sobbing. 'CARRIE! Are you alright?' Marje's voice had real concern in it.

'Yes, I'm alright,' Carrie croaked. 'Just coming… sorry.' She dabbed at her wet face and composed herself as best she could before descending the wide staircase into the hall, wondering all the time how she got upstairs without knowing it. She smiled bravely. 'Sorry, Marje. Got carried away up there where I used to live.' Marje didn't miss the look on Carrie's face but understood that not questioning it was probably the best thing to do.

'I was getting very concerned about you. I know it's a big place but you were gone ages.'

'It didn't seem long to me, I must admit. Come on, let's go home.' As their car crunched along the driveway towards the main gates, Carrie couldn't help reflecting on the previous time that she had done precisely the same thing. Only on that occasion it was the Farleigh limousine she was in and Stan was at the wheel.

What a mess her life was then! All her hopes, her future, everything had been in ruins. The image was fixed in her memory, vivid and clear like a dreadful dream. The scents and emotions of it were still there at the manor; and would always be, it seemed. On that day the atmosphere in the manor had been icily tense when the Squire's old chauffeur carried her bags out to the motorcar. He seemed completely oblivious to the bizarre circumstances of her sudden departure. Then there was Mrs Trimble's self-righteous smirk as she followed her out, making sure that she left the premises without hesitating. She would never forget that.

She remembered her one last look at the graceful manor house as the motor rumbled across the cobblestones and crunched slowly along the gravel drive in the morning mist, and the small tear she had to wipe away. Seeing the Squire staring dispassionately from the drawing room window had made her bottom lip tremble, and she nearly lost control of it altogether when the stable boy gave a final wave and blew her a cheeky kiss. Then Edward had thundered across the lawn on Prince, straight past the car, tight-lipped and staring stoically ahead.

He knew his father was watching and he simply spurred his horse and galloped away without a backward glance, fading into the swirling morning mist, with clods of earth flying up from the horse's hooves in a shower behind him. The sight left an impression of absolute fury and finality that she would never forget.

Just an hour later at Dorchester Station, she was saying goodbye to Stan and buying a ticket; something she had never done before in her life. Then there was the pungent, unfamiliar smell of coal smoke and the hissing and clanking of railway engines. It had jarred her senses, contrasting starkly as it did with the clean fresh air and the tranquillity of the manor. That was when it hit her: a feeling of bewilderment and desperate loneliness in an unfamiliar world. Her heart sank to the pit of her stomach then, and it was still sitting there like a lump of cold lead.

Somewhere deep inside, she was saying goodbye to the countryside she had grown up in and under which her parents were resting, and she wondered with a heavy heart where life would lead her. What if Aunt Ethel refused to put her up? What then?

'Off for a holiday?' His voice had jarred her out of her thoughts and caught her off guard. It was the helpful foreign-looking stranger, smiling pleasantly and speaking with an accent far removed from the continental country her imagination had placed him in.

'Yes... visiting my aunt in Gosport. Do you know it?'

He had looked pleased. 'I live there... and I have a business there,' he added, rather proudly. She noticed his gaze moving to her clasped hands, searching for a ring. He extended his hand. 'My name is Guy, by the way... Bill Guy.'

Carrie smiled to herself at the memory of that moment.

For most of the journey home, Marje chattered on in the background about what she had seen, while Carrie sat quietly with her thoughts as she held Kate who was worn out and sleeping soundly. 'Well, what have you decided to do with that massive empire of yours, darling?' The question startled Carrie and penetrated her dreamy thoughts. 'If it were mine, I'd be there like a shot. I was made for that kind of life.' Carrie smiled.

'You'd soon get fed up with it on your own, Marje – rattling around like a pea on a drum. It would be very lonely, believe me.'

'Mmm...I suppose so. But wouldn't it be lovely to play Lady Muck – just for a week?' Marje carefully studied her friend's face. 'What's the matter, darling – unpleasant memories?'

'No...no, quite the opposite really. It's just...' she struggled to find the right words.

'Empty?'

'Yes, empty. Empty and forlorn. I really thought it would be different. I was afraid that when I saw it again, it would make my decision even more difficult – but it didn't. I was scared that Farleigh Manor would suck me back inside it again – albeit on the other side of it, "above stairs" this time.'

'And...?'

'Instead, it looked like some great dinosaur: magnificent and huge belonging to an age long ago: something that can't be relived or resurrected.'

'I think I know what you mean. They do say, you know, that it's people that make places.'

'That's the very point, Marje. The people aren't there anymore – good or bad, it already feels as if it belongs to someone else. I never thought I'd miss Mrs T, but I can see now that she was a part of my life there, and it wasn't *all* bad. I couldn't possibly live there...or bring children up in it. It's...it's...'

'Disappointing?'

Carrie looked at Kate, tenderly. 'Yes. Although it's ours now, we don't belong there after all. I'd know what to do there, and how to do it, but I don't want to. I'm glad I came. It cleared my mind. We'll come and see it again, one day. But we'll never live there.'

They lapsed into silent thought for a while, staring out of the windows. Marje had a question on her mind. 'Darling, what if George were to be in your life right now?' Carrie rounded on her with a forlorn expression.

'Oh Marje, why did all this have to happen the wrong way round?'

'You still miss him then?'

'Of course I do,' she sighed heavily, 'now more than ever. I need someone strong like George to help me with all this but what's the use? He's gone. What a mess I've made.'

'But what if he hadn't?'

'George is somewhere on the North Sea, Marje. He'll probably be there until the war ends. By then, he won't even remember who I am!' Marje had a knowing twinkle in her eye. Carrie turned in time to catch it.

'He came back to Portsmouth, Carrie. I've seen him – and I think he's still there. And I think I know how he feels, because I caught him staring up at Bill's window one night, hoping to catch sight of you no doubt.'

Carrie looked excited. 'Really?'

'Yes!'

'Oh, bless him!'

'If you really wanted to see him… if that would really make you happy, I'm sure a casual meeting at the weekend could be arranged.'

Chapter Twenty-two

GOSPORT
Saturday, January 8, 1916

It was *9:30 am* when they met outside Portsmouth barracks. Carrie was quite shocked when she saw George again. He looked pale and defensive, and he had a dreadful cold – as did most of *Argyll's* survivors. After his bright blue eyes had finished examining her features carefully and lovingly, they flicked away as if they might be punished for lingering too long. She could see pain in them still, and his manner reflected his anger and cynicism. He seemed uneasy with her and anxious to move on. He crouched down in front of the pushchair and extended a hand to Kate's face, smiling softly.

'Carrie, this isn't a good idea,' he said, keeping his attention on Kate. 'I don't know what you expect. I've nothing more to give... nothing you would want, that is.' The remark stung her, but she understood why he made it. Unbridled thoughts were galloping through her mind like wild horses as she looked down at him and tried to see beyond the barrier of resentment he had put up. Was there any love left inside all that self-pity?

She suddenly felt unsure of herself and her intentions. She could feel tears coming, and struggled to keep them inside. The situation had the poignancy of a very last chance, and she knew she had to convince him now or accept that he would walk away for good. 'George, I love you.' It seemed the simplest, most direct way to tell him what she felt. He glared up at her, not caring to hide his resentment.

'Where have I heard that before!'

'No...really.' She remembered using precisely the same words before. Embarrassed, she searched for others that would sound convincing. 'I mean it, George. Do you love me?' He stood up. His stare probed the depths of her mind like a searchlight.

'I did, Carrie… you'll never know how much. All I wanted was the chance to tell you, to show you, but I was clearly not worthy enough.' His eyes focused somewhere down the road.

A strange smile tugged his lips. 'Then, when you said you loved me too, the whole world lit up. Nothing else mattered… nothing, but I was really stupid, wasn't I? I really believed in you and I trusted you with my deepest feelings. I even betrayed my best friend. With you, I let my armour down and left myself with nowhere to hide.'

He looked directly into her eyes, his gaze smouldered angrily. 'I would have done anything for you, Carrie… gone anywhere, given up anything – just to know that I would always be with you.'

He paused and shook his head slowly. 'But what was that worth to you? Nothing…because all you wanted was the one thing I couldn't give you – money! So, you just *cancelled* your love – switched it off. That's all I was worth.'

Carrie bit hard on her lip. Inside, she was screaming that it was not true – she had only done that because she was confused, making stupid decisions. Now things were so different!

If only he knew.

If only she could tell him that she had enough for both of them now. But she could not.

At all costs, her new wealth and the manor had to be kept out of it. They looked at one another, both still very much in love, and wondering if there was a way back, or if they had reached the end already.

She quickly brushed a tear from her cheek. The sadness in her eyes melted his anger and he began to regret the wounds he was inflicting. 'I love you, George, and I want you,' she said, quietly. 'Do you still love me?'

He gazed into her eyes for what seemed an eternity, his mind busily conversing with his heart. She looked beautiful, and he still felt helpless and vulnerable in her presence. Losing her had been the worst thing that had ever happened to him, and he knew then that he would never really get over her. 'Yes, I do. I always will – whatever you do, wherever you go – wherever I am. I can't help that – even when you taunt me.'

'George, I'm not taunting you. Please believe me. Ever since that day in the park, I've missed you like mad. I made such a mistake, and I'm sorry…so sorry. Please forgive me. Everything is different now!'

'Nothing's really changed, Carrie. How can it be different?'

'It is different – believe me. I've changed. I have no doubts now.'

He searched her eyes for truth, wanting to believe her.

The extended pause while he looked at her drove her to do something that she would normally have found unthinkable. 'George, will you marry me?' The words tumbled out with no further thought.

He looked at her in amazement – not certain that he had heard correctly. 'What?'

'I want to marry you. Will you have me? Will…you…marry …me?' Wide-eyed, she held her breath. Her awesome eyes, sparkling like pale emeralds, took his breath away and sent his pulse racing.

The tension was unbearable, but he did not answer. His mind was racing behind his bland expression. This was not what he had expected. It had taken him off balance. A frown suddenly flashed across his face.

'Carrie! For God's sake! You are proposing to me. Why are you doing this? I don't know, I don't know. I need time.' Her face fell and the excitement visibly drained out of her.

'Are you saying no?'

'No. No, I'm not. I need time to work it out that's all. I've only just got used to being without you, and my feelings have been up and down. Now you've knocked me sideways with a proposal. I just need to catch my breath.'

She was crestfallen and looked down at Kate. 'I really thought you wanted me,' she said in a small voice. 'I had this stupid picture in my mind that everything would be fine – happy ever after – as soon as I told you what I am feeling.'

He was quick not to shut the door but his thoughts were spinning. 'Carrie, please let me work out what it is I'm feeling right now. I need to sort out the muddle in my head.' Inside, George was excited and thrilled more than he could say. To be married to her was all he had ever dreamed of but two things were holding him in check – one being a lack of money. What he would give, not to have that problem!

To marry Carrie would be the happiest ending he could imagine for the agony of losing her, but to rush into it now would be a mistake. 'Carrie, please can we just spend today together? I'll be back at sea soon and I want something pleasant to remember.'

As Carrie looked into his eyes, her expression softened and lost its anxious look. She understood that he needed to collect his thoughts. She knew she had sprung this on him, and had she not broken his heart the last time they had met? She owed him some time to find himself again. She smiled.

'Yes, of course, George. Let's all have a great day together.' His spirits began to lift immediately, and he felt happier than at any time since they last held hands.

At this very time, 1,500 miles away, there was an echo of George's emotions in many men's hearts. The Gallipoli Campaign was over. As George and Carrie were strolling hand in hand down the road towards Southsea, the last British soldiers to leave Turkish soil were speeding away from the beaches on the first part of their journey home.

THE SOUTHERN ZONE OF GALLIPOLI
January 8, 1916

By a coincidence that was as unfortunate for the Allies as it was prescient for the enemy, the Turks, as a precursor to their renewed assault on the British and French positions had launched a general bombardment of the area on Friday, January 7. Under the weight of the return fire from British warships, however, and with the prospect of sacrificing themselves to an enemy they realised finally had retreated from the northern zone, the Turkish troops on the ground failed to respond wholeheartedly to an order to attack with fixed bayonets.

As if they had no plans to leave, British and French troops launched a fierce counter-attack and pushed them back again – then slipped away in the night.

The plan created by Admiral de Robeck and General Munro had worked.

On every day of the withdrawal, the Turks had seen British reinforcements arriving in droves from the warships and transports at sea. What they had not realised was that these were just some of the many more troops that had been embarked during every night, which the Turks could not see in the darkness. By taking as many as possible off the beaches in the darkness of night – and landing a fraction of them back each day – the British convinced the Turks that they were pouring ashore.

With the exception of the rearguard, by the morning of January 8, every fighting man of the Expeditionary Force, complete with all animals and most of the equipment, had left Turkish soil.

Explosive charges were laid around the few pieces of equipment that could not be taken out and fuel was poured over the remaining stores on the beach. A great final bonfire was then lit as the last men left. The battered hulk of *River Clyde* was abandoned on "V" beach for the departing warships to shell to pieces.

It was the final battle of the campaign. In it, the Allies lost 6 officers and 158 men killed or wounded: a miraculously small number relative to the thousands of casualties anticipated and the enormity of the task of removing two whole armies from an enemy's beaches.

Four factors contributed to the successful evacuation and the relatively minor losses – the skill and courage of the British and French Navies, the courage and spirit of the troops, a decisiveness of planning that, ironically, was apparent only in the closing stage of the campaign and the fourth contribution was made by Fate.

At around midnight on January 8, the British battleship *Prince George* was heading out of the Straits with 2000 evacuated troops on board when an enemy submarine attacked her. One torpedo fired struck her hull solidly, but failed to detonate. She proceeded safely on her way. Lieutenant Oc Asquith, the Prime Minister's much-loved son, was among the men evacuated.

Although George would never know, Lieutenant Cartwright did not come home. He had occasion to go back to the front once more and, with several of his men, wandered into the darkness between the lines and was never seen again.

It was finally over.

Nothing at all had been gained – but it was over at last and the survivors were coming home.

GOSPORT
January 8, 1916

As George and Carrie strolled along the Southsea promenade, they talked and laughed as if they had never been apart. They hardly noticed the biting winter wind but, for Kate's sake, they decided to make their way over to Gosport. George splashed out on lunch, and as the afternoon slipped through their fingers, they found their way to the local park, close to home. George had a confusion of thoughts cascading through his mind... did she really mean it this time? Could he stand being rejected, if it were to happen again? Did it really not matter to her that he had no serious money? Could he really live without her? More importantly, would she do it all over again?

It seemed like an eternity, but when the answers to his questions finally tumbled out of his confusion, they seemed so obvious that he wondered why he needed to think about them at all. 'Carrie, I don't know how I can live without you... but I must. I can't marry you now.' Carrie's face fell and the brightness deserted her eyes.

'Oh George...' It was all she could manage before something caught in her throat. 'Why not? Please tell me.' Tears were welling up in her eyes.

'I'm so sorry,' he began, knowing that he owed her an explanation but not knowing where to begin. 'It's just that we are very different people... you've shown me that a few times. It isn't that I am bitter any more about being ditched but we both know, for sure, that if we stayed together it would happen again at some time in the future. There would be another time when you would want to move on to where there was more "security"' – he spat the word through his teeth with mock emphasis – 'for someone with a better paid job than mine, perhaps – someone who could give you more than I ever could. It's a matter of trust, Carrie, and I couldn't go to sea wondering if my wife would be there when I got home.'

She tried to protest but he kept going. 'And maybe you deserve someone better now that Kate is around. Let's face the truth... you set your heart on creating the perfect future for yourself and Kate and I know you well enough to realise that you are going to achieve that one way or another. You're a woman on a mission and, as much as I love you and admire your determination, I know you would not be happy living on a common sailor's pay. I'm just a simple bloke doing the best I can, and I don't even know if I will be alive at the end of this war.'

Kate looked up at her mother, apprehensive at seeing her cry. George held Carrie in his arms as she began to sob, and he struggled to swallow the indigestible lump that had suddenly taken root at the back of his throat. Carrie was suddenly prepared to risk everything by telling him about her newfound wealth but realised that it would just make matters worse. She kept it to herself and quietly cursed Fate's cruel ways.

George waited for her tears to stop then kissed her on the forehead.

Carrie took comfort from seeing his eyes glistening as she and George said their final, awkward goodbyes, and as she watched him walk away she wondered if she would ever see him again. It was over, and she just had to cope with it in her own way.

George didn't look back.

Epilogue

It was also over for some people in high places. The first eighteen months of the war had exacted a heavy price from them.

Although Asquith was still Prime Minister, Venetia Stanley had broken his heart for all time. His life was never to be the same again. He was still in politics, but his political influence was declining and destined never to recover.

Edwin Montagu, who lost his cabinet place when the coalition was formed, returned in January 1916 as Financial Secretary to the Treasury. Sadly, his marriage to Venetia was not the success it promised to be.

Winston Churchill became isolated and disconsolate from the moment the new Coalition Government Cabinet came to office without him on May 25, 1915. His spirit suffered badly from the lack of authority and inactivity associated with his new position as Chancellor of the Duchy of Lancaster and the unfair blame heaped upon him for the failure of the disastrous Dardanelles Campaign where many men died – 37,930 allied officers and men killed and 75,191 wounded. The Turks suffered comparable losses, and the total killed in the battle for the Peninsula rose to over 60,000.

By November 1915, Churchill could stand it no longer. With all hope gone of reversing the situation and restoring his status as a politician, he resigned his position and rejoined his regiment on the Western Front. By January 1916, he was pursuing his war on the front line, in command of the 6th battalion of the Royal Scots Fusiliers.

Lloyd George, having resigned as Chancellor of the Exchequer in order to assume control of the new Ministry of Munitions, was responsible for great changes in the armaments industry during the latter part of 1915. By January 1916, shell shortages were a thing of the past, and the British Army went into the New Year confident of its supplies.

Following his final resignation from the Navy in May 1915,

Jacky Fisher went to ground in Scotland's Lennoxlove Castle, the family seat of the 13th Duke of Hamilton, to spend his time with his close friends, the Duke and Duchess. By January 1916, Lady Fisher was unhappy and concerned about the amount of attention he was paying to the Hamiltons: the Duchess in particular. Her instincts served her well. In spite of his advanced years, his extended stay in Scotland marked the blossoming of a wild love affair with the Duchess. He never deserted his wife, but his love for the Duchess lasted for the rest of his days and led some people to suspect that he – not the Duke – had fathered her son, the 14th Duke of Hamilton.

He continued to make a nuisance of himself in the corridors of power with his eternal quest for control of the Royal Navy, but it was to no avail. Finally defeated on this front, he poured his talents into the workings of the new Inventions Board, over which he was presiding, focusing its attention on improvements to the Navy's undersea capabilities: principally, the development and detection of mines and the advance of submarine technology.

Of many, the Board's most significant achievement was ASDIC: the sonar device whose pinging voice eventually became the scourge of all submariners. Its name came from the Anti-Submarine Detection Investigation Committee that Jacky Fisher fostered and hounded into action.

In a force nine gale off the Orkneys coast of Scotland in the early evening of June 16, 1916, the battlecruiser HMS Hampshire carrying Lord Kitchener to Russia was sunk by a mine laid by a German submarine. Many bodies and a few survivors were washed up on the beaches the following day but Lord Kitchener was not among them. Armed guards were posted on the shores and cliffs to keep the public away from the beaches. This incident was a bitter blow to the British war effort.

William Daysh M.B.E

Following a long career in the Fleet Air Arm, William retired from the Royal Navy in 1971. Although primarily an Aircraft Engineer Officer, he also flew a lot and was a qualified Ship's Diving Officer.

After the navy he worked in London as a Financial Services Branch Manager. Combined, his naval travels and experiences on and under the sea and in the air, plus such hobbies as 'am-dram', skiing, squash, grass hockey and a Guildford University creative writing course, provide a good basis for his creative writing which began in 1969 with short stories.

Acknowledgements

I am grateful to my partner Linda, whose encouragement and hours of patient proofreading helped me finish this book... and to John Treneman and the Elmbridge Writers' Group who, like my children Sam and Sophie, spurred me on to write it and my son Mark who served aboard a Royal Navy warship in the 1982 Falklands war.

My thanks also to the editors whose eagle eyes and enquiring minds kept me on my toes as together we turned a manuscript into a book and to U P Publications for trusting me as an author.

Bibliography

My grateful thanks to the following authors and publishers whose books and websites I referred to in my extensive research for this book.

Beaver, Patrick *'A History of Lighthouses'* (1971) P Davies

Brock, Michael and Eleanor, Editors *'Asquith's Letters to Venetia Stanley'* (1982) Oxford University Press (Quoted with permission)

Coward RN, Cdr. B. R *'Battleship at War'* (1987) Ian Allan, Shepperton, Surrey

Gilbert, Martin *'In Search of Churchill'* (1994) Harper Collins

Hogg, Ian & Batchelor, John *'Naval Gun'* (1978) Blandford Press, Poole, Dorset

Howarth, David & Time-Life Editors *'The Dreadnoughts'* (1979) Time-Life Books Inc.

Lloyd George, David *'War Memoirs of David Lloyd George V.1'* (1933) Ivor Nicholson & Watson, London

MacKay, F *'FISHER of Kilverstone'* First edition (1973) Clarendon Press, Oxford

Massie, Robert K *'Dreadnought: Britain, Germany and the Coming of the Great War V.1'* (1992) Jonathan Cape

Mumby, Frank A., Hist, F. R. *'The Great World War: A History, Vols. I – IX'* (1917 –20) The Gresham Publishing Co Ltd., London

Nicholson, Chrisopher P *'Rock Lighthouses of Britain'* (1995) Whistles Publishing

Peel O.B.E , Mrs C. S. *'We Lived Then 1914-1918: A sketch of Social and Domestic life in England during the war'* (1929) John Lane The Bodley Head Ltd.

http://www.firstworldwar.com (2011)

http://www.anzacsite.gov.au/ (2011)

Lightning Source UK Ltd.
Milton Keynes UK
UKOW021312141211

183777UK00004B/6/P